Unspeakable

MICHELLE K. PICKETT

CLEAN TEEN PUBLISHING

Cover Design by: Marya Heiman
Typography by: Courtney Nuckels
Editing by: Cynthia Shepp
ISBN: 978-1-63422-020-0

For Bre'Anna, Evan, Aleigha, and Alana.
You are loved.

For more information about our content disclosure, please utilize the QR code above with your smart phone or visit us at www.cleanteenpublishing.com.

If you press me to say why I loved him,
I can say no more than because he was
he, and I was I.

~Michel de Montaigne

Jaden

"I want a life without you in it. I want memories that don't include you. I want a heart that never loved you. I want a mind that doesn't know you. And I want a new me who never knew you."
~Willow

BREATHE. NO ONE WILL BREAK ME. I'M STRONG. BREATHE. JUST breathe.

It wasn't always that way. Him. Us. I knew people wondered. But it used to be different. It was sweet, loving, and everything a girl wanted from a boy. But he learned my secret and in that second, he wasn't my wonderful, perfect boyfriend anymore.

He was my jailer.

I watched Jaden celebrate on the field with the rest of the football team. Another victory—the Cougars were on their way to another undefeated season. Jaden stuffed his blue-and-gold helmet under his arm and jogged across the football field. He swiped a bundle of red roses off the team's bench as he passed. He'd had roses there for me the first time I ever went to watch him play.

I waited at the fifty-yard line after the game just as Jaden had asked. Sweat dripped off the ends of his dirty-blond hair and his cheeks were still flushed from running the last play, but he stood in front of me and butterflies swarmed in my belly. Bright, beautiful butterflies. Fluttering their multi-colored wings, tickling me on the inside.

"These are for you." He held out ten magnificent, long-stemmed red roses tied in a shimmering, white ribbon. "Um, I made sure there were no thorns." A small smile tipped the corners of his lips, giving me a tiny glimpse of his dimples.

I sucked in a breath. "They're so pretty, Jaden, thank you." I took the roses from him. Goose bumps ran up my spine like someone had tickled me with a feather, and my fingers trembled when I grazed them over the velvety petals. "But shouldn't I be the one buying you something? You just won the game." I peeked at him through my lashes.

Jaden shook his head slightly and wiped away the sweat on his forehead with his arm. "No. I had to buy something for my good-luck charm. Something beautiful for the most gorgeous girl here."

I felt my cheeks warm and couldn't help my nervous giggle when he slid a lock of hair behind my ear. Crossing one foot over the other, I brought the flowers to my nose. "Why ten?" I asked, my nose buried in the blooms. Ten seemed an unusual number, not that I minded.

"I read on the internet that red roses were for *love,* and ten meant *you're perfect.*"

"Oh," I breathed just before his lips descended on mine.

After that night, at the end of every game, he'd meet me at the fifty-yard line and give me ten long-stemmed red roses.

"Hey." His voice brought my thoughts back to the present, and he leaned in for a kiss. "Some game, huh?" He pressed the flowers into my hand. A thorn bit into the soft flesh of my palm, and I winced.

"Yeah, you were great." I knew that was what he really wanted to hear.

He gave me one of his swoon-worthy smiles before jogging toward the school. "I have to shower. Wait for me in the car," he called over his shoulder before grabbing a scrawny kid by the arm. "Do you have money?" he asked him. He shook the kid's arm to punctuate his question.

"Ye…yeah," the kid answered.

"Good, buy her a Coke." Jaden shoved the boy toward me, almost knocking him over.

Rushing forward, I outstretched my arms to catch the boy before he fell face-first in the mud. I frowned at Jaden's retreating back. "Are you okay?" I asked the boy.

"Yeah. Here." He shoved two wadded-up bills at me.

"No, no, you don't have to buy me anything to drink. Don't

listen to him." I shook my head, pushing the money away.

"Ha! Yes, I do. I don't want him handing me my ass." The boy's eyes were wide as he shoved the money at me. It fluttered to the ground when he turned and jogged away. He acted like I had the bubonic plague. It was close. I dated Jaden.

I looked at the ground where the money had fallen. With a sigh, I knelt to pick it up just as a black boot landed on top of the two bills. I jerked my hand away and looked up into blue eyes so bright they seemed to glow in the darkness. The owner of the eyes squatted next to me.

"Yours?" the guy asked.

"No... I mean, not really..." I looked for the kid who gave it to me, but he'd already disappeared into the crowd. I sighed. "Yeah, I guess."

His lips twitched into an amused grin. A lock of dark hair fell over his forehead. "Well, I'm glad we cleared that up." He picked the money out of the mud, wiping it across the leg of his black jeans before he stood and handed the bills to me. "There you go."

"Thanks. I'm Willow."

"Brody. See you around, Willow."

"Who's that?" a voice boomed behind me, and I stumbled forward.

"Jeez, Karen, don't sneak up on people like that."

"I wasn't sneaking. You were preoccupied staring at the Scooby snack." She smiled and quirked a pierced eyebrow, colored black to match the black stripes in her long, blonde hair.

"No, I wasn't." I could feel the blush creeping over my cheeks and was glad we were standing in the shadows so she couldn't see it.

"Whatever. Personally, I don't give two shits if you look, but you'd better not let Jaden see you scoping out some random guy."

"You're seeing things. I wasn't looking at anyone." I stuffed the money into my pocket.

Maybe I can find the kid at school and give it back to him.

"I'm supposed to make sure you're waiting at Jaden's car." Karen linked her arm around mine and pulled me toward the parking lot.

"What, you're his personal spy and wrangler now?" I rolled my eyes. "I was on my way to his car. It's not like he's gonna hurry or anything. He takes longer than a girl to shower and change."

Karen laughed. "True, but he wants you safely in the car while you wait for him to pretty himself up for you."

The gravel parking lot crunched under our feet as we made our way to Jaden's car. Karen kept her arm linked with mine like we were besties. We so weren't. I could smell the reefer in her hair and cheap liquor on her breath.

When we reached Jaden's cherry red Mustang, I slid into it and, with a sigh, sank into the soft, black leather seats. I waited thirty minutes before Jaden sauntered out of the school and slipped into the car. He leaned over, wrapped his hand around the back of my neck, and pulled me to him for a hard kiss, his tongue invading my mouth. Lifting his head, he smirked. "Hi. Sorry it took me so long," he murmured, his hand snaking under my shirt.

Whatever. I'm used to waiting.

"That's okay." I held my e-reader between us. "I read while I waited."

"You always have your nose in a book. Live a little." Soft lips grazed across the skin of my neck.

"It's kind of hard to live life on the wild side while I sit in your car and wait for you to blow-dry your hair, Jaden."

Pushing away, he glared at me. "Check the attitude." He started the car and pulled out of the parking lot, taking a left, the opposite direction of my subdivision.

"Where are you going?"

"There's a party at Jamieson's."

"I'll miss curfew. I need to go home." My hands balled into fists in my lap. I took a deep breath to stay calm. "Just because you don't have a curfew doesn't mean you can ignore the fact that I do."

"Damn it, Wills, I'll miss half the party if I have to take you home," he said through clenched teeth.

"Don't call me that. I have to go home, Jaden. You know I have a curfew. Why do we have to fight about this every time we're out?"

With a curse, he made an illegal U-turn, tires screeching against the pavement. I grabbed the dash to steady myself. He didn't speak to me the rest of the ride, and when he pulled into my driveway ten minutes later, he shifted the car into reverse and waited for me to get out. I barely had time to shut the door before he squealed out of my drive and sped away.

Breathe. He won't break me. Breathe. I'm stronger than he is. Breathe. Just breathe.

"Willow? Is that you?" my mom called when I walked through the door.

"Yeah."

"Did you have a nice time at the game?" She walked around the corner and smiled at me.

I shrugged a shoulder. "I guess. We won."

"That's good, huh? Why the sad face, then?" She cupped my chin in her hand, lifting my face to look at her.

"Jaden. He's mad that I couldn't go to a party because of curfew." I blew my hair out of my eyes.

"Oh. Well, next time, just call me. You could have gone. As long as you're with Jaden, I know you'll be okay." She patted my cheek and kissed the tip of my nose.

If you only knew. "I will next time. He'll like that."

"Better hurry up to bed. It's getting late," she told me, "but try to be quiet. Ralph has another migraine."

That was code for *he drank himself into oblivion and passed out.* So we tiptoed around the house and spoke in quiet voices—we did not want to wake the beast.

Nodding, I gave her a hug. "Night, Mom."

I climbed the stairs and went into my bedroom. Closing the door behind me, I flipped the lock closed and tossed my things on my bed, before going into my bathroom to wash my face and brush my teeth. I crawled in bed, closed my eyes, and braced myself for the nightmare that was sure to meet me in my sleep.

The same scenes played over and over in my dreams. The secret no one could know—the one Jaden used to blackmail me. The one Ralph taunted my mom with. The secret that changed our lives. No. Ruined our lives. If she'd only done something. Anything. But she just stood there and watched. Listened. And then it was over... and the real nightmare began.

Breathe. Just breathe.

"Hey, Willow, I didn't know you'd be here tonight. I thought Jaden hated these school dances?"

I sat down next to Jenna. "Jaden didn't come with me." Looking at her date, I smiled. "Hi."

He nodded in greeting. Most guys didn't speak to me. I dated Jaden. I was off-limits, and he made sure everyone knew it—and since most people were scared of him, they stayed at a safe distance.

"Oh. He let you off the leash tonight, huh?" Jenna asked. Sarcasm laced her words.

"Something like that." I shrugged and picked at the plastic covering on the tables set up in the gym for the school's fall welcome back dance.

I took in my surroundings. The gym was decorated in oranges, yellows, and reds. Streamers hung from helium balloons floating overhead and brightly colored silk leaves were spread across the tables. Twinkle lights were strewn everywhere. A photographer had set up a photo booth in one of the corners, complete with bales of hay, dried cornstalks, and pumpkins.

"Who's on the decorating committee this year? These decorations are a disaster, and the photographer's booth looks more like a farm threw up in it than a fall scene."

"I know, right? It's heinous. The head of the decorating committee should be put in front of a firing squad."

"You're so funny." I bumped my shoulder into Jenna's. "You did a great job, Jenna, except for the photographer. I still say he missed the memo on the theme." Giggling, I watched the girls perch on top of the hay bales while their dates stood next to them, waiting for their photo to be taken. All they needed was a pitchfork to hold and the look would've been complete.

"Yeah, well, it was either him or one of those giant, blow-up pumpkins you see in people's yards."

Jenna and I met in sixth grade, just after the first week of junior high. We shared a table in science class, and it didn't take long for us to become besties. Now we shared everything—well, almost everything.

There was one thing no one knew, not even my best friend. And it had to stay that way. Only, somehow Jaden found out. The thought made bile rise in my throat, leaving a fiery trail behind. And that was why I stayed with him—so he'd keep my secret.

"Hey!" Jenna snapped her fingers in front of my eyes. "What world were you visiting?"

I looked at Jenna and smiled. With her flawless mocha skin and warm chocolate eyes, she was stunning. Her soft ringlets were styled in a perfect up-do to show off the backless soft pink, silk dress she didn't just wear—she owned. When Jenna walked into a room, people noticed. She would dominate America's Next Top Model. I told her she totally needed to audition for the show after graduation.

"I'm here, just looking around at everyone. No one really changed over the summer." I waved at some friends across the gym.

"Nope. Look at Kirsten dancing with Jason. Her dress is about to ride up so high that she's gonna give everyone a peek at what color her thong is. She's as skanky as ever."

I laughed. "Yup, and Jason still loves it."

"Well, most guys are pigs. They're probably all looking to see if they can get a peek."

Her date huffed next to her. "I'm going to get something to drink." His chair screeched across the floor when he stood.

"Who's the guy?" I watched him stalk to the snack table and grab a cup of punch.

"Earl. He's the one I told you moved down the street a few weeks ago. My ever-so-helpful mother told his mom that I'd show him around. They thought it'd be cute if we came to the dance together, so I could introduce him to people. After all, I didn't have a date or anything." Jenna rolled her eyes. "Sometimes, I think my mother hates me."

"So, why aren't you mingling so he can get to know the high school hierarchy?" I twirled my finger around the expanse of the gym.

"Because I don't particularly want to encourage another date, so I'm trying to make this one miserable for both of us. He has the personality of a rock." She dropped her forehead against the table, banging it several times, making the leaves shuffle across the plastic, orange table covering.

"Keep knocking yourself in the head like that and your personality will match your date's. You can be rocks together," I said with a chuckle.

Her head on the table, Jenna turned and looked at me. "At least he's easy to look at even if he is boring as sin."

"Not as easy as that one." I nodded my head toward the guy standing at the door, guiding a girl out with his hand on her lower back.

"Holy rippled abs, Batman. We have a new hottie on campus."

"Don't get your panties in a wad, ladies." Tim leaned his hip against our table. "That's Brody Victor. He just transferred from Stanton High. He's the bad boy your mamas are always warning you about. You know, the love 'em and leave 'em type. Rumor has it he'll date you 'til he does you, and then he'll drop you cold." Tim shrugged a shoulder and inspected his fingernails. "At least that's what my cousin who goes to Stanton told me. And I have it on good authority that he did her and dropped her."

"Hey, Tim, when'd you get here?" I hugged him before he sat next to me.

"Don't hug me. My features are too delicate. They couldn't withstand a run in with Jaden's fist," he whispered, looking around the gym.

"Jaden's not here." I bumped my shoulder into his. "You know he doesn't do these dances."

"How'd you manage to get him to let you come without him?" Jenna glanced at me over the rim of her paper cup.

My gaze fell to my lap, and I mumbled, "What he doesn't know won't hurt him."

"No, it'll just hurt you if he finds out." Jenna puffed out her cheeks and let out a breath.

"Well, we'll just make sure he doesn't find out, chickie." Tim smiled and patted me on the hand. His mop of brown curls fell over his forehead and into his eyes, and I had to bite my bottom lip to keep from giggling. Sometimes, he reminded me of my neighbor's labradoodle. But even with his untamed curls and puppy dog eyes, he was one of the nicest people who ever lived in my opinion. He was my closest friend, next to Jenna.

Jenna looked over her shoulder. "Karen's here."

"No way!" My voice cracked, and my heart dropped to my toes. "She's supposed to be out of town with her parents. That was the reason I came tonight. I didn't think the little hussy would be able to spy on me and report my every move to Jaden." My stomach felt like someone put it in a blender, and sweat beaded under my hair at the back of my neck.

"You have the worst luck, Willow, I swear," Tim said.

"Don't I know it." My gaze wandered and landed on the school's new hottie. I watched as he led his date out of the gym. "I saw him at the football game last night."

"Who?" Tim looked up from the napkin he was tearing into strips and lighting on fire with a lighter he'd had in his pocket.

Jenna grabbed the pieces of napkin away from him. "Jeez, Tim. People are going to think you're a pyromaniac if you don't knock it off."

"Yeah, I'm the chess club captain, first-rate nerd, math geek, and pyromaniac. I think I have my bases for unpopularity covered. My life mission is complete."

I shook my head and laughed. "The new guy. He was at the game last night, and he introduced himself to me. Sort of."

"Clearly, he's new to the school if he dared to introduce himself to you," Jenna said. "He must not know about the Jaden property laws."

"Stop it. I'm not his property and he knows it." Jenna and Jaden didn't play well together. Jenna was convinced he treated me like a piece of meat. Although I wouldn't admit it, I didn't totally disagree.

"Come on, Tim. Dance with me." I pulled Tim from his chair by the arm. "You're the only one that would get a free pass if Karen tells Jaden I was here."

"Why?"

"'Cause Jaden thinks you're gay," I answered, leading him to the dance floor. I heard Jenna laugh so hard that she choked on her punch.

Tim and I swayed on the dance floor. His arms were wrapped loosely around my waist. I placed my hands on his shoulders. We kept a safe distance between us, so we didn't give anyone the wrong impression. We were just friends dancing together. Nothing more.

I didn't see him come into the gym. It wasn't until he was right behind Tim, ripping his arms away from me that I knew I had a problem, and my heart did a nosedive.

"Put your hands on her again and you'll lose them," Jaden shouted. He always liked to make a scene.

"Jaden, you know Tim and I are just friends," I said with a frustrated sigh.

"Get outta here," Jaden growled at Tim through clenched teeth before grabbing me by the arm and pulling me off the dance floor.

"Knock it off. I wasn't doing anything except dancing with a friend." I tried to jerk away from Jaden's grip. He tightened his hand around my arm.

"We're leaving."

"No. I'm staying. You can leave."

Jaden turned and looked at me. A vein throbbed in his neck. "I'm not having my girl stay at some cheesy school dance embarrassing me. There's a party at Jamieson's house. His parents are out of town. My people are there, not at some dumpy, loser-filled school dance."

"I'm not going to the party. It's just an excuse for everyone to get drunk and hook up." Jerking my arm from his grasp, I stepped away from him. I could feel the tips of my cheekbones heating. Adrenaline bounced off the walls of my veins.

Jaden jerked my purse off the chair and jammed it in under his arm. "Did you drive?" he asked quietly. That tone scared me more than him yelling.

I swallowed down a thick lump. "Yes."

His hand shot out and grabbed my arm before I had an opportunity to move. "Let's go. I'll bring you back for your car later." Jaden pulled me to the door of the gym. I looked back at Jenna. Her lips were pressed in a straight line. I hated what I saw in her eyes when she looked at me. Disappointment.

I wish I could tell you, Jenna. I wish you knew why I put up with his shit. Why I can't kick the jackass in the nuts and lay him out on the floor like he deserves. But he knows. And as long as I do what he wants, he promised not to tell.

"How'd you know I was here?" Out of the corner of my eye, I saw Karen smirk. The bitch.

"Karen texted me. Do you know how embarrassed I am to have you at a dance full of geeks and losers?"

Like your cousin, Karen?

"Oh, and yanking me off the dance floor and dragging me out isn't embarrassing?" I pushed at his hand, trying to pry it off me.

"Get in." Jaden opened the door of his Mustang.

"I'm just going home," I told him. "Let go of my arm, Jaden. You go to your dumbass party, and I'll go home. Problem solved."

Jaden put a hand on my head, pushing it forward, and an arm under my legs. I let out a small scream when he lifted me off the ground. He shoved his knee against my hip to move me sideways into the car. "You're going. Get. In. The. Car," he said through clenched teeth. He slammed the door, walked around to the driver's side, and slid into his seat. I sat with my arms crossed over my chest and stared straight ahead. "Fasten your seatbelt." Jaden drummed his thumbs on the steering wheel. "I'm not asking again, Willow." The muscles in his neck were corded, his lips were puckered in a frown, and I knew he wasn't giving in.

With a sigh, I pulled the strap across my body and clicked the buckle into place. "I don't want to go to the party. Just let me go home."

"I don't care what you want."

"Willow, Jaden's here," my mom called.

I skipped down the stairs to meet him. He was gorgeous standing at the bottom of the stairs waiting for me with a bouquet of flowers. In it were two Birds of Paradise.

"This is for you." He smiled and handed me the flowers.

"Birds of Paradise." I fingered the flowers. "You remembered." I looked at him and smiled wide.

It'd been weeks ago that we'd walked through the shops downtown. We passed a flower shop with a display of Birds of Paradise in the window. I'd never seen them before, and I told Jaden how beautiful I thought they were. How unique—their odd shape that really did resemble a bird at certain angles.

"Of course I remembered. I remember everything you say, Willow." He brushed a lock of hair from my face.

I glanced at him through my lashes and smiled.

"Here." My mom took the flowers. "Let me put these in a vase so you two can get going."

"Thanks, Mom." Jaden and I started out of the door. "So, where are we going?"

He threaded his fingers with mine as we walked to his car. "Well, Jamieson is having a party, but I know you aren't really into those, so I thought we'd see a movie instead."

I smiled up him and emotions filled me—so many I couldn't identify them all.

That was the night I fell for Jaden. I thought he was the most perfect boyfriend on this planet, or any other. Not many guys would give up a party with his football teammates for a girl. Just my guy.

I couldn't believe how lucky I was.

Jaden squealed out of the parking lot, breaking through my memories and thrusting me back to the present. He cut off another car. The driver honked, and Jaden flipped him off. I held on to the dashboard as he sped down the road, swerving in and out of traffic, driving at least twenty miles over the speed limit.

"How much have you had to drink?" I asked, gripping the center console so tightly that my fingers turned white.

"Not enough."

"So you've already been to Jamieson's party." He didn't answer me. "So it's okay for you to go to a party by yourself, but I can't go to a stupid school dance? Who were you hooking up with? Sarah?"

"Jealous, baby?" He smirked.

I rolled my eyes. "Disgusted."

Jaden pulled up to Jamieson's house. Cars were parked along both sides of the road. Jaden pulled into the driveway and took a sharp right into the front yard. He wouldn't park his precious car near anyone else. Someone might touch it.

He threw the car in park and got out, not waiting to see if I'd follow.

The party was in full swing. Music blared, and people danced on the front lawn, laughing and acting like a bunch of drunken fools. One girl, I didn't know her name but I'd seen her around school, was on her boyfriend's shoulders, her tank top wrapped around her stomach. Her boobs on display for anyone who cared to take a peek. And Jaden did.

Closing my eyes, I turned my face away. Tears pushed the back of my eyes, demanding to be let free. I squeezed my eyes tighter.

"She's pretty." I watched the tall blonde walk across the room. She'd been crowned a member of the homecoming court during halftime at the game. "Her." I nodded my head in her direction.

Jaden gave her a quick glance and shrugged a shoulder. "She's okay. I think you're beautiful." He kissed the side of my neck up to my ear. "You're the only girl I have eyes for."

Jaden elbowed me to get my attention. "Get me something to drink, Wills," he said, dropping down on the porch steps next to one of his friends from the football team. They bumped fists and ogled the Vegas-showgirl-wanna-be.

Well, he certainly has eyes for other girls now... at least their boobs. Crap. I hate these parties.

"Don't call me that." I hated Jaden's nickname for me. He knew it, and I was certain that was why he used it.

I pushed my way into the house and through the crowd of people to the kitchen, where the kegs and a variety of other liquor were laid out. I grabbed a Coke from the fridge and a beer for Jaden. When I shoved my way back through the crowd to the porch, I saw Sarah in her tight mini skirt and clingy, white T-shirt—barely long enough to cover her boobs—sitting next to Jaden. She had one arm wrapped around his waist, her finger hooked in a belt loop on his jeans, while the fingers on her other hand twisted a lock of his blond hair around them. I took a deep breath and sighed before walking to them.

Skank. And Jaden isn't much better. And I have to sit around and watch. There's nothing I can do about it, and Jaden knows it.

There were always girls throwing themselves at Jaden, and I was positive he'd caught a few. There were plenty of rumors about him hooking up with some girl or another at a party.

Our relationship had run its course months ago. I tried to break things off with him more than once, but he wouldn't leave me alone. He'd show up at my classes and follow me, making sure no guy came near me. I was off-limits whether we were dating or not.

Then, one Monday morning, he handed me an envelope just before my first period. Inside was a newspaper clipping and a note that simply read: *'I know and I'll tell.'* I knew I was screwed. I was his bitch. Do what he wanted, say what he wanted, go where he wanted, and make sure the world revolved around Jaden—or he'd tell what she did. So breaking up with him wasn't an option. I was stuck.

But it wasn't all bad. After all, what girl didn't want to date the captain of the football team and the most popular, not to mention gorgeous, guy in school? Me, that's who.

I'd been at Jamieson's party for two hours watching Sarah throw herself at Jaden. She didn't seem to care that I was there. Of course, she was so drunk she probably didn't know her own name. Jaden drank beer after beer and was almost as drunk as Sarah was. I sat by, sipped my Coke, and watched them.

I didn't drink alcohol. Well, I should say that I didn't drink anymore. I had my fair share of hangovers after Jamieson's parties, but I didn't like losing control. My inhibitions flew out the window when I was drunk. I lost control and it wasn't a cool. Plus, my mom drank a little too much and I had a stepdad before my mom married Ralph—my current stepdad—that drank way too much. Ralph did his share of guzzling, too. I saw—lived—with what booze did to them. No thank you. Not for me. Call me a prude, or whatever else you wanted to, but I was sticking with Coke. Just Coke.

"Me and Sarah are going to find somewhere quiet to talk," Jaden whispered in my ear. His breath reeked of booze, and I turned my face away.

Yeah, talk. That's what you'll be doing. Sure.

"Come with us." He pulled me up by the arm.

"Nope." I pushed his hand away and sat down on the porch step.
"Come on, Willow. It'll be fun. I promise."

Um, I'm not into that.

"Go do whatever it is you're gonna do, Jaden. I'm not going with you."

"He's gonna do Sarah," Jamieson slurred, leaning so close to my face I could smell the stench of liquor and cigarettes clinging to him.

Everyone around us laughed. I walked away and wandered aimlessly around the huge yard, looking at the flowering bushes and flower garden surrounding a gazebo in the far back corner of the yard. It was beautiful and I made way toward it, admiring each new type of flower as I passed. The gazebo was wood, painted white. There was an intricate design in the railing and the eaves. The roof was rounded before it came to a point at the top. It looked like part of the Kremlin in Russia.

Preoccupied with the beautiful gazebo and the flower garden, I didn't pay attention to who might be *inside* and almost walked in on two people who most definitely did not want my company. The term *"get a room"* took on a whole new meaning. It seemed *"get a gazebo"* worked well, too.

Yelling my apologies over my shoulder, I ran down the walk and across the yard until I came to the back deck of the house where I found a swing. Dropping into it, I leaned my head back and closed my eyes, swaying gently. The swing jostled when someone sat next to me, and my eyes shot open.

Please don't be gazebo guy. I saw enough of him tonight.

"Great party, huh?" Natalie, a girl from my English class, said with a frown.

I made an I-hate-every-second-of-it face, but said, "Yeah. It's wonderful."

"I saw Jaden and Sarah. I'm sorry."

I braced myself for the pity I'd see in her eyes. Instead, I saw disgust and, for one tiny second, I didn't feel so alone. "Thanks." I shrugged a shoulder. "I'm used to it. He's a real douche when he's drinking."

"They all are." She took a drink from the Dr. Pepper can she had in her hands. "You want to get out of here? I could drop you at your house."

I let out a huge sigh. "If you could drop me at the school so I can pick up my car it would be wonderful. Thanks so much."

When I got home, I went straight to my bedroom and fell across my bed. My phone chimed that I had a message. I knew it was from Jaden, and I wasn't in the mood to talk to him. So I turned my phone off, slipped into my boxers and T-shirt, and climbed into bed.

I closed my eyes and waited for the nightmares to begin.

Breathe. You're strong. Breathe. Just breathe.

Two
Biology

"He entered my life... and I knew I'd never be the same."
~Willow

I WALKED INTO SCHOOL MONDAY MORNING, BRACING MYSELF FOR THE fallout after Jamieson's party. The gossip chain at Cassidy High was wicked. Everyone would know about Jaden and Sarah. I hadn't talked to Jaden since the party. He called and texted all night Saturday and all day Sunday. I ignored him.

"Hey, baby." Jaden sauntered up to my locker.

"Hi." I slammed the locker door shut and spun the dial.

"Are you mad? I'm sorry about Sarah. I was drunk. You know how it goes, but I swear nothing happened." He reached out and brushed my hair away from my face, leaning in for a kiss. I turned away.

"It doesn't matter if anything happened or not. Everyone thinks something did."

"I'll set them straight. You know you're the only girl for me."

I walked around him and into my classroom, dropping my books on the table.

"I'll make it up to you. Go out to dinner with me tonight," he called from the doorway.

"Maybe."

He smiled and held his arms out from his sides. "You know you want to. Come on, Wills, I said I was sorry."

"Fine." There was really no sense in arguing with him. He'd bug me until I said yes. Or threaten me.

He gave me one of his cocky grins. "I'll pick you up at six. See you at lunch."

Whatever. Did I really have a choice?

I was looking through my notes when a piece of wadded-up paper landed in front of me. I looked over and saw Tim smiling. He nodded at the paper. I smoothed it out and read the note: '*Look up.*'

Frowning, I looked at Tim. He pointed to the front of the class with a smirk.

My gaze followed his finger and my breath hitched. The hottie stood next to the teacher's desk. Looking back at Tim, I smiled with a shrug of my shoulder. Tim batted his eyelashes and sighed, and I covered my mouth with my hand to keep from laughing.

"Sit anywhere you can find an empty seat," my biology teacher told him.

I watched as the dark-haired hottie turned and looked around the room. His eyes fell on me, and a corner of his mouth tipped up in a half grin. He walked to the table where I sat and tossed his book down, pulling out the chair next to me. I cringed when it screeched against the tile floor.

"Hi, Willow," he murmured. I stared at him. He turned and looked at me, an amused grin playing on his lips. "This is when you say hi."

"Hi, Brody."

"Mind if I sit here? You're the only familiar face I see."

"Um, no. It's fine. I'll finally have a partner when we do labs." I smiled quickly and looked down at my notes.

Oh jeez, Jaden is gonna bust a nut.

"Sounds good," Brody said, opening his book. "What page are we on?"

"Forty-two."

We didn't talk the rest of the class. When the bell rang, Brody swiped his things off the table and walked away.

"Later," he said over his shoulder.

"Bye," I whispered, watching him disappear in the crowded hallway.

"Whoa, he's taking his life in his hands sitting next to you," Tim said behind me, making me jump. "What do you think Jaden will do?"

"For Brody's sake, I hope he doesn't find out."

Tim chuckled. "Yeah, right. With the gossips around here? He probably knew before class was over."

Dinner with Jaden. Not how I wanted to spend my evening. I was still pissed about him and Sarah, even though he promised me over and over nothing had happened. Still, Sarah sat with us at lunch, flirting with him even though I sat right next to him. The skank.

Rushing home from school, I took an extra-long shower, painted my toe and finger nails, and got dressed for my night out with Jaden. Curling my wavy, dark brown hair, I put it up with curls framing my face. I picked a jean skirt and green, paisley pheasant blouse with flowing sleeves that Jenna said brought out the green in my hazel eyes.

Not too bad, I guess.

I curled up on the black-and-white cushioned window seat in my bedroom with a crime novel I'd gotten at the library that afternoon. The story quickly drew me in, and I lost track of time. It wasn't until my phone chimed that I had a text message that I glanced at the clock. It was past seven. Jaden was over an hour late. Nice. I grabbed my phone, expecting the text was from him with some lame excuse. I frowned when I saw Tim's name on the screen.

TIM: JUST SAW JADEN.

ME: WHERE?

TIM: AT THE DIVE.

The Dive was a local burger joint where everyone hung out after school and on weekends. They had the best burgers in Middleton, the small Michigan town where I lived, and their milkshakes were to die for. I gained weight just thinking about them.

ME: NICE. WE WERE SUPPOSED TO GO TO DINNER.

TIM: SORRY.

ME: WHO'S HE WITH?

TIM: FOOTBALL TEAM.

ME: SARAH?

TIM: NO.

ME: I GOTTA GO. SEE YOU TOMORROW.

TIM: BYE.

Jaden didn't text me until nine that night. I didn't answer. He texted every few minutes after that. They went from apologetic to irate that I was ignoring him. I turned my phone off and got ready for bed.

I lay in bed most of the night, thinking about Jaden and his crap. This wasn't the first time he'd missed a date because something better came up. But I was expected to sit at home—alone—and wait on him. God forbid I go out without him. And it wasn't the first time something had happened like the thing with Sarah.

Independent. That was me. Did my own thing and made my own decisions. Keeping up with trends wasn't on my to-do list. I didn't care if people thought I was cool or not. Expensive, designer clothes didn't overflow my closet—dressing for comfort was my thing. That meant sweats, my funky-print Converse sneakers, and T-shirts with sarcastic sayings. Even though I dated the star football player, I wasn't a cheerleader. The chess club was my peeps.

But when it came to Jaden, I was trapped. It felt like a boulder sat on my shoulder, pushing me down a little more each day, drowning me in the secret I was forced to keep. The secret only two other people knew besides my mom and me—Jaden and Ralph.

Get it together. This is the life I was given. Time I put my big-girl panties on and deal.

"I hear you have a new friend," Jaden said, leaning against the locker next to mine the following morning.

I made a face. "What are you talking about?"

"The new guy you're cozying up to in biology." His voice was low and hard. Anyone else would think we were having a normal conversation. I knew better.

"We sit at the same table. That's hardly cozying up. What happened to you last night?" I slammed my locker door shut and turned to look at him.

"I met some of the guys at The Dive and lost track of time, which you'd know if you'd read my texts. Don't ever do that again. When I text you, I expect you to text back." He flicked my shoulder. It stung, but I didn't acknowledge it.

"Well, when you tell me you're going to pick me up for dinner, I expect you to show up. So I guess neither of us got what we expected last night."

Jaden grabbed me by the wrist and pulled me behind him. I had to take two steps to every one of his long strides. I was practically jogging to keep up with him.

"What are you doing?" I tried to jerk my hand free. He tightened his grip.

"Walking you to your class."

My heart rate increased, and I tried to pull him to a stop. "Jaden, just leave it alone."

I knew what was coming. Brody was new to the school, and he made the mistake of daring to sit next to me in class. Jaden was on his way to set Brody straight. He pulled me into biology. Strolling into the classroom like he owned it, he dragged me to my seat and shoved me into my chair. Brody was already sitting at the table, watching with a raised eyebrow. He reached out to steady me. My eyes met his, and I shook my head once. He withdrew his hand.

"So you're Brody, huh?" Jaden asked.

Brody tipped his head in acknowledgement.

"I just wanted to set some rules in place."

"Rules? This should be interesting," Brody said with a half grin. He leaned back in his chair, his fingers laced behind his head.

"Willow's mine. Keep your hands to yourself." Jaden leaned over the table.

Brody just stared at him with a somewhat amused look on his face.

"Mr. Smith," my biology teacher called, "I don't believe you're in this class. Make your way to your own class."

"Yes, sir," Jaden said. With one last glare at Brody, he turned and left.

"Big head, little brain. I could almost hear it rolling around inside that oversized skull of his," Brody said with a chuckle.

"Keep talking, Ace," I muttered.

"What, are you going to run and tell your big, bad boyfriend?" Brody dropped his arms and leaned forward to look at me.

"No, but someone will. There's a whole classroom of people listening to you right now."

He shrugged a shoulder. "Let them. I've seen his kind before. Jaden doesn't scare me."

He should.

The rest of the hour was uneventful. The teacher droned on about the dissection of an earthworm we'd be completing later in the week. I pretended to be riveted by his lecture—a hard feat—and tried not to look at Brody. Maddeningly enough, my eyes had a mind of their own and my gaze kept wandering to him. I dipped my head toward my notebook, pretending to take notes, letting my hair fall in front of my face to hide my eyes so I could stare at him.

Brody reclined in his seat, his long legs stretched out in front of him, his ankles crossed. He drummed his thumb against his thigh and looked completely relaxed. I eyed him up and down. His perfectly mussed dark hair fell over his forehead and curled slightly around his collar—he had the whole messy bedroom hair thing going on—his lips held a small grin. He was tall and lean, and his black T-shirt—snug in all the right places—hinted at a firm, muscular body underneath.

Jeez, get a grip. I'm acting like some kind of ho-bag... like Sarah. Crap.

But my eyes wouldn't stay away. There was no denying he was good looking... beyond good looking, in fact. But there was something else about him that drew me in. He had a kind of quiet confidence about him. I saw it in the way he stared at Jaden. It set me on edge, made me feel off-balance, and I felt a little stirring of butterflies in my stomach as I watched him from behind the curtain of my hair.

Then he opened his mouth, and the butterflies scattered.

"Like what you see?" he murmured, not looking at me.

Feeling my face flame with a red-hot blush, I hoped he couldn't see, I opened my mouth to shoot a witty comeback just as the bell rang.

He flipped his book closed, looked at me, and smiled. "See you tomorrow, Willow. You can stare some more then."

"Don't flatter yourself."

Ugh, that's my comeback? Weak, very weak.

He winked and walked to the door. "Later."

That was when I knew I had a problem. Brody Victor. He was gonna cause trouble. I could feel it.

Bowling

"Life is the art of drawing without an eraser."
~unknown

"SO TELL ME ABOUT HIM," JENNA SAID AFTER SCHOOL. WE WERE AT MY house, supposed to be doing homework.

I lay on my back across my bed, my feet propped against the electric pink-and-black striped wall. "Who?" I dodged.

"Play dumb all you want, Willow, but Tim told me all about you checking Brody out this morning in biology."

"I was not checking him out." I huffed. "Okay, maybe a little." Looking at her, I smiled. "How can any woman with a pulse not check him out?"

"So?"

"He's easy to look at."

"Yeah, that much I can see for myself. He's almost illegally hot. Tell me something I don't know." She leaned forward, pushing her math book out of the way.

"He has an ego the size of Montana."

"Yeah, the pretty ones usually do." She sighed. "Has he talked much?"

"Nope. We just sit next to each other. That's it. Nothing exciting."

"You should ask him out." She nudged my shoulder with the eraser on her pencil.

"What? I'm with Jaden. I can't ask some random guy out."

"Jaden, yeah, yeah." She waved her hand in the air. "Dump him and go for the biology hottie."

24

Oh, you have no idea how fast I'd dump Jaden if I could. He'd be like shit on a shoe.

"No," I said, laughing.

"We could do a group thing and invite him along. We can tell him it's a way for him to get to know people."

I sat up, folded my legs under me, and tucked the loose strands of my hair back into my messy bun. "That sounds good... have fun." I flopped back on the bed.

"What do you mean?" She shoved my shoulder. "You're coming, too."

"Jenna, you know I can't. If Jaden ever found out, he'd flip, and I can't take him with me. He'd do something to ruin the whole thing. You should ask Brody out. You're single."

"Maybe, but I think the group thing is the best idea. We can plan it on a night Jaden has football practice. He never pays attention to what you do when football's involved."

"Willow! Dinner!" my stepdad hollered from downstairs.

"It's dinner already? I should go." Jenna gathered her things, blowing her hair out of her face.

We walked down the stairs together, Jenna still trying to talk me into going bowling with her and checking out Brody.

"You need to unburden yourself of the wart named Jaden." She gave me a big grin. "Think about it. You know you want to."

I laughed. "Okay, okay. I'll think about it."

"Hey, Jenna, I didn't know you were here," my stepfather, Ralph, said with a smile. He wrapped one arm around her and pulled her in for a hug. "Why don't you stay for dinner?"

"Hi, Mr. McKenna! I wish I could stay. I could smell your meatballs all the way upstairs. They smell delicious. But my mom already gave me strict orders to be home by five."

Ralph looked at his watch and tsked. "You've got two minutes."

"Gotta motor," Jenna called as she slipped out of the door. "Bye!"

Ralph and I called goodbye, and he shut the door. I turned toward the kitchen when I was yanked back by my hair. I let out a small scream before I bit my lip to hold it back. He liked it when I screamed. He liked it more if I cried. I tried like hell not to do either.

Ralph pulled me backward by my hair, arching my back, and put his face in mine. His breath was hot when it hit my face, and I wondered how much he'd had to drink already. The more he drank, the harder it was for me.

"Who do you think you are making plans to go out with your friends to meet another boy?"

I cringed when he pulled my hair tighter. "I'm not. I just told Jenna I'd think about it so she'd stop asking."

He paused, eyes narrowed at me. My back muscles quivered and burned. If he didn't let go soon, my feet were going to give out. It felt as though he was pulling my scalp from my head where his fist was wrapped around my hair. "I don't believe you." His voice was quiet. That scared me more than his yelling. He let go of my hair, and I collapsed on the floor. "You're nothing but white trash like your mother." He kicked me hard in the back. Pain radiated through my body, like a thousand needles on fire.

Crawling to the archway leading into the formal living room, I used the wall to pull myself up. I tried to dodge him by cutting through the living room, but he grabbed my arm and yanked me backward. I slipped on the polished wood floor and fell on my hip. Sliding across the floor, I slammed into the front door, the handle burying itself into my shoulder.

Ralph grabbed me under the arm and hauled me off the floor. He stood in front of me, his finger poking me in the chest. "I'm the only reason a nice boy from a decent family will even look at a piece of trash like you." Grabbing my cheeks and squeezing hard, he pulled my face to his. My skin stretched over my cheekbones where his fingers pinched it together. I could smell whiskey and the sweet stench of cigars on his breath. "My stepdaughter is not going to date some piece of crap kid from a nothing family. I have a reputation to uphold. Jaden is doing you a favor. You'd do good to remember that." With one last shove, he turned and sauntered into the kitchen.

"Willow?" My mom's soft voice came from the stairs. I turned toward her. She stood with a hand at her throat, her eyes wide. "Are you alright?"

"Yeah, Mom. I'm great," I whispered.

Thanks for your help, by the way. I love how you stepped in for me. So loving.

I gave her a fake smile and made my way to the kitchen, where the three of us would sit at the dinner table and eat Ralph's homemade spaghetti and meatballs and pretend like nothing had happened. Just another happy family living in suburbia.

After dinner, I texted Jenna and told her I was game for a group of friends going out and inviting Brody along. Screw Ralph. And Jaden.

JENNA: YAY! YOU SLUT.
ME: IT'S JUST A BUNCH OF FRIENDS.
JENNA: YOU SO WANT THE BIOLOGY HOTTIE!
ME: SHUT UP.

Wednesday. Jaden had football practice after school. Afterward, he and the team always went out together, usually to Jamieson's house to play pool and raid his dad's liquor cabinet. Jenna and I decided it was the perfect night to get a bunch of people together to go bowling and out to dinner.

Jenna pulled her books out of her locker. "Ask him in biology," she said.

"No! You have to ask him. I can't risk someone overhearing me and telling Jaden."

"I don't know him," she complained.

I shut the locker and looked at her. "So follow me to biology. I'll introduce you and then you can ask him when you mention it to Tim. It'll look like a last-minute thing." Jenna stared at me with a smirk. "What?"

"You're sneaky."

I picked an invisible piece of lint off my shoulder and flicked it away. "I prefer to call it problem solving."

"Okay, let's go do some problem solving." She pushed me in the direction of my classroom.

I threw the strap of my messenger bag over my shoulder. "So where are we going?"

"Let's go to Super Bowl and then we can grab something at The Dive afterward."

We walked into my class, and I tossed my bag on the table. "Brody and Tim aren't here yet. Perfect. When Tim comes in, we can call him over and I can introduce you both. Then you can start talking about tonight to Tim and casually invite Brody."

"How come I never knew how devious you are?" she asked, raising an eyebrow at me.

I smiled and winked. "I have many wicked skills that you are unaware of. One day I will pass on my knowledge to you." Looking over Jenna's shoulder, I saw him stroll into the classroom. "Here he comes," I whispered. "Tim's right behind him."

Jenna turned and gave a bright smile. "Hey, Tim, come here."

"What's up?" He leaned his hip against the table next to me. "Hi," he said to Brody.

Perfect opening. Thank you, Tim.

"Brody, this is Tim and Jenna. Guys, this is Brody," I said, trying not to stare at Brody when I made the introductions. Jenna, however, was openly staring. I think I saw a drip of drool run down her chin. Yep, she was officially a member of the Brody fan club. If she kept drooling, I was going to have to get her a cup.

"Hi," Brody said, one side of his mouth lifted in a small grin. I almost groaned. It was the sexiest smile I think I'd ever seen.

Jaden, I'm with Jaden. I can't think Brody's sexy... but oh crap is he ever hot and smells so freakin' good, like sun and the ocean and something totally male.

Jenna just smiled at him. Maybe his grin had rendered her speechless.

"Hey, man," Tim said.

Jenna kept staring at Brody. I cleared my throat and glared at her. She didn't notice, so I plunged forward.

"Jenna was just saying we should go to Super Bowl tonight and bowl a few games before grabbing a burger at The Dive. You game?" I asked Tim.

"Sure. What time?"

"Let's meet there around five. Sound good?"

"I'll be there sporting some horrendous and awfully odorous shoes, that only God knows what's growing in them and whose foot last occupied them." Tim shuddered.

"Thanks, Tim. I think I'll wear two pairs of socks," I said, wrinkling my nose. "Gross."

"Hey, you should come, Brody," Jenna finally said. "A group of us are going. It'd be a good way for you to meet people. Plus, there are always people hanging at The Dive."

"I don't think so. Thanks for asking, though."

Jenna's face fell. It was almost comical. She wasn't even trying to hide her interest in him. "Come on, I won't take no for an answer."

Brody glanced at me. "Are you going, Willow?" When I nodded, he sighed and said, "Okay, give me the address and I'll see what I can do." He flipped his notepad toward me.

"Where do you live?" I asked. He raised an eyebrow at me and his grin was back. I rolled my eyes. "I need to know where you'll be coming from to give you directions."

"Rosewood Estates."

"We're practically neighbors," I murmured as I wrote down the directions to the bowling alley. I turned his notepad back to him. "I live in Rose Creek."

He looked at the directions and the small map I drew, furrowing his eyebrows. "I think I know where this is. Give me your cell." He held his hand out. When I just looked at him, he let out a sigh like he was dealing with a toddler. "This is when you give me your cell phone so we can exchange numbers. That way, I can text you if I have trouble finding the bowling alley."

"Oh. Sure." I handed him my cell, and he programmed his phone number into my contacts. I added my number and address in his, handing his phone back to him. Jenna plucked it out of my hand before he could take it.

"Here's my number. You know, in case Willow doesn't answer." Jenna smiled and handed Brody's phone back to him.

"Thanks." He didn't give her his number.

"Okay. I guess I'll see you later. Gotta get to class," Jenna said. She walked backward toward the door—still staring at Brody—and ran smack into my biology teacher.

I covered my mouth with my hand to stifle my giggles. Brody chuckled next to me, shaking his head, and Tim picked up his books, mumbled something about Jenna's ditziness, and walked to his seat.

Smooth, Jenna. Way to make an impression.

It was the slowest day in history. I didn't think school would ever end. When the last bell finally rang, I rushed to my locker and stuffed my books inside before jogging to the student parking lot and climbing into my Chevy. I wanted to get home and finish my homework, so I could shower and change before I left for the bowling alley.

After going through what felt like a hundred outfits, cussing out my hair because it wouldn't lay right, and carefully applying my makeup, I grabbed my keys and headed for the door.

"Willow? Are you going somewhere?" my mom called.

I went into her bedroom. She was lying across the bed on her stomach, two empty beer bottles on the floor beside her and a full one in her hand. "A bunch of us are going to the Super Bowl and then The Dive for burgers after. I asked you earlier, remember?"

"Tonight's not a good night."

Breathe. It's gonna be fine. Breathe

"What… why?" My heart sank. "You said it was okay for me to go."

"It just isn't a good night to go out. You know how things go. Your dad wants tonight to be a family night."

"He isn't my dad," I muttered.

Ralph walked out of the bathroom attached to their bedroom. "You have no idea how happy I am that I'm not your real dad. And I don't give a rat's ass what your mom said about you going out tonight. You're staying in unless you're planning to meet Jaden." He looked at me with raised eyebrows. When I didn't answer, he smirked. "I didn't think so. You're not going anywhere."

I looked at the bed. "Mom—"

"I said no," Ralph shouted, and I flinched.

Breathe. Just breathe.

"Fine." Running back to my room, I locked the door behind me. After I threw my stuff on my bed and stripped out of my clothes, pulling on a pair of boxers and a tank, I texted Jenna.

> ME: CAN'T MAKE IT TONIGHT.
> JENNA: WHAT? WHY?
> ME: HOME STUFF. SEE YOU TOMORROW.
> JENNA: I'M SORRY.
> ME: NO BIGGIE. HAVE FUN.

I used the rest of the night to do schoolwork and wonder if Brody showed up at the bowling alley. I finished my homework for the next day, including the extra credit. It was too early for bed and I was too keyed up to sleep anyway, so I worked ahead in calculus and biology and finished a paper on the Civil War for American history that wasn't due until the next week.

I'd hoped to get a text from Jenna telling me about how her night was, so I waited until midnight before I crawled into bed.

That night, images of Brody's bright blue eyes and amused grin haunted my dreams. It was better than the nightmares that usually invaded my sleep.

Just breathe.

Scheduling

"I don't like you. I don't. You're sarcastic and irritating. But, oh, how I look forward to seeing your face every day."
~*Willow*

I LOOKED IN THE MIRROR THE NEXT MORNING. MY DARK HAIR WAS A MESS. The normal waves hung limply to my shoulders. Dark circles surrounded my eyes, their hazel color washed out from lack of sleep. I sighed. I didn't have the energy to care what I looked like. After I ran a brush through my hair, I twisted it into a messy bun at the back of my neck. I dabbed a little makeup around my eyes to hide the circles and slashed on some mascara. A swipe of lip gloss and I called it good.

I pulled on a pair of sweats, a pink tank top that said, *Zombies Eat Brains (You're Safe)*, a zippered hoodie, and my hot pink sequined tennis shoes and forced myself to go to school.

"You look like crap," Jenna said. I glared at her and grabbed my books out of my locker. "And I am going to burn those shoes the next time I'm at your house."

"Thanks. You're a sexy beast, too."

She leaned her shoulder against the locker next to mine. "Missed you last night. It wasn't nearly as fun without you."

"Thanks. Brody show up?"

"Yeah." She sighed. I swear her eyes glossed over and pink cartoon hearts floated above her head. I wouldn't have been surprised if violin music had started playing, cartoon rabbits scampered around her, and bluebirds landed on her shoulders. It was sickening... I was totally jealous.

You are an amazing person no matter what ☺

"So, what's he like?"

"Eh."

I glanced at her. "What's that mean?"

"He's the tall, dark, and handsome that smutty romance novels describe. He must top six feet, and he seems to be the whole package—brains, looks, and wicked funny. All the girls swooned over him."

"A real ladies' man, huh?" I rolled my eyes.

Jenna shrugged a shoulder. "I guess. He stayed for one game and then left with Tanya."

"Great taste in women. I suppose if the stories about him are true, he's gonna know how to find the easy girls."

"Time will tell, I guess. See you in history."

I shut my locker and jumped when I came face to face with Jaden. "So Jenna's gaga over the new guy, huh? Big surprise. She'll go after anything with a pulse. Sometimes, I wonder if a pulse is even needed." He laughed at his lame joke.

"I'm late, Jaden. I'll see you at lunch."

He pushed off the locker and fell in step with me. "I'll walk you to class."

We were silent on the way. When we got to my classroom, I looked over my shoulder. "Bye. Save me a seat at lunch."

Jaden grabbed my wrist, pulling me backward against his chest. He wrapped his arm around my waist, nuzzling his face behind my ear before turning me around and kissing me. His mouth was hard against mine. Putting my hand on his chest, I pushed him. He smirked and walked away.

I turned and walked into class. My eyes met Brody's. He rolled his and made a disgusted face. "I like your shirt," he said when I reached the table.

I had to look down to remember which one I was wearing. "Oh, thanks. I wore it just for you. You know, to comfort you in case of a zombie attack."

He laughed. My heart nearly stopped at the sound. Dear God, it was like music from Heaven.

It was movie day in biology. I was looking forward to sleeping during it. Folding my arms on my book, I laid my head on top of them, closing my eyes. Near the end of the movie, Brody scooted his chair close to mine and interrupted my nap. "So, you date the captain of the football team. You're one of those," he said quietly.

"One of what?" I asked, not bothering to open my eyes.

"A bimbo jock chaser."

"Hmm, and you're one of those."

"I can't wait to hear this," he murmured. "One of what?"

Sighing, I opened my eyes and looked at him. "A piss poor athlete who's jealous of the real jocks. At least you know you'll always have a job when you finish school."

"Oh?" Brody looked at me and quirked an eyebrow.

"Yes, Mr. Victor, I'm sure you've heard the saying, '*Those who can, do, those who can't, teach*.' So you don't have to worry about your athletic shortcomings. You can rest easy with the knowledge that you'll always be able to teach."

Brody laughed. "Nice. I'm glad to know I'll be a productive member of society."

"That remains to be seen. How was Tanya?"

He grinned and shrugged a shoulder. "I've had better."

"Ugh, you're a pig."

"You asked." He leaned close to my ear and murmured, "So you've been asking around about me?" He tapped his pencil on the table.

My heart skipped a beat.

He can't possibly know that. I've only talked to Jenna and Tim. They'd never tell anyone I'd asked about him.

"You're delusional. Why would you think I've been asking about you?"

"You know my last name. I didn't put it in your contacts when I gave you my cell number," he whispered. He was so close his breath fanned over my neck, moving wisps of hair. His cologne swirled around me, sun, salt water, and something all him. "And you know about Tanya."

Smiling at him, I used my thumb to flick off the top of my pen and reached over, drawing a large circle around his name on his homework.

"No, Mr. Victor, I just know how to read. You should learn. And everyone knows about Tanya. She's as easy as you are."

The bell rang. I shoved my things in my bag and threw it over my shoulder, walking away without looking back. But I wanted to look back. He was quite nice to look at, but he was off-limits. He was also maddening to the point I wanted to scream. So I kept my eyes focused straight ahead and settled for picturing him in my mind.

I can't believe I'm stuck with him in biology for the rest of the year. Ugh. I wonder how much a hit man costs. I have my college fund... maybe that'd be enough.

Jenna was waiting for me outside biology. "I see you and Brody are talking. Anything interesting?"

"Is that jealousy I hear in your voice?" I teased with a smile. "Don't worry. It isn't like we were having a conversation about anything important, unless you consider him calling me a bimbo important."

"He did not!"

"Yeah. He's already activated my bitch-mode, and I've only known him two days."

Someone chuckled behind me. I looked over my shoulder and let out a frustrated sigh when I saw Brody.

"He's behind us, isn't he?"

I smirked at her. "Now's your chance, Jenna. Ask him out," I said loud enough for him to hear.

She elbowed me in the ribs, glaring at me before ducking into her classroom. Laughing, I waved and jogged up the stairs.

"Where should we sit?" he asked when I turned the corner into my next class.

"What are you doing? We don't have this class together," I said through clenched teeth.

Brody twirled his pencil between his fingers. "We do now. My schedule changed. So, where do you sit?"

I didn't answer him. Walking to my seat, I threw my books down.

Brody looked at the girl in the seat next to me. "Bummer. I thought we could be table buddies again."

"You do realize this is AP English, right?"

"Yes. Oh, look! There's an empty seat behind you. We can pass notes during class." He winked as he walked by.

Ugh, he gets more annoying every time he opens his mouth.

I turned in my seat and looked into his eyes. And forgot what I'd wanted to say. His eyes were such a brilliant shade of blue, framed by the longest, blackest lashes I'd ever seen. Girls would kill for his lashes.

He quirked an eyebrow at me when I didn't say anything.

"What class do you have after this one?" I finally asked.

"Computer science. Should I save you a seat?"

"Thankfully, we don't share that class."

"If I didn't know better, I'd think you didn't want me in your classes."

"Ya think?" I turned toward the front, grinding my teeth when I heard him chuckle softly behind me.

As soon as English class was over, I grabbed my bag and walked out of the classroom, trying to disappear in the crowded hall.

"What's wrong with you? You look like you're going to explode," Jenna said as soon as I walked into American history.

"Two words. Brody. Victor." I ticked them off on my fingers.

"What about him?"

"Evidently his class schedule was changed, and we now share the same English class."

"You lucky bitch!"

I moved out of the way of someone trying to get down the aisle before looking at Jenna and nearly yelling, "Lucky? He called me a bimbo! How am I lucky to be sharing classes with him?"

"Do you sit together in English, too?"

"Ugh! Are you listening to anything I say? He's a tool."

"Yeah, but he's a gorgeous tool." She laughed.

I dropped into my seat. "Can't deny that."

This day sucks.

I didn't realize how much my day was going to suck until I

walked into my next class.

"I saved your seat for you." He gave me an amused grin. I wasn't sure what was so funny to him. I was pissed.

"Why are you here? How'd you know I was in this class... and where I sit?"

"I figured it was a good bet that since we are in the same AP biology and English courses that we'd share other AP classes, as well." He shrugged a shoulder. "As far as knowing where you sit, I asked."

My heart skipped a beat, and not in a good way. "Who'd you ask?" I whispered.

"Why? Are you okay?" Brody stood and reached for me.

I flinched away from his hand. "Yeah, I'm fine. Why?"

"You're pale and look—"

"Who'd you ask?" I asked him again. If Jaden found out he'd been asking about me, it was going to cause problems... for both of us.

"I didn't ask anyone. I saw the seating chart on the teacher's desk."

I sighed. "Good," I said, distracted. Putting my books down, I slipped into my seat next to Brody. "That's good."

We didn't speak to each other the rest of the class period. It wasn't until I was gathering my things to leave that he spoke.

"I guess I'll see you after lunch in AP calculus," Brody said, walking past me.

"Yeah, lunch will give me time to mentally prepare myself for your annoying presence. I'll save you a seat."

After lunch, I sat in my usual seat in calculus. I looked up just as Brody walked into class. I moved my messenger bag from the seat next to me. He hesitated, looking around. I looked down and flipped through my textbook. Seconds later, I felt him pull out the seat next to me and sit down.

"I thought you were kidding about saving me a seat," Brody said.

I shrugged a shoulder. "I figured I was fighting a losing battle. There are other open seats. You aren't obligated to sit here."

"Am I welcome to?"

I glanced at him. "What do you mean?"

"Do you want me to sit here?" he asked quietly.

"Why would I care where you sit?"

He grinned. "Just curious why you saved the seat for me."

"Like I said, there are other open seats. Take your pick. And for the record, I didn't save the seat for you. It's an open seat. No one sits there, so it didn't need saving."

He folded his arms behind his head and leaned back in the chair, stretching his legs out in front of him. "I like this seat. I think I'll stay here."

"Whatever," I muttered. "What class do you have next period?"

"Why? Are you gonna save me a seat?"

What constitutes the insanity plea for murder? Could I strangle him and claim temporary insanity?

"Nope. I want to know if this torture is going to continue." I flipped through my notepad and tried to ignore him. Impossible.

He laughed, and I felt a little flutter of something in my chest. I bit my bottom lip to hide a grin.

When calculus was over, Brody and I went our separate ways. I was sure I was done with him for the day, and I let out a sigh of relief. I hated how he made me feel off balance, how he was able to get under my skin. And I especially hated the flutters I felt whenever he laughed or leaned close to say something. It confused me. Like it or not, I was with Jaden and even if I wasn't, Brody had a reputation. I wasn't looking for a one-night hook-up, not even with the gorgeous Brody Victor.

I walked into the library for independent study, a glorified name for study hall. Most seniors skipped out on the last hour. I usually spent it in the library, working on homework. The less time I spent at home, the better.

I always sat at a table in the back of the library where it was quiet and isolated. Putting in my ear buds, I turned up my iPod. Spreading my calculus notes out, I flipped open my textbook and started working out the homework problems. Concentrating on solving the problems, I didn't notice him until his shadow fell across my papers. I looked up, and my heart skipped.

I watched Brody's lips move and him gesture with his hands.

I pulled the ear buds from my ears. "Really? You're here, too? Look, this is my area. There are dozens of cubicles in the library where you can study. Find one, preferably the one farthest from me."

"What happens if I like this side of the library?"

"Brody." I sighed. "Your village called. They want their idiot back. Run along now." I flicked my fingers like I was shooing a fly away.

A ghost of a smile crossed his lips just before he winked at me and walked by. "See you tomorrow, Willow," he said over his shoulder.

Ugh, tomorrow. I think I hate school.

FIVE
Football

"There are no dead bodies hidden in the closet...unless you're volunteering"
~*Willow*

FRIDAY NIGHT. ANOTHER NIGHT OF FOOTBALL. I'D LOVE GOING TO the games if I could spend the time with Tim, Jenna, and our other friends, eating too much junk food, gossiping, and ogling the football players in their tight uniforms. Instead, every move I made was watched, scrutinized, and reported to Jaden later.

Then there was the inevitable fight. There was a party if our team won—the Cassidy Cougars were undefeated, so there was always a party—and Jaden would want to go. I couldn't because of curfew, which would cause a fight. Every Friday, it was the same thing. It would've been so much easier if I drove myself to the games each week, but Jaden insisted on driving me himself. Possessive.

"Hey," Jenna said, sitting down next to me. She handed me a Coke.

"Ooh, caffeine and sugar. Just what I like. Thanks."

"Where's your watchdog?"

"Karen is two rows up, directly behind me." I sighed.

Tim wandered over and sat next to Jenna. He was loaded down with candy and the biggest cup of pop I'd ever seen.

"Think you have enough sugar to get you through the game?" I asked with a smile.

"I'm not sure. I think I'll make it to halftime, but beyond that remains to be seen. Here, I bought this for you." He handed me a stick with a big blob of pink cotton candy on the end.

"Yum! I love cotton candy. Thanks. You are officially my best friend."

"Hey!" Jenna scowled. "Brought you a Coke, remember?"

"Hmm, I guess you guys are even then," I said, shoving the pink sugar in my mouth. "This is good."

"Hi, Willow," a smooth-as-velvet voice glided over me, making me shiver like a finger had just slid up my spine. I turned toward him, cotton candy filling my mouth and a handful melting between my fingers, making them a sticky mess.

Swallowing the gooey candy, I said, "Oh, hi, Brody." His eyes followed my tongue when I ran it across my lips, licking the sticky sugar from them. Something fluttered deep in my stomach. "What do you want?"

"Just stop to say *hi*," he said.

I looked next to him. Sarah sat pressed against him, her hand high on his thigh.

Ew, she really gets around.

"What happed to Tanya?"

He shrugged a shoulder. "That didn't quite work out."

"Ah, so you've moved on to your next conquest. How nice for you."

"Something like that."

"Well, I advise you to get a good supply of penicillin. You're gonna need it."

"That's so sweet. You're worried about my health." He reached up, slipping a lock of hair behind my ear, and a grin pulled at his lips. "Don't worry, I have it covered. Literally."

"Ugh. You know, after meeting you, I'm thinking of becoming a lesbian. You're disgusting."

Laughing, he stood. "Later." He walked away, Sarah following him like a puppy with her tongue hanging out.

"He's with Sarah now? He'll do anybody," Jenna said, popping a piece of popcorn in her mouth.

"I guess so." I shuddered.

He's gonna drive me insane by the end of the school year.

When the game ended, I waited for Jaden on the sidelines like always. He jogged over to me, but instead of giving me roses and kissing me like always, he left the roses on the bench and jerked me to him. His fingers dug in to my arm, and I bit the inside of my cheek against the pain. He whispered in my ear, "Wait for me in the car." He let go of me so fast I stumbled backward.

Great. He's in a mood.

I wandered back to where Jenna and Tim were standing. "What was that?" Jenna asked.

"No idea." I shrugged a shoulder.

Tim glanced at the players' bench. "No flowers tonight? That's new. He always gives you roses. He's pissed about something. What'd he say to you?" Tim forced another stick of cotton candy at me.

I shoved some of the spun sugar in my mouth and talked around it. "He told me to go wait in the car. That's it." I pushed more of the sticky candy in my already full mouth. I ate when I was nervous or upset. I was both. Jaden had a temper, and I was afraid I was on the wrong side of it.

"Let me drive you home, Willow. You don't need to put up with his crap. Let's just leave." Jenna pulled me toward her car. More cotton candy went in my mouth.

"I can't just leave. He'll harass me until I talk to him. I'll just get it done with now." Another bite of cotton candy. The big cloud of pink sugary goodness was already half gone.

"Dump him, Willow," Tim said under his breath. "You don't need him or his hang-ups. Your relationship isn't healthy. No one should be that possessive."

"I know." I sighed. "I know." I shoved a huge piece of cotton candy in my mouth. "I need to go. I'll text you both later," I said.

I wish I could explain it to you. Tell you everything. Why I can't leave Jaden.

Jenna's face was pinched with worry. She raised her hand and waved. Tim just shook his head and turned to leave. Neither of them understood. I knew Jaden was an idiot. But even though he had his bad traits, he was a good guy—somewhere deep, deep inside. When we first started dating, things were different, better. He was loving and caring.

I answered the door, and a shy smile curved my lips. He was gorgeous as always. His cologne drifted in with the breeze. I took in a big breath. He smelled spicy, woodsy.

"Hi."

"Hi, Willow. You look beautiful. Every guy is going to be jealous of me tonight." Jaden reached out, took my hand, and helped me down the porch stairs and into his car. He slipped into the driver's side and turned to me. Cupping my cheek, he kissed me. So soft, tender, and filled with emotion.

The driver's side door swung open, startling me out of my memories. Jaden jumped in the car, his hair still wet.

"That was fast. You didn't blow-dry your hair," I said, looking at his face set in hard lines. Jaden always dried his hair after his shower.

He grunted something in reply. I couldn't make out what he said or even if it was an actual word. He started the car and peeled out of the parking lot, the car fishtailing in the gravel. I grabbed the dash for support.

"Jaden! What's wrong with you?"

He drove toward my house, not even asking about Jamieson's party. Pulling in my driveway, he threw the car in park, jerking us both forward.

"I saw you talking to him." They were the first words he'd said since getting in the car.

"Who? Tim?" He knew Tim and I were friends. He'd never had a problem with it before.

"No. Brody Victor. Sitting there, on the bleachers, where everyone could see." Jaden's hands gripped the steering wheel so hard his knuckles were white.

"We talked all of two minutes, and it wasn't even friendly. We don't even like each other, Jaden." I laid my hand on his arm.

"It didn't look like nothing. He touched your hair." He pushed my hand away, and I flinched at the sound of his raised voice in the small space.

"He was with Sarah. She was practically hanging off him," I yelled. "I'm so tired of this possessive crap. Get over it." I got out of the car and slammed the door.

He rolled down his window and yelled, "Watch your mouth and check your attitude. You have no say in this relationship, Willow. The sooner you figure that out, the better it'll go for you."

He screeched out of the driveway and down the road. I sank to the porch steps. My elbows on my knees, I put my head in my hands and fought the tears that threatened to fall.

Breathe. You're strong. Breathe. You won't be broken. Just breathe

"How'd it go with Jaden last night?" Jenna asked.

I looked down and wiggled my toes in the lavender footbath my feet were soaking in. Jenna and I were having our monthly spa day. I loved the pedicure, soaking my feet in the silky water that smelled so good, and then having them massaged. There was nothing better in the world. It was total bliss.

"So? Are you gonna tell me or what?" she prodded when I didn't answer.

"He was pissed that I was talking with Brody. He saw Brody reach out and push a piece of my hair behind my ear, and it sent him into a freakin' fit."

"You talked to him for like three seconds!"

"Doesn't matter. Jaden saw it. Can we not talk about him? I want to enjoy my footbath." I leaned back in the chair and closed my eyes.

"Okay, let's talk about Brody," Jenna said.

"Why?" I opened one eye and looked at her.

"I can't believe you share five classes with him. That's fan-freakin-tastic!" Jenna practically shouted.

"Shh! Jeez, Jenna, get a grip. You are way too over the top when it comes to Brody." I laughed.

"Well, have you seen him?" she said, her eyes bugged out and eyebrows so high they disappeared under her ebony bangs.

I laughed harder. "Yes, sheesh, I've seen him. And, yes, he's gorgeous—"

"He's smokin.'"

"Yeah, that too, but he's a pig," I said.

"I heard he dropped Tanya like yesterday's news. Didn't even kiss her goodnight when he took her home, which, by the way, had to be a blow to Tanya's ego." Jenna held her hand out and inspected her manicure.

"Who'd you hear it from?"

"Luce."

I opened both eyes and raised my eyebrows. "Luce? You're kidding?"

Luce was the person to go to if you wanted the scoop on anyone at school. She knew everything about everyone—almost before they knew it themselves. If she said it, it was almost certain to be the truth. I'd never known her to be wrong. Of course, there was always a first time for everything.

"Nope. And word going around the texting world last night was he dumped Sarah at home right after the game without so much as a *see ya later*. When someone asked him about why he went out with Tanya and Sarah in the first place, he said he was still trying to figure out the hierarchy of datable girls." Jenna looked at me and shrugged a shoulder. "Maybe he's not as big of a player as people have made him out to be."

"Oh no, he's a player. He just wants to screw a higher class of girl, that's all."

"So. He's only playin' ya if you don't know it. Maybe it's time for the player to get played." Jenna smirked.

I narrowed my eyes at her. "What are you talking about?"

"I'm just saying the tables can be reversed."

I shook my head. "That would require him to become emotionally involved in someone. From what I've heard, that doesn't happen."

"Okay, so cut out emotions. Just use each other for fun." Jenna grinned and winked.

"Who are you talking about?"

"You and Brody… keep up."

I rolled my eyes. "I'm with Jaden. We've been over this before. Several times, in fact."

"Yeah, but you don't want to be." I opened my mouth to argue, but Jenna cut me off. "Please don't try to deny it. I've been your best friend for too long. I can tell the spark fizzled on that romance a long time ago. You just stay with him because it's easier than breaking up with him. But if someone came along that interested you, you'd drop Jaden in a hot second."

I shrugged a shoulder. "And what makes you think Brody is the guy that interests me? I don't even like him. And I definitely don't want a relationship with him considering his reputation."

"I didn't say relationship. I said fun. Think of him as your rebound guy. The bad boy we all need before we find the good guy we want a real relationship with."

"I think you've lost your mind," I told her.

Jenna tapped her bottom lip with her fingernail and stared at me. Finally, she said, "You're scared."

"Scared? I am not."

"Yep, you've been with Jaden so long you know what to expect from him. There's nothing you don't know about him. You, my friend, are in a rut, and you're scared to climb out of it. You're scared of the unpredictable, of losing control."

"We're not in a rut. We're comfortable in our relationship."

Jenna barked a laugh. "Delude yourself all you want. You need to get your freak on with someone who'll turn your world upside down. Comfortable is for wusses."

Monday. I looked through my T-shirts to find one with an appropriate saying for the day. I chose one that said, *I hear voices and they don't like you.* I thought that would get my message across to Brody. Passive aggressive, but I didn't care. I slipped into my jeans, pulled a zippered hoodie on, and drove to school.

"Sending a message, I see," Jenna said when she saw me in the hall. "The question is to whom, Jaden or Brody? Hmm?"

I smiled. "Shut up."

I walked into biology and sighed. He was already there. "You're here." Dropping my books on the table, I plopped in my chair.

"You're here, too," Brody said with a hint of a grin.

"I was hoping I'd be alone today," I muttered.

He frowned. "Why wouldn't I be here?"

"You know, you could develop a case of malaria or jungle fever or some type of disfiguring disease and wouldn't be able to come to school for, oh, the rest of the year." I dropped my head on my books.

He laughed. "Sorry to disappoint."

I grunted in reply and closed my eyes so I didn't have to look at him.

Why does he have to look so freakin' awesome? And smell... wow. I wonder how I can ask what he's wearing so I can get some for Jaden? Because he smells beyond yummy.

"Did you hear me?" Brody asked.

"Huh?"

"I said it was a good game Friday. I didn't see you at Jamieson's afterward. I saw Jaden, though."

Yeah, I bet you did. I wonder who Jaden hooked up with.

"I didn't go to the party," I mumbled.

"Why? Don't you usually go with Jaden?"

"No."

"Oh. I thought you'd—"

"Do they ever shut up on your planet?" I snapped. A surprised look crossed his face, and he leaned back from me like I'd hit him. I sighed. "I'm sorry. It's just, it's Monday, I haven't met my caffeine quota for the morning yet, and my head is already pounding. I didn't mean to snap."

Yes, I did. I don't want to talk about the damn party. And I don't want to talk to you. You're being... nice. It's freakin' me out.

"No problem. Here." Brody reached in his backpack, pulled out a Red Bull, and handed it to me. "That should help with your caffeine problem. It might hold you over 'til lunch."

I sat up straight and immediately felt like the biggest jerk. He was actually being sweet. "Thank you. I need this so bad." Our fingers brushed when I took the can, and my hand tingled from the contact. My mind wandered to a different time, a different boy, and I tried to remember if I'd ever felt the same sensations with him.

A quiet knock sounded against the door. I opened it immediately. I'd been waiting for him in the living room and saw him drive up.

"Hi." Jaden smiled down at me. "You look gorgeous." He pulled his hand from behind his back and showed me a can of Red Bull. Condensation ran down the sides. My throat could already feel the citrusy goodness sliding down it and the punch of energy I'd get to help me navigate my morning classes. Some people drank coffee or tea. I drank Red Bull.

I reached for the can, but Jaden pulled it away. "First a kiss?" he asked softly.

"Always. You don't have to bring Red Bull for that. But it's always a good incentive."

He laughed and gave me the can. "Good to know." His mouth took mine in a slow, soft kiss. His tongue dipped between my lips. Something in my chest trembled and warmth radiated from it.

Wrapping the arm holding the can around his neck, I fisted my free hand in his shirt. I leaned into him, and he deepened the kiss with a low growl.

Jaden moved his lips from mine and skimmed them along my jaw to my ear. "You're killing me, Willow. We have to go to school, and all I'll be able to think about is this kiss and the small sighs you make that drive me freakin' insane."

I smiled and cupped his cheek. "I guess Red Bull is right up there with oysters. A great aphrodisiac."

Jaden nuzzled the curve of my neck a few seconds longer before threading his fingers through mine and pulling me outside to his car.

The memory fizzled, and I remembered I was sitting in my biology class with Brody staring at me. "What?" I asked.

"Oh nothing. I'm just trying to imagine you with a personality."

So much for being sweet.

I pushed the unopened Red Bull across the table toward him and gave him a tight smile. Turning my face away, I lay my head back on my books until class started. I managed not to speak to him for the rest of the class period or through English.

It was lunch, and I stood staring at the vending machine when I heard his voice. We hadn't spoken since the Red Bull incident and, for reasons that confused me, I missed talking to him.

"I figured I'd find you here," Brody said behind me, his body so close to mine I could feel the heat radiate off him. His breath moved wisps of my hair. I stepped to the side. "Come to get your caffeine for the day? I'm surprised you made it until lunch without killing someone... or is there a body or two stuffed in the janitor's closet I don't know about? You certainly seem to have the demeanor to pull off a homicide when you're caffeine deprived." He grinned, his blue eyes sparkling.

Keeping my expression neutral, I turned and stared at him. I let my eyes glide slowly over his face. My breath stalled in my throat and my mouth dried. What started as a sarcastic comment quickly turned into something more. My eyes sucked in his rugged features. Brody was undeniably attractive, but not in a soft, baby faced way. He had a raw sexuality. It showed in the way he carried himself, the way he stood, and the way he gazed at me—intense and knowing. A lock of dark hair fell over his forehead, giving his strong features a small touch of boyishness. My eyes skimmed downward, from his mussed hair to his bright sapphire eyes, framed by thick, black lashes. I took my time memorizing the contours of his high cheekbones and slightly crooked nose, like it'd been broken at some point. I bit my bottom lip when my gaze fell to his full lips that begged me to taste them, and the slight scar on his chin that I wanted to follow with my tongue.

Oh, I need to stop this now. Jaden, Jaden, Jaden... nope, that doesn't help. Brody. Why does that feel right?

Brody shifted from one foot to the other. "What? No snarky comeback? Did I catch you at a loss for words? This must be a first for you." There was that amused grin. I was beginning to like it, even if it did irritate me.

His deep—just throaty enough to be sexy—voice grabbed my attention. "Oh, sorry," I said with a wave of my hand. "I was visualizing duct tape across your mouth."

His smile widened. "First, you tell me to shut up in class and now you want to duct tape my mouth. I'm beginning to think you don't like my conversational skills. If I wasn't so confident and didn't have a healthy sense of self-esteem, it could really hurt." He put his hands over his heart.

I shrugged a shoulder. "I don't mind that you're talking as long as you don't mind that I'm not listening." Putting my money in the machine, I made my purchase and walked away. I heard him chuckle behind me. I couldn't help but smile on my way to my seat.

Wait... when did trading jabs with him go from dislike to mildly funny?

"What are you grinning about?" Jenna asked me when I sat down across from her and next to Jaden.

"Nothin'," I said too quickly, looking at her over the rim of my drink.

"Uh-huh." She smiled at me before looking across the room at Brody. Seconds later, my phone chimed.

> JENNA: HE'S LOOKING AT YOU.
> ME: HE'S NOT AND I DON'T CARE.
> JENNA: YES, HE IS AND YES, YOU DO.
> ME: UGH!

Friday—biology lab. I hated biology labs. I never had a partner, so I had to do double the work. Now Brody was my partner, and I wasn't sure if labs would be any easier or not. I'd have a partner, but it wasn't one I particularly liked. Right? Right. I definitely didn't like him. He was a player. A conceited, self-absorbed bad boy. But... we'd been trading insults back and forth all week and somewhere in there they went from *"I hate you"* to *"you might be tolerable."*

He called me a bimbo. He's definitely not a person I'm going to be friends, or anything else, with. We'll do the assignment and that's it.

Standing at my closet, I looked through my dozens of shirts to pick out my thought for the day. I loved T-shirts with sayings on them. I usually bought one every time I went to the mall or one of those weird magazines came in the mail with pages and pages full of them. I had a closet full. It didn't matter what my mood was, I had a shirt to match it. Grabbing a long-sleeved T-shirt, I slipped it on with my jeans. I finished my hair and makeup and drove to school.

"Willow, you're gonna have to wear a regular shirt one of these days, you know?" Jenna said when she saw me shoving my stuff in my locker.

"Nah, I have dozens of these. I bet I can go six weeks without wearing the same one twice."

"Let's not try it. Be normal. Wear something without a sarcastic comment plastered across your boobs." She grabbed my arm to turn me around and I flinched, sucking a sharp breath through my teeth. Jenna jerked her hand back and looked at me with wide eyes. "What's wrong?"

"Nothing. I just fell and hit my arm against the porch steps. It's nothing." Jenna narrowed her eyes at me, but she kept her thoughts to herself. "Anyway," I continued, "I'm dating Jaden and I'm around Brody all day. I have to let out my sarcasm somehow. So I use my shirts." I threw up one arm and let it slap against my thigh.

"Oh, so dramatic this morning." Jenna rolled her eyes. "You must have doubled up on the caffeine when you drove through Starbucks," she said with a laugh.

I smiled and grabbed my books. "See you in history."

I got to biology before Brody so I grabbed the microscope and slide set we'd need for our lab, starting to set it up. I smelled him as soon as he slipped into his seat beside me.

"Hi Brody," I said, not looking up.

"How'd you know it was me?"

I felt a blush crawl across my cheeks. "I smelled you," I said quietly.

"What are you, a cocker spaniel?"

I looked up and shrugged a shoulder. "You wear the same cologne every day."

"And you wear the same kind of T-shirt every day. What does today's say?" I turned so he could read it. "Huh. '*If you knew what I was thinking, you wouldn't be smiling.*' Interesting. And what are you thinking, Willow?" He braced one hand on the table, his other on the back of my chair, and leaned in to me.

That I love how my name rolls off your tongue in that low voice that you seem to only use when you're talking to me—half whisper, husky and smooth at the same time. That it confuses me that, all of a sudden, I've gone from hating you to being intrigued by you. That I want to scream and cry that I have this secret hanging over my head, ruining my life, because I want you, not Jaden.

"Hmm?" he whispered, leaning closer to me, and I realized I'd been staring at him too long.

"I'd love to explain all my thoughts to you, Brody, but I don't have any crayons," I said finally, giving him a small smile.

He grinned and turned to the equipment I'd laid out for our lab. "Good to go?"

I nodded, and we got started on the lab. We didn't talk the rest of the class period other than what was needed to complete the assignment. There was an uncomfortable vibe between us. Each time our hands or arms would brush against each other when we reached for a slide or turned a page in the textbook, goose bumps would break out over my skin. I was thankful I'd worn a long-sleeved shirt so he couldn't see. I was having a hard enough time hiding my shaking hands, and my voice that seemed way to breathy and soft. He seemed completely unaffected, naturally.

I'm such a fool. What am I doing? I can't fall for him. I'm with Jaden. Jaden who, with just a few words, could destroy everything.

Jaden always liked an audience. He was the captain of the football team, after all. He thrived on attention.

We were sitting at a table in the school cafeteria, Jenna, Tim, and I, along with Jaden and his dumbass friends from the football team. I never took the time to learn their names since they didn't bother to call me anything but *'Jaden's girl.'*

"It's an away game tonight," Jaden told me.

I speared a piece of cucumber in my salad and inspected it. "I know," I answered.

"Hi, Willow," some friends from class called as they walked by.

I smiled and waved. "Hi, guys!" That was when I saw him.

Oh please, please don't say anything. Just keep walking, Brody. Don't say anything, don't stop, and don't wave.

"Hey, Willow. See you in class." Brody raised his hand as he walked by.

"What the hell?" Jaden yelled.

"It's nothing. Leave it alone." I put my hand on Jaden's arm, trying to divert his attention.

"The hell I'll leave it alone." He threw my hand off. My injured arm hit the edge of the table. I gritted my teeth and grabbed it, holding it to my side. "What's going on between you two?" he yelled, standing up.

Brody's face registered surprise and then anger. I looked at him and shook my head, pleading with my eyes for him to leave it alone. Brody looked between Jaden and me. "Are you okay?" he asked me. Brody looked at where I held my arm and raised an eyebrow.

"You don't need to worry about her," Jaden shouted. He reached out and shoved Brody's shoulder.

Brody looked down where Jaden's hand had been. I prayed he would walk away. Then I saw his hands ball into fists.

Oh, crap. Crap. Crap.

Brody took a step forward. I stood up so fast my chair flew backward, hitting the floor with a clang. Jenna reached out for my arm.

"Willow, stay out of it!" she called.

I reached out and grabbed Jaden's arm. It was rigid. I looked at Brody. A vein pulsed in the side of his neck.

"You're messing with the wrong girl, Victor," Jaden said through clenched teeth.

"I think Willow can make up her mind who she wants to be friends with without asking your permission."

Jaden took a step toward him. Brody stood his ground.

Oh, this can't happen. Back down, Brody, please.

"No! Jaden!" I stepped in front of him. "Stop it!" He pushed me out of the way with one arm, like a windshield wiper swiping a bug away. I stumbled backward. One of his friends reached for me. I ducked under his arm and ran in between the two testosterone-filled idiots who insisted on fighting with all the 'B' lunch students watching.

"Stop! Brody, just go." I looked over my shoulder. "Please."

"Yeah, Victor, run along." Jaden twiddled his fingers at Brody.

"Jaden, stop it!" I yelled. "I'm freakin' fed up with your crap!"

"Watch your mouth, Willow." Jaden moved his arm, and I flinched away.

Brody reached out, pulling me against him. "Don't raise your hand to her. You hit her, and I will end you. Make no mistake about that," he said quietly. His hand around my arm, he walked out of the cafeteria, pulling me with him.

"I expect you to be home tonight, Willow. If you're not at the game, you're home," Jaden yelled after us. "We'll finish this later, Willow."

"Great," I groaned, trying to pull away from Brody. "What are you doing?" I yanked my arm away and turned back to the cafeteria.

"Where are you going?" he asked.

"Back inside."

Brody stepped in front of me. "What? Why? He was going to hit you!"

"He wasn't going to hit me." I tried to step around him.

"He pushed you against the table!"

I shook my head, looking at the floor. "Not intentionally."

Brody blocked the door to the cafeteria. "Don't go back in there—"

"Don't you see you've just made things worse by dragging me out of there?" I yelled. "He's gonna see it as an embarrassment in front of his friends, and I'm the one who's gonna pay for it! So thanks for your help. I know you meant well, but just stay the hell out of it!"

Breathe. Just breathe

Saturday night, Jaden and I were at The Dive. As usual, it was packed with people from school, most I knew, but some were just familiar faces. We said our hellos as we walked to the back where the quiet tables were. I saw him almost instantly when we walked in. It was as if my eyes sought him out and once they found him, they wouldn't let him go. We hadn't spoken since our conversation in the hall outside the cafeteria, not even in class. I tried not to look at him. If Jaden saw me glance in Brody's direction, it would start another scene like the one in the cafeteria, so I kept my gaze on the floor and let Jaden pull me through the crowd.

When we walked by his table, I couldn't help raising my eyes just for a second. Our eyes met and butterflies swirled in my stomach, a feeling I hadn't had with Jaden in months. I tried to push that thought from my head as I forced my eyes away from his.

We sat at a table in the very back of the restaurant. The waitress came over to take our drink orders.

"We're ready to order," Jaden said.

"Okay, go ahead."

"I'll have a Coke, a Big Splash Burger with everything, and a side of fries. She'll have a Coke and the Mini Splash Burger, no pickles, no onions, extra cheese. And a side of fries."

"Mustard, ketchup, mayo?" the waitress asked.

"Mayo on both," Jaden answered, handing the menus to the waitress.

Ugh. I hate it when he orders for me. I can order my own damn food. And I hate mayo. How can he not know that by now? And I want a stinkin' order of onion rings. Onion rings!

"Did you like the movie, Jaden?" I asked, trying to divert his attention from our waitress' ass.

"Yeah, it was okay."

Okay? I just sat through two hours of bombs blowing up, appendages flying off, blood and gore splattering everywhere, all of which would have been fine if there had been a plot, and all he says is it was okay? Great. Lovely.

"Did you like it?" he asked, not looking at me.

"Yeah. Loved it, especially the part where the guy was wandering around, looking for his arms. That was classic."

"Yeah." He laughed. "That was great."

Note to self— sarcasm is ineffective on Jaden.

"I need to use the restroom. I'll be right back." Sliding out of the booth, I turned to the restrooms, catching a glimpse of Brody and his date.

Brody's dating Kara? I know her. She's nice. They're sharing an ice cream sundae. How sickening sweet can you get? Ugh… I'm totally jealous. Oh. Kill. Me. Now. I can't be jealous. I'm with Jaden. Jealous, possessive, overbearing Jaden.

Walking down the small hallway where the restrooms were located, I pushed through the door into the ladies' room. I didn't need the restroom. I just wanted a minute alone. Bracing my hands on either side of the sink, I stared at myself in the mirror.

How did this happen? What did I do to get here? This is my life, but I don't remember making the decisions that brought me here. If she hadn't done it… but she did… and now we're both screwed. Suck it up. Stop whining.

After washing my hands, I checked my makeup before pulling the door open to leave. I froze when I stepped into the small hallway. I'd never realized how small it was until I was standing there with him. He filled it, not only with his body, but also with his very presence. Butterflies swarmed my stomach.

"Hey." He gave me a small grin.

"Hey, Ace."

"I just wanted to check on you after yesterday in the cafeteria. You okay?" Brody asked, his eyes searching mine.

"Yes. Thanks." I started to walk away, but stopped and turned to look at him. "And thanks for yesterday. I know you were trying to help."

He nodded once and rubbed the back of his neck with his hand.

I smiled and walked back to my table, trying to put Brody Victor out of my head.

Jaden and I ate our dinner. Then he left me alone in the booth to visit with every football teammate that came through the restaurant. Thankfully, I'd brought my e-reader with me. But there was a time if I'd brought it with me, it would've stayed, unused, in my purse.

"How's your hamburger? I'm sorry I got mayo. I'll remember next time not to order yours with mayo." Jaden reached across the booth and caressed my fingers with the pad of his thumb.

I took a sip of Coke and tilted my head to the side. "It's good. Even with the mayo." I grinned.

Jaden's fingers moved over my hand, drawing invisible circles on my skin. His blue eyes stared into mine.

I took another sip of my Coke, chewing on the end of my straw. "What?" I asked when he continued to stare.

"I just like to look at the prettiest girl here."

He opened his mouth to say more when he was interrupted by three guys from the football team. They pushed their way into the booth with us. One next to Jaden, and two next to me. I was flattened against the wall to make room for them.

"Hey, bro, what's going on?" one of the guys asked.

Jaden's jaw worked, and I saw his pulse beating in a vein bulging on his neck. "Kind of on a date."

"Oh. Sweet," one of the other stinky guys said. They smelled like they'd just walked off the field after hours of football practice and forgot to put on deodorant. I was gasping for fresh air where I was trapped between the wall and the armpit of one guy. "You wanna hang?"

"Did you not just hear me? I'm on a freakin' date. And you weren't invited. So there's the door." Jaden jerked his thumb toward the front of the restaurant.

"Whoa! My man, Jaden. You must be getting some happy-happy if you don't wanna hang with your dawgs. That's cool. We'll catch ya on the flip."

The three guys eased out of the booth and said their goodbyes. I watched Jaden's eyes track them as they made their way from table to table, laughing and joking with other guys from the football team.

I squeezed Jaden's fingers. "Do you want to go say hi to your football friends?"

Jaden turned to me and smiled, his dimples winking at me. "Now why would I want to spend time with them when I have you? I'm with them all the time. They're crude, rude, and stink. You're sexy, smart, and smell good. I'm definitely happier here."

I sighed at the memory and flipped on my reader. By the time Jaden took me home, I'd read three chapters. Three *very long* chapters.

Jaden pulled in my driveway and put the car in park. He leaned over the console and kissed me gently, cupping my cheek in his hand. He took the kiss deeper, skimming his hand down my side, gripping my hip and pulling me closer to him to trail kisses down my neck and across my chest.

"Willow!"

Breathe. Breathe. I'm fine. I'm strong. Breathe.

"Get your ass in the house now!"

Jaden let go of me with a frustrated groan. "I'll text you later."

"Okay. Thanks for tonight."

"Sure." As soon as I got out of the car, he pulled out of the driveway and drove away.

I hurried to the house. "Hi, Mom."

"Hi, honey. You know how I feel about you and Jaden sitting in the car making out."

"I know. I'm sorry."

"Did you have a good time?" She smoothed my hair from my face, a lit cigarette dangling from her lips.

"It was okay." I shrugged a shoulder.

She took a long drag on her cigarette and blew the smoke out of the side of her mouth. Looking at the floor, she nodded. "He isn't the catch everyone thinks he is, is he?"

"He's okay. I mean, you know. He's good." I kissed my mom on the cheek. "I'm really tired. I'll see you in the morning." I climbed the stairs to my room and eased the door closed behind me, clicking the lock in place.

Breathe. You're home. Just breathe.

Heading into my bathroom, I washed my face and brushed my teeth for bed. I changed into a pair of pajama pants. I slipped out of my shirt and looked at the bruising on my arm and shoulder. It was deep shades of purple and black. I let out a breath and pulled my sweatshirt on over my head, trying not to move my arm any more than I had to. Popping two painkillers, I went into my bedroom and crawled in bed.

I'd just turned the light out when my cell phone chimed. I thought about ignoring it, but if it were Jaden, he'd have a fit if he thought I was ignoring his messages. With a frustrated groan, I grabbed the phone off its charger and pressed the message button.

BRODY: I'M SORRY FOR STOPPING YOU AT THE DIVE.

ME: WHY?

BRODY: DID JADEN SEE?

ME: NO. KARA'S NICE. DON'T BE A JERK.

BRODY: NOT ALL REPUTATIONS ARE DESERVED.

ME: ?

BRODY: NEVER MIND. GOODNIGHT, WILLOW.

ME: NIGHT.

Brody is gonna cause me so much trouble.

Calculus

"What harm could it do? It's just a slushie."
~Willow

ONDAY. CRAP. SHUT UP, STUPID, ANNOYING ALARM. I slammed my hand on top of my clock until the incessant beeping stopped. Rolling out of bed, I stumbled to the shower. I washed with a body soap that promised to energize and invigorate. It lied.

Mondays should be illegal. I think that would make a great T-shirt. I'm so gonna go to the mall and have one made. Maybe today. Right after I have a nap.

I pulled on a black, long-sleeved tunic with a cowl neck and black leggings, lined my eyes in black liner, used midnight eye shadow and painted my nails in onyx polish. After adding my black boots and black leather messenger bag, I was totally rockin' the vibe I was going for. I slipped my earrings in, a hoop with a skeleton key dangling from it in one ear and a hoop with a heart-shaped lock dangling from it in the other ear, grabbed my keys, and ran out the door.

"Who died?" Jenna asked when I walked into school twenty minutes later.

"Here." I handed her a Starbucks caramel macchiato and slipped off my sunglasses.

"Holy wow. Are you working the Goth look today or what?"

"No. I'm working the I-hate-Monday-mornings-and-I'm-mourning-the-death-of-the-weekend look."

"Well… you're working somethin'. Thanks for the macchiato."

"No problem. See you in history." I slipped on my sunglasses and walked to biology, standing in the hallway sipping my Starbucks before going into class.

"What are you doing?"

I looked up to see Jaden standing in front of me. "Drinking my caffeine before class starts," I said, holding the cup up so he could see it. "I'm not allowed to take it in the classroom. You want to do something this afternoon?"

"Like what?" he asked, narrowing his eyes at me.

"I didn't know there were limits on what you were willing to do to spend time with your girlfriend."

"Well…"

"Forget I said anything." Dropping my half-full cup into the trash, I walked into the classroom. I flung my bag on the table before dropping onto my seat.

Jaden, being the idiot that he was, followed me. If he'd been smart, he would've taken the hint that I was done talking when I threw away a half cup of caffeine.

"What do you want to do?" he said with a sigh, as if it was a major imposition to spend time with me.

"Nothing, Jaden, I don't want to do anything. I told you to forget it."

"So now you're mad at me?"

"Nope." I started to pull stuff out of my bag. I was so irritated I grabbed things I didn't need. I had a pile of five highlighters and was still pulling more out, slamming them on the table between Brody and me.

"Then what's the matter, Wills?"

"Don't call me that. Nothing's the matter. It's Monday, okay. I hate Mondays. I'm in a crappy mood. Just forget I said anything." I pushed my bag away and threw my sunglasses on top of it, leaning back in my chair.

"Are you PMSing or something?"

"What? Seriously, you did not just ask me that! Just leave."

"See ya at lunch." Jaden bent down to kiss me. I turned my head at the last second, and his lips landed on my cheek. "Now you're starting to piss me off."

"Whatever." I watched him leave the classroom. "Ugh!" I put my hands together like I was strangling him, shaking them back and forth.

Brody chuckled beside me. "Are you okay?"

"Yeah. Why wouldn't I be?"

"Did your hamster die or something?" he asked.

I blew out a frustrated breath. "No one died. I'm mourning the death of the weekend."

"Oh. That's cool."

"I'm so glad I have your approval of my dress code," I snapped.

"Well, there is one thing. If Jaden doesn't want guys looking at you, then you shouldn't wear that push-up bra." He put his elbow on the table and rested his cheek in his upturned palm. His teeth bit into his bottom lip, his eyes traveling from my chest to my eyes and back again.

"Ugh, you're a pig and completely lacking in the IQ department."

"Not that I care what you think, but I'm a member of the honor society." He twirled his pen on the table.

"That's not a surprise," I murmured. I laid my head on my book and closed my eyes.

"No?"

"I'd heard they'd lowered their standards."

He chuckled. "You've got a mouth on you."

I opened one eye and looked at him. "Most people have mouths. Just thought you'd want to know that little fact, you know, before the next honor society meeting."

Brody smiled and turned to face the front of the class where the teacher had started droning on about the earthworm dissection we'd be doing.

Sounds like so much fun, except for the poor earthworm.

"You want to go to the mall?" I asked Jenna as we walked out of school that afternoon.

"Always."

"Good. I have a T-shirt to make."

She threw her arms in the air and sighed. Loud. "Willow, if I'd known you were making another corny T-shirt, I'd have said no," she said, her hands falling with a *thwack* against her thighs. "You must've had a babysitting job, and now you want to throw your hard-earned money away on a stupid T-shirt."

"Don't hate the T-shirts," I said with a laugh. "Besides, you're gonna like this one. But first, a makeover."

"Oh, thank the good Lord. Your makeup is killing me."

An hour later, we left the boutique. We'd been scrubbed, exfoliated, peeled, plucked, moisturized, and had our makeup reapplied. I had to admit they did a much better job than I did. No black eyeliner. Instead, a soft sable that blended better with my hair and fair skin. And even though I always promised myself I wouldn't buy anything when Jenna and I got makeovers, I bought the eyeliner and shadow the make-up artist used—and it was way overpriced. Naturally.

Now if I can just take her home and have her put it on for me every morning before I go to school, I'd be doing okay.

"All right, let's go get this shirt you're so excited about," Jenna said, stuffing a gigantic piece of soft pretzel in her mouth.

"Attractive, Jenna." I winked at her.

"Yeah, like you looked so sexy inhaling that corndog a minute ago."

I laughed and bumped my hip into hers. "After my T-shirt, I say we get slushies and really overload our bodies with junk food."

"Sounds good. The pretzel I ate is lonely." Jenna patted her stomach and pouted. I rolled my eyes.

Fifteen minutes later, I was armed with a new purple, long-sleeved T-shirt that read '*Mondays should be illegal,*' and Jenna and I were on our way to the food court to satisfy our slushie craving. We walked around a corner and I came face-to-face, or rather face-to-chest, with Brody. I stopped just before I ran into him.

"Oh! Hi," I said.

"Hey."

"You're, um, shopping?" It seemed odd that he'd be mall hopping by himself. Most guys avoided the mall like it housed a flesh-eating virus.

He shook his head. "No, I'm just running an errand for my mom."

I looked at the bag he was carrying from a well-known and very upscale cosmetics store. "Well, you're either running an errand or you're a drag queen when you aren't at school."

"How'd you know?" One side of his mouth curved up in a crooked grin.

"Lucky guess," I said with a laugh.

"Are you leaving?" Jenna asked.

"Yes," Brody answered, still looking at me. I felt my checks pink from a blush, and he smiled.

"We're about to leave, too, but first, we're going to satisfy our slushie craving. Come on and have one with us." Jenna grabbed Brody's arm, pulling him toward the food court. He looked at me over his shoulder. I schooled my expression.

I'm gonna kill her. I'm going to hurt her and then kill her. I cannot believe she just invited him to have a drink with us. She will die a long, painful death. I think I'll put that on a T-shirt before I leave.

"So…" Jenna started after we sat down with our drinks.

Brody and I both looked at her, waiting for her to say something epic to break the awkward silence.

"What did you buy?" Brody nodded at my bag.

"Oh, um, a T-shirt."

"Another sarcastic saying on the front?" he asked. I bit my lower lip to hide a grin. His eyes followed the movement. "What does it say? Oh, lemme guess. It says, *I date dumb jocks.*"

I sighed. "That comment really shows your maturity level, Brody."

"Yeah, my advanced maturity level must shock and amaze you considering who you date."

I stood up. "Let's go, Jenna."

"I'm not done—"

"Bring it with you."

"See you tomorrow," Brody called.

I wonder if it's too late to be homeschooled.

"You guys so like each other. It's amazing," Jenna said as soon as we got in the car.

"What the hell are you talking about? We can't stand each other!" I nearly screeched.

"Nope. That's chemistry. You're fighting it. When you stop fighting, there are gonna be fireworks… like I said before, you need someone to rock your world. Turn it upside down. Brody Victor is gonna do that and more."

The next day, Brody and I snapped at each other like always. In biology, Jaden walked me to class. When he left, Brody asked, "Is it hard carrying on a conversation with him? I mean, it must be like talking to a toddler all day."

"You know, Brody, you are the best proof that reincarnation does occur, because no one could be that big an idiot in just one lifetime."

After that, we didn't talk to each other for the rest of the day. We dropped our books on the table, flipped through pages harder than necessary, slapped our pens down, shoved our things in our bags, and made it known to each other, and anyone around us, that we were not happy to be near one another. It wasn't until independent study that we spoke to each other.

I had my ear buds in, listening to music, when he walked up to the table where I worked. Taking out an ear bud, I looked up at him. "What?"

"Do you mind if I sit with you?" Brody asked.

I shrugged a shoulder, looking away from him, which was hard considering he was so *very* easy to look at.

He pulled out the chair next to me and sat down. "Calculus, huh?"

"Mm-hmm." I popped a baby carrot in my mouth.

"Oh, you're a rebel. You're not supposed to have food in here." He smiled.

"Why do you think I sit in the back, genius? Want one?" I held out my container filled with veggies and dip.

Brody looked at it like it was poisoned. "What is that?" He made a face and glanced up at me.

"They're vegetables. Surely, you've seen one or two before. You know, they're those things your mom makes you eat."

"Not the veggies. The other gunk." He took a celery stick and poked at my dip.

"It's hummus. Do you want some or not? I'm not sitting here all day while you play with *my* food."

"I'll take a pass. Thanks."

"Whatever." I dipped a piece of broccoli in the hummus and ate it. Brody watched me with his nose scrunched. "It's good," I said, my mouth full.

"Okay. I'll take your word for it." He opened his calculus book and pulled out his notes. "Did you understand the chain rule we went over today?"

"Yes." I tried not to look at him.

"I hate to admit it, but I didn't completely get it."

"Oh."

"Willow, do you think you can use more than one-word answers when you talk to me?"

I put my pencil down and looked at him. "Maybe."

Brody laughed. "You don't like me much, do you?"

"Not particularly."

"Whoa, was that a two-word answer? Progress."

I rolled my eyes and put my ear buds back in, hoping to end our conversation and focus on my assignment.

Out of the corner of my eye, I watched him look at his textbook and tap his pencil against his notebook a few times before he looked at me. He reached out and pulled an ear bud from my ear.

"Hey!"

"Would you mind helping me out?" he asked.

"Really? You're asking me to help you with your homework? You, a member of the honor society, are asking me, a bimbo jock chaser, for help?" I looked at him with an arched eyebrow.

He cleared his throat. "Yeah, I'm sorry about the bimbo comment. That wasn't cool."

"Ya think?"

Brody lifted his book and looked at me. "Please?"

I sighed. "I can explain it to you, but I can't learn it for you."

He tilted his head to the side and considered what I'd said before laughing loudly. "I deserved that," he said when he stopped laughing. "I promise, I'll try to keep up."

"Let me see what you've got." I leaned over to look at his calculations and nearly groaned. He smelled so good. He looked beyond good. I had the overwhelming urge to touch him.

Focus. Calculus. The chain rule. Think about that and block out Brody. Yeah, like that's gonna happen.

I forced myself to look at his work. "Okay, the chain rule allows us to differentiate a function that contains another function."

I reached over and pointed to his calculation as I explained the problem. He strained to see what I was pointing at before he reached out and pushed the sleeve of my hoodie up my arm.

"Don't!" I jerked away.

"Sorry." He held out his hands, palms forward. "I was just trying to move it so I could see. That's a pretty nasty bruise," he said, pointing to my forearm.

I pulled my sleeve down, not looking at him. "I don't like to be touched."

"Okay, no problem. I'll just turn the page sideways so I can see what you're pointing to. Is there anything else I'm screwing up?"

I took a deep breath to steady my racing heart. "Um, yeah, remember if one function depends on another, and can be written as a function of a function, then the derivative takes the form of the derivative of the whole function multiplied by the derivative of the inner function."

"So basically, I've messed up the entire thing," he said with a grin, looking at me.

I sucked in a breath when I looked in his eyes. I'd never seen eyes quite like his before. I was so close I could see that they weren't just blue, but striations of different shades of blue. Leaning back in my chair, I looked down at my own work.

"You didn't do too badly. It's a hard concept to grasp at first," I said.

"You didn't seem to have any trouble… for a bimbo, I mean."

I glanced up, and he smiled at me. I laughed. "Please take a moment to appreciate my vast knowledge and experience."

"I'm amazed by your exceptional calculus skills." He chuckled.

I inclined my head. "As you should be, Mr. Victor."

The bell rang, and I started gathering my things. I shoved everything in my bag, threw it over my shoulder, and stood to leave.

"Thank you for your help, Willow."

"Sure."

"See you tomorrow."

"'Bye, Brody."

The next morning, while getting ready for school, I pulled on a pair of black skinny jeans and a black tank with an emerald lightweight sweater that fell off one shoulder. Jenna bought it for me for Christmas, saying it made my hazel eyes look green. Scrunching my hair, I blew it dry, letting it fall in waves. I lined my eyes with my new eyeliner, smudging on some smoky green shadow on my eyelids. I looked at myself in the mirror and didn't think I looked too terrible.

Jenna cornered me at my locker when I got to school. "You are totally going for it!" she whispered.

"Going for what?"

"Brody. The fireworks." She smirked at me, her eyes twinkling. "This is gonna be so much fun."

"I am not," I hissed.

"Then why are you dressed to the nines this morning?"

I bit my lower lip to keep from smiling. "I'm not. Jaden likes this outfit, and this happens to be one of my favorite sweaters. You bought it for me if you remember."

"Uh-huh. Whatever you say," Jenna said over her shoulder as she walked toward her class. "I expect details. Lots and lots of details," she sang as she walked away.

What am I doing? I don't normally dress like this. What am I thinking?

I started to go into the bathroom to wash my face, but the first bell rang and I didn't have time.

Crap.

I walked into biology. Brody glanced up quickly before returning to his notes. His head shot back up, and he looked at me a second time. His eyes stayed on me, watching as I made my way from the door across the room to our table.

A slight smile touched his lips. "Hey."

"Hi," I said. "How are you?"

"Good. You?"

"Fine. Better than the poor earthworms are gonna be. It's a deadly day for—"

A hand roughly grabbed my arm. I winced as I was swung around. A second hand wrapped around the back of my neck before a mouth descended on mine in a hard, demanding kiss.

I turned my face away, pushing against the person with both hands. "Jaden," I said through clenched teeth.

"Damn, baby, you look hot. I'm gonna have to follow you around all day to make sure guys keep their eyes and hands to themselves." His hand traveled down my arm to cup my rear. I stepped away.

"Jaden, not in class."

"Later, then." He winked at me before he left.

"Just how short a leash does he have you on, anyway?" Brody asked, watching Jaden leave the room.

"That isn't something you need to worry your little brain over, Ace. It's overworked as it is. Just concentrate on biology and leave the rest alone," I snapped.

"Where's your collar to go with your leash?"

"Mind your own business," I bit out.

Brody chuckled. "Whatever. Such a waste."

"What is?" I asked with an exasperated sigh.

He shrugged a shoulder. "Nothin'. Let's start carving up this earthworm. You're not gonna get all girlie on me, are you?"

I rolled my eyes and slipped on a pair of gloves, making the first cut on the worm. The outside was covered in sticky slime. I pinched my gloved fingers together, opening them slowly, watching the slime stretch between them. I looked at Brody and smiled.

He tilted his head and watched me. "What?"

I darted my hand out and wiped it across the blue button-down he wore open over a soft, gray T-shirt. "How's that for girlie?"

"Okay, so you're not squeamish." He laughed and shrugged out of his shirt. I nearly groaned when I saw his taut biceps flex, especially when I got a glimpse of a tattoo encircling one perfectly toned muscle.

Oh, he's got ink. Can he get any hotter?

For the rest of the class period, we worked on the earthworm dissection. When we finished early, we turned in our work and sat silently at our table, working on other classwork. The silence was awkward and uncomfortable. I spent the majority of the time pretending to read over my notes, trying not to think about him sitting next to me, inhale in his direction and smell him, or, for the love of all of that was holy, look at him, while I counted the seconds until the bell rang and released me from biology Hell.

I was sitting in my usual spot in the library during independent study on Friday when Brody came over and drummed his fingers on the tabletop. "Can I sit with you?" He stood next to my shoulder where I worked on my calculus homework.

I looked up at him and nodded once. "You need more help with the chain rule?"

He didn't look at me when he answered. "Ah, no, actually, I think I have that under control."

"I figured as much. I saw your quiz score. I don't think you had as much trouble as you led me to believe."

"Guilty."

I let the top of my pencil drop onto my paper and looked at him. "The question is why?"

He shrugged. "I wanted to sit with you."

"It's a free country. If you wanted to sit at this table, you didn't need my permission or an excuse."

Brody shook his head. "No, you're not listening. I wanted to sit with *you*. The table is inconsequential."

"Is there a particular reason you are insistent on sharing a table with me, Ace? We don't particularly like each other."

Brody smiled and leaned forward on his forearms. "Who says I don't like you?"

"Okay. I don't like you, then." I drummed my pencil on my paper. "Besides, I'm dating someone. So if that's what you looking for, I'm not interested." I shrugged a shoulder.

"You want me," he said with a grin. "Admit it. You want to go out with me."

I didn't answer right away. Instead, I took my time to write my name on my homework. Silence stretched between us. Finally, I looked at him. "You're absolutely right. I've just been pining away for some guy with a reputation for doing 'em and dropping 'em to come along and sweep me off my feet."

"Nah, you don't care about reputations. You'll go out with me."

"Keep telling yourself that, Ace."

The last bell of the day rang, and Brody smiled at me. He started to shove his things in his backpack. When I didn't move, he stopped and looked at me. "Staying?" I nodded. "Why? Is there something going on I don't know about?"

"Well, if you don't know about it, then you probably aren't invited." I gave him a tight smile.

He chuckled, just a soft rumble in his chest. "Okay. I guess I'll see you Monday, Willow. Have a nice weekend."

Oh, crap. I should keep my mouth shut.

"I have a competition this afternoon and then the football game. It's easier to stay than go home and come back."

He stopped and looked at me over his shoulder. "What kind of competition?"

I felt my cheeks turn pink, and I looked down at my paper.

Why did I bring it up, and why do I care what he thinks about it, anyway?

"A chess tournament. Usually they aren't on Fridays, but this one had to be rescheduled and today was the only available date."

He turned and looked at me. "Chess?"

I squared my shoulders and lifted my chin. "Yeah, so?"

"Nothing. It's, um, I think it's great. It's just not what I expected."

"For a bimbo, you mean," I said through clenched teeth.

"Am I ever gonna live that down?"

I bit my lip to keep from smiling. "Probably not."

"Ah, I see." He smiled. "You're not as pissed as you want me to think you are."

"Oh, no, I am. It's just funny… a chess-playing, honor-society member, bimbo." I couldn't stop myself from laughing.

Brody rolled his eyes. "I did apologize for that comment. So you play chess and are a member of the honor society?" Walking back to the table, he stood next to me. "And you date the captain of the football team." He drummed his thumb on the tabletop.

"Yes. Do you have a point?"

"You just seem more like you'd be his tutor than his girlfriend." Brody shrugged a shoulder.

I tried not to laugh, but did anyway. "That's how we met."

Brody chuckled and nodded. "So, does he watch your tournaments?"

I snorted. "No."

He drummed his thumb against the table again, looking to the side. He glanced at me quickly before looking down. "Ah," he cleared his throat, "would you mind if I stayed and watched?"

"Oh, um, why?"

Brody shrugged a shoulder. "I don't have anything better to do." *What's his angle? I can't figure him out. Do I want him to stay?*

"I can't stop you from staying," I said slowly.

"That's not exactly what I asked." He looked at me, his gaze locked on mine.

"I guess I don't mind if you stay."

What? Why did I just say that? He gave me an out. I just had to say no! Stupid, very stupid.

"Maybe we can grab a burger after?" he asked.

"I don't think that's a good idea—"

"Just as friends. Nothing more," he said quickly.

"Maybe. I'm not sure…"

"How about this—if you win, we get a burger and celebrate. If you lose, well, you go do whatever it is you do after a tournament and I'll leave you to it."

"So you're encouraging me to lose, then?" I asked, looking at him through my lashes.

He laughed. "I was hoping you'd see it as encouragement to win, so you'd get to eat dinner with me and enjoy my sparkling personality and wit."

"Yeah, whatever you say, Ace." I gathered my things and we walked out of the library, toward the gym where the tournament would be held.

"So, how good are you?"

I looked up at him. "Why?"

He opened the gym door for me and put his hand on my lower back, guiding me inside. I tried to ignore the currents of electricity that ran up and down my spine. "I want to know what my chances are of getting a burger." He looked down. "I'm hungry."

"I'm pretty good," I said quietly. I didn't add that I'd been on the chess team since fourth grade and was more than pretty good. In fact, there was only one person on the team better than I was—Tim, who was the team captain. I didn't want to seem like I was bragging, but the chances of us getting a burger after the tournament where high... too high.

"I'll bet you're more than pretty good. I have a feeling you're more than pretty good at whatever you do," Brody murmured, his hand still on my back.

"Thanks. Ah, you sit on the bleachers. I have to go over there." I pointed to the corner of the gym where the chess team had gathered. As I turned and walked away, his hand slipped from my back. My skin instantly felt cold from the loss of his touch, and I felt a prickle of disappointment I had no right feeling. "Oh, Brody?" I called over my shoulder.

"Yeah?"

"I forgot to tell you. We're playing Stanton High."

He grinned and winked at me. "In that case, I hope you slaughter 'em."

"Hey, Willow, I was wondering where you were," Tim said when he saw me walk up. "Here's the assignment sheet."

"Ugh, Paul? Really?"

"You can beat him."

"I know I can beat him, that's not that point. He's just a sore loser. I have to listen to him whine through the whole game. It's supposed to be a silent game, but he mumbles under his breath the entire time. I just want to reach across the table and shove his chess pieces down his throat to shut him up."

Tim laughed like I was joking. I wasn't. The guy I was playing was a total crybaby. I'd played him before and won. But Paul made my life, and the judge's, miserable with his whining, insisting there was no way he could be in checkmate. It was maddening, frustrating, exasperating, aggravating, irritating, and any other adjective I could think of. Needless to say, I wasn't looking forward to a repeat performance.

I walked to my table like I was walking to a guillotine. Paul and I shook hands before we sat down. Folding my hands in my lap, I stared at the chessboard in front of me, trying not to look toward the bleachers to see if Brody decided to stay and, if so, where he was. I failed. My eyes darted to the side. He was sitting directly beside my table, about five rows up on the bleachers. He caught me looking at him and grinned. I smiled back and quickly looked back at the board, waiting for the signal to begin the games.

The buzzer sounded and thoughts of Brody drained from my mind. I was completely focused on the game in front of me. There were approximately fifteen games being played at the same time, but the gym was silent, other than the clicking of the chess pieces and the pressing of the timers.

Thankfully, a judge hovered near our table. It kept Paul quiet. Our game was over quickly. Instead of insisting on rehashing every move, trying to disprove my win, he knocked over his king and shook my hand before he returned to his school's corner to sulk.

In the corner designated for our team, I grabbed a Coke out of the cooler the PTO set out for us and a granola bar. When I turned to sit down, I glanced at Brody in the bleachers. He was looking at me with a smirk. He gave me a quick thumbs-up. I smiled and felt my cheeks heat with a blush.

Why am I blushing? It was just a stupid chess game. I'm dating

Jaden. Jaden... who would probably plow through all the chessboards if he knew Brody was here watching me play. Jaden... who's never bothered to show any interest in my chess tournaments—ever.

My next two games weren't quite as easy as the first. The second I did well, but the third, I made an error early on that almost cost me the game. It was a very stupid mistake that made me wonder if I was thinking more about Brody than the game.

After the final game, I grabbed my things and started toward the door. I felt a twinge of disappointment when I didn't see Brody anywhere. Sighing, I hefted the strap of my messenger bag over my shoulder and started to leave.

I'm dating Jaden. I should be happy Brody isn't around. I don't need the hassle. Jaden. Jaden. Jaden. Yeah, I gotta keep reminding myself of that. Jaden... who knows my secret and would have no problem going through with his threat of telling everyone if I break up with him. Yeah, Jaden, the love of my life.

"You are stupid good." Brody's breath was so close to my ear that it tickled when he talked. I felt his hand on the small of my back, making my skin tingle. His other arm reached out and opened the gym door for me.

"Stupid good?" I laughed.

"Yeah, and that means I'm getting a burger. Good thing, too. I'm starving. Which car's yours?"

"The black one." I pointed. He guided me toward my car with a slight shift in pressure from his hand.

"Stow your stuff inside and I'll drive," he said when I unlocked the door. "I mean, if that works for you. I just figured if you generally stay at school on Fridays, certain people would expect to see your car here."

Jaden. Jeez, Brody's thinking more about my boyfriend than I am.

"Ah. Yeah, that works for me." I tossed my stuff in the backseat. All of a sudden, I was nervous. I was fine thinking I'd drive myself to and from the restaurant and we'd just sit and eat together, but riding in a car with him... that was different.

"I'm over here. The Jeep Grand Cherokee."

"Hey, it's Jaden's girl! How ya doing?" a deep voice boomed

across the parking lot.

I looked over my shoulder and froze. Four guys walked toward us.

"What's wrong?" Brody asked.

"You have to go. Just turn around, walk to your Jeep, and don't look at them. They're on the football team. If they see you and me together…"

"Can I text you later?"

"Yes. Just please go before they get any closer."

Brody ducked his head and jogged to his Jeep, slipping in and driving away before the guys walked past me.

"Hey guys." I tried to sound normal. "Where's Jaden?"

"He's still inside, grabbing his gear. Who was that?" The guy pointed in the direction of Brody's Jeep.

"I'm gonna go find Jaden before he leaves. Good luck tonight!" I hurried toward the school, pushing through the doors. My heart hammered in my chest; it was almost painful. I leaned against the wall next to the doors, trying to calm my breathing while I waited.

"Hey. What are you doing here?" Jaden asked when he saw me.

"I just came to wish you good luck," I said with what I hoped was a convincing smile.

Jaden bent and kissed me. "Thanks, baby. I'll text you later. Maybe you can talk your mom into letting you go to Jamieson's for a while tonight."

"Yeah, I'll ask her." I wouldn't.

"See ya," Jaden said. He pushed through the doors and jogged toward the field.

Oh, that was too close. Way too close. If I'm lucky, they won't say anything to Jaden about seeing me with someone. Please, let me be lucky for once.

SEVEN
Hit

"I wanted to be your friend. I dreamed of being your lover."
~Willow

I WAS RESTLESS AT THE GAME THAT NIGHT. JITTERY. I POPPED A PIECE OF cotton candy in my mouth, already on my second stick and it wasn't even halftime yet.

"Okay, spill," Jenna said, grabbing the candy from my hand.

"What? Give me that!" I scrambled for my candy like a heroin addict would their next fix.

"You only eat this crap when something is bothering you. And even then, you don't mow through it this fast. What's up? Tell me now or I'm throwing this candy on the ground."

"Give it to me," I hissed.

Jenna dangled the stick of cotton candy from her fingertips. I watched it sway back and forth precariously. "Tell me."

"He stayed to watch my chess tournament, and we almost went out for a burger afterward. I would have gone with him, but some of Jaden's teammates walked out of the school just as we were leaving and saw us," I blurted out all in one breath. "Now give me my damn candy."

"Who?" she asked, a frown pulling on her lips.

"Brody," I whispered. "Who else?"

"Oh, holy hottie, Batman! Give me some of that." She grabbed a handful of my cotton candy and shoved it in her mouth.

"I know." I took a bite of my candy, but it melted on my tongue too quickly. It wasn't giving me the high I needed. "This isn't enough.

I need something stronger. Time for chocolate." I made my way to the concession stand. My gaze fixed on my feet while I waited impatiently for my turn to order. "Three chocolate bars, please," I said when it was my turn. "And the biggest Coke you have. With an extra side of caffeine."

"Sure thing, sweetie," the old woman behind the counter said, smiling at me. She pushed the chocolate through the small window and took my money, handing me my change and Coke. "And, sweetie?"

"Yes?" I looked up at her.

"Whoever has you drowning your sorrows in chocolate and caffeine probably isn't worth it."

I smiled at her. "Thanks." Turning, I came face-to-face with Brody. He looked down at me, and his lips tipped in a grin.

"Got a sweet tooth?"

"Ah, yeah, a little. Did you get dinner?"

"Are you worried about my eating habits?" Brody asked with a quirked brow. "How sweet and totally unnecessary."

Sighing, I tried to walk around him. "Forget it." I couldn't figure him out. This afternoon he was sweet and friendly, and now he was back to antagonizing and irritating.

I walked through the concession stands on my way back to the bleachers when someone grabbed my arm and pulled me into the shadows behind one of the concession booths, making me drop my Coke.

"I'm sorry. I didn't mean to be a jerk back there. I just didn't want anyone overhearing us actually talking like… we like each other," Brody murmured.

"Oh." I hated how my voice sounded all breathy and my mind spun from the closeness of him. "You made me drop my Coke."

That's what I say? Deep. Real deep. Earth shattering, actually.

Brody laughed. "I'll buy you another."

I shrugged. "At least it wasn't my chocolate." I smiled.

"So, to answer your question, no, I didn't get to eat. Do you think you could get away for a while?"

"Um." I drummed my fingers against my leg, opening my mouth

to answer, and then closing it again before finally asking, "Why?"

"'Cuz I could grab us a couple of burgers from the concession stand, and we could eat them in my Jeep. You do owe me a burger," Brody reminded me, like I'd actually forgotten.

"Ah, where are you parked?"

"Way in the back. I decided to come at the last minute, so I think I got the farthest parking space there is. In fact, I think it's actually in another county."

I laughed. "Okay. I need a minute to see what I can do."

"I'll get the burgers. What do you like?"

You. Oh, crap, where did that come from? I'm seriously walking on a very thin line.

"No, don't get them yet. I'm not sure if I'll be able to come back or not."

"I'll take my chances. I'll meet you over there?" He nodded at an unlit part of the parking area behind the last concession stand.

"Okay, but if I'm not back in five minutes, you'll know I couldn't get away." I forced myself to walk calmly to where Jenna and Tim sat on the bleachers. As I walked, I opened one of the candy bars and threw the candy under the bleachers, keeping the wrapper. I did the same with half of another. I sat down between Jenna and Tim.

"Got your candy fix?" Jenna said with a laugh, looking at the chocolate bars.

"Yeah."

"Uh-oh. I know that look. You're gonna hurl, aren't you? You ate too much of that crap and nothing else." She picked up the empty wrappers and looked at them.

"Yeah, I'm not feeling too hot." I purposely talked loud enough that Karen, who was sitting a row behind us, would hear me. She would tell Jaden everything as soon as the game was over. "Do you think you can take me home?"

Jenna gave me a funny look. "Yeah. What about Jaden? He'll be looking for you."

"I'll tell Karen to tell him I'm sick and had to leave. He'll be fine with it. He won't have to worry about my curfew and can go to Jamieson's party after the game."

"Okay." Jenna grabbed her things.

I turned to Karen, who, like I figured, was listening to our conversation. "Karen, I'm not feeling so great. Too much candy, I guess. Can you get a message to Jaden that I went home and tell him I'll text him after the game?"

"Sure." She studied my face. I tried to look sick.

"Tell him I said to have fun at Jamieson's party."

"I'll tell him." She watched Jenna and me walk down the bleachers after we said goodbye to Tim and the others in our group.

As soon as we rounded the stands, Jenna grabbed my arm. "Spill. Now."

"I'm having a burger with Brody. You were the only cover I could think of. I know you don't really like the games anyway, so I didn't think you'd mind leaving early." I cringed, waiting for her to say something.

"Nope, don't mind at all. He'll give you a ride home?"

I nodded. "I think so."

"Well, have fun." She winked and walked to her car. "I expect a full and very detailed report. It's the least you owe me."

"You're the very bestest friend a girl can have, you know that right?" I gushed with a smile, swinging my clasped hands back and forth and batting my eyelashes.

"Of course," she said and waved.

I ran to the back of the last concession stand where I was meeting Brody. He stood with his shoulder leaning against the wall, one thumb hooked in his belt loop. His other hand held a tray of drinks and a bag. He smiled when he saw me.

"I was just about to give up," he said quietly and pushed off the wall.

"Sorry. I tried to hurry."

"No problem. Let's go. When do you have to be back?"

"Here, let me carry something." I took the drinks from him, and my stomach growled.

Brody laughed. "You sound as hungry as I am. So? How long do we have?"

"Oh, um, I don't have to be back. I said I was leaving because I was sick from too much junk food." I smiled.

"Ah, three chocolate bars and a Coke on an empty stomach can make anyone sick."

"Yeah, well, I'd already had two things of cotton candy, an ice cream cone, and a bag of chili cheese corn chips. Oh, and that was my second Coke." Brody looked at me with raised eyebrows. And I shrugged. "I eat when I'm nervous," I said.

"Are you even gonna have room for a burger?"

"Oh, yeah, I'm hungry for something that's not full of sugar." I grinned. "Something dripping in fat sounds good."

Brody laughed and unlocked the passenger door to his Jeep, holding it while I got in and shutting it after me. I groaned. The Jeep smelled like him—oh so good. It surrounded me like a cloud. I wanted to open a window and let in fresh air because I knew I wouldn't be able to concentrate on anything but his smell as long as I was in his Jeep. Brody opened the door and climbed in the driver's seat. The smell of burgers filled the space, masking his smell, and I could breathe again. My head started to clear and stopped spinning.

"I didn't know what you liked, so I had them put everything on the side," he said, pulling out a tray full of lettuce, tomato, pickles, and cheese, putting it on the center console before reaching in and grabbing a handful of condiment packets. He took out a burger and held it out to me. I couldn't stop staring at the mini buffet of burger toppings. "Hey, earth to Willow, do you want this?"

"Huh? Oh, sorry." I took the burger and unwrapped it.

Brody started piling his burger with lettuce and tomato. He stopped when he noticed I just watched him. "Do you eat yours plain? Or did I not get what you like? 'Cuz I can run up there and get whatever you want."

"No. No, this is great." I put a piece of cheese on my burger, looked at it, and then grabbed another. I piled my burger with lettuce and squirted mustard all over it before taking a bite. "This is so good," I said when I swallowed, chasing it down with a gulp of Coke. "Jaden always orders my food for me, and it's never what I want. I like mustard—he orders mayo. I want onion rings—he orders French fries. I can't believe you did this." As soon as the words were out, I wanted to suck them back in.

"He doesn't let you order your own meals?" Brody asked around a bite of burger.

"Sorry, I shouldn't have said anything. Let's not… I don't want to talk about Jaden."

"No problem. So, how long have you played chess?"

"Fourth grade."

"No wonder you're so good. I used to play in middle school," Brody said, before taking a sip of his Coke.

"Why don't you play anymore?"

"We moved around a lot. It made it tough to do any extracurricular activities."

"Ah. And now? Does your family still move around or are you going to be in Middleton for a while?"

"I think we're here to stay."

"Then you should join the chess club. I mean… ah, never mind." I shook my head, taking another bite of my hamburger.

"What? Tell me what you were going to say."

"Well, the chess club isn't exactly something that would… your reputation isn't one that would suggest… I'm not sure you'd enjoy chess club, that's all."

Smooth. Way to stick my foot in my mouth. Never mind just one foot—I just shoved them both in there. Jeez.

Brody looked at me for what seemed like hours before he spoke. "And you believe everything you hear about reputations? You judge people based on them?"

"I wouldn't say I judge them—"

"Why are you here? If my reputation is such an issue for you, why are you here? Oh, wait, I get it. We're in a car in a dark parking lot where no one can see you slumming it with the bad boy of Cassidy High, right?"

"No! That's not it at all."

"Then enlighten me, Willow. Why are you here?"

"You asked me."

Brody blew out a breath and looked out the window. Throwing his half-eaten burger in the bag, he started clearing the remnants of the toppings and condiments from the Jeep's console.

I opened my door and slipped out of the Jeep, throwing what was left of my sandwich into the field behind the parking lot. "I'm sorry... I..." I shook my head, turned, and walked toward the stadium.

Brody got out of the Jeep and called after me. "Where are you going? I thought you told them you were leaving?"

I shrugged. "I'll tell them I'm feeling better and decided to stay. No big deal. I'll see you Monday, Brody. Thanks for the burger."

"Willow," he called, just loud enough for me to hear. "Don't go."

I stopped with my back to him. "Give me one reason to stay."

"Because I don't believe you care about reputations, and I don't want you to go."

"That was two."

"Then I should get extra credit." I could hear the smile in his voice.

"I can't, Brody. This was a mistake. I'm sorry." Back in the stadium, I sat down next to Tim.

He looked over at me. "I thought you weren't feeling good and were going home?"

"I'm feeling better. I didn't want Jaden to worry, so I decided to stay." I was surprised at how easily it was becoming to lie to everyone. I hated myself for it.

I pulled out my phone and texted Jenna.

> ME: ARE YOU HOME?
>
> JENNA: HAD TO PULL OVER. WAS DRIVING. NO. NOT HOME. WHY?
>
> ME: DIDN'T WORK OUT. STILL AT THE GAME. COME BACK?
>
> JENNA: YEAH. BE RIGHT THERE.

Monday. I dreaded seeing Brody. I thought about texting him a million times over the weekend. If I had known what to say, I would have, but I didn't, so I didn't.

I stood in front of my closet, trying to decide what to wear. Make a statement and wear a T-shirt with a message on it or dress in something normal, as Jenna would call it? I opted for the message. I was in a crappy mood. It was a Monday, after all. So I pulled on a pair of black jeans and a black tank that read, *I'm allergic to stupidity so I break out in sarcasm.* I wore a long-sleeved, red button down that matched the lettering on my tank. Tying it at the waist, I left it unbuttoned so people could read the tank. I slipped on my red plaid converse tennis shoes that Jenna despised, but I loved, and grabbed my messenger bag, darting out my bedroom door.

I came face-to-face with my mother. Her breath smelled like stale alcohol and cigarettes. Her long, bleached-blonde hair was matted to one side of her head and hung in knots, like she'd just rolled out of bed. "Watch where you're going, Willow," she snapped.

"Yes, ma'am. Sorry."

She pulled the collar of my red shirt back and looked at my chest and shoulder. "When'd you get that one?"

"Friday night. He was mad about curfew."

"Well, you have to do better to stay on his good side, won't you?"

"Yes, ma'am."

"Make sure it stays covered. Better get before you're late and he sees fit to give you another one."

I hurried down the stairs and out to my car. When I was inside and the doors were locked, I let out the breath I was holding.

Breathe. Just breathe.

Brody was already sitting at our table when I walked into biology. He looked up when I walked into the classroom.

"Hey," I said, hanging my bag on the back of my chair.

"Hey yourself."

"Did you have a good weekend?" I looked at him, sitting down and angling my body toward him.

"Not particularly. You?"

"No. Not really. I did have another chess tournament Saturday."

"Yeah? How'd that go?" he asked, looking down at his notebook, doodling on a sheet of paper.

"I lost two out of three games." I shrugged a shoulder.

He turned his head to me. "You lost? What happened?"

"I guess I didn't have any incentive to win. There were no promises of a burger afterward." I gave him a small smile, trying to break the ice between us. It felt like the iceberg that took down the Titanic was sitting between our chairs.

He didn't smile back. Sighing, I bent over to grab my biology book and notebook. I flipped open the flap of my bag and reached inside when Brody's hand darted out and grabbed my wrist. His other hand moved my shirt to the side.

"Don't," I whispered, pushing his hand away. He waved off my hand, his eyes never leaving the mark on my chest. He made a fist with his hand, placed it over my chest, and inhaled sharply.

"Who did that to you?"

I opened my mouth to answer, but nothing came out. I just shook my head.

"Willow, who did that to you?"

"No one. I mean, I just got pushed in the crowd at the football game Friday night. It's no big deal."

Brody's face turned hard. "You're lying," he said through clenched teeth. "That's not from getting pushed. That's from a hit."

Pushing Brody's hand away, I pulled my shirt back over my shoulder before anyone walked by and saw the bruise covering it.

"Who did it?" he asked again.

"I don't want to talk about it."

"Willow—"

"Just drop it. Don't say anything to anyone. Please."

Running his hand through his hair, he let out a frustrated sound before flipping his book open. He stared at it a few seconds before slamming it shut so hard I flinched. He stood quickly and his chair rocked backward, hitting the table behind us. I watched him as he stalked out of the room without a word.

Class was half over before he returned. After handing a tardy slip to the teacher, he sat down next to me. He didn't look at me the rest of the class period and when the bell rang, he slid his things off the table and left the room. He didn't speak to me in English class, leaving as soon as the bell rang.

"How'd things go this morning?" Jenna asked on our way to history.

"They didn't," I mumbled.

"That good, huh?"

"Yup. I think we're back to square one. Open hostility. Brody Victor and I just aren't meant to be friends, or anything else. We just don't gel." I stared at the floor so she couldn't read the disappointment in my eyes.

"What about Brody Victor?" Jaden hurled himself over the railing of the stairs and landed in front of me. He slipped his arm around my waist, kissing my neck.

"He's a jerk and a royal pain in the ass," I said and smiled at Jaden, turning my face up to his for a kiss.

Brody and I sat next to each other in every class for the rest of the day except one, and he didn't speak to me in any of them. I wasn't sure why he was upset with me—it wasn't any of his business—but it was obvious that he was pissed. It wasn't until independent study that he spoke to me. We'd gotten in the habit of sharing a table in the back of the library. It was quiet and secluded. Generally, we worked on our homework separately, sometimes we'd work on our assignments together, and occasionally, we'd talk—although that didn't happen often without one of us insulting the other.

"Is it Jaden?" Brody asked. He pulled out a chair, flipped it around, and straddled it.

I sighed. "No. Please, just drop it."

"Who else knows? Jenna? Tim?"

"They know some, not everything."

"And they're fine with it?" he asked, his voice rising.

"Shh! No, they aren't fine with it, but they respect my privacy and understand that, while they might not agree, it's still my decision to handle it the way I want."

"The bruise on your arm the other day, that wasn't from a fall, was it?" When I didn't answer, he nodded. "And the long sleeves even when it's warm outside, that's why you wear them. You're hiding bruises." It wasn't a question, so I didn't answer. "There are places to get help—"

I fiddled with the pages of my open textbook. "I'm fine."

He reached out, gently took my chin in his hand, and pulled my face around so I was facing him. I closed my eyes. I didn't want to see pity in his.

"Look at me," he whispered. "Willow, look at me."

I opened my eyes. There was no pity in his eyes, only concern. "I want to help. Let me be here for you. Anyway you need me, just let me help."

I plastered on my best fake smile. "Thanks, but I really am fine."

"A bunch of people are going to The Dive," Jenna said as we shoved our books in our locker after school.

"What's the occasion?"

"It's the end of this freakin' horrible Monday, that's what the flippin' occasion is," she muttered, mashing her notebook on her overstuffed shelf.

"Sounds good to me. I'm in," I said. I had homework in calculus I really should've taken home and worked on, but it wasn't due until Wednesday and I didn't feel like doing it. "Screw it." I shoved the book in my locker.

I'll do it tomorrow in independent study.

I drove to The Dive. The place was already jumping by the time I got there. Music was blaring from the large speakers hanging in the corners, and the noise from people talking was almost deafening. I looked around until I spotted Jenna and Tim sitting in a booth in the corner of the restaurant.

"How'd you score this booth? It's my favorite," I said, scooting in. It was a circular booth that looked like it'd been pushed into the wall. It was nearly surrounded by windows overlooking the outdoor eating area, which was always hoppin' during the summer.

"Someone got here before us and saved it," Tim said. He didn't look at me when he answered. That was my first clue something was up.

"Oh, yeah? Who?"

Jenna shrugged and changed the subject. "Hey, look, there's

Sarah. I wonder who she's doin' today." That was my second clue.

I opened my mouth to ask them again who saved the booth, but I felt someone slide in next to me, and then I smelled him. Third clue and *ding, ding, ding.* The light bulb went off.

Oh. Just. Kill. Me. Now. It can't be him.

"I'm going to hurt you," I whispered to Jenna.

She smiled and shrugged a shoulder. "He asked us to sit with him."

"Hey," Brody said, his voice both husky and smooth at the same time, which, of course, sounded ridiculous, but somehow he pulled it off. And, holy Hell, it was sexy. My stomach fluttered every time he spoke, and, yes, even when we traded insults.

I looked over my shoulder. "Hey back." I smiled at him. "Um, I don't mean to be rude, but I need to get out of here. Jaden will go apeshit if he sees me sitting with you."

Brody leaned in close. His lips skimmed my ear when he spoke. "Is that when he hits you? Will seeing you sitting here make him mad enough to hit you again?"

I inhaled a sharp breath and pulled away. "Move."

Brody slid out of the booth and let me pass. I looked up just as Jaden walked through the door, followed by a group of his football buddies.

Yeah, this'll be fun. Sitting with a bunch of belching, farting, horny football idiots hitting on skanks like Sarah. Why did I bother coming?

"Jenna?" I turned and looked at her.

"No way. I'm staying right where I am."

"Thanks a lot." I rolled my eyes and walked to Jaden. He pulled me into his arms, kissing me deep and hard. I felt nothing. No butterflies fluttering, no sizzle, no jolts of electricity. Nothing. Unless you counted the way my mind was still swirling with thoughts of Brody. Not good, not good at all.

I sat and drank the strawberry malt Jaden ordered me—I wanted vanilla—and listened to Jaden and his friends talk endlessly about football. I talked with the girlfriends of the other players, but I didn't know them well. They were all cheerleaders and had their own little clique. I was the odd one out.

When Jaden started mingling from table to table, I got up and wandered to the booth where Jenna and Tim were. Brody was still there, along with some of my other friends. Kara was next to Brody.

She's so close that her shoulder is touching Brody's. She has plenty of room on the other side to scoot over. She doesn't have to sit so close. Why am I so jealous? I don't care. I'm with Jaden. Jaden, who isn't paying any attention to me. Jaden, who knows my secret and holds me prisoner.

As soon as I walked up to the table, Brody told Kara to scoot over. He moved so I could sit next to him. I looked into his eyes and then at the seat. I opened my mouth, but closed it without saying anything, shaking my head slightly and hoping he saw that I wasn't rejecting him intentionally when I walked past, sitting next to Tim on the other side of the booth. I glanced at him under my lashes.

"Are you ready for the calculus exam?" I asked him, reaching out and lightly touching his hand, which was lying on the table in front of me. He glanced down where I touched him, but didn't move his hand. I hoped that was a sign that he understood why I didn't sit next to him.

"Yeah, I think so. Although, that chain rule is a bitch," he said, looking into my eyes.

I smiled. "It's tricky. You have to be careful."

Brody nodded and turned to look out the window. Kara took that as her cue to talk. She and Brody flirted back and forth a half an hour before I couldn't stand listening to it any longer and stood up. "I have to get home. I have homework. See you guys tomorrow." I walked away, not waiting for their goodbyes. Jaden was talking to a bunch of football players when I found him and told him I was leaving. He barely stopped talking long enough to pull me down for a kiss goodbye.

I was halfway across the parking lot when I heard someone call my name. Looking over my shoulder, I saw Brody jogging after me. I turned and kept walking. "Brody, you're gonna start something with Jaden if he sees you out here. Go back inside."

"I'm not afraid of him."

I sighed. "I didn't say you were. I just don't want another scene."

"If he wants to start something, let him. I'm willing to take the risk," Brody said, reaching out to touch my arm.

"Don't you get it? I don't want to see it! I don't want to take the risk, okay? Look, you might think you're hot snot on a golden platter, but you're really just a cold booger on a paper plate. Go back inside."

He laughed loud and free. "I don't know what to say to that except, go out with me," he asked when his laughter faded.

I took a step back "Wh-What?"

"Go out with me."

"I'm not interested in a booty call, Brody. I'm not the type of girl you're looking to hook-up with."

"You don't know what type of girl I'm looking for. Go out to dinner with me or a movie. Even the mall if you want. You can drag me through all the stores looking at every piece of clothing, or we can play board games with your parents on family game night. I don't care what—just spend time with me. I think about you all the time, Willow. When we're apart, I count the minutes until I can see you again."

"I'm with—"

"I know you're with Jaden, damn it! I don't know why. You aren't happy, and it kills me to see you with him. You're hiding something. I can see it in your eyes, but I'll respect that you have your reasons for staying with him, and I'll keep everything just friends. That's all. But I want to spend time with you. I *need* to spend time with you." He paused, looked at the sky, and took a deep breath like he was deciding what to say next. When he looked at me, his face was open, vulnerable. "You're special, Willow. We belong in each other's lives."

I looked down at the ground, making circles on the pavement with the tip of my tennis shoe. There was so much I wanted to say to him—that I felt the same way. That I thought of him all the time too. That I thought we could make a great couple. He got me, understood me, more than anyone else. And I wanted to say yes. I wanted desperately to tell him I'd go out with him. It was all I could do to keep the word from popping out of my mouth. Things were fluttering in my chest, and my hands were shaking. My brain was screaming at me to take a chance... to give him a chance.

"I can't. I'm sorry. I'm dating someone else."

"As a friend. No expectations. Not a date. Just friends hanging out, spending time together. We can invite Jenna and Tim if it makes you feel more comfortable. I just want to spend time with you."

Jaden burst out of the door with a couple of his football buddies. They were laughing and talking, not paying attention to Brody or me. I looked at them over my shoulder and then back at Brody standing in front of me. "Text me," I said just as I felt Jaden's arm fall over my shoulders.

"I thought you were leaving?" Jaden asked.

"I am." I smiled up at him.

"You want to go for a ride?" He grabbed my chin with his hand and held it while he kissed me. I didn't close my eyes. Instead, I looked for Brody. He was in his Jeep, looking at me. Our eyes met for a brief second before he drove away.

"I can't," I said when Jaden broke the kiss. "I have too much homework." Standing on my tiptoes, I kissed him gently.

"Okay. Another time." He smiled and patted my rear like I was one of his teammates. I hated that.

EIGHT
ER

Breathe. Breathe, Willow. This won't break you. Breathe.

I DIDN'T KNOW WHO ELSE TO TEXT. JENNA WASN'T ANSWERING ME, neither was Tim. I didn't trust anyone else. I wasn't even sure why I trusted Brody, but I did. So I texted him and hoped he'd answer me.

ME: CAN I ASK YOU SOMETHING?

He texted me back almost immediately.

BRODY: YES.

ME: IF I NEEDED A FAVOR, WOULD YOU DO SOMETHING FOR ME WITHOUT ASKING A LOT OF QUESTIONS?

BRODY: ?

ME: I'D ASK SOMEONE ELSE BUT JENNA AND TIM AREN'T ANSWERING. I DON'T KNOW WHO ELSE TO ASK. PLEASE. I JUST NEED SOMEONE WHO'LL DO THIS AND NOT ASK QUESTIONS.

BRODY: OK. WHAT?

ME: I NEED A RIDE HOME.

BRODY: WHERE ARE YOU?

ME: ST. MARY'S ER.

BRODY: ON MY WAY.

I was sitting on a bench outside the emergency room when I saw Brody jog across the parking lot. Standing, I walked toward him.

Please don't let me start crying. I can't cry.

"Wait. I'll drive around and pick you up," he called.

I shook my head. "I'm fine." I cursed the slight tremor in my voice.

He reached me, and we stood staring at each other in the dark parking lot. An awkward silence hovered between us. "Um, so you said not to push you, but does that mean I can't ask if you're okay?" Brody finally asked.

I smiled. "No, you can ask that."

"Are you? Okay, I mean?"

I bit my lower lip when it started to tremble and nodded. My eyes started to fill with tears. I tried to blink them away.

"Do I get to know why you're here?" he asked, studying my face.

I moved the hospital paperwork I'd been holding in front of my hand. I heard him suck in a breath. "It's not as bad as it looks. The fingers are just jammed, not broken. The doctor just wrapped them to keep them immobilized for a couple of days, so they'll heal faster. But, hey, bonus, it's the hand I write with, so I'll get a free pass on some of my assignments unless someone writes them out for me or I peck them out on the computer." I turned my hand over and looked at the fingers that were immobilized and wrapped with medical tape. "You want to sign it like people do casts?" I joked.

Brody reached out, but let his hand drop before he touched me. "What the hell happened?"

"You promised."

He ran his hand through his hair, giving it that perfect bedhead look. "Yeah, okay. You're right. Where do you want me to take you?"

"Home."

"Where are your parents?" Brody asked, his voice hard.

"They were out when I called. My mom's cell went straight to voice mail. She probably forgot it. She never remembers to take it with her."

Brody held his Jeep's door open and helped me get in. Truthfully, I didn't need any help getting in, but I figured since my hand hurt like hell, I was going to let him touch me and not feel guilty about it.

Brody slipped in the driver's side and started the Jeep. He turned toward my subdivision. We drove in silence for a few miles when I finally spoke. "Do you have a curfew?"

He glanced at me. "No. Why?"

"I don't want to go home yet. Do you think we can go somewhere?"

"Sure. Are you hungry?"

"Starving and I could drink one of the Great Lakes I'm so thirsty."

"Um, Willow, why didn't you call Jaden tonight?"

"You promised," I whispered.

Brody nodded. "Okay. That's what I thought. Ah, I'm not sure where we should go that we wouldn't run into—"

"Just a minute."

> ME: HEY HANDSOME!
>
> JADEN: HEY.
>
> ME: WHAT ARE YOU DOING?
>
> JADEN: WATCHING A MOVIE.
>
> ME: OH. AT A FRIEND'S?
>
> JADEN: NOPE. SEE YA TOMORROW.
>
> ME: BYE.

"He's home," I said, looking out the side window.

Brody grabbed my cell phone out of my hand. "Nice. He's not much of a conversationalist, is he?"

"I don't think he could spell conversationalist." When I realized what I'd said, I clamped my good hand over my mouth.

Brody burst out laughing. "Ah, so you aren't convinced it's a match made in heaven either. Hmm, interesting."

"What do you mean by *either*?" I asked.

"Just that you seem to be the only person in the entire school that doesn't realize what an odd couple you make, well, and Jaden, of course. When you finally come to your senses and drop him, it'll mean that some other idiot, like me, will have a shot with you."

"Oh." I wasn't sure what to say to that.

"Now I've made it weird, huh?" Brody chuckled, rubbing a hand over his face.

"No," I lied and smiled at him. "But I'm gonna make it weird."

"Okay..." he pulled the word out.

"You know I only called you because we're friends, right? This isn't anything else. I'm with Jaden, even if everyone thinks it's a weird relationship. That hasn't changed."

"Yeah, I know," he murmured.

I smiled at him. "Good, because I think I like spending time with you. You know, when you aren't insulting me."

"I don't insult you." He rolled his eyes. "Okay, maybe a little, but I didn't know you then and you were just as insulting."

I laughed. "True."

Brody pulled into a small pizza place and told me to wait in the Jeep. He ran in and brought back a small pepperoni pizza and two giant Cokes. We sat in the Jeep, listening to the radio and eating while we talked. By the time he took me home, I realized I actually liked Brody Victor.

"Thank you for tonight," I said when Brody pulled into my driveway. "The pizza was good. The conversation wasn't too bad either. There's actually a chance if I got to know you better, I'd find out you're not a complete idiot."

Brody laughed. "And let the insults begin." He shook his head and rubbed the back of his neck. "So, are you gonna test that theory?" he asked quietly.

I nodded. "I'm willing to take the risk."

"So, what message are you going to send me tomorrow?" When I just looked at him, he said, "Your shirt. What message are you going to send?"

"Oh, I don't know. Maybe I'll dress normal," I said with a shrug.

"Normal?"

"Yeah, Jenna says I have to dress normal at least one day a week, meaning something without words on the front of it."

"I like your T-shirts. They suit you," Brody said, gently pulling on the hem of my tank top. All of a sudden, it became hard to breathe, and the inside of the jeep felt very, very small.

"Hmm, well, I'll surprise you then."

I looked at him, and his gaze locked on mine. My shirt still between his fingers, a chill ran down my spine, and the air seemed to crackle around us. Brody's eyes dropped to my lips, and my tongue darted out to moisten them. He inhaled sharply, pulling lightly on my shirt, leaning toward me. His free hand hovered next to the side of my head, the tips of his fingers barely skimming my hair as if he were afraid to touch me. I fought the urge to lean into his hand. My body seemed to crave his touch; it was drawn to him. Some invisible force pushing us together—it felt wrong to fight it, like I was denying myself a part of me.

He let go of my shirt, skimming his fingers lightly up my arm and over my shoulder. When he reached the side of my neck, his fingers touched bare skin. I sucked in a breath, let my eyes close briefly, and soaked up the feeling of his skin gliding over mine. The tips of his fingers continued moving and slid across my jaw until he reached my lips. My body burned from Brody's touch. It felt right. And I wanted to stay cocooned in his Jeep forever. Just like that. His hands on me. No one in the world but us. No Jaden. No secrets to protect. Just Brody and the trail of fire his touch created.

His thumb caressed my bottom lip. My lips parted, and he groaned a curse. Cupping the side of my face, he gently pulled me toward him. He met me halfway. His lips were so close to mine that I could feel his breath tickling them, smell the mint he'd been sucking on. Just as his lips touched mine, I turned my face to the side. We sat unmoving for a moment before Brody started to pull away. I reached for him. Holding his face between my hands, I kissed the corner of his mouth.

"I'm sorry, Brody. Just friends. That's all I can do right now."

He pulled back, rested his forehead against mine, and blew out a breath before leaning back in his seat. He nodded once. "I know. I'm sorry. I didn't mean—"

"It's okay."

"No, I've made things awkward between us."

I shook my head, reached out, and squeezed his hand. "Nope. I kiss all my guy friends at least once. Ask Tim." I grinned and opened the car door. "I'll see you tomorrow. Thanks again for tonight. It was perfect."

Except the kiss. That could've been perfect if I'd been brave enough to let it happen.

Breathe. Breathe, Willow. You're strong. Breathe.

They were waiting for me when I opened the door. The sweet stench of cigars and expensive perfume filled the foyer.

I closed the door behind me and leaned against it. My eyes darted between them.

Ralph stood in the middle of the foyer. I wasn't getting by him unless I ran upstairs. One problem, though. My mom sat on the stairs.

"Let me see it." Ralph motioned with his fingers for me to show him my hand.

I lifted my hand up, but kept it close to my chest. And kept my mouth shut.

"I said I wanted to see it." He grabbed my hand and yanked me to him, twisting my arm back and forth to see the damage. I bit the inside of my cheek to keep from making any noise from the pain. "Broken?"

"No, sir," I answered quietly, "Just jammed."

My mom moved from the stairs to my side so she could look at my hand. "How'd you get—?"

The slap was loud and hard. She stumbled backward several steps, a look of surprise on her face. She cradled the side of her face in her hands.

"Damn it!" Ralph shook the hand out he'd just slapped my mother with. "That stung. If you'd both learn to just keep your mouths shut, you'd make my life so much easier. It's not a hard concept to grasp. Even ignorant white trash like the two of you should be able to understand it. Just shut. Up. When I want your opinion, I'll give it to you. When I want to hear you speak, I'll tell you. Otherwise, silence." He slashed his hand through the air.

"What did you tell the doctors?" Ralph looked at me. When I didn't answer right away, he shoved my shoulder hard enough that I lost my balance and fell against the door behind me, cracking my head against the wood. He rolled his eyes and let out a long, exasperated sigh. "Well? How did you explain your hand?"

"I jammed my fingers playing basketball."

He nodded. "And when they asked who your ride was?"

"They didn't ask me," I answered.

Ralph nodded. He started whistling, turned, and walked away.

I slumped forward. My heart raced in my chest, and I took several deep breaths to calm myself.

"What'dya go and do this time? You can't just shut your mouth and do what you're supposed to, can you?" my mother hissed. It wasn't a question she expected an answer to, so I didn't give one. "You need to learn to be quiet and do as you're told. Men want you to be seen, not heard. Things will go a lot smoother for you when you learn that."

This gem of advice from the woman whose husband just smacked her senseless for daring to ask a question.

"I'll do better." I hated the quiver in my voice. I hated that I wanted my mother to wrap me in her arms, hug me to her, and tell me everything was going to be okay. That she'd fix it. That the secret would go away and we could leave Ralph. I hated that sometimes I hated her for what she did. That I blamed her. I hated that she could drown the problems of our life from hell in alcohol and pills. I didn't have that luxury. And she only had Ralph to deal with. I had Ralph and Jaden. And most of all, I hated feeling like I was a whiner.

This is life. Get over it. Suck it up and deal.

"You'd better. He's a good guy. Start treating him with respect." She turned and walked away.

"Yes, ma'am. Goodnight," I said to her retreating back.

"Goodnight, Willow. I love you."

Yeah, okay, whatever. Sometimes, you have a really shitty way of showing it.

"I love you, too, Mom."

Breathe. Just breathe.

NINE

Friendship

"I'm supposed to be riding the 'just friends' bus. But I cashed that ticket in a while ago. I sit on the curb, watch the bus drive away, and wonder... which bus are you on?"
~*Willow*

"SURPRISE HIM. OKAY, WHICH ONE SHOULD I WEAR... WHAT MESSAGE do I want to send?" I stood in front of my closet, looking through my shirts. I finally decided on sending a safe message to Brody and hoped Jaden wouldn't notice or ask about the shirt. I pulled out a pink tee that read, *He's just a friend,* and slipped it over my head before I could change my mind and grab the other one I was debating on wearing that read something about kissing me... which would definitely send mixed messages after the night before in Brody's Jeep. But, oh, how I wanted to wear that shirt—wanted to finish that kiss.

Maybe I'll have a T-shirt made that reads, I just dumped my dumbass jock boyfriend. Will you kiss me senseless now? *Yeah, that's sounds like a perfect T-shirt. I'll get right on that... sure.*

I pulled on a thin, zippered hoodie—I had a ton of them to go with the T-shirts and tanks. They were great for covering the cuts and bruises. Thankfully, he didn't usually hit in the face. The hoodie was a light blue and matched the lettering on the tank top. I pushed my feet into my blue paisley Converse high tops. Another fashion faux pas I had that made Jenna cringe—my shoes. I went for comfort more than style. I loved my Converse, especially the ones with the funky prints. Not Jenna. She nearly had heart palpitations every time she saw me wearing them. I thought it was hilarious. She thought I'd lost my mind.

After running a brush through my hair, pulling it into a messy bun, and swiping my teeth with a toothbrush, I was ready for school.

I opened my door slowly and peered down the hall. My mother wasn't anywhere in sight. Stepping into the hall, I made my way to the stairs. I was careful to avoid the boards I knew would make noise with the slightest change in pressure. I didn't want to wake her up and get another lecture on how to keep men happy so they wouldn't smack me around.

As soon as I'm eighteen, I am out. Of. Here. I don't care if I have to flip burgers every day and babysit every weekend for four years to put myself through college. I'm leaving Middleton far behind.

I walked toward my locker when Jenna turned and saw me. "What are you wearing? I told you, shoes make or break an outfit. Those are breakin' it. They are even worse than that horrid pink monstrosity you call a shirt." She finally freed her book and papers from the mess overflowing from her shelf. I had to stifle a laugh.

"What's so funny?" Brody peeked around the locker door at me.

"Oh, Jenna is just being… Jenna."

"Ah. How's the hand?" Brody asked.

"It's okay. It makes getting my pants on and off interesting. Ugh… I can't believe I just said that." I laughed, feeling my cheeks heat with a blush.

"You're cute when you blush." He smiled. "I'll see you in class. Oh." Stopping, he looked over his shoulder. "I don't like that particular T-shirt. Just so you know." He winked and walked toward our biology class.

"What happened to your hand? And what the hell was that between you and Brody?"

"I jammed two fingers. No big deal. And Brody and I are… just… we just are. Like the T-shirt says. That's all."

"Mm-hmm. Sure, just friends." A small smile curved her lips. "And how'd you jam your fingers?"

"Oh, you know, the usual."

"Willow—"

"I'm fine. Really. I'm just fine," I lied.

I sat next to Jaden, twirling my fork in the salad I was eating for lunch. Brody was across the room with some people I recognized from a few of our AP classes. Jenna and Tim sat with them, the traitors.

"I can't believe you, like, eat that," a blonde cheerleader said to me, cracking her gum as she talked. She was a girlfriend of one of the other football players—Sasha, or something like that.

"What?" I asked, looking at her.

Jeez, is it a requirement that all cheerleaders possess abnormally perfect genes? Big blue eyes, wavy, blonde hair, big boobs, and a tiny waist, yeah, I feel incredibly sexy next to her. She does wonders for my self-esteem. Sure. At least she's dating a butt-ugly football player.

"The salad dressing. It has, like, a million calories and, like, a ton of fat in it," she said, horrified.

"Oh, I don't really pay attention to that. I just eat what I want." I shrugged a shoulder.

"You must workout constantly to stay so thin."

She thinks I'm thin? Has she looked in the mirror?

"I don't work out, actually—"

"Not unless you count moving chess pieces around a little board working out, huh Wills?" Jaden laughed.

I faked a smile and imagined stabbing him in the eye with my plastic fork. "Yup, that's about as close as it gets."

"Oh, you're on the chess team?" the cheerleader asked.

"Mm-hmm." I went back to twisting my fork in my salad.

"That's cool," she said before turning and talking to the girl sitting on the other side of her.

I flipped my fork into my plate and stood up. "I'm going to go say hi to Jenna and Tim," I whispered close to Jaden's ear, kissing his cheek and quickly stepping away before he could pull me in for another.

Dumping my tray, I tossed it on top of the bin and, wiping my sweaty hands up and down my thighs, walked toward the table where

Jenna sat. I didn't think Jaden could see Brody from where he was, but I couldn't be sure. I'd know in about two minutes.

"Hey." I sat in an empty seat next to Brody.

"Hey back to ya. Aren't you living life on the wild side by sitting here?" Brody asked.

"A little. I don't think he can see this part of the table from where he is. Or that he's even paying attention."

"Ah." Brody nodded, looking down. He let his arm slip from where it rested on the table's top. His hand brushed across my thigh before he propped it on his knee. My eyes darted to his; he was watching me through his lashes, a small grin touching his lips. He leaned back in his chair, stretching his legs out in front of him.

"So what's happening on the other side of the world?" Jenna asked.

"Apparently, I eat too much dressing on my salad because, like, it has, like, a million calories and, like, fat." I imitated her voice, bobbing my head back and forth. "And I should workout more because, according to Jaden, moving little chess pieces around a board is all I do… or something like that." I rolled my eyes.

"Like, really?"

I laughed. "Like, yes. And, predictably, as soon as chess was mentioned, her eyes glazed over and she started talking to someone else."

"That's, like, too bad," Tim said with a laugh.

"Like, I think I'll, like, put that on a T-shirt. Wanna go to the mall?" I looked at Jenna.

"No. I'm done being your enabler. If you want any more of those crazy T-shirts, you'll have to get them by yourself." Jenna shook her head.

Brody chuckled, twirling a straw on the table.

"Eh, whatever. I'll break you before the day is over. You'll be begging to go to the mall with me. Begging." I leaned back in my chair, pulled my knees up to my chest, and wrapped my arms around them.

"You're delusional." Jenna looked away.

"Okay. You'll be home doing homework while I'm browsing the

clearance racks."

Jenna shrugged. "There can't be too much new stuff. We were just there."

"Eating a soft pretzel and drinking a slushie while I get a pedicure, soaking my feet in a lavender footbath—"

"You're a bitch."

"I know." I laughed.

"But I can't go to the mall tonight even if I wanted to," Jenna said.

"Yeah." I sighed, smacking my hand down on Brody's straw when he spun it in front of him. "I can't either. I have way too much calc. homework due tomorrow." I popped Brody's straw in my mouth and chewed on the tip, grinning at him. "But you have to admit, it'd make a great T-shirt."

Oh. Holy. Hotness. Chewing on his straw is almost like touching his lips. His lips touched it and now mine… okay, I'm officially losing it.

"They wouldn't get the joke," Brody murmured with an amused smile.

"I know. That's what makes it the perfect T-shirt." I nudged his thigh with my foot and winked at him.

He laughed.

I love that sound.

I was lying across my bed, working on my calculus homework and grumbling at myself for waiting until the last minute to do it, when my phone chimed. I thought about ignoring it, but I was happy for the interruption. It felt like I'd been doing the same calculus homework for a week.

I grabbed the phone off the table next to my bed and smiled. My heart started doing all sorts of weird things and butterflies immediately started tickling the sides of my stomach and some other places that were… very new to the sensation.

BRODY: WHATCHA DOING?

ME: CALC. YOU?

BRODY: SAME. WANNA TALK?

ME: SURE.

My phone rang just a few seconds later. I jumped and almost dropped it. "Hello?"

"Hey," Brody said, his voice sliding over me like velvet rope. It caressed me as it squeezed the air from my lungs.

"Hi." I cringed when my voice came out all squeaky and breathy. "When you asked if I wanted to talk, I thought you meant texting."

"Oh. Sorry, we can hang up and just text."

"No! No, it just surprised me when the phone rang." I giggled. *Jeez, I'm giggling like a little girl. I need to get a freakin' grip.*

"How much more calc. do you have to do?" Brody asked. I could hear papers rustling through the phone.

"I'm on the last three problems. You?"

"I have five left."

We fell quiet. I could hear him breathing on the other end of the phone. Every so often, he'd adjust the phone or I'd hear papers rustling. I'd worked through the three problems I had left and picked up my things, throwing them in my bag. Rolling over on my back, I closed my eyes and listened to Brody breathe.

"Are you finished?" he asked.

"Yes."

"What are you doing?"

I felt my cheeks heat, which was silly since he couldn't see me. "I'm just lying here, waiting for you to finish." I left out the part that I was enjoying listening to him breathe—that sounded a little like a freaky stalker.

"I'm finished," he said. I could imagine him flipping his pencil into his book and flicking it close like he did at school.

"So, what did you want to talk about?" I asked him.

"What are you wearing?" he whispered.

"Um, what?"

He laughed loudly into the phone. "I'm kidding, Willow," he said when his chuckles faded.

"Oh, you were kidding? I was totally gonna to tell you if you told me…" I let my words trail off.

I heard him inhale. "Oh. Okay."

It was my turn to laugh. "Kidding."

"Bummer. I was hoping you were going to start telling me about your Victoria's Secret lingerie."

"Well, I am wearing this little pink—"

"Um, I think we need to move on to safer, more friend appropriate topics."

I laughed. "Okay, you pick the topic."

"You want to see a movie?"

"I can't."

"Do you have a TV in your room with satellite?" Brody asked.

"Yes."

"Good. Turn to channel 235."

Turning on my television, I flipped to the channel Brody suggested. "Oh, I've wanted to see this movie." I pulled the blankets back on my bed and slipped under them, bunching the pillows behind my back.

"Good, I haven't seen it yet either. We can watch it together."

"Are you in bed?" I asked.

"Yeah." His voice came out huskier than normal.

"Me, too. Hey, pause the movie for a minute." An idea sparked, and a tingle of excitement ran through me.

"Okay. Why?"

"We should pop some popcorn. Do you have any?"

"Yeah," he answered. I heard his blankets rustling through the phone as he climbed out of bed, and I had to force myself to stop imagining what he might look like. I really did want to ask him what he was wearing.

Stop it! Jeez.

"I can hear yours popping through the phone," Brody said with a chuckle when we were standing in our separate kitchens, each waiting for our popcorn. "What kind is it?"

"Extra butter."

"Yeah, mine too. What's the point of eating it if there isn't butter dripping off it?"

"I know, right? It should be a law that all popcorn has to be buttered," I said, smiling when I heard Brody's soft chuckle.

Popcorn made, we chatted as we made our way to our bedrooms

and got comfortable before restarting the movie.

"This is new. It's kinda fun. Only, there's one thing missing," Brody murmured.

"It is fun. What's missing?" I was disappointed he wasn't having as good a time as I was.

"You. I wish you were here, not there."

"Oh." I wasn't sure what to say. I was glad he couldn't see me because I was grinning like a fool. "Look at that. That is so ridiculous. There's no way that could happen."

"That's why they call it entertainment, Willow. Movies defy the rules of everyday life."

"Still, that's just cheesy," I said, tossing a piece of popcorn in my mouth.

"It's a movie about zombie aliens. I think we passed cheesy a long time ago. Oh, look at her. Now we're getting somewhere."

"You're such a perv."

"What? I'm a guy and she's hot. If she's going to walk around naked, I'm gonna look and appreciate the fine job God did assembling her."

"Ugh. Whatever." I rolled my eyes.

"Stop rolling your eyes."

"I didn't."

"Yes, you did. I heard it in your voice," he said with a laugh.

"Oh! What do we have here? My, my, my, I do believe we have the male species joining the bimbo in the shower. Mmm, he's nice to look at. Great butt." I sighed.

"Now who's the perv?"

"Me. I never said I wasn't."

Brody laughed. "Good to know." He cleared his throat, and his voice was a little huskier than normal when he said, "Love scene."

For some reason, our easy teasing ended and we floundered for something to say. The television played a very hot love scene—how it got only an R-rating was a miracle. I watched it on my television, hearing the moans and sighs from Brody's television echoing through the phone. Awkward.

I could hear every breath Brody took. I could tell when his

breathing sped up. I heard the small groan he made and the rustle of blankets and I wondered what was making him uncomfortable, the love scene or watching it with me on the other end of the phone. I tried to keep my breathing steady, but it was hard listening to the changes in Brody's and thinking of his reaction. I was glad we weren't watching the movie in the same room because I would have embarrassed myself by throwing myself at him. Yeah.

"You want to know a secret?" I whispered.

I should stop talking now. Shut up! Shut up!

He sighed. "About you? Always."

"I really do want to know what you're wearing." I bit my lip, waiting for him to say something. The sounds of the love scene still filtered through the phone.

"Mm. You're making it very difficult for me to keep things G-rated between us," he murmured.

"I know. I feel the same."

"Fight scene. Ooh, did you see that arm fly across the screen?" Brody asked a little too loudly.

"Yeah. Gross."

Finally. That love scene was killing me. I never thought I'd be so happy to see arms and legs blown off.

"Willow? Willow?" I heard Brody call softly. "Wake up, beautiful. The movie is over."

"Oh. I fell asleep. Crap, did I snore?"

Oh, how embarrassing. If I snored, I won't be able to face him in the morning.

"No," Brody murmured, "you didn't snore. You sighed a few times. It was cute."

"Okay. Good."

"You did talk a little though."

Oh, no.

"What'd I say?" I squeezed my eyes shut and cringed.

"Oh, just that you thought I was incredibly intelligent, handsome, and irresistibly sexy."

My mouth dropped open. I tried to tell from his voice if he was kidding or not, but without seeing him, it was impossible to tell, and, the truth was, I did think all those things.

"I did not," I said.

"Okay, if you say so." He tried to hide it, but I could hear the smile in his voice, and I let out the breath I was holding.

"I need to go. It's late."

"Yeah. Goodnight, Willow."

"'Night. Thanks for the movie."

Wait, did he call me beautiful?

Thursday morning. I was so tired and was bitchin' at myself for staying up so late. And then I remembered what I was doing and smiled. Movie night with Brody. I got goose bumps just remembering it.

Jaden and I had never done anything like that. He'd have thought it was stupid. We hardly talked on the phone, or even texted. But Brody and I had fun. It was easy. I didn't have to try. I could be myself, and that was enough for him. Jaden always seemed to want more from me. I was never sure which girlfriend I was supposed to be when I was with him—the football-loving girlfriend, the attentive girlfriend that waited on him hand and foot, the girlfriend that gave him his space, the girly-girl, or the tomboy. He thought I should be able to fill any of those girlfriend types, and I should automatically know which one he expected me to be. I never felt like I could just be myself—that was never enough. I was never good enough. But Brody didn't make me feel that way. He actually seemed to *want* to know the real me. Maybe even like the real me.

"Okay, what to wear today? Something that says, *Had a great time last night; next time, let's do it in the same bed*? No, not a good idea." I slid my shirts across the closet rod, looking for something to wear. Nothing jumped out at me. For once, I couldn't find a sarcastic shirt that matched my mood. So I picked a black, long-sleeved T-shirt that had three, neon-green alien heads on the front. Beneath the aliens it read, *The aliens made me do it.*

When I walked into biology, Brody looked at me and laughed. "Huh. Just what did the aliens make you do?"

"I don't think you could handle knowing what they made me do," I said with a grin. When I bent over to hang my messenger bag over the back of my seat, I leaned over a little further than necessary so my mouth was near his ear. "I had a lot of fun last night." My voice was soft and quiet, and I heard him draw in a deep breath. He turned his head, and our faces were just mere inches from each other.

"I did too. We'll have to do it again." He looked in my eyes. "But next time, I'd rather we be in the same bed."

A small smile curved my lips, and I had force the next words out of my mouth because it wasn't how I felt. At. All. "We're just riding the friend bus, remember?" The truth was my ticket on the friend bus was about to expire. Every second I spent with Brody, he stole a piece of me. No, that wasn't true. I opened my heart and invited him to take what he wanted. Piece by piece, I let him dismantle me and rearrange the pieces so I was whole again. Not the shell I'd let myself become. Brody was bringing me back to life.

"Yeah, yeah, I remember, but a guy can dream, right? And besides, since when do girls ask their guy friends what they're wearing?" He smirked and winked.

I'm with Jaden. I need to keep reminding myself of that because Brody's grins, smiles, and little comments make my heart twirl inside my chest and butterflies flutter inside my stomach. I'm starting to wish more than anything I was with him and not Jaden. But Jaden knows. He knows what she did. And he can't tell. So what Jaden wants, Jaden gets.

The instructor walked into the room and saved me from answering. Since I didn't know what to say, it was better to say nothing at all anyway.

I'd hoped for a movie day so I could sleep through class. I was so tired from staying up late the night before, but unfortunately, the teacher droned on about our next dissection. I hoped Brody was listening because I sure wasn't. My mind was wandering, mulling over the comment he'd made.

About halfway through class, I couldn't stand it any longer. I reached over and pulled his notepad toward me. At the bottom of the page, I wrote, *So, what's the answer?*

Twirling the notepad around so he could read it, I watched his face as his eyes skimmed across my note. A small smile touched his lips.

He leaned over, put his lips against my ear, and all but growled, "Just boxer briefs."

"Mm, the torture," I whispered. He pulled back and held my gaze a moment too long before returning his attention to the front of the class.

That's it. I'm officially unable to concentrate on anything except the knowledge that I was talking to Brody while he was in just his boxer briefs while in bed! Why did I ask?

Brody and I teased and talked through our classes the rest of the morning. There weren't any more little comments about what each other was wearing—or not wearing—the night before. I wasn't sure if I was happy about that or not.

"What are you doing after school tonight?" Jenna asked at lunch that afternoon.

I shrugged. "Nothing, I guess."

"Well, I know this afternoon is football practice, so you'll be Jaden free for the day. We should do something."

"Oh, I almost forgot, today's chess club. I can't do anything after school." I twirled a fry in a puddle of ketchup on my plate.

"We could always do something after," Jenna said, grabbing a fry off my tray.

"Maybe. I'll have to see what time I get out of chess club. I'll be right back. My bloodstream is severely depleted of caffeine."

I jogged to my locker to get my afternoon dose of Red Bull. While I was walking back to the commons, I saw Brody talking to Jenna. She smiled and looked at me. Nodding her head, she said something to Brody. He went back to his seat and sat down, quickly glancing at me over his shoulder.

What the heck was that?

I found out during independent study when Brody sat down next to me at our normal table in the back of the library. We were working separately on our homework. For some reason, the air seemed filled with tension. At least, I felt it. He seemed unaffected, as always.

"So…" He continued writing in his notebook, not looking at me. I put my pencil down and watched him. The scratching of his pencil lead across the paper was the only sound, and it grated on my nerves as I waited for him to finish his sentence.

I let out an exasperated sigh when my nerves grew so taut I felt as though I'd fly around the room like a snapped rubber band. "What?"

He shrugged a shoulder. "I was wondering if it would be okay with you if I watched you at chess club today?"

I stared at him for a minute, trying to process what he was asking and why. "I guess. But why? It isn't a tournament today."

"I know. I just want to go and watch." He put his pencil down and his gaze found mine.

"You can come, but you'll be bored," I said.

He grinned at me. "I don't think I'll be bored."

When the bell rang, we gathered our things and he followed me to the classroom where chess club was held. I sat at a table in front of a chessboard. He pulled out a chair next to me and sat down, scooting it as close to my chair as possible. I hung my bag over the back of my seat and looked at him.

"Is this okay?" he asked me. "If you want me to sit somewhere else, I will."

"No, this is fine."

It's totally not fine! I'm not gonna be able to play with him sitting so close to me, smelling his cologne, feeling his thigh brush against mine. I'm not going be able to concentrate on the game when I'm concentrating on him. I'm so going to lose and embarrass myself.

Tim walked over to me and said, "We have an uneven number of people. Too many people are out sick."

"I don't have to play today." I started picking up my things to leave.

"I'll play you," Brody offered.

I glanced up from gathering the game pieces and placing them back in the box. "How long has it been since you've played?" I twirled a rook between my fingers.

Brody shrugged. "A while."

Tim looked at me. "I don't mind if you don't mind."

"I guess so."

Brody walked around the table and sat down across from me. We set up the pieces on the board. "Your go," he told me.

I made my first move, and he followed with his move. The game progressed quickly, and I was surprised at how well he played. I beat him the first game, and he beat me the second.

Brody rubbed his hands together and stared at me over the table. "All tied up. Third game's the tiebreaker. Let's make it interesting."

"What did you have in mind?" I leaned forward and tilted my head to the side.

"If I win, you have to go get something to eat with me," Brody said with a grin.

"And if I win?"

Brody shrugged a shoulder. "What do you want?"

Ohmigosh, if he only knew what I wanted. Things I shouldn't be wanting. I'm with Jaden. I shouldn't want kisses from Brody, but that's exactly what I want.

"I'll tell you after I win the game, Ace."

Brody laughed. "Pretty sure of yourself, aren't you?"

"Yup."

"Okay, challenge accepted."

I spent the whole game trying to figure out what it was I was going to ask for when I won. I was so distracted, I lost the game. Brody was not gracious winner. He laughed and said, "Looks like it's burger time. I think I'm gonna have a cheeseburger with the works, and a chocolate milkshake. Maybe two. Oh, and onion rings. Can't forget the onion rings."

I rolled my eyes, but I couldn't help but grin. Secretly, I was glad he'd won. I really wanted to spend time with him, but I wasn't going to examine my reasons why too closely. I shouldn't want to go get a burger with Brody, but I did. More than anything

"Just out of curiosity, what would you have asked for if you would've won?" Brody asked.

I smiled and winked at him. "I'll never tell."

"Ugh, you're such a tease."

"Let's just say, you should have let me win."

Brody groaned.

We gathered our things and walked out to the student parking lot. Brody unlocked the door of his Jeep and held it open for me to get in. I felt a little awkward. Jaden never held the door open for me and we were freakin' dating—sort of.

"Thanks," I said, climbing into the Jeep. I watched Brody in the side mirror as he walked around the back. He twirled his keys around his fingers on one hand, the other tucked in his jeans pocket. "So, where do you want to go? The Dive?" I asked when he got in the Jeep.

"No, I didn't think you'd want to go to The Dive." He put the keys in the ignition and angled his body toward me. "I know we're going as friends, but your boyfriend doesn't seem the type to allow you to have guy friends. The Dive is going to be full of people from school. Someone will tell Jaden we were together."

I looked out the window and blew out a breath. "Um..."

"Hey, it's okay. I know a little place not too far away. I doubt anyone from school would be caught dead there. At least, no one in your social circle."

I swung my gaze back to his. "I don't have a social circle."

"No? Are you sure about that?"

"No. I mean, yes, I'm sure. I hate that people assume just because I date Jaden, I belong to a certain clique. Did you already forget I'm a member of the chess club? One of my best friends is the captain of the club? I fit in more with him than I do with any of Jaden's friends." I shoved my things to the floor of the Jeep with a frustrated breath. "I don't know why I'm even bothering to explain myself to you. It's not like it matters what you think. Let's just go and get this over with." I fell back against the seat and stared out the side window. Suddenly, the idea of going anywhere with him lost its appeal.

"Hmm, and I wouldn't know anything about stereotypes, huh? I'm just the bad boy, man-whore of Cassidy High," he murmured.

I turned to face him, and his sapphire gaze locked onto mine. "I guess you were judged before you even stepped foot in school," I whispered. He didn't answer, but his gaze held mine captive. I lay my hand on his arm and skimmed my fingers over his skin. "I'm sorry. I was one who judged you, and I'm sorry."

He didn't answer me for a long time. The silence stretched between us, awkward and uncomfortable. I fought the urge to squirm in my seat. And then he did something that caught me completely off guard and threw me totally off balance. Brody took my hand from his arm, turned it over, and kissed the inside of my wrist, letting his warm, soft lips linger against my skin just a moment longer than necessary for a normal kiss. But it was no normal kiss. It was a silky whisper caress of his lips across my skin that sent my body into a frenzy.

I sucked in a breath. My insides did all sorts of weird things. Forget butterflies, I had balls bouncing around my stomach— bounding from one side to the other, hitting the wall and springing back again. My heart beat so hard it hurt and if someone had asked me about Jaden, I would have said, "Who?" Not good, not good at all. And so very dangerous.

I slowly pulled my hand away, still looking into his eyes. "Just friends, remember?" My voice was barely a whisper.

"That was my just-friends kiss. If it was my kiss for more than friends, we wouldn't be talking right now." He turned and started the Jeep.

I let out the breath I was holding and tried not to think about the more-than-friends kisses he would give.

Houston, I definitely have a problem.

We drove in silence for about five minutes when Brody pulled into a small, gravel parking lot. I looked around. "This is a bar," I said. "They're not going to let us in here."

"Don't worry. My aunt owns the place. She makes the best burgers in town. Makes The Dive's look like dog food… and her milkshakes? Don't even get me started."

We walked into the small, white building. It was much larger than it looked from the outside, and it wasn't at all what I thought a bar would look like. It wasn't dark and smoky inside. It was light, without being too bright. And the smell of burgers filled the air, not the smell of cigarettes and stale beer like I expected. A large, square bar sat in the middle of the room with bar stools surrounding it. Booths lined the left wall and tables were scattered throughout the remaining area, with the exception of the right side of the room, which was full of pool tables, a couple of air hockey tables, and arcade games.

Brody took my hand and pulled me gently with him as he made his way to the back of the building where a small counter was located. A petite woman, who couldn't have been much taller than five feet, greeted him with a broad smile.

"Hey, Brody! Whatcha up to today?"

"Hi, Aunt Bess. I'm just in the mood for one of your awesome burgers," Brody said with a smile, dropping my hand so he could give his aunt a hug over the counter.

"And who's this?" The woman glanced at me and then back to Brody.

"This is my friend, Willow. Willow, this is my Aunt Bess."

"Hi, sweetie," Bess said, turning her smile on me.

"Hi. It's nice to meet you." I smiled back at her. Her smile was contagious.

"So, you're here for burgers, huh? Let me guess. A big Cheesy and a chocolate milkshake for you, Brody?"

Brody laughed. "I guess I'm getting too predictable. I'm going to have to switch it up one of these days. Keep you on your toes."

Brody's aunt winked at him before turning to me and asking, "And what would you like, Willow?"

"Um." I looked at Brody. "Why don't you order for me?"

"Nope." He shook his head. "I know how much you hate that."

I tapped the counter with my finger and read the menu under the glass on the counter. "I think I'll try the little cheesy, and I'd like an order of onion rings, please, with a Coke."

"Good choice." Brody's aunt wrote everything down on a ticket. "I'll bring it right out to you, but, Willow?"

"Yes?"

"You really should have a milkshake. They're the bomb, if I do say so myself," she said with a giggle.

"Okay. I'll try a chocolate," I said, smiling at her giggles. I immediately liked Brody's aunt.

"Do you want to play pool while we wait for our burgers?" Brody nodded at the pool tables. "Do you know how to play?"

I shook my head and concentrated on schooling my features. "No," I lied.

"Well, I can teach you. I'm not too bad."

Score. That's what I was hoping you'd say.

Brody racked the balls and selected our cues. "You want to break?" He handed me a pool cue.

"Um, sure, I can break." I took the cue from Brody and stood in front of the pool table, pretending like I had no idea what I was doing.

"Here, let me help you line up your shot." Brody moved beside me and wrapped his arms around me, holding the pool cue with me. "Here, place your hands like this." He adjusted my grip.

Oh, yeah. This is exactly what I was hoping for. Not a good idea, but, oh, it feels so good not to be right.

His warmth scorched my skin, and my body soaked up the feel of him to relive later. I was thoroughly enjoying having Brody's arms around me. Pool was my new favorite game.

I've died and went to hell, because now I know what it feels like to have his arms around me. This was a bad idea, a very bad idea.

We pulled the pool cue back to make the shot. I nearly groaned as I felt his muscles flex and contract against me. The ball rolled down the pool table and cracked against the balls at the other end, sending them flying across the felt. Three balls sunk into the pockets. Brody looked at me and smiled.

"Good job. Do you want to be stripes or solids?"

"Well, since I sunk two stripes, I guess I'll pick stripes." I gave his shoulder playful nudge with mine. Well, sort of. My shoulder didn't actually reach his.

"It's still your shot," Brody said, studying the table. When he decided on our next shot, he held his arm out to me. "This looks like a fairly easy one."

I walked into his outstretched arm, my heart racing. Brody immediately wrapped both arms around me to help me take the shot. We bent over the table to line it up. It was an easy play and I normally would've made it, but I missed. My hands were shaking. My mind was numb, but my body hummed. I couldn't concentrate on pool. I could barely remember my name.

Brody took his turn, sinking shot after shot. I wondered if I would get another turn. It was obvious he spent a great deal of time at his aunt's bar playing pool.

"You're pretty good, Ace."

Brody looked at me and grinned. "I'm around here a lot. My mom travels a lot on business, so I spend time with my aunt. She makes sure I get fed when my mom's gone."

"What does your mom do?"

"She's a sales rep. for a pharmaceutical company." He took another shot, and I barely held in my groan as I watched his muscles in his shoulders and back.

"Do you have any brothers or sisters?" I asked.

"Nope. It's just me."

It was my turn again. I looked over my shoulder. "Sounds kind of lonely," I told him. My voice was all breathy and soft, so very embarrassing. It was hard to talk with his arms around me.

"Sometimes. But think of all the wild parties I can have." Our faces were close. His eyes dipped to my mouth, and then back to my eyes.

I took—and missed—my shot. "Ah, I think I just found out the reason for your bad boy reputation," I said, as Brody's arms slid away from me.

"Pssh, too bad all my parties are study sessions. That's about as wild as I get."

We finished our game of pool—he won, of course—just as our burgers arrived. We slid into a booth as the waitress placed our burgers in front of us. We didn't talk much as we ate. Our eyes would meet across the table every so often, and we'd smile at each other before looking away.

"Mm, you're right. Your aunt's burgers are the best. And this milkshake is to die for," I said, scooping out the last of my chocolate shake.

"I told you. Willow..."

I looked up and raised my eyebrows when his voice trailed off.

He let out a breath and threw his napkin on his plate. "I'd never lie to you."

"Okay," I said slowly, pushing my plate away and focusing my attention on him.

"I hope you and I are past the love-to-hate-each-other phase of our relationship and have moved into a friendship." He looked at the dark green table and spun his fork in circles.

"I think it's safe to say we have," I answered.

And then some.

"So, I hope you'd never lie to me." He looked up at me through his lashes.

"I wouldn't."

Except about not being able to play pool, but that was for a very good reason.

He let out a frustrated breath. "I saw the bruises." I stiffened. "When I bent over to help you line up your shot. Your shirt pulled back and to the side, and I saw the bruises on your back."

"Oh." I looked down at the table, making circles on it with my finger.

"Look at me. Willow, look at me. Please," Brody said softly. I slowly raised my eyes to his. "Who's doing that to you?"

I opened my mouth to answer, but I snapped it shut before I said anything. Shaking my head, I fought the tears pushing at the back of my eyes. I bit my lip and squeezed my eyes closed.

I won't cry. I'm stronger than that. Tim and Jenna ask me about my bruises. I don't cry then. I won't cry now. But the look in his eyes... he really looks like he cares.

"You can tell me. Is it Jaden?"

"I don't want to talk about it, Brody. I promised I wouldn't lie to you, but if we keep talking about this, I'll have to break that promise... and I don't want to. Just... It's okay. I'm fine. Let's leave it at that, okay?"

"No. It isn't okay. Someone is hurting you. That's not okay." He reached across the table and took my hand, rubbing his thumb over the top of it. "There are places that can help, people you can talk to."

"Trust me, it wouldn't help. I need to get home. Are you ready?" I asked, grabbing my purse.

Brody stared at me for a second before he stood up. "Yeah, I'm ready."

We said goodbye to Brody's aunt and walked silently to the parking lot. Brody unlocked and held the passenger door of the Jeep open for me. He slammed it shut, and I flinched. We didn't speak during the short drive back to the school where I'd left my car. He pulled up beside my car and threw the Jeep in park, jolting us both forward. I reached for the door handle.

"Wait," Brody said, his tone clipped. I pulled my hand back. He climbed out of the Jeep and walked around to open my door for me. "Give me your keys." He took them from my hand, unlocked, and opened the driver's side door of my car. As he held it open for me, he said, "You're wrong, you know."

"About what?"

"There's always something or someone that can help." He dropped my keys in my hand and closed the car door. Jogging back to his Jeep, he drove away.

No, Brody, you're wrong. This is one time where there isn't anyone who can help. The damage is done. Only bad things would come from telling anyone. Some secrets should stay buried, no matter how much it hurts.

Movie

> "Thank you for reminding me how to laugh, and live. I'd almost forgotten how."
> ~*Willow*

*F*RIDAY. *I STOOD IN FRONT OF MY CLOSET, LOOKING THROUGH MY* clothes. I was supposed to dress *normal*. Jenna texted me early that morning and told me I'd worn my limit of sarcastic T-shirts for the week. She said I was absolutely dressing in something that didn't have words on it to make up for wearing the awful shoes I wore all week. I told her I'd see what mood I was in. Her next comment wasn't very pretty and sounded a lot like she was PMSing, which was a dangerous time of the month for those of us close to Jenna. So I decided to try to find something she would consider normal and stay on her good side.

I finally chose a forest green moleskin shirt and jeans. I wore my brown, distressed leather, calf-high boots that matched my messenger bag. If that wasn't normal enough for Jenna, she'd have to come over and pick out my clothes for me every morning.

I showered and blew my hair dry, scrunching it so it hung in waves. Put on a little makeup—I never wore too much—and called it good. When I got to school, I swiped some lip gloss on my lips and made my way to my locker.

"Jeez, it's about freakin' time," Jenna said, rolling her eyes. "Finally, you look like a normal person. Nice choice, by the way. Love the boots."

"Thanks." I grabbed my books from my locker. "I figured if you didn't like this, you were going to have to start dressing me yourself."

"Well, if you insist on wearing those damn T-shirts and ugly ass shoes all the time, I just might," she snapped.

Yeah, definitely sounds like PMS. Note to self—buy Jenna chocolate at lunch.

"See you in history." I bit the inside of my cheek to keep from laughing and walked toward biology.

Brody's chair was empty when I got there. I felt a pang of disappointment. The first bell rang, and he still wasn't in class. He was always there by the first bell. I wondered if he'd be at school and realized how lonely my day would be without him sitting next to me, trading teasing insults.

I heard him before I saw him. "I mean it, Victor. Things will get ugly," Jaden shouted.

"Your empty threats really scare me, Jaden. Really. I'm trembling like a little girl," Brody shouted back before he walked into the classroom and slammed his books on the table.

"I need to talk to you." Jaden looked at me. When I didn't get up, he grabbed my arm and yanked me from my chair. "Now."

Brody was around the table so fast I wasn't sure what was happening. He shouldered Jaden. "Don't yank her around like that."

"Stay out of this, Brody," Jaden said through clenched teeth. A vein in his forehead bulged and pulsed in time to his heartbeat as he pulled me out of the classroom.

"I want you to stay away from him. Someone saw you two together yesterday. I don't know what you're up to, but I won't have my girl running around with that piece of scum behind my back. Stay away from him... or there'll be trouble." Jaden smirked, rubbing his chin with the side of his hand. "You don't want me to start talking, do you, Wills? Because I'm starting to feel kinda... chatty—like I have a lot to say. And I think there are some people who'd be really interested to hear it."

Jaden shoved me back into the classroom. I stumbled backward. Two hands caught me before I fell. I looked up to see Brody holding me. His face hard.

"Let go of her," Jaden ordered.

"If you can't treat her right, she'll eventually come to her senses and find someone who will. Your days are numbered, Jaden." Brody said, his voice measured.

"Willow isn't going anywhere until I say she is. Period. I have the power in this relationship, and she knows it. She's mine." Jaden walked away, slamming his fist against a locker.

Brody rubbed his hands gently up and down my arms. Turning me around, he stared in my eyes. "Are you okay?"

"Yeah." My voice cracked, and I closed my eyes for a handful of seconds to calm myself.

"Why do you stay with him?"

I shrugged a shoulder and tried to smile. "It's easier than trying to leave him."

Everyone stared as we made our way back to our table in class. My eyes darted to Tim. He looked at me with an expression of concern. I smiled and mouthed that I was okay. He didn't smile back. He wasn't a member of the Jaden fan club any more than Brody or Jenna was.

I sat with Jaden and the same bunch of football players and their cheerleader girlfriends at lunch. I tried to start conversations with them, but as usual, it was a no go. I felt more and more like an outsider in Jaden's world, and he did nothing to change the fact. Either he didn't notice, or he didn't care. I leaned to the latter. Jaden was all about himself. He wouldn't sympathize with my discomfort.

"You're drinking a diet shake today?" the same cheerleader who had a fit about my salad dressing asked.

"Yes," I said, holding up the can.

"That's much better than all that icky dressing you had on your salad," she said, scrunching up her nose, making her face look like one of those wrinkly dogs.

"I figured this might save me some time on the treadmill," I mumbled.

Not that I'd ever be on a treadmill.

"Good thinking." She nodded, her blonde curls bouncing around her perfect face. Turning to the girl next to her, they started an in depth conversation about the newest cheer they were learning. I sighed.

"Jaden, I'm going to go say hi to Jenna," I said, laying my hand on his shoulder to get his attention.

"Yeah, whatever." He waved me away with a flick of his hand. "Oh, Willow?"

"What?" I looked at him over my shoulder.

"Tonight's an away game. I expect you to be home if you aren't at the game."

I sighed. "I know the rules, Jaden." He narrowed his eyes before turning his back to me.

I plopped down in a chair at the table where Jenna and Tim were sitting and dropped my head down on the tabletop, covering it with my arms.

"That good, huh?" Jenna asked.

"Just peachy," I said, my words muffled.

"Drop his ass," Jenna whispered.

"You know it's not that easy, Jenna. I've tried. More than once."

"Hey." I jumped when I heard his voice. He hadn't been at the table when I sat down. Brody eased into a chair next to me, and I groaned. If Jaden saw him, there'd be hell to pay.

"Hey, Ace," I said, not looking up.

"How ya doin'?"

"That seems to be the question of the day. I'm fine. Just great. Everything's great. Just great."

"That's a lot of greats. Who are you trying to convince—me or yourself?" Brody asked quietly.

I turned my head, moved one arm so I could look at him, and blew a strand of hair out of my eyes. "Who knows?"

He gave me a small smile and ran a finger down the back of my hand, sending goose bumps up my arm and straight to my heart, which starting racing. Damn it to Hades and back. I hated my reaction to Brody. I wasn't supposed to feel anything for anyone. Jaden was easy. He didn't ask questions. He didn't pay attention. As long as I kept him happy, he'd keep his mouth shut. Win/win. Brody... well, he was a different story altogether.

"What are you doing tonight? Are you going to the football game?" Jenna asked, twirling her cup on the table.

"Nope. It's an away game," I said.

"Oh, so you'll be locked away at home, huh, Rapunzel?" Tim bit out.

I shrugged. "That's the assumption."

"Meaning?" Brody asked.

"Anything can happen. Maybe something will come up, and I'll decide to go out."

Jenna dropped her drink on the table, and ice flew across the top. "You're kidding, right? If he catches you out…" She didn't finish her thought.

"What?" Brody asked, looking at Jenna. When she didn't answer, he looked between Jenna and Tim. "He'll what?"

"He won't be happy," Jenna said quietly.

Tim snorted. "Yeah. That's putting it mildly. Willow, if you leave the house tonight, make sure you're in disguise and you aren't anywhere someone from school will see you. Like, you know, another country."

It was seven o'clock, and I sat on my bed watching a rerun of a stupid sitcom on television while I texted Jenna. My phone chimed that a text had come through. I clicked to read it, expecting it to be from Jenna. My heart started palpitating when the name across the top was Brody's.

BRODY: HEY.

ME: HEY, ACE. WHAT'S UP?

BRODY: WHATCHA DOIN'?

ME: TEXTING JENNA. HOLD ON.

I sent Jenna a quick text, telling her that Brody was texting me and I'd talk to her later. Her last text was a threat that I'd better cough up all the details of what was said between Brody and me. At my promise that I would, she told me to have fun and added a little winky face next to it. I rolled my eyes but giggled, quickly switching back to my conversation with Brody.

ME: OKAY. I'M BACK.

BRODY: WHAT'D YOU DO?

ME: TOLD JENNA I HAD TO GO.

BRODY: WHY?

ME: UM... SO I COULD TALK TO YOU.

BRODY: AH.

Huh. Maybe that was too much information. I shouldn't have said anything. Crap.

BRODY: I'M GLAD. NOW I HAVE YOU ALL TO MYSELF.

Or maybe not. I just got major chill bumps everywhere.

ME: SO, WHAT ARE YOU DOING?

BRODY: THINKIN' ABOUT YOU.

Oh, wow. My chill bumps just got chill bumps and now I have flutters in my chest.

BRODY: WERE YOU SERIOUS ABOUT GETTING OUT OF THE HOUSE?

ME: MAYBE. WHY?

BRODY: I HAVE AN IDEA. NO DISGUISE NEEDED.

ME: OK. I'M GAME.

BRODY: YOU DON'T EVEN KNOW WHAT IT IS.

ME: I TRUST YOU.

BRODY: PICK YOU UP IN 10.

ME: DON'T COME TO THE DOOR.

BRODY: ?

ME: MY PARENTS ARE OFFICIAL MEMBERS OF THE JADEN FAN CLUB.

BRODY: AH. THEY WOULDN'T LIKE YOU GOING OUT WITH ME.

ME: RIGHT.

BRODY: I'LL PARK IN FRONT OF YOUR NEIGHBOR'S.

ME: I'LL BE WAITING.

I jumped off the bed and grabbed a pair of yoga pants and a long shirt, trying to pull them on at the same time I pulled off my pajamas. Putting on a loose belt, I let it sit on an angle over my hips, just tight enough to make my shirt look like something other than a paper sack hanging from my shoulders. I looked in the mirror and groaned. My hair was flat on one side and a frizzy mess on the other. Quickly pulling it into a knot at the base of my neck, I tried to fix what little makeup I still had on. As I grabbed my purse and phone, I saw headlights shine through my window. I shot off a text to Jenna.

> ME: COVER FOR ME. WE'RE AT THE MALL. GOING OUT FOR A WHILE.
>
> JENNA: BRODY?
>
> ME: YEAH.
>
> JENNA. K. BE CAREFUL.
>
> ME. LOVE YA.
>
> JENNA: LOVE YA BACK.

I hurried to my mom's bedroom and knocked before sticking my head inside. "Mom?"

"What?" she answered, her voice hoarse. It sounded as if she'd been crying.

"Um, Jenna asked me to go to the mall with her."

"Have fun."

"Are you okay? I don't have to go if you need me here."

"I'm fine. Go," she said. "Just remember curfew."

"Thanks, Mom."

I hurried out the front door and down the walk. Brody pulled up when he saw me. For once, he didn't get out of the Jeep to open the door for me—thank God—and he had the interior lighting turned off. He drove away as soon as I was in the Jeep.

"Hey." He looked at me and smiled.

"Hey back. So, what are we doing?"

"It's a surprise."

"Okay." I settled back into the plush leather seats.

"You aren't going to try to get it out of me? Beg, plead, whine, until I tell you?" he teased.

"Nope. I told you, I trust you. But I'll beg, plead, and whine if it makes you feel better," I offered.

"No. Please don't start whining." Brody chuckled. How could just a small rumbling in his chest affect me so much?

"Okay. I'll stay whine free." I smiled and watched him drive.

"Let me ask you a question. If I was Jaden, and I didn't tell you where we were going, would you go with me with no questions asked?" Brody coasted to a stop at a red light. He turned to me, his eyes catching mine and holding them.

I bit my lip, trying to decide how best to answer the question. "Honestly, probably not. But that's because Jaden would most likely take me to some football game, football museum, football hall of fame, or something else football related, in which case, I'd have to fake an illness and skip out on him."

Brody laughed hard and loud, making me laugh with him. "Well, now I know if I ever ask you out and you tell me you're sick, that you're blowing me off."

"Somehow, I don't think that would be a problem," I said, and then immediately wanted to slap my hand over my mouth. Brody just gave me a crooked grin that melted my heart, but he didn't say anything.

"We're here." He pulled into a small driveway surrounded by trees. After he drove a few hundred yards, the trees fell away. We were in the middle of a field surrounded by trees on all sides. Completely secluded.

"Where's here?"

"It's my aunt's property. She plans to build a house here one day. No one will bother us. Wait there." Brody got out of the Jeep, walked around to my door, and opened it for me.

"Where are we going?"

"The backseat."

"Huh?"

Brody grinned. "Not for that. Although, I wouldn't be opposed to it." I rolled my eyes. "Okay, okay, you'll see when you get back there. It's a surprise, remember?"

I sighed and climbed into the backseat. "It's nice back here. Roomy. Is this yours or your mom's?"

"It's mine. Well, actually, it was my aunt's until she got a new one. Then she sold me this one at an enormous discount," Brody said as he grabbed a pillow out of the back and slipped it behind me. "There's no way I could afford a Jeep Grand Cherokee otherwise. I work at her place washing dishes and stuff like that to pay her."

"That's nice of her."

"Yeah, she's great." Brody grabbed a bag from the very back of the Jeep before sliding next to me. He took a blanket out of the bag and settled it over us. Next, he brought out a large bowl sealed with a plastic lid, sliding closer to me, until our thighs touched—oh, holy hotness!—and then he balanced the bowl on our thighs.

"Okay, what's up, Ace?"

He held up a finger for me to wait. Reaching into the bag once more, he pulled out a case. When Brody opened it, it folded back to reveal a video screen. "I hope you haven't seen this one." He handed me a DVD before he pulled the lid off the bowl and the smell of buttered popcorn filled the Jeep's interior. "I brought you Coke since that's what you order every time I've been with you." He reached in a cooler and gave me a can. "I know how much you hate for people to order for you, but I didn't know what else you liked."

I held the Coke by the tips of my fingers and stared at him. My voice stalled in my throat, and my gaze held his for a few beats. I mapped the striations of blues in his eyes before my gaze skimmed over his face, committing every feature, every curve, every line, to memory. I didn't want to forget how he looked at that moment. The very moment I knew he'd taken all there was of me.

Oh, shiznit. I'm falling in love with him. No, no, I can't be. I hardly know him. So it can't be love. It must be lust, then. He has a body hotter than Hades itself, but that's not it either. I don't know what it is. It's more than lust, but not quite love. What comes in between lust and love? Whatever it is, that's what I am. I'm in between lust and love with Brody.

"What?" Brody asked, looking at me with his head tilted to the side.

"I just can't believe you went to so much trouble for me just so I didn't have to sit alone on a Friday night," I whispered. I laid the Coke can in my lap and raised my hand to his face, hovering just a millimeter away from his skin, but not touching him. My fingers trembled, whether from nerves or the need to touch him, I wasn't sure. Maybe both.

"I told you the next time we watched a movie, I wanted you with me. Technically, I said in my bed, but since that isn't possible, this will have to do."

"Thank you." My hand skimmed over his jaw to the back of his neck. I leaned to him and hugged him tightly, laying my head on his shoulder.

Brody wrapped his arms around me, resting his head on top of mine. When I ended the hug and pulled back, Brody cupped my face in his hands. I froze, and we looked in each other's eyes. I could feel Brody's breath against my lips. It came in fast puffs, matching mine. I wondered if his heart was beating as hard as mine. If he'd leaned in for a kiss, I wouldn't have moved. I'd have let him kiss me—I'd have kissed him back.

He pulled me toward him. My tongue darted out to moisten my lips, and Brody groaned. Just before his lips touched mine, he pulled my head down and placed his mouth against my forehead. I sighed, partly from the feel of his lips on my skin and partly from the disappointment that it wasn't on my lips.

"You're welcome. It wasn't a big deal. A few bags of microwave popcorn and a cooler full of Cokes, no biggie." Brody shrugged a shoulder, pushing a lock of my hair behind my ear. "Have you seen this movie?"

"Nope." I wanted to forget the movie and pull him to me. Brody made me feel things I'd never felt with Jaden. And it wasn't just physical, although he was hot as Hell. It was everything. Brody made me feel wanted, cared for, special, respected, all things that a girl could wish for from a boy.

"Good. Let's pop this sucker in and fill our faces with popcorn dripping in butter."

"Sounds good." I leaned back against the pillow and got comfortable.

We sat in Brody's Jeep in the dark field watching a horror movie. I jumped at every little sound, and Brody laughed at me.

"Come here," he said, putting his arm around me and pulling me into the crook of his arm. "I'll keep the monsters away." An amused grinned pulled on his lips.

"You couldn't pick a comedy to watch while we're out in the

middle of nowhere in the dark?"

"That's no fun." He squeezed me tighter to him and tickled my side.

I giggled and squirmed against him. "Yeah, if you say so."

I stayed snuggled against Brody's side. His hand gently grazed up and down my arm, and I wished I could have worn short sleeves so I would've felt his skin sliding against mine. Since I'd started noticing the effects Brody was having on me, I'd wondered if I was having the same on him. Yes, he'd tried to kiss me, but he was known for his steady stream of romances. And no matter how hard I tried to put that out of my mind, I couldn't get past him dating Sarah, Tanya, and then Kara right after school started. But every time I moved against him as the movie played, I heard his heart rate speed up under my ear, or his breathing change… and I knew. Brody Victor was not immune to the effects of our attraction to each other. He was feeling it as strongly as I was. That made me happy, and a little scared.

"That was pretty good," I said when the movie was over.

"How would you know? You had the blanket over your eyes most of the time." Brody grinned.

I moved to sit up so he could take care of the video, but his arm tightened around me. I settled back against him.

"I did not."

"Okay, whatever you say." Brody pulled the blanket around me. "Are you getting cold?"

Ha! If he only knew how *not* cold I was. "No."

"So…" He drummed the thumb of one hand on his knee.

"What?" I pushed the strands of hair that had worked their way out of the knot at the base of my neck behind my ear and looked up at Brody.

"Jaden. He's quite a piece of work, that one."

I sighed and pulled away from him. This time, he let me go. "I was hoping we were going to avoid this conversation."

"What? Just sit, watch the movie, and never bring up the thousand-pound elephant dangling over our heads?"

I glared at him. "I was hoping."

Brody nodded. "Okay. Sure, if that's what you want. I just

don't get you. You seem so self-assured in everything you do. So independent... until it comes to him. And then it's like all your common sense and intelligence flies out the window. You roll over and just let him treat you like dirt. It doesn't make sense."

"I know. What time is it?"

"It's after ten."

"I need to get home. My curfew is eleven."

Brody sighed and sat up. We were silent as we folded the blanket and picked up the empty pop cans and popcorn bowl, putting everything back in the bag in the rear of the Jeep.

It wasn't until we were driving home that Brody spoke. "I overheard you saying to Jenna that you'd tried to break up with Jaden before. What happened?"

"I've tried more than once. He made my life a living hell. He'd follow me from class to class when I was at school, and I'd catch him following me even outside of school, at the mall, the movies, and places like that. He threatened any guy who came within ten feet of me. And forget asking me out, no guy would dare do that. They'd barely speak to me. That's why I sat alone in all my classes before you came along. No one would risk getting on Jaden's bad side. So they stayed away."

"So he bullied you into getting back together," Brody said, his voice hard.

"I guess so."

"You're home." He stopped in front of my neighbor's house and turned out the lights.

"Thanks so much for tonight. I had a lot of fun." I looked at Brody and smiled. "It sure beat sitting at home all night."

Brody grabbed my hand, laced his fingers with mine, and squeezed. "Anytime."

I slipped out of the Jeep, our fingers sliding slowly away from each other's. Shutting the door, I walked home. I saw Brody flip on his lights and slowly pull away from the curb as I closed the door behind me.

"You made it home before curfew tonight. There's a first time for everything, I guess." I jumped at the sound of Ralph's voice behind me.

Ralph owned two successful car lots and was on the Cassidy Independent School Board. He was highly respected in the social circles in Middleton. My mother, however, was not. She was white trash from the wrong side of the tracks. Everyone assumed she was nothing more than a gold-digging hussy. If they knew the real Ralph McKenna—not the front he put on when he was around other people—they'd know there were easier ways to dig for gold. They'd also know gold digging went both ways.

Ralph and my mother married just six months after meeting. Six months after my stepdad died in a car accident. She was working as a waitress, trying to keep a roof over our heads and food on the table until the life insurance benefits and the inheritance from my stepdad's will was finally distributed. She planned to go back to school and finish the degree she started before her surprise pregnancy with me caused her to drop out. But she met Ralph, and it was love at first sight. A whirlwind romance, an elopement in Vegas, and they've been happy ever since. Or that was the story they told everyone.

"Yes, sir," I said, inching my way to the stairs and hoping he'd just let me go up to my bedroom.

"Jaden called looking for you. Didn't seem too happy that you weren't home after you told him you would be. He's on his way over now."

My heart sank.

Jaden's coming here? Ralph told him I wasn't home. Crap.

Breathe. Just breathe.

I'd barely gotten to my bedroom when the doorbell rang. Turning, I went back to the stairs. I could see Ralph and Jaden talking in the foyer below. Ralph laughed at something Jaden said and clapped him on the back. I sighed, forcing my feet to go down the stairs. My heart beat in my ears, the blood whooshing behind them. My hands were slick with sweat and slipped on the bannister.

"Hey," I said to Jaden, smiling.

He didn't speak to me. Instead, he looked at Ralph and said, "I know Willow's curfew is eleven, but do you think we could take a drive? I'll have her back by midnight."

"Sure, Jaden, that's fine," Ralph said, clapping Jaden on the back again like they were long-lost buddies. Ick.

Jaden gripped my upper arm and guided me out to his car. He didn't say a word. We'd driven through my subdivision before he pulled into a convenience store parking lot, jammed his Mustang into park, and turned to glare at me.

"Where were you?"

"Out," I said, raising my chin.

"With?"

"A friend. What difference does it make?"

"I know you weren't with Jenna like you told your mom and Ralph," Jaden said quietly. It was almost scarier than if he were yelling at me. "Karen saw you."

"Should have known your spy was out on patrol."

He turned toward me so fast I flinched against the car door. "Check the attitude, Willow," he said, pointing a finger in my face. "Who were you out with?"

"A friend."

"What friend?" He nearly spat the word *friend*.

"None of your freakin' business, Jaden," I yelled. "You go off and party with Sarah and God only knows who else whenever you want. I think I'm entitled to visit with a friend if I want to."

"You aren't entitled to anything—"

"Take me home."

"We aren't done."

"I am. Either take me home or I'll walk." I narrowed my eyes at him. When he didn't start driving, I said, "Now."

"You're making this harder than it has to be," he warned. "You do not want to push me. I don't want to be the bad guy, but I will be if you don't play by the rules."

"No, you're making things harder, Jaden. You and your rules are full of shit. Things are going to change. I'm not putting up with your possessive bullshit anymore. Get over yourself. I'm going to start doing what I want, when I want to do it, without getting permission from you... and you're going to keep your mouth shut about what you know. If you don't like it, then maybe we should break up now and get it over with."

"I won't keep my mouth shut. I'll tell everyone." Leaning toward me, he whispered, "Everyone." He planted a quick kiss on the end of my nose. "And you and I both know who people will believe."

"Well, here's the deal." I smoothed out my shirt and adjusted my belt before I looked at him. "You've known what happened for... hmm, how long? Weeks? No, longer than that. Months? No, even longer." I shook my head and tsked. "Gee, I don't think the police are going to like it when they find out you had this information and didn't come forward."

Jaden's face turned red, and a vein bulged in his neck. It was definitely the wrong thing to say. And he made sure I knew it.

Jamming the car into drive, he squealed out of the parking lot. He didn't say another word to me on the drive back to my house. When he pulled into my driveway, he looked at me and finally broke the silence. "You seem to have it all figured out. But if you were so sure it would be that easy, you would have done something before now. To me. To Ralph. But you haven't. So I call BS on your little threat, Willow. Now get the hell out of my car." I'd barely got out and shut the door when he gunned the engine, peeled out of the drive, and sped down the street.

"Ass," I muttered, running my hands over my tear-stained face. *Breathe. Just breathe. You're strong. Breathe.*

Fallout

"Just because I keep a secret doesn't mean it didn't happen. No matter how much I wish that to be true."
~Willow

ONDAY MORNING AND THE SHIT WAS ABOUT TO HIT THE proverbial fan. I looked at my face in the mirror, still foggy from my shower. I could see the purple splotch even through the condensation.

Makeup isn't gonna cover that. What's my story? I took an elbow while swimming. Yeah, that'll work.

I blew my hair dry straight, angling it toward my face. Maybe if it fell forward, it'd help hide what makeup couldn't. Not likely.

I put on my makeup, trying to use concealer around my eye to hide as much of the bruising as I could. It was a lost cause, and, besides, no amount of makeup could cover the swelling.

I grabbed a pair of black yoga pants and the new T-shirt I had made when Jenna and I were at the mall that said, *Mondays should be illegal.* Once dressed, I grabbed my things and left for school.

Jenna had texted repeatedly since Friday night. I sent her one text telling her things were okay, and I'd tell her more Monday. Other than that one text, I hadn't talked to anyone since Friday. Sitting in my car in the student parking lot, I pulled out my phone. I knew I needed to warn them before they saw me, especially Brody.

I felt sick. I hated lying to them. I hated how weak it made me look… how weak I was.

Jaden texted me over and over during the weekend, reminding me that he knew my secret and he had no problem telling people. And even if they didn't believe him, they would believe Ralph. With every text he sent, my stomach roiled. Bile rose in my throat, scorching it. I felt pathetic and useless. And pissed. And not for the first time, I thought I'd just tell him to go ahead. Tell everyone. I didn't care anymore. Just do it and get it over with. Whatever the fallout was, it couldn't be any worse than living with the secret hanging over me.

> ME: HAD AN ACCIDENT OVER THE WEEKEND. DON'T FLIP WHEN YOU SEE ME.
> JENNA: YEAH. AN ACCIDENT. OK.
> ME: TELL TIM FOR ME.
> JENNA: SURE. WHATEVER.

I sat looking at the screen on my phone, tapping my fingernail on the back. I knew I had to text Brody. I couldn't just walk into biology without warning him. He'd have a fit. These were always the hardest bruises to explain. The others, I could hide with clothes, but my face, I couldn't. That was why he didn't normally hit in the face. I guess that shows how much I pissed him off Friday night.

Breathe. Just breathe. It won't break you. Just breathe.

I took a deep breath and started typing.

> ME: HEY, ACE.
> BRODY: HEY BACK.
> ME: I NEED TO TELL YOU SOMETHING AND YOU HAVE TO PROMISE ME YOU'LL BE COOL.
> BRODY: OKAY.
> ME: NO. PROMISE.
> BRODY: I PROMISE. I'LL BE COOL.
> ME: I HAD AN ACCIDENT OVER THE WEEKEND. DON'T FLIP OUT WHEN YOU SEE ME.
> BRODY: I'M GONNA KILL HIM.
> ME: YOU JUST PROMISED ME. COOL REMEMBER? OR I'LL LEAVE.
> BRODY: DAMN IT, WILLOW. OKAY. I'LL TRY.
> ME: TRY HARD. FOR ME.

Sighing, I opened the car door. I reached in the backseat to grab my bag. When I turned around, I saw Brody jogging across the parking lot toward me.

Oh, jeez. I was hoping to put this off until we were in class where he wouldn't make a scene.

"I saw your car when I pulled in. What happened?" His voice trailed off when he got close enough to see my eye. "What the hell?"

"I had an accident—"

"Don't lie to me, Willow. Remember sitting in my aunt's bar and telling me you wouldn't lie to me? So, let's try again. What happened?" Brody reached out and took my chin in his hand, moving my head to the side so he could get a better look at my mangled eye. He gently smoothed the hair away from my face.

I bit my lip and looked away from him. If he didn't want me to lie to him, I wouldn't say anything at all. That was the safest thing to do, anyway.

"You're not going to answer me?"

I looked in his eyes and shook my head slowly. "No," I whispered. Tears overflowed from my eyes.

He let go of my chin and nodded once. "Okay. Then answer this. When's the last time you've seen Jaden?"

I sighed. Afraid Brody would hear from someone else that Jaden was over Friday night, I decided to tell him. I thought it would be better for him to hear it from me. Maybe I could do some damage control. Yeah, right. "He came over after the football game Friday night. His cousin Karen saw me in your Jeep. He wanted to know who I was out with. I guess she didn't see you."

"Son of a bitch. And you're asking me to look the other way and do nothing?" He flung his hand toward my eye.

"Yes. I'm asking you, as a friend, to overlook it."

Brody glared at me. His jaw worked back and forth as his eyes roamed over the bruises and swelling covering my eye. "You're scared of him."

"Yes." My answer was mostly the truth.

"Willow, you don't have to be—"

"Please, just do this for me." Grabbing Brody's hand and threaded my fingers with his, I skimmed my lips over his knuckles. "Please." I hated how my voice trembled, the desperation I could hear in it.

"Fine," he said through clenched teeth. He grabbed my book bag, slung it over his shoulder, and stalked toward the school.

"Brody, wait. Give me my bag." I hurried after him, taking two steps to every one of his long strides.

He stopped abruptly and turned. "Why? Because he'll get angry that I'm carrying it?"

I took a step back at how hard his voice sounded. "Yes."

He let the bag slide from his shoulder. It hung from his flattened palm. "Here."

"Don't be mad at me," I called when he turned and walked away.

"I'm not," he said over his shoulder.

"You're acting like it." I hated the tremor in my voice, but I couldn't stand him mad at me. His opinion, our relationship, was important to me.

He stopped, and I nearly ran into his back. "I'm disappointed, Willow. I didn't figure you would let someone treat you this way without fighting back."

I sucked in a sharp breath. It felt like he'd physically knocked the air from my lungs. Disappointment was so much worse than anger. "That's not fair! There's more to it than you know."

"Then tell me," he shouted. Turning to look at me, he held his arms out from his sides. "Tell me, what's not fair? What don't I know?"

"I can't," I whispered.

"Whatever." His arms dropped with a smack against his thighs. He walked away and left me standing alone in the middle of the parking lot.

Walking slowly into the building, I made my way to my locker. I focused on the tiles on the floor and putting one foot in front of the other, so I didn't have to look at everyone staring at me. It was bad enough I could hear their whispers.

"Yoga pants? Really, Willow?" Jenna asked, looking at me. Then I raised my head. "Oh, shit."

As soon as I saw Jenna, the tears started. I hadn't cried when it happened. I hadn't cried all weekend. But there, standing in the middle of the school's hallway, in front of my locker, I started blubbering like a damn fool. Like I hadn't given people enough to talk about already, I had to give them more ammunition.

"Let's go to the bathroom. C'mon." Jenna put her arm around my shoulder and held me tight against her, guiding me to the restroom. When we got inside, I slid down the wall and sat down on the dingy, tiled floor with my knees pressed against my chest, my arms wrapped around them. I laid my head down on my knees. "You wanna talk?" Jenna asked softly.

I shook my head. "Nothing to talk about." Jenna handed me some tissue. I wiped my face and cursed. "All the makeup I put on to cover it up, and I'm crying it all off." I half laughed and half sobbed. I heard the warning bell ring. Three minutes until classes started. "You should go. I don't want you to be late."

"No freakin' way." She shook her head. "I'm not leaving you like this."

"I'm fine, Jenna. Go. I don't want you to be late. You get detention enough on your own. You don't need me helping you by making you late for class." I smiled, wiping my tears on the back of my hand. "I'm just going to splash cold water on my face, and then I'll go to class."

"You're sure? 'Cuz I don't want to leave if you need me—"

"I'm sure."

She gave me a kiss on the cheek. "Text me if you need me. It doesn't matter what class I'm in. If you need me, just text and I'll be there." She hesitated in front of the door. "Promise me you'll text me, Willow. I hate leaving you like this." A tear slid down the side of her face.

I went to her and hugged her tight. "I promise I'm okay, but if I need you, I will text. No matter what. I'll see you in history."

With one last hug, Jenna wiped her tears and slipped out the door. Alone in the bathroom, I sat down on the floor again. I had no intention of getting up and going to class.

Sometime later, I don't know how long, the door squeaked open, and I turned my face from it. I wasn't in the mood to answer any questions, and I damn sure didn't want to see pity in anyone's eyes. I just wanted to sit on the dingy, pea-green tiled floor for the rest of the day. Maybe for the rest of my life… or at least the rest of the class period.

"You gonna sit here all day or what? 'Cuz if you are, I can make a Chinese run for lunch." He eased himself on the floor next to me.

"What are you doing here, Brody?" I asked, trying to wipe away my tears before he saw. Because, although the tears were because of the circumstances that led up to my majorly black eye, I was also crying because of him. His reaction to me in the parking lot. I was hoping for a little more empathy, rather than disappointment. That stung. And maybe hit a little close to home, too, because, if I faced the truth, I was disappointed in myself.

"Jenna told me you were in here. She said if you weren't in class in five minutes, I was supposed to text her so she could check on you."

"Of course she did. So why are you here instead of her?" I turned my head to look at him, but kept my arms in front of my face to block his view.

He shrugged a shoulder and wrapped the hem of my shirt around his finger. "I wanted to be the one to check on you."

"You do realize you're sitting on the floor of the girls' bathroom?"

"So are you," he pointed out.

I sighed. "Yes, but I *am* a girl. You most definitely are not."

"Thanks for noticing." He gave me a lopsided grin, and I couldn't help but let out a small laugh.

"Believe me. I've noticed, along with the rest of the female, and some of the male, student body."

"Well, it goes both ways. I've definitely noticed the fact that you're a girl. A very beautiful one at that." He slipped a finger under a lock of my hair and twirled it around his fingers as he looked around the room. "So, what's it gonna be? Are we staying in here all day or are we going to brave biology?"

I shrugged and dropped my arms, forgetting that not only was my eye totaled, but I'd also been crying so my face was undoubtedly red and splotchy too. *Yeah, America's Top Model, here I come. No need to vote. I'll just accept my winnings now. Sure.*

I heard Brody suck in a breath when he looked at me, and his fingers stilled.

"Yeah, I guess I look busted, huh?" I said, wrapping my arms around my legs, pulling them tighter to my chest.

Brody shook his head. "Nope." He swallowed and cleared his

throat. "Not unless the term busted means something different to you than it does to me, because I think you look effin' gorgeous."

I rolled my eyes—the good one, anyway. "Whatever. What happened to your vow to always tell the truth?"

"It's still in place," he murmured, sliding a lock of hair behind my ear. He let his fingers glide gently along my jaw and down my neck, following it with his eyes. I shivered under his touch and watched him roll his full bottom lip between his teeth. I nearly groaned out loud.

I'm losing it. I have a mangled eye, a splotchy face, no makeup, I'm sitting in a dirty school bathroom, and I'm getting turned on.

"You deserve so much better than this," Brody whispered, cupping the side of my face. He ran his thumb over my bottom lip, eyes following. I let the tip of my tongue touch the pad of his thumb, and he groaned deep in his chest.

He moved in front of me so fast, I gasped. Grabbing my upper arms, he slid me across the tiled floor until I was sitting between his legs with my legs over his, wrapped around his waist. His hand traveled up my back, sliding under my T-shirt. I hummed at the feel of his skin against mine. His other hand cupped the side of my face, his fingers delving into the hair falling in front of my eyes, holding it back.

His eyes roamed from mine to my lips and back again. My breath was trapped in my chest. His touch made it impossible for me to breathe, and my chest burned. My heart pounded as though it were trying to breakthrough and hand itself it Brody, because at that moment, he surely held my heart in his hands.

I wasn't sure how much time passed. Brody's hand ran up and down my spine. My hands moved up his arms to his shoulders, and then my fingers sifted through his silky dark hair like I'd wanted to do so many times. Time and place melted away. We were no longer in a school bathroom, but encased in a solitary cocoon where we were the only two people alive.

Brody's hand left my cheek and moved to cup the back of my neck, nudging me forward. He leaned his cheek to mine. I could feel his warm breath moving wisps of my hair. Turning slightly, he kissed my cheek, moving along my jaw to my ear, kissing the sensitive spot just behind my earlobe. My head started to swim, and a tremor ran through me.

"Brody," I whispered so low I wasn't sure if he heard me.

He pulled back and rested his forehead against mine. His breathing came in short gasps, his eyes closed. His fingers opened and closed around the hair at the back of my neck, gripping it tighter and tighter.

I knew the moment he decided. His breathing changed. His grip on my hair loosened. He splayed his hand between my shoulder blades. He groaned a curse, moving his mouth to mine. Pressing his lips to the corner of my mouth, he hesitated, giving me time to stop him, but my mind had been made up before that day. I knew if Brody Victor ever tried to kiss me again, I wouldn't stop him. My body craved the taste of him and wouldn't be satisfied until it had him—and even then, I knew one taste wouldn't be enough.

He pulled back just far enough to move his blue eyes, dark with desire, to mine. Seeing his desire mirrored in my gaze, he leaned forward just as the bathroom door flew open, hitting the wall beside it with a crack before bouncing off.

"Oh, sorry," a girl dressed all in black with blue hair said, looking down at us. "You know, there are better places to make out than the slimy bathroom."

Scooting away, I stood, keeping my back to the girl. I didn't need any reports getting back to Jaden of my bathroom tryst with Brody.

"Thanks," Brody murmured, rolling off the floor. He placed his hand on the small of my back and guided me out the door.

I made it through the rest of the day without hiding in the bathroom. Brody and I never mentioned the best damn kiss that almost was.

When I left school that afternoon, Jenna, Tim, and Brody waited at my car. "What's this? An intervention?" I asked, only half kidding.

"Today's football practice," Tim said, as if that explained everything.

"Yeah, and we're taking you out," Jenna chimed in.

"Where?" I eyed the three of them.

Jenna cringed. "It pains me to do this. I want that noted for the record. I'm only doing it because I'm awesome like that."

"That goes without saying," I said, pursing my lips to keep from smiling. Jenna was a diva of the highest form.

She gave an exaggerated sigh. "We're taking you to the mall and buying you one of your damn T-shirts."

"Really? I have the best besties in the world!"

"Yeah, yeah, it wasn't my idea so don't get your mush all over me. I still despise your shirts."

I looked at Brody and smiled. "Thank you."

"What?" he feigned innocence.

"I know it was your idea. Jenna hates the shirts. Tim has probably never paid enough attention to even realize I wear them—"

"Not true!" Tim said.

"That leaves you, Ace. The one person who's told me they fit my personality. So, thank you." I glanced around the parking lot to make sure we were alone and then stood on my tiptoes and kissed Brody's cheek.

His hand glided over my hair when I kissed him. "Yeah, well, don't go getting all girlie or anything."

"I have some things I have to do first, so let's meet in the food court in about an hour?" Jenna suggested.

We all agreed, and Jenna and Tim left for their cars. Brody held back. "What's up?" I asked.

"Um, I was wondering if your parents would be home this afternoon?"

"My stepdad won't be, but my mom probably will be home. Why?"

"Oh. I was thinking we could ride to the mall together. I could follow you home so you could drop your car off and we could take mine, but if your mom's gonna be there it wouldn't be a good idea."

"No, it wouldn't. Sorry. I would've liked riding with you."

"Yeah?" He looked at me with a grin.

"Sure. Mall traffic is horrible this time of day."

"Ha. Nice. Here I thought you wanted to spend time with me

because of my charming personality, but you just want me for my superior driving skills."

I laughed. "I'm a sucker for a guy who follows all the traffic laws."

If you've ever seen yourself drive, you'd know why I want to ride with you. You ooze sexiness when you drive. I'm in so deep with you it's pathetic, and you don't have a friggin' clue.

"Well, if you want, we can drop your car off at my house and leave for the mall from there. My mom won't be home and even if she were, she wouldn't care," Brody said, leaning his back against my car door.

Alone. With Brody. At an empty house. With beds. No parental guidance whatsoever. What could go wrong? Yeah. I hope he has an unlimited supply of condoms. Jeez, Willow, get your mind out of the gutter... or the bedroom—whichever. It's no different from being alone with him in a parked car in the middle of a field after dark. Except this time, there'll be beds. Nice, soft, beds. I should tell him no.

"Sure. That sounds great." I smiled.

I'm so going to Hell for sexual immorality.

I followed Brody to his house. When we pulled into the drive, I got out of my car and went to Brody's Jeep. He got out, and I thought he was just coming around to open my door for me like always. No such luck. Ugh.

"You want to go in and get something to drink? We have time before we need to meet Tim and Jenna."

"Um." I looked at the door and then back to the jeep, twisting my fingers in front of me. "Okay."

Oh, no. This is so bad. We should leave now and get something to drink at the mall... where there aren't any beds and there are lots of people around. Not here, where we are alone, with beds in the house. Why can't I stop thinking about the damn beds? I'm starting to sound like a hussy scoping out the beds.

"You're sure your mom won't mind us being here alone?"

Brody inserted the key into the house's door and unlocked it. "I don't remember saying that exactly. It's not like I'm going to call her up and tell her I have a girl alone in the house. I just said she wouldn't mind you parking your car here while we went to the mall. Slight difference."

"Then we should leave." I started to get in the Jeep when he grabbed my wrist and pulled me gently away from it.

"She's out of town. It's fine. Let's get a Coke." He threaded his fingers with mine and led me into the house. "Besides, I need to change clothes before we go. Someone squirted mustard on my jeans at lunch, remember?"

She's out of town. Oh, well, that makes it so much better.

"Huh? Oh, that was an accident," I said absently. My mind was still focused on the fact that Brody's mother was out of town.

We're on the friendship train. Nothing more. Just friends. Yeah. That's why we were practically mauling each other this morning in the girls' bathroom. If Brody can make the girls' bathroom a sensual, seductive place, just think what he could do in a bedroom. I'm thinking about those damn beds again! I need a distraction.

"This is a really nice house. Just you and your mom live here?"

"I guess. It isn't ours. We're just renting until we find a place of our own. My mom likes this side of town. I kinda like it here, too." He glanced at me and grinned. I was sure something melted inside me—a vital organ, no doubt, because my body started doing all kinds of weird things in response. My hands started shaking, my breathing was shallow, and my heart was skipping every other beat. My mind tried to stay immune to Brody Victor—even though it was failing miserably—but my body had completely lost control. Wherever he was, my body was like a homing beacon, picking up his signal. Missiles locked and loaded. I was ready... for what, I had no idea. But I assumed it had something to do with the beds.

Yup, I'm a lost cause. Just give me a gallon of chocolate chip ice cream and a spoon now. I'm going need them. No need for a bowl. This heartbreak will call for eating it right out of the carton.

We walked into to a huge two-story foyer with a curved staircase on one side and a formal living and dining room on the other. Brody led me to the back of the house where there was a great room with a family media room, and a huge kitchen with an attached sunroom. A second staircase was located off the kitchen.

"Wow." I looked around. "I didn't know this subdivision was this upscale compared to mine."

"It's just a house. I've lived in more houses over the years than I can count. None of them ours, so they've never really been homes, you know?"

Yeah, more than you can imagine.

I sat down at the breakfast bar and watched Brody grab two Cokes out of the fridge. He pulled down two glasses, filled them with ice, and handed one to me along with the can.

"Thanks," I said, smiling up at him.

He didn't say anything, and he didn't smile back. I forced myself not to squirm in my seat. He turned back to the fridge and pulled something out of the freezer. Turning around, he handed me a bag of frozen peas. "You need to ice that." He gestured to my eye.

"Peas?"

"I don't know where the ice pack is and I don't like peas." He shrugged a shoulder.

I laughed. "Okay, peas it is, then."

"I'll be right back. I'm going to change. Make yourself at home." He jogged up the stairs

I dropped my head on the granite countertop. "Ugh, he's changing. Distraction. I need one. Now."

"What?" Brody's head peeked over the balcony.

"Nothing," I said a little too fast and loud.

"I thought I heard you say something."

"Nope." I smiled, praying he couldn't see the flaming blush I could feel crawling across my face. I smacked the bag of peas to the side of my face and cringed.

His head disappeared, and I let out the breath I was holding. I dropped the melting bag of peas on the counter and wandered around the family room. My arms were held ramrod straight as I clapped my hands against the sides of my thighs, a nervous habit I'd had since I was a little girl. It made me look like a chicken trying to take flight. That thought threatened to make me giggle so I forced my arms to go limp, putting one hand over my mouth to hold in any laughter that might try to escape.

I came to a collection of eclectic framed photos on a table in the family room. I stood looking at them, picking them up one at a time so I could examine the faces smiling back at me. I smiled when I came to one of a baby smiling at the camera while it ate an ice cream cone. Vanilla ice cream dripped from its chin and onto its bare belly. One chubby hand held the ice cream and the other twirled its dark hair between its fingers, filling it with ice cream.

"It's you?" I asked when he walked up behind me. He hadn't said anything, but I knew he was there. My body was becoming more and more in tune with his presence. I could feel his warmth radiating from him, smell his scent, and feel the slightest shift in the air as he moved.

"Yeah. How'd you know I was here?" he asked. I looked over my shoulder and saw his amused grin—one of my favorites out of his many smiles.

I looked back at the photograph and shrugged a shoulder. "Why? Were you trying to sneak up on me, Ace?"

"No, not really."

"Not really?" I asked, putting the frame back in place on the table.

I felt his hands settle gently on my hips and froze. He hesitated for a few beats. Whether he was giving me a chance to move or was deciding his next move, I didn't know, but the next thing I felt was his warm breath moving over the back of my neck, then his lips skimming over my skin. Sucking in a breath, I gripped the edge of the table. I felt him smile against my skin just before his fingers dug into my hips. He pulled me closer and placed an open-mouthed kiss on my neck, touching my skin for the briefest moment with his tongue.

"Brody," I whispered.

He wrapped one arm around my waist, hooking his finger through the belt loop on my jeans. I reached over my head and ran my fingers through his hair, holding his head to me, letting my head fall forward. Brody cursed and pulled me harder against him. He kissed from the back of my neck toward my shoulder. His free hand moved slowly up my arm to the collar of my shirt. When he started moving my collar out of the way, it was as if someone threw a glass of ice water in my face.

"No!" I reached up and brushed his hand away. His grip on me loosened briefly, and I slipped by him. "We… we can't," I said, my breath coming in small pants.

He turned and looked at me. First confusion marred his face, and then understanding. "Move your shirt."

"What?"

"You heard me, Willow. Move your damn shirt." He took two strides toward me. I backed away from him, bumping into the wall behind me. He stood in front of me, his hands planted on the wall on each side of me, caging me in. "Do it."

I looked up at the ceiling and bit my lip, trying to decide if there was any way I could distract him from wanting to look under my shirt. Problem was, the only way I could think of was by taking my shirt off—which was exactly what I was trying to avoid. Totally messed up.

I watched him as I reached up and pulled my shirt collar away from my neck far enough that he could see what he already knew was there. He didn't say anything, but his look turned hard. He reached up and placed his hand over the bruises, moving it around until he found how it fit the pattern. "The other side too?"

I nodded but stayed silent.

"It's fresh. When? Friday… when you were hit in the eye?" I looked at him, not answering. His fist hit the wall next to my head. I flinched and squeezed my eyes closed. "Damn it, you don't get to just not answer."

"I said I wouldn't lie to you. If I answer, I'll have to lie." My voice was strained from the lump in my throat, and I was trying—unsuccessfully—to keep my tears from falling.

Brody let out a loud sound of frustration, almost a growl, and ran his hand up the back of his head, resting his hand on top, his other hand low on his hip. "You are so frustrating."

"I'm sorry. I'll just go." I'd just opened the door to leave when I heard him move behind me. His hand slapped against the wood, pushing the door closed. I stiffened.

"I don't want you to go," he murmured close to my ear, kissing the hollow behind it. "I promised you a visit to the mall." I felt his lips curve into a smile against my skin.

"Yes, you did."

"Let's go then. All of a sudden, I have a craving for a blue raspberry slushie." I looked over my shoulder and gave him a shaky smile. "Okay?" Nodding, I followed him to his Jeep.

When we got to the mall, we met Jenna and Tim in the food court. Jenna looked back and forth between us with a raised eyebrow. "Meet each other in the parking lot?" she asked.

"Sure did," Brody answered.

"Uh-huh." Jenna looked at Brody, who was doing a much better job of keeping a straight face than I was.

"The ease with which you're able to lie is scary, Ace," I whispered to Brody as we walked from the table to get our slushies.

"What? I wasn't lying. We did meet in the parking lot. You got out of my Jeep and I met you at the door in the parking lot."

I laughed. "Okay. Whatever you say." He reached down and took my hand, folding it in his. I looked down at our intertwined hands.

"Sorry." He started to let go and I squeezed his hand, holding it in place. We stood in line holding hands and not really caring who might see. When it came time for us to order, Brody ordered two blue raspberry slushies.

When he tried to let go of my hand, I tightened my grip on his. He bent down to my ear and whispered, "I love holding your hand. I really do. You have no idea how much. But I need my hand back so I can pay."

I shook my head, and he chuckled. "I thought of that already." I fished in my back pocket, pulled out a twenty, and handed it to the clerk. "See, no reason for you to let go." I smiled and bumped my hip into him.

"I love how your mind works." He kissed my temple, and I shivered. "That shiver had nothing to do with your slushie." Brody smirked.

"Pretty sure of your skills aren't you, Ace?"

"When your body does that, yeah, I am."

If he only knew that little shiver isn't even half of what my body is doing right now.

The four of us sat at a table in the middle of the food court, eating soft pretzels and drinking slushies. We joked and laughed for nearly two hours. I was amazed at how easily Brody fit in with Tim and Jenna, in a way Jaden never had. In fact, Jaden had never tried to fit in with my friends. It was expected that I make the effort to fit in with his friends. They were the only people that mattered in Jaden's world—other than himself, of course.

We finally left the food court. Brody and Tim got sidetracked by a music store and Jenna by a makeup counter. While they were preoccupied, I made my way to the T-shirt Factory.

It was a small store filled with racks of T-shirts. Some already had sayings and jokes printed on them, and some were left blank for the customer to design. A person could get something as simple as a saying on the shirt, to something as complex as a drawing or logo. If you could think it up, Mr. Rafferty could get it on a shirt. The walls were covered in samples of T-shirts that he'd made. One of my designs was even hanging up.

Mr. Rafferty smiled when he saw me. "Back for another one, huh Willow? I swear you keep me in business." He chuckled.

"Yeah, just can't get enough."

"Nice shiner. Everything okay?"

I raised my fingers to my eye. I'd almost forgotten about it. Glancing over at Mr. Rafferty, who was probably my grandfather's age and looked like a bald Santa Clause, I shrugged a shoulder and said, "Just took an elbow in gym class."

"Gotta watch out for those stray elbows. Let me know when you're ready."

"Actually, I'm ready. I want to get a long-sleeved shirt in this burgundy color with this printed on the front." I handed him a piece of paper.

He read it and glanced at me. "Okay. I don't get it, but I don't get much of what you kids want these days." Shaking his head, he walked to the back of the store. "Give me fifteen minutes," he called over his shoulder.

"Thanks. I'll be back."

I found Jenna, Tim, and Brody sitting on a bench outside the music store. "Hey, where were you?" Brody asked, walking over and taking my hand.

"I know where she was. The T-shirt Factory. Right, Willow?" Jenna smiled.

"Yeah. I have to go back in fifteen minutes."

"Why didn't you let us go with you?" Brody look down at me.

"Because I don't want you to know what it's says until it's done."

Brody quirked an eyebrow at me and smirked. "Should we be alone?"

I laughed. "No, Ace. Nice try though."

After I picked up my shirt, Jenna and Tim followed us to Brody's Jeep. Jenna forgot what part of the lot she'd parked in, and Brody offered to drive her around until she found her car.

"I thought you were paying attention, Tim," Jenna snapped as we walked to the Jeep.

"You drove. You should have been watching where you parked." Tim rolled his eyes.

"Yeah, I was driving. That means you weren't doing anything but riding, so you had less to do. That means you should be able to remember where the car is." Jenna threw up her arms and let out a frustrated breath.

"They're a match made in Heaven," I whispered to Brody. He laughed. Jenna and Tim rolled their eyes at me.

"Show us your shirt," Jenna said when we reached the Jeep.

"Not now." I shoved the bag under my arm.

"Yeah, I want to see it," Brody said.

"I don't want you to see it until I'm wearing it, and there's nowhere to change here. I'll wear it to school tomorrow."

"So change in the Jeep. The windows are tinted," Jenna said. I looked at her with my mouth open. "What?" She shrugged. "They won't look." She waved her hand at Brody and Tim.

"Yeah, Willow, change in the Jeep." Brody's blue eyes sparkled with a hint of a dare as he let his keys fall from his hand and dangle from his fingers in front of me. "I won't look. Much."

I glanced at the windows and back at the three of them. Jenna's eyebrows were raised; she was completely daring me to do it. Tim looked bored. If it didn't have to do with chess, it really didn't get him going. And Brody looked amused.

"Fine. Give me those." I swiped the keys from Brody. "You better not look." I pointed at him.

"Wouldn't dream of it."

I climbed in the back of the Jeep and quickly switched from one shirt to the other, smoothing the new one in place before getting out of the SUV. "Okay."

I felt a little stupid standing in the middle of the parking lot while three people read words plastered across my boobs, but there I was.

Brody laughed as soon as he saw me. Jenna and Tim looked at me and said, "Huh?" in unison.

"*'Movies in the back of Jeeps do it better.'* What the hell does that mean?" Jenna said, looking at the back of the T-shirt for the punch line.

"Just an inside joke," I said, biting my bottom lip to keep from laughing.

Jenna looked at my face, which I'm sure was beet red, and then at Brody, who was still laughing. "Uh-huh. Inside joke. Nice color. Really matches Brody's *Jeep.*" She pointed between my shirt and the Jeep.

Brody doubled over with laughter.

Tuesday. I woke up to my phone chiming that I had a text message. Groaning, I pulled my quilt over my head. I still had twenty minutes before my alarm was set to go off. I'd just started drifting back to sleep when my phone chimed a second time. I flipped the quilt off and grabbed my phone. Whoever was texting me was not going to like my response. Then I read the name and smiled. Except him. For him, I'd make an exception.

BRODY: GOOD MORNING, BEAUTIFUL.

ME: HEY, ACE.

BRODY: WERE YOU AWAKE?
ME: NO, BUT THIS IS A NICE WAY TO WAKE UP.
BRODY: ICK. TOO SAPPY FOR THIS EARLY.
ME: WHAT'S UP?
BRODY: WEAR SOMETHING FUNNY.
ME: WEIRD REQUEST. I'M GAME.
BRODY: LATER.
ME: BYE.

Wear something funny? What does he think is funny this early in the morning besides waking me up to tell me I'm too sappy? Guys. God's way of letting women know He has a sense of humor.

I pulled out a blue, long-sleeved T-shirt and a pair of black jeans. Jenna was going to have a fit. It was technically my day to dress normal, but Brody's request outweighed Jenna's, so funny T-shirt it was.

I showered, doing my hair and makeup before getting dressed. Grabbing my blue converse tennis shoes and my book bag, I was just walking out the door when my phone chimed. I looked at the screen, expecting a text from Brody. My heart stopped when I read the name across the top of the message. My hands turned clammy and started to shake. I was so dizzy I had to sit on the bottom step of the staircase before I fell.

There was just one line, but it was going to change everything.

Twelve
Caught

"They must often change, who would be constant in happiness or wisdom."
~Confucius

STARED AT THE TEXT, WILLING MY BREATHING TO CALM. I COULD FEEL myself start to hyperventilate. Tears pressed at the back of my eyes and, for the first time, I realized something. I was happy, happier than I'd been in months, maybe more than a year. And then another truth slammed into me like a linebacker on Jaden's football team. The message I was staring at was going to rip that happiness away.

JADEN: SOMEONE SAW YOU AT THE MALL YESTERDAY.

The letters started to swirl and blur as my eyes filled with tears. My head pounded in sync with the blood rushing behind my ears. I sucked in two deep breaths, letting them out slowly to calm my rapidly fraying nerves. One thought was in the forefront of my mind—I had to warn Brody.

I tried to call him as I drove to school, but my call bounced to voicemail. I hung up without leaving a message. Pushing the speed limit, I drove through yellow lights and rolled through stop signs. I was lucky there weren't any cops around, or I would have gotten one helluva ticket.

I parked in the student parking lot, not caring I took two spaces, and hurried into the building, sliding to a stop when I saw Jaden leaning against my locker. I'd prayed that he'd just let it go. That he'd use this as an excuse to break up with me. Play the part of the jilted boyfriend. Smear my name all over school. I wouldn't have cared. I'd

154

be free of him. That was all that would've mattered.

But I'd known deep in my gut that he wouldn't. He'd make me suffer for the embarrassment I caused him. Breaking up with me would be too easy. He'd want to hurt me—the sadistic streak running through his dark soul wouldn't let him walk away. This was a game to him. One that had just become a lot more fun.

"I don't know what was going on at the mall and I don't care. But it's gonna stop. Now. From now on, I'll walk you to and from your classes. You'll sit with me at lunch—the entire lunch period. Karen will stay and watch your chess practices and tournaments while I'm at football practices, and you will be required to attend all of my football games. If you need a ride to the away games, Karen will drive you."

Jaden paused and scratched his thumb over his bottom lip. "I know you share a lot of classes with Brody Victor. I've already made arrangements with friends to keep an eye on you during those classes to make sure you don't overstep any boundaries. I feel these new guidelines will help keep you in line. There will be no discussion and no negotiations. This is how it will be. Period. And in case you're wondering, I've had a chat with Ralph. He agrees with my terms. Thinks I'm being more than fair considering your behavior. So do we understand each other?"

I didn't know what to say. I was completely blindsided. I nodded my understanding more out of shock than actual acceptance.

"Good. I'm glad you are going to be sensible about this." He grabbed my arm, pulling me behind him to my biology class. Jaden jerked me to a stop next to my seat, and I stumbled into it. He stood next to my table until the first bell rang, and then he left without a word.

Brody leaned over to say something to me. I shook my head, but I didn't look at him. He pulled back. I could see him watching me out of the corner of my eyes. Taking my notebook out of my bag, I scrawled a note across a page.

Jaden found out about us at the mall. His friends are watching. We can talk on the phone or text later.

When the bell rang after class, I gathered my things. I hadn't even left the classroom and Jaden was there to walk me to my next class. It continued all day.

During lunch, I sat at Jaden's table. When I mentioned I wanted to say hi to Jenna and Tim, he stood to go with me. I sat down and told him I'd changed my mind. Brody was sitting with them, and he was who I really wanted to see. But that was impossible with Jaden shadowing me.

I was counting the seconds until independent study so I could talk to Brody. But when I walked into the library, I came face-to-face with one of Jaden's football buddies. How had I not noticed him before? There was no way I could talk to Brody with Jaden's lackey watching me. So I sat at a table in the front of the library, instead of where Brody and I always sat. When independent study was over, Jaden was waiting in the hall. He walked me to my locker and then my car. I was never alone the entire day. He'd completely shut me off from my friends and, more importantly, from Brody.

I was backing out of my parking space when my phone chimed, but I didn't dare look at it. Jaden still watched me. I waited until I was on the main road sitting at a stoplight before I looked at the message.

Brody: Call me.

I dialed his number as soon as I pulled into my driveway. I hadn't even gotten out of the car when he answered.

"What's going on?"

I threw my messenger bag over my shoulder and walked into the house. "Someone saw us at the mall yesterday and word got back to Jaden. I can't believe I was so stupid. He has friends everywhere. I should have known someone would see and tell him."

"So, what, he's going to babysit you every day to make sure you don't talk to anyone?" Brody asked, his voice hard. "Willow, you can't—"

"I know what you're going to say and if it was any other person, I would break up with him, but it's Jaden. He'll make my life a living hell if I try to leave him. And he'll do the same to you. Trust me, I've tried."

"And he's not making your life a living hell now?" Brody challenged. I didn't answer. He was right. "I need to see you," he said softly.

I took the stairs two at a time and hurried into my bedroom, clicking the lock closed behind me. "I can't. He's coming over for dinner. My mom and stepdad are wrapped around his little finger. They'll never let me see you." Blowing out a breath, I threw my stuff on the floor before I fell across my bed.

"Can you get away tonight? After your parents are in bed?"

"You mean sneak out?" I chewed on my bottom lip, running through the scenarios in my head. Once I went to bed, my mother never checked on me and since I had my own bathroom, there was no reason for me to leave my room. But my bedroom was on the second floor. Getting down the stairs and out the door would be a problem. If I ever got caught... "I can do that."

"Don't if you'll get caught. My mom isn't around, so I'm free to come and go. I don't want you getting in trouble."

"No, I'll be fine. Can you meet me down the road around midnight? They should be in bed by then. Or is that too late?" I ran my hand up and down my thigh, waiting for his answer.

Actually, they'll both be passed out by then, but that's beside the point. They won't know I've left the house.

"I need to see you. I don't care what time. I'll be there."

I looked straight ahead through most of dinner. I spoke when spoken to. I smiled when I was supposed to. Answered questions, played the part of adoring girlfriend. All the while, I screamed, railed, and cursed inside. I was trapped, both physically and in my own head. I didn't want to be there. I didn't want to be sitting next to Jaden. I tried not to cringe when he touched me, and I had to force myself not to gag when he kissed me.

I kept looking at the clock. The hands moved so slow it was as if they were moving backward.

"Have somewhere to be?" Jaden asked, looking at me. I looked up at him and noticed he gripped his fork so tightly that his knuckles were turning white.

"No." I shook my head and forced a smile. "I just have a ton of homework tonight. My history teacher assigned another report. Did yours give the same assignment?" I took a bite of dinner, forcing myself to keep eye contact with him and my expression neutral.

"Yeah, she did. It's due Friday."

"Mine too."

"We should work on it together this week after school. I could pick you up after football practice tomorrow and Thursday. We can go to the library and knock it out." He smiled like he knew he'd just one-upped me and taken away any chance I'd had at seeing Brody after school the evenings he had football practice.

"Oh, that sounds great, doesn't it, Willow? You and Jaden haven't been able to spend a lot of time together since football season started," my mom said, looking between Jaden and me.

"Yes, that does sound great." I kept my smile in place and my eyes never left Jaden's.

Jaden didn't leave until eight. My nerves were nearly frayed, and I'd chewed my fingernails to the quick.

I put my ear buds in and listened to music to distract myself as I cleaned the kitchen from dinner and bagged up the garbage, picturing Jaden's face as I stuffed the garbage bag into the dirty garbage can outside.

"I'm done with my chores. I'm going upstairs."

"Okay," my mom said.

"Goodnight."

And then I waited. I heard my mom go to bed at ten-thirty. My stepdad stayed up. Eleven o'clock came and went, and he still hadn't come upstairs. Eleven-thirty passed, and he still hadn't gone to bed.

Adrenaline flooded my bloodstream, and my head began to pound. I paced my room, wringing my shaking hands, and trying to think of other ways to get out of the house.

Can I climb down from my window? Can I climb out of the bathroom window and into the tree next to the house? Is it too far to reach? Can I climb down the trellis or is that something that only works in movies?

And then I heard it and my heart started racing. The floorboards creaked outside my bedroom door as he walked by. I wanted to do a happy dance. I would've if I weren't afraid he or my mom would hear. So I forced myself to sit on the edge of my bed and text Brody.

ME: I'LL BE A FEW MINUTES LATE.

BRODY: I'LL WAIT.

At midnight, I stuck my head in the hallway and looked toward their bedroom door. The light was off, and it was quiet. I slipped out my door, carefully avoiding the floorboards I knew creaked. I'd learned which were safe about a month after moving into the house. It was a skill that had come in handy more than once.

I bypassed the front door because it was directly under their bedroom. Instead I made my way to the back corner of the house and let myself out through the sunroom.

I saw Brody's Jeep parked three houses down from mine. The engine was running, but the lights were off. As soon as I step on the sidewalk, the Jeep rolled forward and I climbed into the passenger's side.

"Hey, Ace," I said and grinned at him. I wanted to touch him so bad. I could hardly keep my fingers to myself. I slipped my hands between my thighs and the seat to keep from reaching out to him.

"Hey back." He smiled at me as he steered away from my house. "Where do you want to go?"

I shrugged. "I don't know. I thought you had this planned out."

His eyes met mine. Open and vulnerable. His voice was soft when he said, "I just needed to see you. I didn't think beyond that."

"Um, there a small park down the road and to the right. We can go there if you want."

We drove in silence until Brody turned into the park's parking lot and turned off the Jeep. He turned sideways in his seat and looked at me.

"So." He rubbed his hands up and down his thighs.

"Yeah."

Why am I so nervous? I've been out with him before. I wasn't nervous the night we drove to his aunt's property and watched a movie. What's different now?

Brody rubbed the back of his neck and gave a short laugh. "I'm freakin' nervous."

"Why? It's just me." I didn't tell him I was nervous too. I thought that might make him more nervous. "Let's go swing." Jumping out of the Jeep, I started running toward the swings. "I'll race ya," I called over my shoulder, laughing.

Brody caught up with me easily. I squealed when he grabbed me around the waist and lifted me in the air

He let go of me, letting me slowly slide down his body. My breath quickened. And desire flowed through my veins. I held on to one of his arms, my other hand resting on his chest, where I could feel his heart beat racing, mimicking my own. I looked into his eyes as he leaned his face closer to mine. My lips parted, and I moistened them with the tip of my tongue. Brody watched my tongue move across my lips and groaned a curse.

He cupped the side of my face with one hand and placed the other on my hip, pulling me closer to him. Placing his thumb under my chin, he tilted my head to meet his. His lips were so close to mine that our breath mingled. Then he moved and kissed just in front of my earlobe.

He let his lips rest in front of my ear and murmured, "I'm not going to kiss you tonight. I'm not going to kiss you tomorrow, or the next night, or the next, or even the night after that. I want to. You don't know how damn much I want to, but I won't. Not as long as you belong to Jaden." He kissed the side of my face again, sucking my earlobe gently into his mouth. I gasped, fisting my hands in his shirt. He pulled his head back and rested his forehead against mine.

He took my hand in his. We walked to the swings and sat down next to each other, swaying back and forth.

"So tell me all about Willow McKenna," Brody said.

"Well, first, my name is Willow Rutherford, not McKenna. That's Ralph's name. He's my stepdad."

"Huh. How come I didn't know that? I mean, I knew he was your stepdad, but I didn't know your last name."

"That's because you were too mesmerized by my beauty and wit to be bothered by things as trivial as names." I flipped my hair and batted my lashes at him.

He chuckled at my pose and kissed me on the nose. "That has

to be it."

"Either that, or you didn't bother to find out my last name because you thought I was a bimbo." I giggled at him.

"You will never let me live that down, will you?"

"Probably not. In fact, I'm thinking about putting it on a T-shirt," I said.

"No way."

"What? You said you liked my T-shirts."

"I do, but you're not going to wear a T-shirt that reads *bimbo*." Brody shook his head. "Nope."

"Oh, I wasn't going to get it for me. I was going to get it for you." I poked him in the chest and grinned.

"Ah, I see how it is." He chuckled. "So Rutherford was your biological father's name, then?"

I twiddled my fingers on the side of my thigh, looking at my feet. "Um, no. Rutherford is my mom's maiden name. I don't know who my biological father is. She was married once before. He was the closest thing I had to a father, but he died in a car accident. Six months later, she married Ralph." I shrugged.

Shut up. Shut up now! You're telling too much.

"Birthday?" he asked.

"Ugh, you're not going to ask me what my sign is, are you?"

"No." He snorted a laugh. "I just want to know when your birthday is."

"May first." I took a few steps backward, lifting my feet to swing forward.

"Really? Mine is April first."

I skimmed my feet against the packed dirt ground under the swings until I came to a stop and angled myself toward Brody. "Your birthday is on April Fool's Day?"

"Yes." A grin tugged at his lips.

I giggled. "So you're just a fool, then."

He looked into my eyes, his blue eyes twinkling. "A fool for you." He didn't smile. There was no trace of teasing in his voice.

"Brody, you're no one's fool." I tried to wave off what he'd said.

I'm with Jaden. Brody and I are just friends. So why did what he said make my stomach do somersaults? And why do my lips tingle with the need to feel his on them? Who am I kidding? Brody and I crossed the friend line a long time ago. And Jaden will never let me go.

We sat on the swings talking for more than an hour before Brody took me home.

"Would it be too greedy for me to ask if you can get away tomorrow night?" Brody asked before I got out of the Jeep.

"I was afraid you wouldn't ask."

He let out a breath and shook his head. "When it comes to you, it goes without saying that I want to spend every second I can with you."

His answer filled me with the most exquisite feeling. I felt it bubble up within me, beginning in my heart and moving through my veins until it touched every part of me. I didn't know what it was, but I'd never felt something so good, so right. "Then I'll definitely be waiting for you tomorrow night. Same time."

I was already looking forward to the next night and wondered what we'd do, what we'd talk about, where we'd go. Jaden never entered my mind.

"Oh, and Willow? The answer to the question is purple." I tilted my head and looked at him, my brow wrinkled. He waved his hand at me. "Your shirt, '*If you choke a Smurf, what color would it turn?*' It'd turn purple."

"I don't even want to know how you know that." I shook my head slowly and jumped from the Jeep.

Brody chuckled. "See you in class."

"Bye, Brody."

I was still smiling when I climbed into bed. When I fell asleep, I dreamt of bright blue eyes looking into mine, as if they could see directly into my soul.

Wednesday. I dressed normally for Jenna. Well, I guessed you could call it normal. I called it my mourning outfit, a short, black shirt, black leggings, a black belt sitting diagonally on my hips, black boots, black nail polish, and black eyeliner. I looked like I'd just come from a funeral. Totally the vibe I was going for. I slipped in my skull and cross bone earrings that Jenna had bought me as a joke on Halloween the year before, and left for school.

Walking into the school building, I saw Jaden leaning against the locker next to mine. Jenna was pulling out her books from her locker. Papers and pens were falling from the shelf. Jaden stood there watching her, shaking his head. The idiot didn't even try to help.

Handing Jenna a Starbucks caramel macchiato, I picked up the pens and crap falling out of the locker, stuffing them back on the shelf. "Thanks," she said over her shoulder. "Holy black hole, Batman. Did a funeral throw up on you?"

I glanced at Jaden and then back at Jenna. "Something like that."

"Ah. Your mourning outfit. How could I forget?" Jenna nodded.

"Doesn't my girl look hot in black?" Jaden asked, wrapping his arm around me and kissing me hard on the lips. I felt nothing. Empty. Dead.

Brody set my body on fire with just a look. Jaden turned it cold with the sound of his voice. He made me feel dirty with his touch. Being with him was wrong. But he knew, damn it all to hell. He knew... and I didn't know how to get out from under his threat of exposing what she did—what we did. That one night... one decision. Every day, I wish we could go back. I'd make her do something. Something other than what she did best—watching.

I grabbed my biology book out of my locker and walked to class, Jaden following close behind me. Stopping outside the door, I stood with my back to the wall and one foot propped against it. I could see Brody watching me out of the corner of my eye.

"Aren't you going in?" Jaden asked.

"Nope." I took a sip of my macchiato

"Why not?"

"I'm drinking my caffeine. I can't take it in with me," I said and looked around the hall, saying hi to people as they passed.

"I don't want to stand in the hall while you drink your macchi-whatever the hell it is. Let's go." He grabbed my arm, pulling me toward the door.

I yanked free of his grasp. "If you don't want to stand here, don't.

Go to your class. I'm finishing my drink. I can't take it in the room with me, so that means I'm staying out here until I'm done. Don't like it? Tough." I took another sip of my Starbucks, watching him over the rim of my cup. I braced myself for his outburst, but he was too smart to do anything in school. He'd wait until after, and then he'd mete out his punishment.

"Fine. We'll do it your way today. But from now on, make sure your drink is gone before you get to school. I'm not waiting in the hall for you to finish your coffee again."

"Macchiato."

"Whatever," he snapped.

I deliberately drank as slow as humanly possible. When the first bell rang, Jaden started getting nervous. He shifted from foot to foot, scanning the hallway.

"You're going to be late for class, Jaden. You know if you're tardy too many times, you'll be benched." I looked at him with a raised eyebrow, knowing he wouldn't risk not being able to play in his precious game.

"Go in and sit down," he said through clenched teeth.

"I will. I still have some drink left," I lied. My macchiato had been gone before I even got to the door of the classroom.

He turned with a huff and stalked away. I grinned behind my cup. As soon as he was out of sight, I walked past the classroom door. Brody got up and walked into the hall.

"Hey, Ace," I said with a smile. "Tired?"

"Nah. I could stay up all night." He let his hand brush against mine quickly. I wrapped my finger around one of his and squeezed.

"We'd better get in there, I guess."

"Is your Starbucks gone?"

I laughed. "It was gone before I even got here."

"Sneaky. You go in first. I'll wait a minute and follow."

I squeezed his hand one more time and walked into class, dumping my cup in the garbage on my way to my seat. I didn't look up when Brody walked in and sat down next to me. We didn't speak in class, and we scooted our chairs as far from each other as possible.

It was all about appearances. That was my life. Smoke and

mirrors until I wasn't even sure what was real and what wasn't.

Ugh. Midnight will never get here. They've been in bed for a half an hour. I'm sure they're out for the night.

I stood at my window, overlooking the street, waiting for Brody to drive up. As soon as I saw his Jeep, I hurried out of my bedroom and slipped out of the sunroom door. I jogged to his Jeep and hopped in.

"Hey you," he said, with a smile. Jeez, he could stop hearts with that smile.

"Hey back."

"Wanna go to my aunt's property? I want to show you something."

"Sure." I didn't tell him that I'd go just about anywhere with him if he asked.

He pulled into the field and parked in the same place he did the night he brought me there to watch the movie. Grabbing a blanket out of the back of the Jeep, he opened my door to help me out. Again, I was perfectly capable of getting out myself, but I wouldn't give up the chance for him to touch me. Even an innocent touch sent my body into a frenzy, creating feelings I'd never felt before. Feelings that confused me, but felt oh, so good. And I greedily took as many as he was willing to give.

He gripped my waist to help me down, and I put my hands on his arms. His biceps flexed under my hands, and I nearly groaned out loud. He pulled me close to him, and our faces were so close that I had to remind myself to breath. It was heady, heart stopping, and made me feel completely off balance. And I wanted it. I wanted it all. I wanted him.

Is he trying to torture me?

When he set me on the ground, we stood there, our bodies touching, looking in to each other's eyes. He reached up and placed a lock of hair behind my ear before grabbing my hand and pulling me away from the Jeep.

He spread the blanket on the ground and sat down on it. "Wait until you see this. You'll love it." After he pulled me down on the blanket next to him, he laid down on his back. "Lay down."

I eased myself next to him. "What am I looking for?"

"Just look up," he whispered.

"It's beautiful." The sky was so black, not like in the city where the lights turned it into a murky gray. Stars were sprinkled across the inky sky, bright and beautiful, twinkling like they were winking at us. "I've never seen so many stars."

"You can't see them in town with all the lights."

"It's amazing."

"I come here sometimes to think. It calms me," Brody murmured.

"Thank you for bringing me." I looked at him. He stared at the sky. I took my time looking at his profile, my eyes roaming over his face. He hadn't shaved and a day's worth of stubble covered his cheeks, giving him a sexy, rugged look.

He reached out and threaded his fingers through mine. I turned and gazed at the stars. It was perfect, lying with him in the dark, the stars shining above us. I wasn't sure how long we lay there silent, holding hands. It could have been seconds, minutes, hours—it didn't matter. I could have stayed there all night with him. It felt right.

"Why do you stay with him?" Brody asked quietly.

I opened my mouth to answer, but closed it and shook my head. My eyes filled with tears. I didn't have an answer to give him. Not a good one—not the truth, anyway.

Brody rolled to his side and wiped my tears away with the pads of his thumb. "You're not happy with him. Anyone who pays attention can see that. And I swear on my life if he hits you again, I'll kill him."

"Jaden doesn't hit me." I tried to pull away, but Brody held me in place.

"Willow, I've seen the bruises. Everyone has."

"He's never hit me. He's a jerk sometimes, yeah, but he's never hit me. I'm just clumsy, and I bruise easily. I'm fair-skinned, so they look worse than they are."

Please, please just let it go.

Brody shook his head. His hand fell away from my face and he reached down, pushing up the sleeve of my shirt, looking in my eyes. "You can't hide them all with big bracelets and long-sleeves."

His fingers lightly traced the bruises circling my wrist. His touch was so gentle.

"I… I stumbled and—"

"You said you'd never lie to me. Don't lie for him. These marks are the perfect imprint of a hand." His voice was hard, and I flinched.

What do I say? How do I get him to leave it alone? The truth? Can I tell him the truth? I want to tell him, tell somebody.

"It's late. I need to get home before they miss me."

Brody sighed and let go of my hand. "Okay."

We picked up the blanket and climbed into the Jeep. Brody was silent as he drove me home, stopping a few houses away from mine.

"I'll see you tomorrow." I turned and smiled at him. "Thanks for tonight. It was… perfect."

He didn't smile back. "Willow, it doesn't have to be like this."

Tears pressed at the back of my eyes. "Yes, it does," I whispered before climbing out of his Jeep. I ran to my house, slipping through the door with tears staining my face.

I wish you were right and things could be different. But wishing gets me nothing. He knows what she did. What I did. She could've gotten to him. But she didn't even try… neither did I. Jaden has his hooks in me until I can leave and get as far away as possible.

Breathe. Just breathe. This won't last forever.

Friday night, my favorite night of the week. Or not. I sat on the bleachers right behind the players and watched the football game. Exactly where Jaden told me to be. I didn't get to spend time with Jenna or Tim or any of my other friends. He didn't even want me getting up and leaving to go to the concession stand alone. Karen followed me. I felt like a fugitive.

At least I was going to get to see Brody for more than just an hour that night. I was staying over at Jenna's house. Jaden wasn't pleased, but I told him he could go do something very naughty to himself that involved an 'F' and 'you'. Something I didn't generally say, but it fit the situation and Jaden just brought it out in me. He took the hint, for once, and gave in without too much of a fight.

Jenna was all for Brody and me spending the evening together. She even had the logistics of how I'd get in and out of her house all worked out. I loved her. I just had to wait for the game to end and for Jaden to shower, blow dry his freakin' hair, change, and then take me home. By the time he did that, it would be two hours after the game ended. Jenna and I planned to meet up three hours after the game. She'd pick me up and then drop me off at Brody's house.

It was planned out perfectly. But there was a saying about the best-laid plans. They rarely worked out. Jaden didn't bother showering. He just changed and met me in the car. He wanted to go to Jamieson's party. He knew I was supposed to be at Jenna's that night, so my curfew wouldn't be an issue. When I pitched a fit about having to go to the party, he told me to tell Jenna to meet us there.

"She doesn't want to be at a party with all your skanky friends any more than I do," I snapped. That earned me a smack on the mouth.

"Check the attitude, Willow."

"Take. Me. Home. Now."

He drove to the party, despite my demand to be taken home. I expected no less. When we got to Jamieson's, I rummaged in the kitchen drawers until I found a phonebook to find a number for a cab.

Jaden ripped the book out of my hands and grabbed my cell phone. "What the hell are you doing?"

"Calling a cab to take me home," I said, reaching for my phone.

He held my phone over my head. "You'll leave when I do," Jaden said, tossing my phone at me.

As soon as Jaden walked away, I texted Jenna and asked her to pick me up. She was there in twenty minutes—it was the longest twenty minutes of my life.

We were halfway home when I saw a car that looked a lot like Jaden's Mustang in the side mirror. I turned in my seat to get a better look and could see the cherry red paint when it drove under a streetlight. I was sure it was him. "Crap. Jaden's following us." My voice cracked.

"What do you want me to do?" Jenna glanced at me.

I faced forward and sighed. "Just take me home so I can grab my stuff, and come get me at ten like we planned."

"I don't want to leave you alone with him. He's been drinking, and he's pissed off." Jenna shook her head.

"Everything will be fine. I won't be alone with him. My mom and Ralph will be there, remember?"

"Yeah, we both know Ralph won't give a rat's ass what Jaden does."

Jenna's comment surprised me and I glanced at her, fumbling for something to say. "My mom with be home. It'll be fine. You'll be right back to get me."

"Yeah. Be careful." Jenna dropped me in front of my house. "I'll see you in an hour," she said before she drove away.

Jaden was out of his car before the tires finished squealing in my driveway. And he wasn't happy.

ME: IS YOUR MOM HOME?
BRODY: NO. WHY?
ME: JUST ASKING. GOTTA GO.
BRODY: EVERYTHING OK?
ME: YEAH. SEE YOU LATER.
BRODY: K.

Jamming my phone in my pocket, I slipped out of my bedroom. I crept through the house and out of the sunroom door. If I rode my bike to the field between our subdivisions, I could cut through the yards and get to Brody's house quicker than if I stayed on the roads.

I rode my bike to the field. There was a trail carved out where neighborhood kids rode their bikes, jumping off ramps made out of cinder blocks and old plywood. I flew down the trail, dodging the bike ramps. My teeth clamped together when my bike jumped over the bumps and ruts in the ground. Thank goodness, I had a mountain bike. Nothing else would have been able to handle the wicked trail. When I got across the field, I dumped my bike against a fence before jumping it.

I darted through the backyard, jumping over toy cars, pails, and shovels littering the ground next to a sandbox. When I came to the road, I turned right, making my way to Chestnut Trail and taking a left. I ran to the end of the street where a beautiful Victorian house sat. Climbing the stairs to the large wraparound porch, I bolted to his door, sagging against it. I stood there, trying to catch my breath, blinking back the waves of nausea and dizziness washing over me. I felt like I'd been on a tilt-a-whirl a few hundred times. I could barely walk straight I was surprised I'd made it to his house at all.

I was still propped against the door when the porch light flickered on. I took a big step backward just as Brody pulled the door open. He stood there in nothing but a pair of sweatpants.

Oh, this wasn't a good idea. He's half-naked and looks so much better in person than in my fantasies—all of which involve him.

"Willow? What's wrong?"

I stepped into the light streaming from the door. Brody's face hardened. I could see his jaw clenching and unclenching.

"I'm gonna kill that sorry son-of-a-bitch." He reached out and pulled me gently into the house, shutting and locking the door behind me. "What happened?"

I started to cry. Not little tears. I sobbed. Brody wrapped me in his arms, my head against his chest. I could hear his heart beating a steady rhythm beneath my ear. The warmth of his skin enveloped me, and I lost myself in him. He held me like that for a while—I don't know how long—smoothing my hair from my face or running his fingers up and down my back.

When my sobs turned to soft sniffles, he led me to the couch. "Sit down and tell me what happened," he said and sat next me, angling his body toward me.

"I need to use the restroom."

"Not until you tell me what's going on." He caught my hand in his when I stood.

"Brody, I really need to use the restroom first." He let go of my hand. "Will you text Jenna and let her know I'm here?" I asked over my shoulder as I walked into the hall bathroom.

Splashing cool water on my face, I wiped the running mascara from my eyes. Then I stood and stared at the face looking back at me.

My eye had a jagged cut above it. Dried blood was smeared over the side of my face. Pieces of hair were stuck in it. The top lid on my eye was already turning a deep purple and swelling. My lip was bleeding where I bit down on it when he hit me, but so far, it wasn't swelling. I didn't look half as bad as I felt.

I finished in the bathroom and walked into the hall. The room tilted to the left and the lights blinked on and off. I felt like I was twirling around and around like I'd done playing as a child.

"Brody?"

He was there in an instant. At least, it seemed instantaneous. But then again, I wasn't exactly sure what had happened. One second I called out to him and then I turned, realizing I was lying on the floor in his arms.

"What happened?" I whispered.

"You passed out. Let's go. I'm taking you to the emergency room."

"No!"

"Willow, you have a gash on the back of your head. Your hair is matted with blood. You probably need stitches. You need to see a doctor."

"No. I'm not going to the hospital. I can't. I came here because I thought I could trust you."

"You can trust me. You can always trust me, but I really think you need to see a doctor."

"No."

Brody sighed and helped me up. "Are you still dizzy?"

"Not as long as you're holding me up." I smiled at him.

"Let's go upstairs. I think there's a first aid kit up there." Brody helped me up the winding stairway and into the master bath. "Sit here." He pulled out a small bench covered in pink brocade.

"I can't sit there. I'll get it dirty."

"It's fine. Sit."

"Stop being so bossy, Ace."

"Then stop being so damn pigheaded and let me take you to the hospital," he snapped.

His arm darted out in front of me, and I flinched away.

"Shit, Willow, I was just turning the sink on. You're not scared of me, are you? Because I'd never—"

"No, I'm not scared of you. You make me feel safe. That's why I came."

Brody straddled the bench next to me and cupped my cheek in his hand. He rubbed his thumb lightly over my skin. His eyes never left mine as he leaned forward. Our mouths were so close that I could smell his minty breath. I dropped my eyes from his and turned my face away.

He sighed and kissed the area in front of my ear lobe. I tried to hide the shiver that coursed through my body at the feel of his lips against my skin.

He nudged my face so I was looking at him. "You're so beautiful."

I let out a half laugh, half sob. "I'm mangled." I was crying again. How could he think I was beautiful? I was damaged. Inside and out.

Brody shook his head, his hand still cupping my face. "I'm looking at a beautiful girl sitting in front of me, one that has driven me wild since the day I met her. You're so freakin' amazing and somehow, you've missed the memo. You're kind, funny, intelligent, and so damn gorgeous. You're perfect, Willow, every part of you."

"I'm not perfect," I whispered.

"You're perfect for me."

Breathe. You're strong. Brody makes you stronger. Breathe.

Looking into his eyes, I smiled. I could feel butterflies filling my stomach—the colorful kind. Beautiful and graceful. No one had ever made me feel as beautiful as Brody did, as wanted, as loved.

"You're so cute when you blush." He smiled, rubbing his thumb over my pink cheek. "Come on, sit next to the tub."

"What are we doing?"

"I want to clean the cut on your head and see how bad it is," he said, throwing towels on the steps leading up to the jetted soaking tub.

"Wow, this is an awesome tub."

"Do you want to take a bath and wash the blood away?"

"Um…" I bit my bottom lip, looking anywhere but at him.

"I meant you could take a bath. You. Alone. By yourself." He shifted from one foot to the other, his cheeks turning slightly pink. "Not that I wouldn't take a bath with you, you know, if you asked me. You'd have to ask real nice." He laced his fingers together and put his hands behind his head, stretching his arms.

Watching his muscles stretch made all rational thought drain from my head. Seconds ticked by, and Brody gave me a concerned looked when I didn't answer. I forced myself to look away and concentrate on the conversation. "No, that's okay. Thanks though."

"Can't blame a guy for askin'. Here, sit on this step, lean back against these towels, and rest the back of your neck on the edge of the tub." Brody sat on the tile ledge and turned on the water. He pulled the retractable bath-head out and ran the warm water over my hair. "Is that okay? It's not too hot? It doesn't hurt, does it?"

"Mm. It's great." I watched his face as he sprayed the water over my hair.

"I've never done this before. Are you sure it's okay?" He looked into my eyes as he drizzled some shampoo on my hair.

"I've never done this either."

I let my gaze wander over him. His arms flexed as he moved the water over my head. His rippled abs were just a finger space away. I let the tip of my finger run across his skin, watching as the muscles contracted and goose bumps covered them. His gaze darted to mine.

I looked up at him as he gently shampooed my hair and then applied conditioner. He pulled his bottom lip between his teeth as he worked, like he did when he concentrated on school work. When he glanced down, he caught me staring at him and smiled. He wiped the blood from the side of my face and above my eye.

"Is this okay?" he asked again.

"It feels good."

Wrapping a towel around my hair, he squeezed the water out before wrapping it in a dry towel and helping me sit up. He placed a soft kiss on my forehead before brushing a droplet of water off my face. "Dizzy? Do you feel okay?"

"I'm good." I smiled.

"Nothing started bleeding again. That's a good sign."

"See, no doctor required."

"I still think—"

"No." I shook my head, immediately wishing I hadn't when pain sliced through it.

"Hurts, huh?"

"Don't be smug. It's not a good look on you, Ace."

Brody helped me stand. I ran a brush through my hair while he grabbed the towels and threw them in a corner—typical guy—then he helped me back downstairs to the kitchen.

"Are you hungry?" he asked.

"Starving."

"So, are you going to tell me what happened?" He set a plate of fresh vegetables and hummus in front of me.

"Hummus?" I smiled.

"Yeah, someone told me it wasn't a gross as it looked. Turns out, she was right. You trying to change the subject?"

"Can you just let me stay here for a while?"

"You should know the answer to that," he said, sitting on the barstool next to me. He put his elbow on the counter and rested his cheek in his upturned palm.

I turned my head slightly and looked at him through my eyelashes. "Okay, then can I stay without talking about… things?"

He opened his mouth to answer, then closed it and nodded. "If that's what you want." He studied me for a moment before saying, "Willow, look at me." I angled my body toward him. He stared into my eyes. "You can tell me anything. You know that, right?"

"I know." I looked down at my plate, pushing the hummus around with a carrot stick.

Brody sighed and stood. "You want to watch a movie?" He held his hand out to me. I threaded my fingers with his. "Come on. Bring the hummus with you." He started climbing the stairs.

"Wait, where are we going?"

"I was watching a movie upstairs when you got here."

"Oh." I walked with him upstairs, to a room at the end of the hall. He walked inside. I hesitated at the door. "Your bedroom?"

He nodded. I stood just inside the door and looked around. His room was twice as big as mine was. The walls were painted a silvery gray, and the curtains and bed linens were navy blue. A flat-screen television hung on the wall across from his bed. One wall held a dresser and a desk with an open laptop on it. The other had built-in bookcases crammed full of books.

Wandering over to the bookshelves, I set the plate of hummus down on the bedside table. I fingered some the books, reading the titles. Some recent titles I recognized, while others were older, classics.

"I have an e-reader now, but I can't part with these," he said behind me, his breath skimming my neck.

"I didn't know you liked to read so much."

"Yeah. Like you," he said.

I turned and looked at him. He was standing so close I could feel his body heat, and I became acutely aware of his lack of shirt. I tried to keep my eyes on his face, but they had little minds of their own and wandered down his chest, taking in his broad shoulders, defined—very well defined—chest, tight, rolled abs, and oblique muscles as they disappeared into his low-riding sweatpants.

Ugh, I think I'm going to hyperventilate. At least if I faint, I can blame it on my head. But holy shiznet is he ripped.

I shook my head and tried to remember what we were talking about... books, yeah, books. "Um... how do you know I like to read?"

"I pay attention." He shrugged one of his totally orgasmic shoulders. "You're always taking books from the library."

I, however, was not paying attention. Not at all. Not to what he was saying, anyway. I was paying a great deal of attention to how he looked, and he looked amazing. Like an underwear model, Greek god, and any other extraordinarily good-looking guy I could think of—but since my thinking was severely limited by the sex rolling off his body, I couldn't come up with any more men to compare him to so I settled for, *oh holy hell is he hot.*

Reaching up, I skimmed my fingertips over the tattoo circling his left bicep. It was an intricate tribal design. I traced it with my finger. He inhaled through his teeth, and goose bumps dotted his skin. I pulled my hand back.

"Sorry," I whispered. "I've just wondered what it looked like since I saw it in class one day."

"It's okay." His voice came out huskier than normal. Reaching out, he took my hand. "Let's watch the movie."

I perched on the edge of the bed. Brody threw pillows against the headboard. "Come here. You'll be more comfortable sitting against the headboard."

I scooted next to him. "What are we watching?"

That was the last thing I remembered.

Brody woke me at four in the morning. "Willow, wake up, darlin'"

"Is the movie over?"

He chuckled. "Yeah. You fell asleep."

"Sorry." I rubbed my eyes, wincing. Dropping my hands, I looked at him. "Did you call me darlin'?"

"Just tryin' it out," he said with a grin.

I scrunched my nose and shook my head. "Nah."

"I didn't think so, either." He smoothed the hair from my face. "I need to take you to Jenna's before her parents miss you."

"Oh. Okay." I climbed out of bed and followed him downstairs, grabbing my shoes. "Hey, do you think we could swing by the field and grab my bike? I rode it over here last night."

"Sure. What's it doing in the field?" Brody asked as he pulled on his Nikes.

"I left it there when I jumped the fence." I looked up when he didn't say anything. He was staring at me. "What?" I asked.

He smirked. "Very badass."

"I just jumped a fence, jeez. You're easily impressed."

"Everything you do impresses me." He skimmed his hand over my hair.

"Well, Ace, the feeling happens to be mutual. Except for one thing."

"What's that?" Brody tilted his head, his brows furrowed.

"I'm not impressed that you woke me up so early. That sucks."

"You can go back to bed when you get to Jenna's."

"Are you kidding? Do you even know Jenna? She'll want to know everything. Everything. Every single second will need to be accounted for. I'll never get back to sleep." I sighed.

"Poor baby," he said, grinning.

"I see you're completely torn up over it."

Jenna was waiting for me at her front door when Brody dropped me off at her house an hour later. She put her fingers to her lips for me to stay quiet—like I was gonna sing and dance—as we made our way to her bedroom. As soon as she closed her door, she swung around and pointed her finger at me.

"Spill. Now."

So much for sleep.

"Ok, but can we have some caffeine first?" I asked.

She ran downstairs, came back with two Red Bulls, and shoved them at me. "Now talk. I want to know everything. Starting with what happened to your face."

THIRTEEN
Free-Falling

"Yeah, you make me happy. In case you didn't know."
~Willow

RODY AND I MET EACH NIGHT AT MIDNIGHT. USUALLY, WE DROVE TO his aunt's property and gazed at the stars while we talked. Some nights, we didn't talk at all. We just lay side by side, holding hands. It wasn't an uncomfortable silence. It fit. Nothing with Brody was uncomfortable, except when he touched me—and that was a good uncomfortable. One my body craved. I needed his touch almost as much as I needed to breathe.

Each night I was with him, I felt myself doing something I shouldn't…

I was falling.

Falling fast and hard for Brody Victor. It felt like a dream. One when I'd jolt awake with the sensation I'd been falling. I wondered if Brody would be there to catch me or if I'd hit bottom. Because the bottom scared me. I knew who waited for me there.

Brody and I talked about everything when we met each night. There was no topic off limits. There was nothing I didn't want to tell him, even though there was one thing I wouldn't. Something no one knew the truth about, except Ralph and Jaden. The two people who had no trouble using it as a way to torment and force my mom and I to bend to their will.

"Favorite color?"

"White," I answered.

"White isn't a color," Brody said. "Why white?"

"Yes, it is a color, and because it's clean, pure. What's yours?"

"Red. Favorite food?"

"Your aunt's milkshakes."

Brody laughed. "Same here. They rock."

"Yes, they do," I agreed. "Where's your dad?"

"Around." Brody rolled to his side and picked up a lock of my hair, twisting it around his finger. "They got a divorce. That was an excuse for him to take off and disappear."

I turned my head to face him. "I'm sorry."

"It is what it is, I guess."

"Yeah, I guess so." I licked my lips. "You and your mom seem to do okay."

"Yeah, my mom's great. What about you? Do you all get along?"

"Ralph and my mom are really… well, they just are, I guess. I'm not sure if it's love or a match made in Heaven or whatever." I rolled toward him and lay my head on his out stretched arm. "But they have someone. So they aren't alone, you know?"

"I suppose. I've heard of couples getting together just for companionship. I guess it depends on the people." Brody shrugged a shoulder. He picked a pebble off our blanket and tossed it. It was swallowed up in the inky blackness surrounding us.

"Okay, here's a question. How did you get your *love 'em and leave 'em* reputation?" I smiled and lifted a brow.

"I dated a cheerleader at Stanton, and we had a bad break up. I dated another girl right after her. It was a rebound thing. It didn't last long. The cheerleader started a rumor that we slept together, and then I dumped her right after. The rebound girl jumped in, said the same thing, and there you go—instant reputation."

"Did you?" I bit my bottom lip, waiting for his answer.

"Did I what? Sleep with her?" He let out a long breath and looked at the stars before his gaze found mine again. "Yes. But it wasn't like she made it out to be. I didn't dump her as soon as we slept together. We dated for nearly a year."

"And the rebound girl?"

"Do you really want to know all the girls I've slept with?" I shrugged a shoulder and picked at the blanket. "I've slept with a few, not that many. I can count them on one hand. And, no, I didn't sleep with the rebound girl."

What is wrong with me? I'm jealous. I shouldn't be surprised. If I didn't want to know, I should've kept my mouth shut. But I'm crazy jealous of those bitches.

"So, what about you, Willow? Have you slept with Jaden? You've been together since, what, sophomore year?" Brody tugged a piece of my hair.

I licked my lips and brushed a piece of grass off Brody's shoulder. "No, I haven't slept with him."

"You're kidding. We're talking about Jaden, right? He's waited all this time?" Brody slipped the lock of unruly hair behind my ear. His fingers trailed down my jaw, leaving goose bumps in their wake. He cupped my jaw in his hand and guided my face to his, massaging the back of my head with the tips of his fingers.

"No, I didn't say he hasn't slept with anyone. I said *I* haven't slept with him, or anyone else," I said quietly.

"Oh. I just figured… I mean, Jaden. I assumed…"

"Yeah, I know. Bimbo." I gave him a small smile. He didn't smile back.

"Sorry," he murmured. His thumb grazed over my bottom lip.

"Hey, I was just teasing." I gave him a playful shove on the shoulder. "You've apologized for that. I just like teasing you."

"If there was something I wish I could take back, it'd be that comment."

I shrugged. "It's not a big deal, Brody. I'm over it. I think it's funny now."

"Can I ask you something?" His eyebrows pulled down over his eyes.

"I thought that's what we were doing. You just asked if I'd slept with Jaden. And I just admitted I'm still holding my V-card. I think you can ask me about anything," I said with a wink.

"Why haven't you?"

"What? Slept with him?" Brody nodded. I placed my hand on his arm and moved it up until it covered his hand. Turning his hand over, he threaded our fingers together and kissed the inside of my wrist.

I let out a small breath. "It doesn't feel right with Jaden. It never has. I guess I've always known he wasn't the one, even when we first started dating and things were different." I paused and gazed at the stars. "I won't do it just to do it. I'm waiting until it means something."

We were at the park in my subdivision. I was on the swing, and Brody was pushing me.

"You don't need to push me, you know. I've known how to swing since I was six."

"I know."

"Then come up here and sit next to me so we can talk," I called over my shoulder.

"And give up the chance to put my hands all over your ass? No way."

I laughed and jumped off the swing. "You're such a perv."

"Yeah, and you love it," he said with a grin.

Oh, that grin is going to be the death of me.

He walked to me, took my hand, and led me to the merry-go-round. We lay on our backs, and Brody used his feet to slowly turn it as we looked at the sky.

"Can't see the stars here like at your aunt's place."

"No," he agreed.

"Everyone thinks you're gay, you know," I blurted.

He rose up on his elbows and looked at me, clearly amused. "Really? I've dated a few girls since I've been at Cassidy. Why would they think that?"

I stretched my arms over my head and grabbed the center pole. "You've only went out with three girls, and you just went out once with each. You didn't even kiss them. At least, that's the gossip."

"I didn't happen to be in the kissing mood."

"Do you have a… I mean, is there someone special at your old school?"

"No."

"So there's no one?" I turned to face him. "That's hard to believe."

He lay back down and rubbed his hand over the top of his head. "I didn't say there wasn't anyone. She just hasn't noticed yet."

I snorted a laugh. "I don't know if you are aware of this, but every girl notices you, Brody. Some guys, too."

"Not this girl. At least, not the way I want her to."

"Then she must be blind and incredibly stupid not to be interested in you."

He shrugged. "She's not stupid, just… preoccupied."

"Maybe you should try dating someone else."

"Have anyone in mind?" he murmured, reaching over and playing with a lock of my hair. I shivered when the tips of his fingers skimmed over my skin.

Yeah, me, please. Oh, how I wish it could be me.

"I don't know. Jenna would be first in line, I think." Jealousy stabbed me just uttering the words. I loved her like a sister, but I didn't want him to go out with Jenna. I didn't want him to go out with anyone, even though I knew it was an unfair expectation.

"Nah, I'm going to wait on this girl for a while. She's worth the time, and I'm not ready to give up yet."

I felt a pang of something. A stab of something in my gut. The green-eyed monster named *Jealousy* bombarded me. It stabbed organs and beat others hard enough that I wanted to curl into a ball right there on the merry-go-round. Whoever the girl was, I was jealous of her. I didn't even know her, and I already hated her. She had Brody's affection. Lucky bitch.

It was Thursday. We'd been meeting every night at midnight for three weeks. We were sitting in the Jeep on Brody's aunt's property, talking. It was raining and we watched the raindrops hit the windshield. Every so often, lightning lit the sky, giving me glimpses of him in the darkness.

"What are you going to do after graduation?" Brody asked me.

"Just a minute. There's something I need to do." I climbed over the center console and into the backseat.

"What are you doing?" he asked with a chuckle.

"Come back here," I said.

He climbed into the back and fell onto the seat. I immediately scooted close to him until the sides of our bodies touched. He sat for a second, looking at me, his arm raised over me like he didn't know what to do with it. I waited, holding my breath. He lowered his arm around me, pulling me closer to him, and I let out the breath I was holding. My body vibrated every time Brody touched me. I'd never felt that before.

"After graduation, I'm getting as far away from Middleton as I can. I've always wanted to go somewhere warm. I hate the winters in Michigan. I applied to UCLA."

"Did you get in?"

"Yeah."

He pulled back and looked at me. "That's awesome, Willow! Congratulations." He paused, and the skin between his eyebrows creased. "You don't seem excited."

"I'm not sure how I'll pay for it," I admitted.

"Your parents have money. I'm sure you'll be fine."

I shook my head. "Ralph won't give me anything for college. I'm not his daughter."

"Oh. Didn't your dad leave you anything before he died?"

"Um, he left me something. I have no idea what. My mom and Ralph control the estate, and they won't tell me. So I'm not counting on that." I shrugged. "But there's always financial aid and scholarships. I might be able to swing it, especially if I find a job."

"Why California?"

"It's about as far from Michigan as I can get. Jaden is going to State on a football scholarship. He thinks that's where I'm going since I've already been accepted. I haven't told him that there's no way I'll be going there."

Brody's hand skimmed up and down my arm. "Ah. I guess he isn't going to take the news well."

"My plan has always been just to get to graduation and then get the hell out. I figured if I could just last with Jaden until then, I could get away from him when I left for college. It wasn't that big a deal to date him until graduation. There wasn't anyone else I was interested in, so that wasn't an issue. But now…"

"But now what?" Brody murmured.

"Now, it's an issue," I answered, my voice soft.

"Why?" Brody shifted in the seat and pulled me around to face him. "I need to hear you say it." He cupped my face, his thumb rubbing across my cheek.

"Because now, there's someone else." I watched his eyes darkened.

He leaned his face to mine. His lips were so close. They were barely touching. I could feel them moving when he spoke. "Then leave him. I want you, Willow."

"I don't… He's gonna—"

He pulled back and dropped his hands. "Look…" He blew out a breath and rubbed his hand over face. "This… thing with you, it's all new to me. I'm crazy about you. You're in me. My day doesn't start until I see you, and I want the last thing I hear at night to be the sound of your voice. I've never had anyone affect me like you. A million girls can come and go, but you'll always be the one I look for, dream about, love. Only you. You're my very heart.

"If you were dating some great guy, I'd be okay with being just your friend. I might not like it, I'd be jealous as hell, but as long as you were happy, I'd be okay with it. Problem is, you're not dating a great guy. He's a loser. A possessive, domineering, condescending jerk who takes you for granted—"

"Tell me how you really feel," I muttered, scooting back on the seat.

"And I'm not okay with it, Willow. I'm not okay with just standing by and being your friend while you date an idiot like him. I don't want to sneak around and see you just at midnight for a couple of hours. I'm greedy. I want all of you. I don't share well."

"What are you saying?" My heart beat doubled and my hands shook.

Is he going to make me choose between him and Jaden? Don't make me choose. Please, please, don't.

"Dump him and be with me. I'm not perfect, but I'm a lot closer than Jaden is, at least for you. You have to know that."

"Or?" I whispered.

"There is no *or*. I won't stand around and watch you self-destruct because of him."

"You want me to choose between you?" I said slowly, looking in his eyes.

"I don't want you to do anything tonight other than think. But tomorrow, yes, I want you to make a choice." His eyes held me captive and his words fell like bricks between us.

I just stared at him. I'm not sure how long. Then I turned and opened the door and got out of the Jeep, leaning back against the door. I didn't even notice the rain hitting me. I just stood there, his words ringing in my ears.

He's making me choose. My choice is him. Brody will always be my choice. But Jaden will tell. He'll make our lives a living Hell. He'll tell everyone what he knows. I can't risk that...can I? Would Brody still want me if he knew?

"Willow," Brody stood in front of me. "Get in the car. You're freezing."

I climbed into the Jeep when he opened the door. We drove to my house, neither of us speaking. It was the first time I felt uncomfortable with Brody. The first time I didn't want to be with him. I just wanted to get home and climb into bed.

"I'll see you in the morning," he said when he pulled up to my house.

I nodded and slipped out of the Jeep.

Fourteen
Choice

"I can't be with someone like him, but be totally in love with you."
~Willow

RIDAY. *It was a home game. I used to sit with Jenna, Tim, and* a handful of other friends. But that was before Jaden's new *rules.* Under the new rules designed to keep me *'in line,'* he expected me to sit behind the players' bench. But I'd decided that it would end that night.

The night before Brody had asked me to make a choice. I'd been up most of the night thinking. When I got up that morning, I intended to ask Brody for more time, but he deserved an answer. So instead of asking, I texted him and asked him to meet me at the football game that night. I'd tell him my choice then.

That morning, I got up early and took extra time with my hair and makeup. I wore my black jeans and a red, scoop-neck sweater. I picked red for a reason, and I hoped Brody would catch the hint. Pulling on my black boots, I grabbed my keys. After a quick trip to Starbucks—I was going to need as much caffeine as I could get—I drove to school.

"Two days wearing normal clothing. What's the occasion?" Jenna asked when she saw me. I handed her a caramel macchiato. "Thanks. I so need this."

"I can't tell you now, but something big is going down today," I whispered.

She grabbed my arm. "What's going on?"

I looked down the hall, saw Jaden walking toward us, and barely

186

shook my head. She looked over her shoulder at Jaden, let her hand drop from my arm, and turned to get her books out of her locker.

"I'll see you in history."

"See ya," I called after her.

"Are you done with that?" Jaden asked, nodding toward my macchiato.

"Nope."

"Then you're throwing it out when we get to your class."

I shrugged and slammed my locker shut, walking away from him. He caught up with me and grabbed my hand. We walked to my class. I stopped outside the door and leaned against the wall, drinking my Starbucks.

"Toss it and go sit down," Jaden said.

"No."

"What you mean 'no'?"

"Did I stutter? I said 'no.' I'm finishing my drink. If you don't like it, go to your own class," I said, my voice rising with each word.

"I told you, I'm not standing out here while you drink your freakin' Starbucks."

"Then don't. You have two feet. Use them to walk away and piss someone else off."

He grabbed my arm and started to pull me into the classroom. I flipped the lid off my drink with my thumb, aiming it at him. When he jerked me forward, the macchiato sloshed down the front of his shirt.

"Shit!" He jumped back and held his arms out to the sides, gaping at the coffee stain.

"Oops. I guess you shouldn't jerk my arm while I'm holding a Starbucks in my hand."

"That's hot, Willow."

"What do you want me to do about it? You were the one pulling on me!" I yelled.

"Look at my shirt!" he shouted.

"Yeah. Hmm. That's probably gonna stain."

"We'll take this up later." He stalked off.

"Doubtful," I called after him and walked into class, dumping what was left of my drink in the trash.

I glanced at Brody. One side of his mouth tipped up in his signature, amused grin. "Nice sweater. I like the color," he commented.

"I thought you would." I sat down and looked to the front of the class.

The rest of the day went by smoothly, even though Jaden gave me the cold shoulder because of his ruined shirt. I chatted and followed him from class to class as if nothing was wrong.

That afternoon, after the last bell, Jaden followed me to my locker. "Do you need a ride to the game?"

"I don't know why you ask me that every week. I have my own car," I snapped.

"Watch the damn attitude. Just making sure." He stared at me.

"I'm going to give Jenna a ride tonight. Just wanted you to know before the game so you wouldn't think anything was going on. Her car's been acting weird. Her dad is dropping it off at the mechanic's this afternoon, so she won't have it for the game tonight." I lied.

"No. She can find a ride with someone else."

"I've already told her I'd give her a ride. I'm not going to tell her no after I've already said yes. It's one week, Jaden. Surely you can trust me with Jenna long enough to drive to the school and back home again."

"Forget it. I'm picking you up for the game. She can find her own way."

"No! I'm not coming up here three hours before the freakin' game starts." I yelled. Out of the corner of my eye, I saw Brody and Jenna walk by. "I'm driving myself, and Jenna is riding with me."

"Like hell you are," he said through clenched teeth.

I leaned in close to him. He was so much taller than I was that I had to almost look straight up to see his face. I pointed my finger, poking him once in the chest. "Watch me."

Jaden grabbed my finger, twisting it around. I bit my lip to keep from crying out. Brody took a step forward. I shook my head. Jenna grabbed his arm and held him back.

"I'm pretty sure if you break my finger on school property, you won't be playing ball tonight." I winced when he pushed my finger back a litter further.

"You better be at the game tonight, and Jenna better be the only one in your car." He let go of my finger and shouldered past me, knocking me into the lockers.

"You're not walking me to my car today, honey?" I called after him. He gave me the finger over his shoulder. "I'll take that as a no."

"Don't provoke him like that, Willow." Jenna came over, grabbed my hand, and looked at my finger. "You know what he can do." She looked in my eyes. "We all do."

I shrugged a shoulder. "I'll be fine." Trying to give her a confident smile, I failed. I could see it in her eyes.

I tried to take my mind off the game that night. I cooked dinner listening to my iPod, singing along with the songs. I did homework. I cleaned my room. But nothing worked. I spent most of the afternoon pacing my bedroom, wringing my fingers. I twisted them so hard my knuckles cracked.

Finally, the first text came through.

JENNA: ARE YOU REALLY PICKING ME UP?

ME: NO. I'LL SEE YOU THERE.

JENNA: OK. YOU'RE ACTING WEIRD.

ME: WHAT'S NEW?

JENNA: TRUE.

I paced some more, redid my hair and make-up and checked my outfit in the mirror twenty times. I didn't consider myself particularly beautiful. I wasn't completely unfortunate looking, but stunning? No. But that night, I was getting as close as I could.

Time for the next text. And it was the biggie. I took a breath and picked up my phone. My hands shook so badly I had to start over twice.

ME: CAN YOU GIVE ME A RIDE?

There wasn't an answer right away. It took three minutes. I know—I watched the clock. My heart thudded in my chest, and my breathing was shallow as I waited.

What if the answer is no? It'll kill me.

BRODY: YES.
ME: BE HERE IN TEN?
BRODY: I'LL BE THERE.

I let out a breath I didn't even realize I'd been holding. My whole insides shook. I was excited and terrified at the same time.

Brody pulled up exactly ten minutes later. I ran out the door before he could come to the house. My mom would never let me leave with him. She didn't know I planned to break up with Jaden, and she wasn't going to be happy about it.

Brody got out of the Jeep and held the passenger door open for me. "You're beautiful," he murmured as I slipped by him.

I smiled, feeling my cheeks heat with a blush.

"And you're adorable when you blush." He grinned. He ran his finger down the side of my face, sending a wave of tingles over my skin. I turned my head, kissing his hand.

Brody cleared his throat, rubbed his thumb over my cheek one last time, and shut the door. I watched him walk around the Jeep, swinging his keys around his finger, a finger on the other hand hooked around a belt loop on his jeans, which were riding just low enough on his hips to send any girl into heart palpitations. Smexy. Smart and sexy. That was Brody Victor. Sex personified. And he was mine. I couldn't help the grin that spread across my face.

He's mine. Holy freakin' shiznit.

"What's that grin for?" he asked when he got in the Jeep.

"Just happy."

"Yeah? I guess I don't need to ask this, but I want to hear you say it. You've made a choice?"

"You're my choice, Brody. Always have been."

He nodded once, and a small grin touched his lips. "That's what I hoped to hear. So, I guess this is our big coming out of the closet, so to speak."

"Yup," I said, rubbing my hands down my thighs.

He watched the movement. "Any idea what you're going to do?"

"Not a clue." I gave a nervous laugh.

"Well, it's always good to have a plan," Brody teased and put the Jeep in gear.

It was official. Brody knew my choice was him. Now, it was time to tell Jaden.

Holy hell. What have I done?

Breathe. Just breathe. I can do this. I just have to breathe.

Fifteen

Done

"When he tells me, 'I'll never find anyone like him,' I'll smile and say,
"Yeah, that's kind of the point."
~Willow

WE ARRIVED AT THE FOOTBALL GAME A HALF HOUR BEFORE IT WAS set to begin. Jenna and Tim were already there. Their expressions were priceless when they saw Brody and me walk to the bleachers and sit next to them, holding hands.

"Oh shit on a shoe," Jenna whispered. "Does he know?"

I shook my head. "Have you seen Karen yet?"

"I saw her wandering around," Tim said. "Hey, can I be there when you tell Jaden?" He bounced in his seat like a little kid.

"Yeah, why not? Everyone here will see it anyway." I pulled my bottom lip between my teeth.

"Damn, I wish I had a camera." Tim laughed and fist bumped Brody.

"Yeah, the more witnesses the better," Jenna muttered, folding her arms in front of herself and rubbing her hands up and down her arms.

Brody squeezed my hand, pulling me closer to him. "I'm going to get us something to drink. Slushie or caffeine?"

"You have to ask? Do you not know me at all?" I rolled my eyes, but smiled.

"Caffeine it is, then." He started to walk away, and our fingers slipped slowly apart.

"Wait!"

Brody turned toward me. I hurried to catch up to him. "I want

192

to go with you." I threaded my fingers with his. "I think I'll need a fix, too," I said, looking at the cotton candy.

"Cotton candy? Or should we go straight to the hard stuff and get the chocolate bars now?"

"Don't mock the calming effects of the combination of pure sugar and caffeine. Hmm…" I tapped my finger against my bottom lip, looking from the chocolate to the spun sugar and back again. "I think I'll get two cotton candy and two chocolate bars, you know, just in case."

Brody nodded. "Always be prepared."

"Exactly." I reached to pay, and Brody shook his head.

"I've got it."

"Thanks," I said, smiling at him. I couldn't stop smiling. My cheeks were starting to hurt, but it felt so good. I felt as if a weight had been lifted from my shoulders. Brody made me happy—giddy, even. I never felt that with Jaden, even when we first started dating. I never realized it was missing until I met Brody, and he showed me how it should feel.

Are my feet even touching the ground when I walk? Cuz I feel like one of those little cupids with the wings on their feet… yeah, I'm definitely a lost cause. He's so gonna break my heart. I'll think about that later, when he's not buying me chocolate. Tonight, not even Jaden can kill my buzz.

When we got our order and turned to walk back to the bleachers, I stopped dead. There, not two feet from me, stood Karen. I knew it would happen. It had to happen. But I was hoping she'd just see us and report back to Jaden. I didn't want to come face-to-face with her.

"Hi, Karen," I said, shoving a huge piece of medication—cotton candy—into my mouth.

She didn't answer. Her eyes traveled down and locked on my hand intertwined with Brody's.

We stood looking at each other for a few seconds. "Well, it's been nice chatting with you. I gotta get back to my seat. It's gonna be a great game tonight. We're playing Stanton. That's your old school, isn't, babe?" I looked up at Brody and smiled.

"Yes, it is. I know who I'll be rooting for."

"See you later," I called over my shoulder as Brody and I walked away. "Well, that went much better than I'd expected." I shoved more cotton candy in my mouth. At the rate I was stuffing it in, I'd deplete my stash before the game started, not to mention have major tooth decay by the time the night was over.

"Babe? Since when do you use pet names other than Ace?"

"Well, Ace didn't sound very loving so I improvised. But don't worry. You'll always be Ace to me." I bumped my hip into his.

"Good, I kinda like it. How long do you think it'll take for her to tell Jaden that she saw us?" Brody looked over his shoulder. "She's already gone."

"Oh, I'd bet money that she's already texted him," I said. More cotton candy went in, and I licked the sticky sugar from my fingers.

Brody put his lips to my ear. "You're killing me. I don't know if I can sit next to you and watch you lick your fingers like that. I might have to scoop you up, take you back to the Jeep, and do all kinds of naughty things."

"Promise?" I peered at him through my lashes.

"Ugh, you're such a tease."

"But I wasn't teasing."

Brody gazed at me, his eyes darkening.

"Hey guys, come on," Jenna called. "Did you see Karen? She walked by here, and she didn't look too happy."

"Yeah, we saw her," I answered, my gazed still locked on Brody's.

"Then Jaden knows. He's gonna have a fit, and it's gonna be epic. We'll be lucky if he doesn't move the earth off its axis." Jenna rubbed her hands together and shivered. I think she was more worried about Jaden's reaction than I was.

When the football players ran through the stupid banner that the cheerleaders held for them, Jaden's gaze immediately found me on the bleachers and if looks could kill, I would've been dead twice over. He wasn't just mad. He was livid. I expected no less. This was going to be fun. Or not.

I still had no idea how things would go down. No plan on how to tell him. I was secretly hoping that seeing me with Brody would be enough and Jaden would just leave it alone, but I knew that wouldn't happen. Jaden's moods were all over the place. I had no idea what type of reaction we'd get. And it scared me. I tried to stay calm in front of Brody. If he knew how scared I was, he'd insist on leaving, and that would only prolong the inevitable. We had to confront Jaden at some point. And like Jenna said, the more witnesses, the better.

We watched the game. Well, I pretended to watch. My mind was reeling with thoughts of what would come after the game ended. My knee bounced up and down with nerves. The closer the game came to an end, the faster my knee bounced. Finally, Brody laid his hand on it and squeezed.

"It's going to be fine," he whispered in my ear.

"Sure." I nodded.

I wish I could believe that. I know he's going to make a scene. And he's going to tell. Years of protecting what I know, putting up with Ralph, dealing with Jaden, all to keep her secret—our secret—hidden. I'm throwing it all away. He'll tell, and everyone will really know what happened that night. But Brody's worth it. I hope he thinks the same of me when he knows the truth.

"Do you want to leave now? He knows. That was the main point of tonight, right? You got the message out. Everyone here is staring at us. We're no doubt the topic of most conversations. People are watching us more than the game," Brody said with a chuckle. "The bad boy steals the good girl from the star football player. Yeah, we're big news. We don't need to hang around."

"I have to face him sooner or later." I hated how my voice shook. I didn't want to sound weak, but Jaden was one area in my life that I'd never been able to control. I'd always let him have control. It kept him happy, and he kept his mouth shut. I needed to stand up to him.

As soon as the game was over, one of Jaden's closest friends and teammates made his way to the bleachers. "You'd better leave now, Willow."

I looked over his shoulder and saw Jaden plowing his way toward Brody and me. His face was red with rage. A thick vein pulsed in the side of his neck. People got out of his way like he was Moses parting the Red Sea.

Too late.

"Thanks for the heads up."

"Willow," Jaden said, looking at Brody's hand holding mine. "What do you think you're doing?"

"We're done, Jaden. Sorry you had to find out like this, but it's over."

"No, it's over when *I* say it's over," Jaden said through clenched teeth. He looked at Brody. "If you want to keep that hand, I suggest you get it off my girl."

"I don't believe you can stake claim to her any longer. My hand's gonna stay right where it is." Brody narrowed his eyes at Jaden.

Jaden took a step toward Brody. Brody didn't move.

"How long, Willow? How long have you been sleeping with this piece of shit?" Jaden spat.

"None of your business."

"You've been seeing him while we've been together?"

I hesitated for a second. I knew if I answered truthfully, Jaden would destroy my reputation, but if I didn't tell the truth, I'd risk hurting Brody. "Yes. We've been seeing each other."

"You slut!" His hand darted out so fast that I didn't have time to react. The pain sizzled across the side of my face, ricocheting through my head. I could feel where his class ring dug into my skin, warm liquid dribbling down my cheek. The impact ripped me away from Brody's grasp and sent me tumbling across the bleachers, scraping the side of my face where it hit the grooved metal.

Jenna and Tim ran to me, helping me up. I looked up in time to see Brody charge Jaden. He slammed into him, sending them both flying across the bleachers.

"What's the matter with you, Victor? You're the one screwing her. If she's gonna act like a whore, she's gonna get treated like one," Jaden shouted, standing up and wiping the dust off his uniform.

"I told you if you ever laid a hand on her, I'd end you," Brody whispered through clenched teeth, shouldering Jaden.

Jaden barreled toward Brody. A group of his football buddies held him back. "He's not worth it, man," one told him.

"She's definitely not worth it," another said, looking at me like I wore a scarlet letter across my chest. Maybe I did. Maybe I deserved one.

Brody took a step toward Jaden. "Brody! Brody, stop!" I yelled, trying to get his attention.

He looked at me, and his face softened. "Let's get you out of here and clean those cuts." Reaching out, he wiped the blood off my face with the pad of his thumb. He looked over his shoulder at Jaden. "If I ever see you touch her again, I will make sure it's the last thing you touch. You won't always have your jughead friends to protect you."

Well, that actually went better than I thought it would. I'm still alive.

SIXTEEN

Freefalling

"Somewhere between our laughs, stupid little fights, and lame jokes...I fell in love with him."
~Willow

RODY TOOK ME TO HIS HOUSE TO CLEAN MY CUTS. *WHEN WE DROVE* up, a strange car was parked in the garage. He pulled next to it, killing the engine.

"Whose car is that?" I looked out of the window at the black sedan parked next to us in the immaculate garage.

"My mom's." Brody climbed out of the Jeep and came around to open my door.

I didn't get out of the SUV. "I don't think we should be here."

"Why not?" Brody's gaze didn't waver from mine. His brows furrowed over his eyes.

"I don't really want to meet your mom when I'm sporting a cut-up face."

"My mom's not like that. She's cool. She'll baby you the whole night." He paused and lowered his gaze. "And, um, I've already told her about you." His eyes traveled slowly up to meet mine. "Don't be mad. I just wanted her to know in advance what your situation was if you ever needed a place to go."

Tears pushed at the back of my eyes. I sniffed and cleared my throat. "And... um, and she was okay with everything?"

"She wasn't okay that someone was hurting you, but she was very okay with you having a safe place to come if you needed one. Don't worry, Willow. She's going to love you."

Brody lifted my hand and kissed the inside of my wrist, letting his mouth linger. Giant butterflies invaded my stomach. My arm tingled under his lips. They were soft and moist. I wanted them on my mine. My lips parted, and I sighed. Brody looked into my eyes and grinned against my skin.

He placed my hand in my lap and wrapped his hand behind my neck, leaning into me. My breath came in little gasps, and my heart did a free fall to my toes. I ran my tongue over my lips, leaning toward him. He kissed the space behind my earlobe. I sucked in a breath and threaded my hands through his hair, gripping his head to me.

"Mm, I love the way you smell," he whispered in my ear. "Like raspberries."

I closed my eyes and let his voice wash over me, concentrating on his mouth on my skin. I think I answered him. I was positive I didn't use an actual word because at that moment, I couldn't put two coherent words together. My lips ached for his. I tightened my hold in his hair and pulled his face to mine. His lips skimmed mine when he spoke, just a whisper of a caress, barely a touch at all.

"We need to go inside," he murmured, reaching up and pulling my hands from his hair.

He pulled me gently from the Jeep and led me to the door. His mother had her back to us when we went inside. She sat on the large couch, watching television. She turned when she heard the door open.

"Brody, you're home early—" She stopped abruptly when she saw me standing behind him. "Introduce me to your friend."

She stood and walked toward us. Tall like her son, she shared his thick hair and color. Hers was cut in a short bob that was businesslike and feminine all at once. Slim, but curvy, and dressed in designer jeans and T-shirt, she looked almost like Brody's older sister, or maybe an aunt, than his mother.

"Mom, this is Willow."

"Hi, Willow," she said with a smile.

"It's nice meet you, Ms. Victor," I said, trying to cover the gash on my check with my hair and standing behind Brody's shoulder.

"Oh, call me Anne. Come on. Let's get that cleaned up. Do I get to ask what happened? I'll be honest, as long as I feel you aren't in immediate danger, I won't call the police or your parents."

"My ex-boyfriend didn't take the news that I was breaking up with him very well," I said quietly, not meeting her eyes.

"Ah. Well, not to worry. We'll get this taken care of. Brody, don't just stand there, get Willow something to drink."

"Sorry. Do you want a Coke?"

I nodded. "Thank you."

Ms. Victor was incredibly nice. Brody was right; she did baby me the entire time I was there. She didn't ask too many questions. Occasionally, she'd slip a question or two in about Brody's and my relationship. I let Brody handle those. I wasn't sure how to answer them yet. At least not to his mother. Brody didn't seem the least bit bothered by them.

"We're dating. That's why Willow broke it off with her ex."

"I see. How long have you been dating?"

"Since tonight. We started out as friends, Mom. Willow broke up with her boyfriend when we decided we were crossing the friendship line. We officially started dating tonight. Right, Willow?" He took a drink of his Coke.

"Right, Ace. I mean, Brody." I could feel my cheeks warm at my unintentional use of his nickname.

He smiled and threaded my fingers with his.

"Ace, huh? Do I want to know?"

I laughed. "Probably not. Let's just say we weren't a match made in heaven when we first met."

"Brody gets that a lot," his mother said and waved her hand in the air, dismissing the comment. "He comes off as arrogant."

"That's for sure. And judgmental," I muttered.

"Hey, I'm in the room, you know?"

"Yes, dear, we know. Well," Anne said with a sigh, gathering her Coke can and the shoes she'd flipped off at some point. "I'm tired. I'm going upstairs to read for a while. It was very nice to meet you, Willow. I hope I'll be seeing more of you."

"It was nice meeting you too, Ms. Victor."

She squeezed my shoulder as she walked by. "Anne, remember?"

I smiled and nodded. Anne climbed the stairs, leaving Brody and me sitting on the couch, alone, in the great room. I suddenly became very nervous.

"So..." Brody let the word trail off and looked at me.

"Yeah."

"You've met my family. My mom and my aunt. When do I meet yours?"

My heart sank. Everything around me slowed. I could hear my heart plodding along in my chest, squeezing blood out like a sponge. The ticking clock slowed. A second felt like a minute. Then, just as fast as time slowed, everything sped up and righted its self.

"My mom and stepdad are Jaden fans. It's going take them a while to adjust to the break up and accept the fact that there's a new guy in my life. I think we're going to have to take it slow if we want them to be okay with us."

Brody stared at me for what seemed like forever. I fought the urge to squirm under his gaze. "Is that the only reason?" he finally asked.

"What do you mean?" I paused. Then it clicked. "Yes! Do you think I'm embarrassed for you to meet my parents? That's not even close. I'm not embarrassed by you. I'll stand on the busiest corner of town and scream that I'm Brody Victor's girlfriend if you want me to. I'm embarrassed by them. I know them and how they can be, especially Ralph."

He didn't say anything, just stared into my eyes, his bright blue ones boring into mine. Finally, a slow grin spread across his face. "You don't need to scream. You can just wear a sign."

I laughed. "Yeah, okay, I'll get right on that." I sighed and stood. "I need to go. I don't want to be late for curfew."

"Okay. How are you going explain your face to your mom?"

My hands stilled for just a moment as I gathered my things. I took a breath to steady myself and looked up at Brody. "It won't matter. She's used to it." I could see his jaw clench. His hands opened and closed in fists. I took one of his hands in mine. "Hey, it's okay." I smiled at him.

He nodded once and tried to give me a smile, but it wasn't one of his easy smiles that made my heart flutter and insides melt. It was forced. I reached up and brushed my hand over his cheek, wanting to wipe away the sadness and anger I saw in his expression. He turned his head and kissed my palm, making my knees feel like jelly and my breath hitch in my throat. Just a simple kiss caused my body to rage with emotions, and I didn't want it to stop.

I could feel his breath quicken against my skin, and it made my heart beat faster. I took a step closer, nearly touching him. He laid his hand on my hip, gripping the waistband of my jeans in his fist. When he wrapped his other hand around my hair, I gasped at the shocks of electricity that sizzled through my body.

I looked into his eyes and watched them darken, his gaze locked on mine. It felt as if the world had stopped spinning. Everything was still, waiting for what came next. It was all I could do not to grab his shirtfront and yank him to me. My lips tingled with the need to feel his lips on them. My very core needed his closeness. It wasn't just a kiss. It was so much more. Emotions were both confusing and all encompassing. I needed him, needed that connection, and I could tell by the way his eyes darkened and lips parted that he felt the same.

He lowered his head toward mine. My heart sang in my chest. But he didn't kiss me. At least, not how I longed for him to. He gently placed an open-mouthed kiss on the curve of my neck, sucking at my skin ever so slightly. I moaned and ran my hand through his silky hair, opening and closing my fingers around the dark strands. He planted soft kisses up the side of my neck until he reached the sensitive area behind my ear. Kissing it gently, he let his tongue touch my skin, pulling another moan from my lips.

"I think I'm falling for you," he whispered.

He lifted his head and looked into my eyes. I cupped his face with both my hands, rubbing my thumbs over his checks.

"I think we're free falling together."

He leaned his forehead against mine before lifting his head and kissing it. "I'd better get you home." He pulled back slowly.

Oh. Holy. Hell.

I put a hand on my chest, trying to slow my breathing. My heart still fluttered. I took two deep breaths and let them out slowly to calm myself.

Jenna's right. He's turning my world upside down, and it feels friggin' awesome.

Brody pulled up in front of my house, and ran around the Jeep to open the door for me. I still couldn't get used to that.

He stood in front me, one hand on the side of the Jeep, the other on the door, blocking me in. "Are you free tomorrow?"

I tilted my head as though I was thinking and tsked. "I'll have to check my schedule, Ace."

"Oh, you have that many appointments, do you?" He stepped closer to me. His cologne swirled around me, invading my senses.

"I'm in demand, but if the right offer came along, I think I could make an exception."

"I was thinking maybe we could go out, you know, on a real date. Maybe something boring like dinner and a movie." His eyes held a question. Would I brave being seen with him after the nasty break up with Jaden and admitting that we'd been seeing each other while I was still dating him—would I go out with Brody when my reputation just got trashed because of our relationship?

"I thought you'd never ask."

He blew out a breath and smiled. "You pick the movie. I'll pick you up around four?"

"Okay, but I'm warning you, I'm going to pick a really cheesy chick-flick."

He grinned. "I'll watch anything with you as long as you wear one of your famous T-shirts for me."

"Deal."

We looked at each a few seconds, minutes, hours, who knew how long?

Just kiss me already! If you don't kiss me soon, I'm going to spontaneously combust. Kiss me!

Finally, Brody let his arm drop from the Jeep's door so I could pass. He grabbed my hand as I walked by and brought it to his mouth, kissing the inside of my wrist and sending fingers of longing through my body.

Damn it. Stop doing that and kiss me. Why won't you kiss me? If you don't do it soon, I won't be held responsible for my actions. I'm gonna jump ya, and it's not gonna be pretty... it's gonna be pretty awesome.

"See you tomorrow." My voice came out all breathy and soft.

He smirked. I think he loved torturing me. "I'll text you later tonight. And probably tomorrow, too."

"You'd better, Ace."

I'd only been home an hour. I was locked in my bedroom, wondering if Jaden would call and break the news to my mom and Ralph. It'd be just like him to call, pretend to be upset, and ask to talk to me. When they'd ask him what was wrong—and they surely would because to them, he hung the moon—he'd tell them I'd broken up with him. And with that, world war three would begin.

I had no delusions that my mom and stepdad would ever accept my decision to break up with Jaden and date Brody. They'd never accept Brody. In my family's mind, Jaden and I were as good as married. The news that our relationship was over was going to go over about as well as a fart in church.

We just had to get to graduation. Then I'd leave Jaden, my mom, and Ralph in Middleton while I went somewhere far, far away to college. There was just one problem. Where did that leave Brody and me?

My phone chimed, and I jumped. I really didn't want to look at it. It could've been anyone texting to find out if the rumors of my break up were true. It could've been Jaden. That thought made me cringe. The only reason I looked was because it could've been Jenna or Tim. I smiled when I read the name.

BRODY: TOLD YOU I'D TEXT.

ME: HEY, ACE. MISS ME ALREADY?

BRODY: ALWAYS.

ME: I MISS YOU.

BRODY: CAN'T WAIT FOR TOMORROW.

ME: ME EITHER.
BRODY: PICK A REALLY CHEESY ONE.
ME: NO DOUBT.
BRODY: GOODNIGHT, WILLOW.
ME: NIGHT.

Jeez, I'm smiling like a fool. I'm already in so deep. Please don't break my heart.

My phone chimed. I was still holding it and pushed the message button without looking to see who it was from.

JENNA: ROCKIN' YOUR WORLD YET?
ME: SHUT UP.
JENNA: I'LL TAKE THAT AS A BIG YES.

I stood in front of my closet and looked at all my T-shirts. Never in my life had I picked out an outfit the night before, but I wanted to find just the right shirt to wear on my date—yes! A date—with Brody. I flipped through them and found a black one that said, *I can't wait to be ashamed of what I do this weekend.* Shazam! That was the one. If that didn't clue him in to the kissing thing, nothing would.

I laid the T-shirt out with a pair of Khaki skinny jeans and my brown riding boots. Dumping my crap out of my messenger bag, I put what I'd need into a small, brown leather purse that matched my boots.

There. That looks good, right? Maybe. I don't know. I'll have to call Jenna. She knows about normal clothes.

I dialed Jenna. When she picked up, I said, "Yes, you were right. There, can we talk about something else now?"

"Yes. As long as you admit I was right, I'm good." She giggled.

"I need clothes advice."

"Why?"

"We're going on a date tomorrow," I said.

"Okay, first off, no writing across your boobs."

"He wants me to wear a sarcastic T-shirt. He specifically asked me to," I said.

"Hmm. Oh, right, I get it," she said.

"What?"

"It gives him a reason to look at your boobs without looking like a perv."

I laughed. Hard. When I finally stopped long enough to talk, I told her, "But, I want him to look at my boobs."

"Slut."

"Who said I wasn't? It's gonna be all over the school by Monday anyway."

"Yeah, well, you'd be surprised how many people don't like Jaden and his crap. I wouldn't worry too much about it, Willow. When it comes down to it, you're the one people actually like between the two of you. No one could figure out why you stayed with him in the first place."

"We'll see."

"So what are you wearing?" She sighed.

"Okay, I have a black T-shirt and—"

"What's the stupid T-shirt say?" Jenna interrupted.

"I can't wait to be ashamed of what I do this weekend."

"Actually, that isn't too bad." She laughed. "It might give Brody a hint."

"That's what I'm counting on," I said.

"You're bad. What else?"

"Okay. I have Khaki skinny jeans, my brown riding boots, and my brown leather purse. How's that?"

"Sounds like I've created a diva. Finally." Jenna huffed. "So where are you going?"

"Just dinner and a movie." I still couldn't stop smiling.

"It sounds like you're a smiling fool."

"You can't hear a smile," I said.

"I can hear the smile in your voice. I hope you're finally happy."

"Thanks, Jenna."

"Ugh, too much mush. I gotta go. Call me after your date and tell me everything, and I mean *all* the gooey details."

"Okay. 'Bye."

I went to bed right after I got off the phone. The sooner I went to sleep, the sooner Saturday would get there.

I'm so totally pathetic.

SEVENTEEN
Date

"Thought for the day: Brody Victor."
~*Willow*

M Y PHONE CHIMED FIRST THING SATURDAY MORNING. I SLAMMED my hand on my alarm clock, wondering why the sound wouldn't stop. Finally, I woke up enough to realize that it wasn't my alarm. I grabbed my phone off the bedside table and looked at the message. A goofy smile spread across my face.

Ugh, my cheeks hurt from smiling.

BRODY: GOOD MORNING, GORGEOUS.

ME: HEY, SEXY.

Wow, I'm getting bold. Maybe, just maybe, he'll take my hints. Kiss me. Please, please, please. Just do it. Man up and pucker up.

BRODY: SEXY, HUH?

ME: MM-HMM.

Why am I blushing? It's not like he can see me or anything.

My phone rang, I jumped, and my phone flew across the bed. I bunched up my comforter, pulling it to me so I could reach it.

"Hello?"

"Hey, sexy."

Oh. Kill. Me. Now.

"Hi, Ace." I snuggled back into my pillows.

"So you think I'm sexy, huh?"

"You asked me that already."

"I know, but it occurred to me that I'd like to hear you tell me in your soft, sexy voice while I'm lying in bed."

Oh, wow. How can he say things like that and not expect my body to go berserk every time he's around me? I need that damn kiss.

"Yes, Brody, I think you're incredibly sexy, with a body to die for, a smell that makes me dizzy, perfectly mussed hair, bedroom blue eyes, and full lips that send me into a frenzy every time they skim across my skin."

Dead silence.

Crap. That was too much. He probably thinks I'm some kind of stalker—or worse, Sarah.

I cleared my throat. "Are you there?" I whispered.

"Yes."

"Oh." I was desperate to find a way to unsay what I'd just said. I'd made things awkward. I felt tears press behind my eyes. I wasn't even sure why I was starting to cry. I'd just opened my mouth to tell him that I had to go when he spoke.

"I'm trying to find the right words to tell you how you make me feel, but I don't think they've been discovered yet. You're sexy, yeah. Beautiful doesn't even begin to describe you. But that's not all. You make me feel, I don't know, whole."

And then, I knew why I was crying. No one had ever said anything as sweet as that to me. No one. Ever.

"Brody." My breath hitched. "I really don't know what I did to deserve you."

"You're just you. That's all you ever needed to do. Just be you."

We talked a while longer, although our conversation veered away from declarations of how wonderful and sexy we found each other to more mundane topics because, as Brody complained, "It's way too much mush for this early on a Saturday morning."

"How can you go from telling me how beautiful I am in one sentence to being such a guy in the next?" I asked with a laugh.

"Um, gee, 'cuz I am a guy?"

"Funny."

"Have you picked out what movie we're going to see?"

"Yup."

"Gonna tell me?" he asked.

"Nope," I answered, popping the *'p.'*

"Okay. Have you picked out what you're gonna wear?"

"Yup, and I'm not going to tell you about that either except that I found something suitably sarcastic just for you." I smiled, picking at my comforter.

He chuckled. "Since you won't tell me what you're going to wear tonight, what are you wearing now?" His voice turned husky.

My hand stilled, and my heart beat a little faster. "Are you seriously asking me? Because now that we're dating, that's totally a question I'll answer, and it might not be one that you'll like. Or you might like it. I don't know your preferences... yet."

He groaned. "Yet?"

"Yet. I plan to find out," I said.

"Alright, Willow, I call your bluff. What are you wearing?" he asked, a hint of teasing in his voice.

"A pair of pink boy shorts with a white tank top that doesn't quite cover my stomach. Nothing else."

"You're not serious."

"I told you I'd never lie to you. Your turn."

"I don't remember what I'm wearing. I can't get the image of you out of my head."

I laughed. He groaned.

Chores, chores, chores. Even they didn't seem so bad. At least they helped pass the time until Brody picked me up. I hadn't come up with a story to tell my mom and Ralph yet. But as luck would have it, my mom told me they'd be going out. Ralph had to attend a business dinner with a reception to follow. So that took care of them for the night. They'd be gone before Brody picked me up. They would most likely still be gone when he brought me home or they'd be sufficiently sloshed that they wouldn't pay attention. Either way worked in my favor.

I listened to my iPod as I did my chores, humming along with the music and keeping an eye on the clock. I must have looked at the stupid thing a million and one times, and it hadn't moved at all. It was the longest day in the history of recorded time.

Finally, it was time for Ralph and my mom to leave. They gave me the standard spiel about no wild parties, remembering curfew, blah, blah, and blah. It was all I could do not to shove them out the door. There was barely an hour before Brody got there. I still had to shower and do my hair and makeup.

I'd just finished up when my phone chimed.

BRODY: I'M HERE. SHOULD I COME TO THE DOOR?

ME: YES.

I ran around my bedroom like a crazy woman, throwing dirty clothes in the hamper and swiping the makeup bottles from the counter into the vanity drawer. Scanning my room one more time for stray underwear or bras, I heard the doorbell ring. One last look at myself in the mirror, and I decided I looked about as good as I was going to. I hurried into the hall and padded down the stairs to let Brody in.

I opened the door and let my eyes roam over him. "Hey, Ace. You look nice. What's the occasion?"

He grinned the crooked way that sent my blood pressure through the roof. "I'm taking this incredible girl out on a date tonight. I just stopped by to cancel our plans."

"Ha. You're so very funny." I pulled him inside.

"Are you sure it's okay that I come in? You've told them about us?"

A twinge of guilt stabbed my heart. "They aren't here. Come on. I'm almost ready. I just need to get my boots on and then we can leave."

"I'll wait here."

I stopped on the bottom stair and turned to look at him. "Why?"

"You're going to your room?"

"Yeah, so?"

"I'll wait here."

"Jeez, Brody, it's just a room. I think we can stand to be in the same bedroom together. We have before, not to mention the backseat of your car and in your bed. Come on."

He followed me upstairs. "This part isn't so bad. The view is spectacular."

"You're such a perv." I laughed.

I went to my closet to grab my boots. Brody stood in the middle of my room, looking around. "Hot pink and black stripes, huh? Doesn't it make you a little dizzy?"

"You're funny tonight. A real comedian."

"I half expected there to be posters with all sorts of sayings all over your walls."

I grabbed my boots out of my closet. "Nope, I just wear those across my chest," I said, and then held in a groan.

What a way to invite him to look at my boobs. Could I have been any more obvious?

"Speaking of which…" He walked behind me, gently turning me around. "I didn't get a chance to read tonight's message."

Watching his face as he read my T-shirt, I could feel my cheeks heat with a blush as his eyes roamed over my chest. Any other time, I wouldn't have thought anything about it. People read my shirts every day, but knowing he was looking, watching him, made it seem personal, like he was reaching out and touching me.

He grabbed each side of my shirt close to where it tucked into my pants, pulling it taut. "You know, now that I think about it, I kinda agree with Jenna. You need to start dressing normal."

I tilted my head to the side. "You said you liked them."

"I do. I just don't know that I like other guys reading them." He let go of my shirt and moved his hands to my hips, sliding them slowly up my sides. He hesitated when his fingers brushed the sides of my breasts, before moving upward to cup my face. I forgot how to breathe.

I was sure I was going to pass out. Brody Victor just passed second base, and we hadn't even kissed yet. How was that possible? Of course, I wasn't sure skimming his fingers over the side of my breasts, through my shirt and bra, for a mere second, counted as second base. I didn't really know what the bases were. I wasn't a guy. And I'd had people accidently bump into me who got more of a feel than that. But that was… just delicious. He'd intentionally touched me, his gaze locked on mine. And my stomach dropped to my toes. I still wasn't breathing.

He stepped closer to me, backing me up against the wall. One hand on either side of my head, he leaned down, his face close to mine. The length of our bodies touched. I dropped my boots. They hit the floor with a dull thud. Wrapping my hands around his arms, I made a moaning sound deep in my throat when I felt his muscles flex. I ran my hands up to his shoulders and across his back, feeling his muscles contract under my touch.

He leaned in closer to me, his mouth skimming my skin just in front of my ear, sending shivers through my body. "Willow?"

I think I said, "Yeah?"

"We're going to be late."

"Mm-hmm."

He kissed my shoulder, moving up my neck, across my jaw, stopping when he reached my lips. His mouth was so close that his breath tickled them, and my tongue slid across to moisten them. Brody cursed under his breath and grabbed my hips, pulling me even closer against him.

The front door opened, and Ralph's voice boomed through the house, followed by my mother's softer voice. My heart skipped a beat, and then another. And not in a good way.

"Did you park in the driveway?"

"No. In the street," Brody said.

"Thank God." I moved to the door and clicked the lock closed. "Just be quiet."

I stood at the door and listened. Someone came up the stairs, the floor creaking when they walked past my bedroom. Judging by the sound of the footsteps, it was Ralph. I squeezed my eyes closed, praying they'd just forgot something and would leave.

My doorknob rattled, followed by a knock. "Willow?" my mother called.

"Yeah?"

"What are you doing in there?"

"Just reading," I lied, rubbing my hand over my face.

"Open the door."

Crap.

Grabbing Brody's arm, I pulled him toward the door. I positioned him behind it before unlocking and opening it, standing in the doorway so my mother couldn't walk into my bedroom.

"Why's your door locked?" she asked.

"Oh, um…" I put my hand on the top of my head; the other held the door so tightly my fingers hurt. "Someone knocked on the door earlier. I didn't know who he was. It freaked me out a little so I locked my door." I let my hand drop from my head and shrugged. "What are you guys doing back so early?"

My mom flicked her hand like she was waving my question away. "We just forgot something Ralph needed, and I forgot my cell phone, like always. We're leaving now. We'll probably be late. I'll see you in the morning."

"Okay. Have fun."

"Yeah, right," she grumbled. She hated going to work functions with Ralph. She knew what people thought of her. It didn't matter if they said it to her face or not. She could read it in the way they talked to her—or didn't talk to her. She'd always be the gold-digging hussy that snagged the most eligible bachelor in Middleton.

I held my breath until I heard the door shut. "Stay here." I crept downstairs, looked out of the window, and saw Ralph drive away.

That was too freakin' close.

Despite Brody's worry that we'd be late, we made it to the movie theater in plenty of time to get our tickets and popcorn with lots and lots of butter.

"I'm glad we have the butter thing in common. It would have been a deal breaker if not."

Brody grinned and squirted more butter on the popcorn. "What are we seeing?"

"Beyond the grave." I gave my best impression of a ghost's voice. I didn't quite pull it off judging by Brody's laughter.

"I thought you didn't like horror movies."

"No. I don't like watching them in the backseat of your Jeep, in the dark, in an isolated field, surrounded by nothing but woods. That," I pointed at him, "by the way, is a scene in most horror movies, and it never turns out well for one or two of the actors."

"You're quirky," he said and kissed the tip of my nose. "I love that about you."

Hold. The. Phone. What did he just say? The L word? And it wasn't Like or Lust. Calm down. He didn't say he loved me, just that I was quirky. Yeah, totally different. So what am I supposed to say back? Nothing? That I love that he loves that I'm quirky? That I love him? Wait! What?

"Hi, Willow."

I looked up and saw Natalie from English class. "Hey, Natalie!" I looked at her date and recognized the guy with the personality of a rock. "Hi, Earl. I remember you from the fall dance. You went with Jenna." Earl rolled his eyes. I guess Jenna's master plan of making his life miserable so he wouldn't ask her out again worked. "Do you know Brody? Brody, this is Natalie and Earl."

"Hey, man," Brody said to Earl, shaking his hand and doing that weird shoulder bump thing guys do. "Hi, Natalie. I remember you from English class." He smiled at her, and her cheeks turned slightly pink.

Yeah, that smile gets 'em every time. And it's mine. All mine. Mine, mine, mine. Jeez, I sound like I'm two. But it is mine.

"I heard you broke up with Jaden and you two are dating now." Natalie looked between Brody and me.

"Yes. I'm sure the whole school's heard by now," I said with a shrug of a shoulder.

"Pretty much. Everyone thinks you two make such a cute couple. Way better than Jaden. What an ass." I blinked in surprise. It wasn't what I expected her to say at all. "Well, I'll see you two in English. We have to go. We have dinner reservations." Natalie smiled at Earl. He actually smiled back. It was the first time I'd seen his face register any type of expression other than boredom.

"Have a nice dinner," I called after them. "Huh."

"What?" Brody asked, looking down at me.

"Nothing, just something Natalie said."

"The thing about Jaden? I told you, no one could figure out why you stayed with him."

Brody and I saw four more people from school, and none of

them seemed the least bit concerned about what happened with Jaden. I was cautiously optimistic that my reputation would survive the break up intact. Then again, one never knew about these things. It was high school, after all.

"Did you like the movie?" Brody asked as we walked to his Jeep.

"Yeah. Did you?"

"Mm-hmm. Are you sure you liked it?"

"Yes, why?"

"Because your face was buried in my shoulder for ninety percent of it," he said with a chuckle.

"It was not. I watched it. It wasn't even that scary. The one—"

Brody grabbed my upper arm and pulled me toward the Jeep. "Let's go. Get in."

"There's the slut. Hey, Brody. Out with your tramp of a girlfriend?"

I cringed when I heard Jaden's voice. "Brody, please just get in the car. Let it go." Brody stood next to the open driver's side door, looking at Jaden. "They're just words. They can't hurt me. Let's just go. Please."

Brody looked at me and grinned. "Of course we're going. I'm not wasting my time on your garbage."

He got into the Jeep, threw it in gear, and drove away, Jaden and the guys with him scattering out of the way. "Where do you want to go eat?"

I looked down at my hands. They were shaking. I slipped them between my thighs and the seat so Brody wouldn't see. Blood was rushing behind my ears, making it hard to hear.

"Let's go to your aunt's."

We pulled up to a stoplight, and he looked at me. "You don't want to go to The Dive?"

"Not really."

"Hmm. Any particular reason?" he asked, an edge to his voice.

"Yeah, as a matter of fact there is. I thought it would be fun to play pool and the last time we were there, I saw a couple of air hockey tables. I thought those might be fun, too. What do I have to do to make you understand I'm not ashamed to be seen with you? Why are you second-guessing everything I do or say? I'm with you tonight, Brody. Here, right now. If you want to go to The Dive, all you have to do is say so and we'll go." The car behind us honked. "The light's green." I turned and looked out the window, crossing my arms over my chest.

"I'm sorry."

The ride was silent. We pulled into the parking lot of his aunt's bar. I reached over and threaded my fingers with his. "I'm getting a chocolate milkshake, maybe two." I smiled at him. "And then we can play pool?"

"Whatever you want." He ran a finger down the side of my face, making me shudder.

Whatever I want. Yeah. Except a kiss. He's a tease. A big, fat tease. If he doesn't kiss me soon, I'm gonna... I don't know what, but something.

We said *hi* to his aunt, who hugged me tight and said how glad she was to see me. When she saw Brody holding my hand, she winked and said she was *really* glad to see me.

The restaurant of the bar was packed and Aunt Bess—she insisted I call her that—said there'd be a wait before our food was ready.

"Do you want to play pool while we wait?" Brody asked.

I looked at the pool tables and bit my bottom lip, trying to keep from smiling. "Um, no, let's play air hockey."

"Okay, but I warn you, I'm pretty good."

"Pretty sure of yourself, aren't you, Ace? Care to make it interesting?" I tossed the puck onto the table.

Brody laughed. "Sure. What're the stakes?"

I raised an eyebrow and put a hand on my hip. "What do you want?"

Brody flipped the machine on. "To see you tomorrow."

I nodded. "Okay. But you didn't have to bet me for that. I'll spend time with you anytime, you just have to ask."

"Good to know. What do you want?"

I drummed my fingers against my bottom lip. "Hmm, so many

possibilities. I'll tell you after I win," I said.

"So secretive." He winked. "Okay, challenge accepted. Three out of five." He slid the puck to me. "You shoot first."

I lined up my shot. It flew into the slot before Brody had time to react.

"Crap. I think I'm in trouble," he said with a laugh.

I won the first three games and the bet. We slid into a booth just as our food arrived. "That really wasn't fair, you know," Brody said, sticking a fry in his mouth.

I smiled and looked down at my plate, pretending to be engrossed in covering my French fries in ketchup. "What wasn't fair?"

"You didn't tell me you knew how to play air hockey."

"You didn't ask." I took a bite of my burger, groaning when the melted cheese oozed into my mouth.

Just wait until you see me play pool. You are so gonna lose, buddy.

Brody took a sip of his Coke and looked at me over the rim of the cup. "So what do you want for winning the bet?"

I smiled and winked at him. "I'll tell you when the time comes."

After we finished eating, we moved on to the pool tables. "Wanna make it double or nothing?" Brody asked with a raised eyebrow.

"Sure."

"I'm not going to help you this time," he warned, selecting a cue.

"Okay. I think I remember everything you taught me last time." I took a pool cue and rolled it between my hands.

He nodded and chuckled. "Okay. You break."

Lining up my shot, I couldn't help but grin. Brody was watching me, his shoulder leaning against the wall, a thumb hooked in a belt loop on his low-riding jeans. He looked sinful. I was still gonna beat him.

I took my shot, and the balls scattered across the felt. Five dropped into the pockets. "See? I told you I remembered. I'll be solids." I lined up my next shot and sunk another ball. Three more turns and two more balls hit the pocket before I missed, and Brody stepped up to take his turn.

He walked in front of me, narrowing his eyes. "You knew how to play."

"Yup." I bit the inside of my cheek, trying not to smile. I couldn't help it. A grin broke out over my face.

"You hustled me?" He laughed.

"I don't think you can call it hustling when there's no money involved."

He drew his eyebrows down and the skin between his eyes wrinkled. "Why did you let me think you couldn't play?"

I leaned close to him, standing on my tiptoes to whisper in his ear. "Because I wanted to know what it felt like to be held in your arms. And it felt fan-freakin-tastic."

His eyebrows rose. "But we weren't... we were barely friends."

"I crossed the friend line a long time ago, Brody." I bit the corner of my bottom lip.

He took the pool cue from me and set it away with his. Turning, he walked toward me until I was pressed against the pool table. With a hand on each side of me, he leaned in close. "When?"

"The day you asked me to help you with your calculus homework and I realized the next day you didn't need my help. That you'd just wanted to sit with me and talk. No one had ever done that before. You know, made an effort?"

"I think I knew the first night I saw you," Brody murmured.

I thought back, trying to remember what happened when we first met.

"Jaden pulled a kid over and demanded he buy you something to drink. You reached out to keep the kid from falling and gave Jaden a death glare. Then you kept telling the kid he didn't need to buy you anything and tried to give his money back to him, remember?"

I nodded.

"I knew you weren't like the normal, spoiled, popular crowd that thinks everyone owes them something."

Brody paused. His eyes roamed over my face, landing on my mouth. He ran his thumb across my bottom lip. His eyes followed his thumb before seeking out my gaze. "I knew that night there was something special about you. Even when we were insulting each other, I was secretly enjoying every second of it because you were talking to me, even though you were wicked harsh."

I laughed. "Yeah, sorry, but you did call me a bimbo."

"Honestly," he huffed, "are you ever going to let me live that down?"

I ran my hand through his hair, brushing it off his forehead. "Maybe. You'll have to do something really epic to make me forget it, though. Are we going to finish our game?"

Brody stood in front of me, not moving. His gaze locked on mine, and all I could think of were sapphires. That was what his eyes reminded me of, brilliant, sparkling, sapphires. He leaned his face close to mine. "Let's call it a draw. You won air hockey, and I won pool. I want you to myself tomorrow. What do you want?"

"I want to spend our date at your aunt's property," I whispered.

"Any reason why?" He leaned in closer. His breath fanned my lips.

"I want you all to myself."

Brody put his hands on my hips and pulled me to him. Every part of our bodies were touching. I just had to tilt my face to the side and his lips would be on mine.

"Well, go on, boy. Kiss her," an old man sitting on one of the barstools yelled. "You two've been dancing around each other all night. Jist do it an' git 'er done."

"You heard him, Ace. Kiss me," I whispered. Brody watched my lips move. His hands tightened on my hips, pulling me even closer to him.

"I will," he murmured, our breath mingling. "But not here and not yet." He let go and took a step back, an odd expression on his face.

I cursed him silently. Then I wondered what was wrong with me. Why he didn't want to kiss me.

"If you're not into the whole kissing thing, that's cool." I tried to brush off my disappointment. "Let's just finish our game because you were dreaming if you thought you were gonna beat me." I didn't look at him when I grabbed my pool cue and chalked the tip. "Whose turn is it? I can't remember. I'll just take a shot." I sunk one ball before missing. I managed not to look at Brody while I took my turn, but when I looked up to tell him it was his shot, I saw him standing in the same place I'd left him, no pool cue in his hand. "You're up, Ace."

We finished our game and Brody drove me home, dropping me off without a kiss.

Something's wrong with me. I'm un-kissable, and I have no idea why.

EIGHTEEN
Sunday

"The hours I spend with you, I look upon as sort of a perfumed garden, a dim twilight, and a fountain singing to it. You and you alone make me feel that I am alive. Other men it is said have seen angels, but I have seen thee and thou art enough."
~ *George Edward Moore*

*I*T'S SUNDAY!

I scrambled out of bed. My foot got tangled in my sheets, and I face planted on the floor with a grunt. Even that didn't ruin my excitement. Another day with Brody, I was in Heaven. The best part of the day—other than being with Brody—was Sunday was Mom and Ralph's day. They always spent it doing something together. What, I had no idea and couldn't care less. The whole idea kind of creeped me out. The less they told me, the happier I was. Their time away left me free for the day. And I was spending it with Brody Victor. But first, I had to untangle my foot and get off the floor. I decided texting him was more important. I reached up, grabbed my cell off my bedside table, and typed in a text.

ME: GOOD MORNING, ACE.

I set my phone next to me, untangled my sheets, and stood up, scooping my phone with me. After I made my bed, I ran downstairs to get a bowl of cereal. When I got back to my room, I checked my phone. No text.

Huh.

My mom stuck her head in my room to tell me she and Ralph were leaving. They were spending the night in Shipshewana, Indiana and wouldn't be home until the next morning. I had to restrain myself from doing my happy dance. Instead, I simply told them to have a nice time and I'd see them after school Monday.

Still no text from Brody.

Jenna called me and wanted every second of my date with Brody accounted for. I spent the next hour telling her everything that happened, twice.

Still no text.

"Should I text him again?" I asked Jenna.

"How long has it been?"

"Almost three hours." I sighed.

"Yeah, text him. Maybe your first one didn't go through."

"What should I say?"

Jenna laughed. "I don't know. He's your hottie boyfriend."

"Yeah."

ME: WHATCHA DOIN'?

I talked another half hour with Jenna before hanging up. Still no text. Brody had never gone this long without answering me. I didn't expect him to answer the second I texted him, but he usually texted back within a few minutes, not hours.

I picked out my outfit. Jenna would be proud. It was something normal and a little sexy—at least I thought it was sexy, but what did I know? Guys baffled me, especially Brody. At least Jaden was an open book, and it was all about him. I couldn't figure Brody out at all.

I laid the off-white sweater and navy leggings on my bed and waited. An hour later, I took a shower. And I waited. I rechecked my outfit, decided I didn't like that one, and picked another. This time, it was a sweater that fell off one shoulder—that had to be sexy, I thought. And I waited.

I was just about to shove my clothes back in my closet and say screw it when my phone chimed. I forced myself not to snatch it up right away and click on the message. He made me wait all flippin' day. He could wait five minutes. I sat on my bed, looking around my bedroom, mentally taking inventory of my things.

Black furniture to match the black stripes on my walls, check. White chandelier hanging from the ceiling to match the white in the white-and-black paisley wallpaper on the bottom half of my walls, check. A hot pink papasan chair to match the hot pink stripes, check.

A hot pink lava lamp, check. Even my friggin' phone is hot pink! Ugh!

I wanted to throw it across the room. Instead, I clicked on his message.

> BRODY: HEY, GORGEOUS. I'M SO SORRY. RUNNING ERRANDS AND FORGOT MY PHONE.

And just like that, my stupid smile was back on my face.

> ME: IT'S OKAY. HOME NOW?
> BRODY: YES. DON'T WANT TO BE.
> ME: ?
> BRODY: WANT TO BE WITH YOU.
> ME: I'M ALONE. COME OVER.
> BRODY: BE THERE IN FIVE.

Holy Shiznit! I gotta get dressed.

I jumped around my room, pulling on my pants—pretty undies, check—and squirming into my sweater—lacy bra, check—I was just putting a swipe of cherry-flavored lip gloss on my lips—just in case—when he rang the doorbell.

I adjusted the sweater so it fell over the shoulder that didn't have any bruises and pulled the door open. My breath whooshed out of me.

It should be illegal for him to look that good.

And then I got a whiff of him, and I might have actually seen those stupid little cartoon hearts float around his head.

"Wow," Brody said. "You look amazing." He walked in and shut the door behind him, his gaze never leaving me.

"I was thinking the same about you, Ace."

"Nope. I'm definitely getting the better deal. Where're your mom and Ralph?"

"Oh, Sunday is marriage day." I used my fingers to make little air quotes. "No kid allowed. They went to Shipshewana to do… whatever it is people do there." I shrugged.

"You've never been?"

"Nope."

"Me either. We should go together," he said.

Together. Yeah. Together. That's a beautiful word.

"We should. Maybe one day after graduation. You know, when

the weather is nice and we'd have all day."

"Sounds like a plan." Brody smiled. "Are you ready?"

I grabbed my military jacket and pulled it on. "Mm-hmm."

We drove to a small pizzeria, picking up a small pepperoni to take with us to Brody's aunt's property.

"Hey, isn't this the pizzeria we stopped at the night...?" I let my words trail off. I didn't want to bring up that particular memory. The part of the night I spent with Brody eating pizza and listening to the radio while we talked was great. The beginning of the night, before Brody, hadn't been.

"Yeah, it is." He looked over at me and smiled, reaching for my hand and kissing my fingers.

By the time we got to Brody's aunt's property, the day, which had been full of sunshine, had turned gloomy. I looked at the sky. Gray clouds swirled over the sun like someone was stirring them with a giant spoon. "Oh, no. It was so pretty earlier. Did you bring your little DVD player?"

"No."

"Well, what's our back-up plan if it starts raining?"

"I don't have one," he said, looking over at me.

"Hmm."

We drove to the field, and Brody parked the Jeep in the same spot we always used. I glanced at Brody and then out of the window. A large tent sat in the middle of the property. "Who's here?"

"I don't know. Let's go find out." He jumped out of the Jeep, came around, and opened my door.

"I don't think we should hang around. I mean, if your aunt didn't say anyone would be out here, we should definitely leave." I didn't move from my seat.

"I want to check on something first." He grabbed me by the waist and lifted me out of the Jeep. Threading our hands together, he pulled me behind him.

"Wait, I don't want to go over there." I tried to push his hand off me.

"It's safer than standing here by yourself." He raised an eyebrow at me. Ugh, he was maddening.

"Fine." I walked behind him, my faced buried in his shoulder. One hand squeezed his and the other wrapped around a belt loop of his jeans, following so close behind him that I kept tripping over his shoes. He walked to the back of the tent. I peeked around his arm and saw a boxy piece of machinery. "What's that?"

"A generator." He pulled a cord that looked like one on a lawn mower, and the generator roared to life. I jumped and looked at the tent, waiting for someone to come running outside. Brody laughed.

"What are you laughing at?" I asked through clenched teeth, still holding on to his arm with a death grip.

He was barely holding back his laughter. "Time to let you in on a little secret." He framed my face and kissed my forehead. "I put the tent out here. I knew it was supposed to rain tonight."

I opened my mouth before snapping it shut. I looked at the tent, then the generator, and back at Brody. "You did this?"

"Yes."

"Why? We could have gone to a movie or something instead."

He shrugged a shoulder. "You said you wanted to come here, and I wanted to give you what you asked for. Besides, you won the bet."

I rolled my eyes. "It was really romantic until you added that."

"You want romance? I'm going to romance the hell out of you tonight. Wait here." He jogged to the Jeep and grabbed our drinks and pizza. I stood where he left me while he disappeared into the tent with the pizza. Seconds later, he came out. "Okay, come here." He reached for me.

He stood behind me and placed his hands gently over my eyes. "You could've just told me to close my eyes."

"You'd peek. Step up and over and bend down. Good."

I could tell I was standing in the tent. The air was warmer and smelled sweeter. Brody let his hands fall from my eyes. I blinked and looked around, taking everything in. "This was what you were doing today when you said you were running errands?"

"Yes. You like it?"

I looked around, trying to find the right words to tell him exactly what I felt. *'Like'* didn't cover the jumble of emotions I was feeling. There was so much more to them than that.

I stood in the middle of a two-room, green canvas tent. The ceiling had clear twinkle lights—the kind you'd find at Christmastime—draped everywhere. It was covered. There was a small table next to me where Brody had put our pizza. A vase of fresh flowers and a candle sat in the middle of the table. I peeked in the second room, and there was a blow-up mattress covered in pillows on the floor in front of a small television and DVD player. More lights sparkled from the ceiling.

"I thought since we wouldn't be able to see the stars, I'd make some for us to look at..." His voice trailed off.

"It's beautiful. I just..." I shook my head, still looking at everything he'd done. All the little details he'd thought to include. "I can't believe you did this."

"I had some help. My aunt's boyfriend helped me set-up a lot of it. This is his tent and generator. He said there was only one rule."

"What's that?" I turned to Brody.

He smirked and ducked his head, looking at me through his dark lashes. "You'd better not come back pregnant."

"Huh." I wasn't sure what to say to that so I said the first thing that popped into my head, which was never a good idea. "Kind of hard since we haven't even kissed yet."

"Not impossible, though."

"Hmm, true." I looked at him and gave him a small smile. "Let's eat before the pizza gets cold."

"Okay." Brody pulled my chair out for me, and I sat at the small table. He sat next to me, rather than across from me. Our thighs brushed against each other whenever we moved. Every so often, Brody would run his hand up my arm and over my bare shoulder, sending waves of tingles through my veins. It made talking, at least coherently, very difficult.

When we'd finished eating, he asked if I wanted to watch a movie.

"You said you didn't bring the DVD player," I said, narrowing my eyes at him.

"No, I think I said I didn't bring the little one. This is a different player."

"Technicality, Ace. Sure, a movie sounds great. What did you bring?"

"A horror film."

I laughed. "Really? But it's not dark out. Doesn't that kill some of the scare factor?"

"Nah, it's a gloomy and rainy day. You'll still get freaked out and end up with your face pressed against my chest through the whole movie." He bit his lower lip to keep from grinning.

That's not a bad place to be.

The movie was scary, and Brody was right. I either had my head turned into his shoulder or the blanket over my eyes.

A tense scene was playing. The murderer was stalking his prey and I had my face pressed against Brody, watching the movie with one eye. My hand was fisted in the blanket, and adrenaline was building in my blood stream as I waited for the inevitable moment when the psycho killer jumped out of the shadows. A bolt of lightning arced across the sky outside followed by a loud boom of thunder. I jumped and screamed. Brody laughed.

"That wasn't funny." I pushed his arm.

"Yes, it was." He laughed harder.

I pursed my lips to keep from grinning and flopped backward on the mattress, trying to get my heart to stop racing.

"Aw, come on, you know you love me," Brody said, rolling to the side so he was leaning over me.

My grin disappeared and a shiver ran up my spine. Brody looked down at me, his expression serious, a look of vulnerability and questioning in his eyes.

My hands gripped his arms, squeezing them in a silent answer. My gaze never left his. I wanted him to kiss me, ached for him to. He was so close. His eyes darkened. I could see the striations of blue in his eyes, feel the heat from his skin singeing mine, and feel his heartbeat, fast and strong, its rhythm keeping time my own.

Dipping his head forward, he slid his lips across mine. He pulled back and looked into my eyes. I raised one hand to rest on his shoulder, the fingers of my other skimming over his bottom lip. His tongue darted out, touching their tips. I pulled in a sharp breath and moved my hand to cup his face.

"Brody." It was barely a whisper, but it was all the answer he needed.

He lowered himself to me. Leaning on his forearms, he cradled my head in his hands. He kissed me like no one had before. There was so much tenderness, yearning, and emotion held in his kiss. I'd never felt so complete, so at peace, as I did in his arms.

"I've waited so long to do that," he murmured against my lips. "You taste so good."

I made a sound deep in my throat, something between a moan and a sigh, and arched toward him, urging him to take our kiss deeper. I was mesmerized by him, his touch, his smell, and now his taste. My body craved them all and soaked up as much as it could hold, and still it wanted more.

His tongue dipped into my mouth, sliding against my own. Exploring, teasing, tasting. It was heady and blissful. Fingers of desire spread through me, warming parts of my body that had never felt a lover's touch. And I realized it was because I was never touched by a lover. A guy, yes. A lover, no. Brody's touch conjured up emotions I didn't realize I possessed. I liked him. I lusted after him. And I knew with certainty, I loved him. And my body knew it and reacted to it.

I slipped my hands under his T-shirt, sliding them across the muscular planes of his back, running my fingernails over his skin. He broke our kiss long enough to reach behind his neck and pull off his shirt in that sexy way only guys can do. My hands roamed freely over his skin, his chest, back, arms, pulling a groan from deep inside him.

Then his hands were on me. He rolled us over so I was straddling him and slid his hands under my sweater, skimming my bare belly. My body sizzled with longing. He pulled sensations from me I'd never felt, never knew existed. I heard noises, muffled moans and whimpers, and realized they were from me. I had the fleeting thought I should be embarrassed by my complete lack of control, but when it came to Brody, there was no such thing as control.

His hands moved higher, skimming up my sides, across my

chest, between my breasts. I sighed his name and he slipped my sweater above my head, tossing it on the floor next to his. He rolled and was above me again, kissing every part of me, and I returned them. Our hands roamed everywhere our mouths touched. I let my hand skim down his rippled stomach to the button of his low-slung jeans. I pushed the button through its hole and his hand covered mine.

"No," he said, his breath coming in gasps. "Pants stay on." I looked at him through the haze of desire. "I won't be able to stop." He shook his head. "I didn't bring you out here to—"

My mouth covered his. My tongue slipped between his lips. I pulled back just enough to suck his bottom lip into my mouth, nipping at it. He took the kiss deeper; it was as if he were consuming me.

And I wanted him to.

We'd kept our make-out session going for almost an hour before Brody cursed and rolled away from me.

"What's the matter?" I asked, confused and worried I'd done something wrong.

"I have to stop now, Willow. If I don't, I won't."

"Oh." At first, disappointment filled me, and then an air of satisfaction. I'd done that to him. I'd driven him to the brink. That knowledge was almost as delicious as his kisses. Almost.

I lay on my back in just my bra and jeans, looking at the lights twinkling above us. Brody was shirtless on his side next to me, drawing slow circles on my skin.

"Brody, why did it take you so long to kiss me?"

"Because I knew once I started, I wouldn't want to stop, and I didn't want our first kiss somewhere meaningless, like in the school parking lot. I wanted it to be something special. And building up to, forcing myself to wait, made it more awesome than I thought it'd be."

I smiled. "Yeah, it was freakin' awesome."

Brody chuckled, leaned his head forward, and kissed my belly.

"What are you doing after graduation?" I asked.

"College."

"Where?"

Brody's hand stilled. He flattened it, splaying his fingers over my belly. "University of Michigan."

It felt like someone sat on my chest. It was hard to breathe, and I could barely get my next words out. "It's a long way from California."

His hand started moving again. "I know," he murmured.

Tears formed in my eyes and dripped from their corners into my hair spread around my head. I didn't move to wipe them away. I didn't want to draw attention to them, hoping they'd stop before Brody saw. I swallowed back the cries my body fought to release, trying to hold still so my shoulders didn't shake and give me away.

It had been an amazing night. And although no one was perfect, Brody was damn near. We were perfect together, but I was scared. Scared about what would happen to us when I left for UCLA and he stayed behind in Michigan. For the first time, I found myself not wishing for graduation. Until that point, it couldn't come fast enough. But realizing I'd be leaving Brody—and I had to leave Michigan—it seemed like the worst day imaginable.

Brody reached up and caught a tear on his fingertip before kissing my eyes, then my mouth. His kiss, so gentle, always gentle, made me cry harder.

"What will happen to us after graduation?" I asked, my voice trembling. My bottom lip started to quiver, and I bit down on it.

"We'll be fine." He placed open-mouthed kisses on my stomach and worked his way up to the space in front of my ear. "I need to tell you something, but I don't want to freak you out," he murmured.

"What?" I held my breath. I had a strange feeling I wasn't going to like what he was about to say, and I wanted to tell him to stop. To not tell me, that I didn't want to hear. But I kept silent.

He pulled back and gazed in to my eyes. "I know we've only been dating for a day," he said with a small laugh. "But we've known each other longer. We've spent time together talking and learning things about each other."

"Yes," I said slowly.

He kissed me, his tongue dipping into my mouth. When he

lifted his head, his gaze found mine. "I'm in love with you, Willow. I know it seems crazy and it's probably way too fast but—"

"I love you, too, Ace."

Brody let out a breath and grinned at me before leaning in for another kiss.

NINETEEN
Bliss

"Our soul mate is the one who makes life come to life."
~Richard Bach

HE NIGHT BRODY AND I SPENT IN THE TENT MADE OUR RELATIONSHIP even stronger. We knew we loved each other and belonged together.

We were nearly inseparable. We spent every free second together. It didn't matter what we did, as long as we were together. I'd even started going with him to work at his aunt's bar. Aunt Bess joked that she was going to put me on the payroll.

"No, being with Brody is enough," I told her.

"Oh, girlie, you've got it bad for him, don'tcha?" she asked, hugging me. "Good thing he's a good kid and he loves you, too. I see it in the way he looks at you when you aren't looking. He can't keep his eyes to himself, that one." She smiled and kissed my cheek.

Each week after that, there was always an envelope in the payroll bin with my name on it. Inside was a check. On the bottom, she'd write the same thing: *This is for all the work you do here and all the happiness you bring. Thank you.*

I opened a savings account and deposited my paychecks each week. I didn't spend a cent of the money. It wasn't because I was going to give it back. That would've offended Aunt Bess. No, I was creating a travel fund. If Brody and I were going to live apart throughout college, I wanted to see him as often as possible. The money I earned working at Bess's was for Brody to travel to California. I didn't know how long it would last, but it would be good for at least a couple of trips and that was better than none. It had to be.

"I want to do something for Aunt Bess."

We were at Bess's rinsing dishes off before loading them in the washer. Brody looked at me. "Like what?" He flicked his finger, sending soap bubbles through the air at me.

"Stop playing or I'll make you do this alone." I tried to give him a stern look, but laughed when he shot more soap at me. "I don't know. What does she like?"

"White chocolate and almond candy bars, but she never buys them because they cost three dollars and she says that's too much money for a stinkin' candy bar." He mimicked her voice, and I laughed.

Magically, a white chocolate and almond candy bar appeared on her desk each Monday. If she knew it was me who put them there, she never said. But she'd always break off a square and hand it to me. There was only one problem. I'd become addicted to the candy bars too.

Brody's mother was another constant in our relationship. I'd grown to love her. Anne was the type of mother every teenager wished for. She respected Brody's need for privacy, but still had firm boundaries in place.

Most of all, she accepted me as part of her family, calling me the daughter she knew she'd have one day.

My mom and Ralph still didn't know about Brody. It bothered him that he wouldn't be accepted into my family like his had accepted me. It broke my heart and I wanted to scream at Ralph and my mother, but knew I was better off keeping my mouth shut.

If they'd found out about Brody and me, they would've done everything in their power to end our relationship. Jaden was their pick. He always would be.

Brody and I had just finished Sunday dinner with Anne. I put the last of the dishes in the dishwasher when Brody asked if I wanted to take a drive with him.

"Sure. Where are we going?"

He shrugged a shoulder and grinned at me.

I knew where he wanted to go. Our spot. The one on his aunt's property to look at the stars together. We went there at least once a week. The tent and generator were long gone, so we took a blanket to lie on. The night sky calmed him, whether from a long week of exams, too much homework, or the stress of constantly seeing Jaden in the halls at school. He'd go to the little spot on the field and watch the night sky. I'd been the only one he'd ever taken with him. He said, "You get it," and he was right. I understood.

Some nights we'd go and lie on the blanket, holding hands and talking quietly, and sometimes we'd go and not say anything at all, just hold hands and look at the sparkling sky. That night, I had something I needed to talk to him about.

"Brody? I need to tell you something." I rolled on to my side so I could look at him. "You know how Ralph owns the car lot?"

"Yeah." He turned his head toward me.

"Well, he's been out of town a lot the past month, and he'll probably be out of town most of next month, too. He wants to add on to his business, so he's spending time researching and visiting different car lots and looking at properties where he might build one."

"Okay, what does that have to do with us?" Brody rolled to his side and laid his hand on my hip.

"I told my mom I broke up with Jaden and that I've been dating someone else," I said in a rush.

Brody tensed. "What'd she say?"

"Not much. She said if it made me happy, she's okay with it." Brody's hand tightened on my hip. "She never liked Jaden quite as much as Ralph. I think she saw his domineering side one too many times, even though he tried to hide it. She wants to meet you."

Brody stiffened next to me. "What about Ralph?"

"We'll do it on a day he's out of town. She agrees that we shouldn't tell him for a while. He's still hung up on Jaden. They act like they're the ones dating." I rolled my eyes.

Brody laughed. "When does she want to meet?"

"Tomorrow. Dinner at my house."

"I'll be there." He smiled at me before pulling me toward him for a kiss, and then another, and another, and another. My head spun and my stomach filled with butterflies. It was intoxicating.

Brody rang the doorbell at precisely five o'clock the next afternoon. I'd warned him not to come early. My mother hated that. I couldn't count the number of times I'd heard her complain, "If I invite someone over at five, I don't want them showing up at four." So when Brody was neither early, nor late, he'd automatically earned a gold star.

I'd been looking out the window, waiting for him to arrive, and answered the door as soon as the bell chimed. It wasn't like I was nervous for him to meet my mother. I was petrified. Brody smiled his crooked smile as soon as he saw me and my insides melted and, along with them, some of my nervousness. After all, who could look at that face and not like him? Then he opened his mouth, all the sweet nuthin's came spewing out, and most people were hooked. You had to have a heart made of stone not to be affected by Brody's charm. Or maybe I was biased.

I looked at the flowers he was holding and raised an eyebrow.

"These aren't for you," he said with a grin. "This is for you." He lowered his head and touched his lips lightly to mine. I breathed him in. His subtle scent filled my nose and peppermint filled my mouth.

Flowers or a kiss? The kiss was definitely the better deal.

When he lifted his head, I ran my tongue over my lips. His eyes followed the motion. I gave him a small smile and looked up at him out of the corner of my eye. His gaze traveled over me. "You taste good," I whispered. He smirked. "I want a piece of gum." I stuck out my hand.

He laughed. "How do you know I have gum?"

"Because you taste like peppermint. Your toothpaste is spearmint." I smiled, waiting for my stick of gum.

"How do you know what kind of toothpaste I brush with?" He gave me a funny look, and I laughed.

I leaned close to him, and he lowered his head so I could whisper in his ear. "Because you've had your tongue in my mouth enough times I've learned your taste. And it's spearmint."

"Huh." He reached in the pocket of his buttery soft, leather jacket and pulled out a piece of gum.

"See? Peppermint," I chirped and stuffed it in my mouth. "C'mon." I took his hand and led him into the kitchen where my mother was flitting around from place to place, baking this and stirring that. You'd have thought she was a great cook by looking at her. In truth, everything she cooked usually came from a box or a can. She was just really good at using spices to make things taste homemade.

"Mom? This is Brody. Brody, this is my mother."

"Hello, Mrs. McKenna. It's a pleasure to meet you. These are for you." Brody handed her the bouquet of roses and lilies. His voice didn't quiver or shake. He didn't stammer or stumble over his words. He seemed completely at ease, not nervous at all, unless you looked at his hand holding mine. He had me in a death grip. I was afraid I was going to lose a finger from lack of blood flow.

"Hello, Brody. It's nice to finally meet you. Thank you for the beautiful flowers!" My mom fingered one of the blooms before smelling a rose. I smiled to myself. Brody just earned his second gold star of the night. "I'll just put these in water, and we can sit down and eat. Willow, hang up Brody's coat."

"Yes, ma'am." Taking Brody's jacket, I went to hang it up in the hall closet. I could hear the steady cadence of his voice as he talked with my mother.

"May I help with anything, Mrs. McKenna?" he asked.

May I help with anything? Wow, he's really pouring on the charm tonight.

"No, thank you. I think I have it under control," my mom answered.

"C'mon, Brody, you can help me set the table," I handed him the plates and led him to the dining room. "May I help with anything, Mrs. McKenna?" I said in a teasing, singsong voice when my mother couldn't hear us.

Brody chuckled and shrugged a shoulder. "Gotta suck up to the woman who brought my soul mate into the world."

"Aw, Ace, you make my heart go pitter-patter," I teased, fanning myself with my hand.

He smirked. "I'll make other things go pitter-patter later."

"Tease."

"Here we are." My mom carried the pot roast into the dining room.

"Oh, Mrs McKenna, that looks heavy. Let me help you with that." Brody darted to her and lifted the platter out of her hands.

"Thank you, dear."

Dear? Whoa, Brody just earned his third gold star of the night, and we haven't even sat down to eat yet. The big schmooze.

Dinner went great. My mom was talkative and asked Brody a million questions. He answered them all without a hint of annoyance. I was the one becoming annoyed.

"Mom, stop interrogating him like you're a member of the KGB or something."

"I don't mind," Brody said with a smile.

"So, what are your plans after graduation, Brody?" My mother dabbed each side of her mouth with a linen napkin.

"College, ma'am."

"And what will you study?"

"Medicine."

Really? How did I not know that? I guess I was too preoccupied about us being separated to ask.

"Ah, a doctor!"

"Actually, I'm going into medical research."

"Still, a very respectable field. Willow is going to study education." She said it like I'd be skimming scum off mud puddles. She thought I was wasting my life on teaching. There were so many more prestigious occupations I could have, especially with my grades. Blah, blah, blah. I didn't care about prestige. I wanted a job that made me happy. "You've been accepted at a college?" my mom asked Brody.

"Yes. The University of Michigan."

My heart did a nosedive like it did any time I thought about where we'd be going to college, so very far away from each other.

237

"Very nice," my mom said, nodding. And Brody earned his fourth gold star of the night. "Willow is going to State."

Not in this lifetime.

Brody looked at me and nodded. I gave him a tight smile.

And so it went throughout the evening. Question after question.

After Brody left, my mom said, "He's a very nice young man. Seems to have a plan for his life. That's important. I like him a lot."

I smiled. "I like him a lot, too."

"I know. I can see it in your eyes. You both have the look."

"The look?" I asked.

"The look, you know, respect, admiration, friendship, love. I can see it when you look at one another. I'm happy for you." She tapped the end of my nose with her finger. "Few people find a relationship like that."

And Brody earned his fifth gold star. Five out of five stars. He had sufficiently won over my mom. I breathed a sigh of relief.

We lay on a blanket on the roof of Brody's Jeep, wrapped in a quilt to keep warm, snuggled together, sharing body heat.

"The stars are pretty tonight," I whispered.

"Mm-hmm."

"I love coming here. Soon, it'll be too cold." I shivered.

"I know. I usually go to the planetarium in the winter. It's not the same, though."

"Do you want to come over and watch a movie? Ralph isn't home this week."

Brody turned his head and looked at me. His face was so close our noses nearly touched. "Your mom won't mind?"

"No. She'll probably be upstairs reading anyway." I scooted forward and kissed him. His lips were cool against mine, but when his tongue slipped into my mouth, it was warm and tasted sweet. It sent my body into overdrive. Every time he touched me, my body reacted in ways that surprised me. But it was more than just physical. It was raw emotion. We didn't hold anything back. We opened our bodies, hearts, and souls to each other and connected in a way that was beyond the physical.

I'd never given much thought to the idea of soul mates. I never knew if I believed there was only one person in the world meant for me. But Brody answered those questions. We connected in a way that I knew he was my other half. There wouldn't be anyone else that would touch all of me the way Brody did.

"You're freezing. Let's go. We'll get a movie on the way to your house," he said when he ended our kiss.

"Okay," I agreed reluctantly. I didn't want to leave. Brody's aunt's property was my favorite place. It was the only place we were truly alone. We spent hours there talking and learning about each other.

And other things... those were good, too. Yeah.

I'd never been happier than I'd been the two months I dated Brody. It was bliss.

"When you jump for joy, beware that no one moves the ground from beneath your feet."
~ Stanislaw J. Lec

TWENTY
Lies

"Don't listen to my words. They are toxic and lies. Gaze into my eyes. They hold the love I have for you. Always you. Only you."
~Willow

URING THE TWO MONTHS THAT BRODY AND I DATED, JADEN WAS relatively quiet. Thankfully, he avoided us. But, like I knew he would, he told people I'd slept around with other guys while we dated. He made it sound as though it happened all the time. I'd known he'd try to trash my reputation. What surprised me was that people didn't believe him. Not only was my reputation not ruined, but people also talked about Jaden sleeping around on me.

The truth was, I wasn't sleeping with anyone. And thankfully, Brody wasn't one of those guys who made up stories about bagging some chick to make their friends jealous or himself more popular. No, he was the type of guy who wasn't embarrassed to tell people we hadn't had sex. It didn't bother him what others thought.

Although Jaden remained somewhat detached from the situation, acting as if it didn't matter—maybe it didn't—he still had moments when he just couldn't keep his mouth shut.

It was a Monday, and Brody and I had just walked into the commons during lunch. We had to walk by Jaden's table to get to my locker for my afternoon dose of caffeine.

"What do you have today, caffeine or caffeine and chocolate?" Brody asked. "I know how nervous you get before an exam. You might need a fix of both before our calc. exam," he teased.

"Ha, you are so very funny. I think I'll stick with the—"

"There's the slut of Cassidy High," Jaden shouted when he saw us walk by.

Brody's fist darted out so quickly that no one had time to react. He landed a hard punch to Jaden's jaw, knocking him off his chair. Jaden jumped to his feet and charged Brody, but his football teammates held him back.

Brody grinned. "Watch your mouth, Jaden." He threaded his fingers through mine and walked away as though nothing happened. "So, what's in your stash?" he asked when we reached my locker.

"You can't do that. It doesn't matter what he says, Brody. You can't do that. Look at you," I grabbed his hand and looked at his knuckles. "You're hurt."

"Nah." He pulled me to him by the belt loops on my jeans and bent down, kissing me slowly. When he raised his head, he looked in my eyes. "I don't like hearing him say things like that about you."

"It doesn't matter what he says. Just leave it alone." When he opened his mouth to argue, I put my finger over his lips. "For me. Please."

He nodded once and leaned his forehead to mine. "Okay. For you." He pulled back and kissed my forehead. "Let's get your caffeine and go eat."

"Have you asked him yet?" Jenna asked in history class. It was Friday, and I was itching for school to end. Brody and I had a weekend full of things planned.

Jenna doodled little hearts across my notepad. I shooed her pencil away. "No. He's coming over after school. I'm going to ask him then."

"Is Ralph home this week?"

I blew a lock of hair out of my eyes. "He's coming home tomorrow."

Jenna started drawing hearts across the table. "You've got to tell him sooner or later."

"I know. I thought we'd wait until the wedding."

Jenna laughed. "Yeah, that might be a good idea." She drew a big heart across the table and filled it with little ones.

"Vandal," I said with a laugh.

"Yeah, I'm a rebel. I have detention this week anyway. I might as well make it worthwhile."

"What'd you do this time?" I asked with a sigh. Jenna was a detention addict. She had detention as much as I had caffeine.

"I needed to use the bathroom in English and old fart bag Malone wouldn't give me the bathroom pass. And I needed to go. It was a woman thing, if you know what I mean."

I nodded. "And?"

"I just left and went to the bathroom anyway. She hunted me down and yelled at me through the bathroom stall. I yelled some four-letter words back. I wanted to throw my tampon at her, but decided that might've got me suspended, so I didn't."

"Good call," I said, trying not to laugh.

I paced my room, waiting for Brody to get there. I was so nervous.

Get over it. It's Brody. He's the last person I have to be nervous around.

The girls' choice dance at school was in two weeks. I'd never been to one. Jaden didn't do dances. This would be my first official school dance with a date. Providing, of course, Brody didn't find them as repulsive as Jaden did. But even if he weren't all that thrilled with school dances, he'd go if he knew I wanted to. Brody was like that.

I took the small slip of paper out of my drawer and read it for the hundredth time. A small smile curved my lips. Brody loved my sarcastic T-shirts, but I couldn't wear one to the dance. So I wrote a sarcastic saying on a piece of paper, planned to show it to him, and tell him I'd pin it inside my dress so he'd know it was there.

The doorbell chimed, and I flitted down the stairs. "Hey, Ace," I said when I opened the door.

"Hey, you." He leaned down to kiss me just as my mother walked into the room. Curse her. He pulled back. "Hello, Mrs. McKenna. It's nice to see you again."

"Hello, Brody. Thank you. It's nice to see you, too. Everything well? School going alright...?" She let her words trail off. I was shocked she'd even said that much.

"Yes, ma'am, I'm fine. School is great, although I find some of the material boring as it's a repeat from my previous school." Brody rocked back on his heels and gave her a small smile.

Although I loved that my mom liked Brody and was interested in him enough to actually start a conversation, I had to break up the Brody love-fest. "Come on, I want to show you something." I reached for his hand and pulled him toward the stairway.

We were halfway up the stairs when the door leading from the garage into the kitchen slammed open. It hit the wall with a boom before it bounced back and slammed shut. I jumped and swung my head in the direction of the door.

"Willow!" he barked.

"Oh shit," I breathed.

"What's wrong?" Brody asked. When I didn't answer, he pulled my face to him. "What?"

"Janine! Where is she?"

"Ralph, what's wrong?" I heard my mother ask in her soft, comforting voice.

"That little slut daughter of yours, that's what's wrong." He spat the words. So full of venom and hate, I flinched as though they hit me.

I felt Brody stiffen beside me, and my heart sank. I knew what was coming, and I knew Brody couldn't be there for it.

"Hi, Mrs. McKenna," Jaden said.

Jaden? Jaden. What is Jaden doing here?

"Jaden." My mom acknowledged. "I didn't expect to see you hanging around." I could hear the false cheerfulness she forced.

"What the hell is he doing here?" I whispered.

Breathe. Just breathe.

I heard Ralph stumble around. His voice was closer, louder. "She's been dating someone behind Jaden's back. The whore. Where is she?"

"No, no, no." I looked at Brody and shook my head. "I didn't… I didn't…" I shook my head, my mouth opening and shutting as I floundered for something to say. "Brody, I didn't… I love you… I…

no." I still shook my head.

I put my fingers on my temple and pushed so hard it hurt. My mind was whirring, putting the pieces together as quickly as I could. Jaden had gotten to my stepdad, the one person who'd always been in his corner. According to him, Jaden could do no wrong, which is exactly why I'd kept Brody a secret from him and Jaden as long as I could.

"Ralph, calm down," my mom said.

"Please, Brody, please, you have to go," I told him, looking over my shoulder. I tried to push him toward the door. It was like trying to push a wooden bookcase full of books across a carpeted floor. He wasn't moving. "We'll talk later," I whispered. "I promise. Please."

"You're back with Jaden?" Brody looked at me, confusion and hurt in his eyes.

I shook my head no. My mouth opening and closing as I tried to think of someway to explain what was going on, but I needed Brody to leave so I said, "Yes." I nearly choked on the word. Bile rose in my throat and I felt my mouth fill with saliva, the kind a person gets right before they puke. It was sickening to say I was with Jaden, even if it was a lie.

Brody nodded once before looking into my eyes. "Tell me why you're back with him and I'll leave."

"I love him."

"You're lying."

"No. No, I'm not. I love him. Now leave, please." I opened the door to push him out; he stood firmly in place.

I heard footsteps coming down the hallway.

Oh, no!

"Brody," I whispered. "Please leave. You can't be here... we can talk later on the phone and I'll explain everything." I pleaded with my eyes for him to go. "If Ralph sees you... please."

He didn't move.

I panicked and said the first thing that popped into my head. "We can't be together. I'm not in love with you. I never loved you. I love Jaden. I used you to make him jealous." I tried to think of anything hurtful I could say to him that would get him out of the house as fast as I could and keep him away.

Please go, hurry, hurry.

"Willow!"

I jumped, sucked in a sharp breath, and slapped my hand over my mouth to keep quiet. I could feel tears pressing against the back of my eyes.

"Brody, you have to go." I jerked him by the arm toward the door. When he didn't move, I looked at him and yelled, "Go!"

"Who are you yelling at, girl? You best be watching that smart mouth. Get your ass in here. Now!" he shouted.

Oh, he sounds really drunk. Please leave, Brody. Somehow, I hope you know I love you. Always will.

Brody walked slowly out the door. His eyes searched mine. Placing a hand lightly on the side of my face, in a broken voice, he said, "I love you."

It took everything in me, but I made myself jerk away from his touch. "Goodbye, Brody." I was screaming inside. '*No, no, no! I love you.*' I couldn't hear anything over the screams in my head and the blood rushing behind my ears.

The first tear rolled down my cheek just as I shut the door. I laid my forehead against the scarred wood and felt a sob ricochet through my body. It sliced through my insides like a shard of glass. Saying goodbye to Brody, hurting him, was more painful than anything I'd ever felt. It ripped through me more than any punch. It stole my breath worse than any kick, tasted worse than my own blood after getting backhanded. I'd gladly suffer through any of those to take back the hurt I'd seen in Brody's eyes. The hurt I'd put there.

But he had to leave. If he'd seen Brody here, he wouldn't have just hurt me. He would have hurt Brody.

I wasn't worth it. I had to make him stay away.

Breathe. Just breathe. You're strong. Breathe.

TWENTY-ONE
Consequences

"I'm sorry I dragged you into my dark and twisted world. I was hoping you'd be the one to give me strength and help pull me out of it."
~Willow

I SAT IN THE EMERGENCY ROOM, MY ARM CRADLED AGAINST MY CHEST. *I'D* been there three hours, waiting to be called back to see a doctor. Ralph dropped me off with an order to call when I was finished. My mother wanted to come with me, but he refused. Said he hadn't seen her all week and didn't want her to spend time in the emergency room instead of with him. Of course, she acquiesced. *Nice. Thanks, thanks Mom. Makes me feel loved.*

Kids screamed around me. Their piercing wails echoed off the tile floors and bounced against the bare walls. My head pounded. The man to my left vomited into a plastic bucket, and blood dripped on the floor from a dish towel covering the teenaged boy's arm on my right. I tried not to look at either of them.

"Willow Rutherford," a nurse finally yelled.

"I'm here." I got up and followed her to an exam room.

"Why are you here today?" she asked. She was pretty and had kind, chocolate-colored eyes. I tried not to look at her. I didn't want to cry, and she had the kind of face that made me want to cry and tell her all of my secrets.

I'd protected my secret for so long, it was like a vital organ in my body. One I couldn't cut out.

"I fell down the stairs and hit my shoulder against the wall."

She wrote something in her file. "Who's with you?"

"No one." I hated how my breath hitched. I wasn't just alone at the hospital, but I was truly alone. Brody's face flashed in front of my eyes. The hurt look. The questions in his eyes. The love. I swallowed down the lump that formed in my throat and tried to pull myself together. One problem at a time. That was the only way I'd get through this. One problem at a time.

She nodded and jotted something else in her file. "Okay, the doctor will be in shortly. Do you want me to turn the television on for you?"

I looked at the small TV hanging in the corner of the room and shook my head. "No, thank you. I'd rather just lie down."

"Okay, sweetie. Buzz if you need anything." She walked out of the room, pulling the door closed behind her.

I looked around. It looked like any other hospital room. Scuffed white walls, scary-looking machinery, heart monitors, IV poles, and stuff I had no idea what it was. I hated it. Laying back on the gurney, I closed my eyes. I breathed deep, trying to ease the pain in my shoulder.

There was a quick rap on the door and a tall, white-haired man walked in. "Ms. Rutherford?"

"Yes?"

"I'm Doctor Sebastian. What brings you here?"

I sighed. I already answered this. "I fell down the stairs and hit my shoulder against the wall."

"Can you move your arm?"

"No."

"We're going to take some x-rays and see what's going on in there."

"Okay, thank you."

Minutes later, a guy that didn't look much older than me pushed a huge piece of machinery into the room. "Rutherford?"

"Yes."

"I'm from X-ray."

He took several shots from different angles. It hurt like hell, and I cried out several times. "I'm sorry," I said, biting my lip.

"It's okay. I'm sorry I have to bend it around. I know it hurts, but I'm almost done."

When he finished, he told me the doctor would be in shortly to discuss the results with me. I waited an hour for the doctor. I sat on the gurney with my eyes closed, trying to focus on something other than where I was and what had happened to put me there. But all I could see were Brody's blue eyes and the hurt in them.

My forehead leaned against the door Brody had just walked out. Tears and flashes of the pain in his eyes were all I could see. I felt like I cut a piece of me out when I hurt him. And I knew I hurt him. I could feel the pain radiate from his body.

He grabbed a handful of hair and jerked me backward. I couldn't hold in my small scream, and he smirked. Next to hitting me, his favorite thing was hearing me cry and scream.

"What the hell were you doing? Cheating on Jaden with some punk. Who do you think you are?" A punch to the side punctuated his question, and the air whooshed out of my lungs. Ralph let go of my hair, and I dropped to my hands and knees. I saw Jaden leaning against the wall at the end of the hall. He smirked at me.

I grabbed the staircase banister and pulled myself up, only to be on the receiving end of another of Ralph's fists.

"You know the only reason someone like Jaden even looks at you is because I'm friends with his family. He'd never waste his time on white trash like you if it weren't for me." He wrapped his hand around my upper arm and squeezed so hard I knew there'd be bruises the next day.

He pulled me to face Jaden. "Jaden has graciously agreed to take you back." He looked at Jaden. His voice softened and he even grinned at him. Grinned. It was sickening, and it made me hate them even more. "Am I right, son?"

"Yes, sir. There will be rules, of course."

"Definitely. Willow needs rules and punishment to keep her in line. She seems unable to make good decisions otherwise." Ralph slapped Jaden on the back like they were old buddies. "Good, good, I'm glad we've got this worked out. Let's go have dinner. I'm starving."

Ralph shoved me toward the dining room. My arm and shoulder hit the doorframe hard, and I felt a pop followed by a searing pain.

I couldn't use my arm throughout dinner, and when I tried to move it, the pain was so intense that bile rose in my throat and I was sure I'd either throw up or pass out from the pain. I squeezed my eyes closed and tried to think of anything other than the agony sawing through my body.

"Willow? Open your eyes," my mom asked when dinner was over, but I hadn't moved from my chair. When I didn't, she knelt in front of me and realized my breathing was ragged and a fine sheen of sweat covered my face. She turned and called to Ralph, who'd already plopped down in his recliner and commandeered the remote. "Ralph! Ralph, I think she needs a doctor!" She silently looked in my eyes and cupped the side of my face before helping me out of the chair.

"Oh, for shit's sake. Anything to make my life more difficult. Let's go." Grabbing his keys, he walked out the door. He didn't look back to see if I needed help.

Jaden stood in the same place he had when the spectacle began. When my mother and I walked by, he twiddled his fingers at me and smiled. "See you at school, Willow."

If I'd been able, I would've kicked him in the crotch so hard he'd have to pee through his nose for the rest of his life.

I jumped when the door opened and Dr. Sebastian, a tall, dark-skinned man wearing a white coat and looking at a computer tablet, walked in. "Ms. Rutherford?"

I looked up. "Hi." I tried to smile. I didn't think I managed it.

"I've reviewed your x-rays and the good news is nothing is broken. The bad news is your shoulder is dislocated."

"Oh. What happens next?" My teeth chattered, and I wasn't sure why. The exam room was warm, and the nurse had given me a heated blanket.

"Well, we need to set your shoulder, then we'll take another x-ray to make sure everything looks okay, and then you can go home."

Two nurses entered the room and the doctor took hold of my arm. I couldn't really say what happened next. All I knew was it was the worst pain I'd ever felt in my life. I tried not to, but I screamed. A lot. And loudly. Then it was over.

"You did good, honey," the pretty nurse told me. "Listen, Willow, is it okay if I call you Willow?" I nodded, and she smiled. "Are you sure there isn't something you'd like to tell me about what happened?"

"No. I fell down the stairs." I was getting good at lying. Once I decided what my story was, I almost believed it myself.

She patted my leg and smiled. "X-ray is here." She left, and the same guy rolled the x-ray machine into the room.

He asked me how I'd hurt myself while he took the x-rays. I repeated my story to him.

A few minutes after X-ray left, an older woman who wore too much perfume and was wearing a blue suit that didn't quite fit came into my room with my nurse.

"Hi, Willow. I'm Joyce. I'm a case manager for the hospital."

"Okay," I said slowly.

"I just want to make sure we understand exactly what happened to you today. Can you tell me in your own words what led up to your accident?"

No, but I can lie to you.

"I was rushing down the stairs to answer the door. My foot missed a step. I fell down them and hit my shoulder against the wall at the bottom of the stairs."

"Are you sure?"

"Yes, ma'am."

"Who's with you today?"

"No one."

"How are you getting home?"

"My stepdad said to call him when I was finished and he'd pick me up," I whispered.

All through our conversation, Joyce wrote in her file. When she'd finished with her notes, she looked at me. "If something else happened, you can tell me. Anything you say in here is strictly confidential."

I shook my head and bit a hangnail on my finger. "Nothing else happened," I lied.

"Okay. The nurse will get your discharge papers ready."

"Thank you," I said, my gaze locked on the floor.

An hour later, I was in the car with my mom riding home. My arm was in a sling to allow the tendons and crap time to heal. I didn't know. I didn't really listen. They gave me something for pain, my discharge papers, and told me to see my regular doctor in a week. I wouldn't.

My mom let me stay home from school Monday, partly because my shoulder still hurt and the pain pills made me sick, and partly because I think she felt guilty.

She should have stopped it. She should have done something, anything, except what she did. She just stood there and did nothing, because if she did something, he might expose her secret. Tell what she did. And then people would know she was something so much worse than white trash who snagged the most sought after bachelor in Middleton.

Tuesday was my first day back at school. The first day I'd see Brody since telling him I didn't love him. I dreaded going into biology. I tried to rearrange my schedule so I could avoid him—seeing him every day was going to be torture—but there was only one AP biology class, so I was stuck.

Brody wasn't there when I walked into class. Jenna carried my books for me. She laid my bag on the table in front of my chair and gave me a quick kiss on the cheek. "I'll see you in history. If you need anything, text me. I don't care what it is, Willow. Text me. I mean it."

Nodding, I sat down. I didn't look at anyone, and I didn't speak. I just sat staring straight ahead at the whiteboard, waiting for the teacher to start his mind-numbing lecture. Steeling myself for Brody's arrival.

Someone slipped into the chair next to me, and I stiffened. I let out the breath I was holding when he spoke. "Hey, chickie. How ya doin'?" Tim asked, giving me a kiss on the cheek.

I shrugged a shoulder—my good one. Tears pressed behind my eyes. I knew if I said anything, I'd start to cry. Again. So I didn't say anything, and Tim was okay with that.

"Um, we switched seats. I thought it might be easier for you," Tim murmured. I nodded again and looked away. "I'm only gonna say this once because I know you won't want us to keep bringing it up, but I'm really sorry. You got a shit deal, Willow. I know you love Brody. I don't know what happened with Jaden, but I know this isn't what you want." He looked at my arm. "It isn't what any of us want."

I didn't say anything. The single tear that ran down my cheek said everything for me. I swiped it away before anyone other than Tim saw. He rubbed his hand up and down my back before he got my book out of my bag for me.

I couldn't concentrate during class. All I did was wonder if Brody was sitting in Tim's old seat—two rows behind me and the table to the right. I wanted to turn and look. I didn't.

After class, Tim helped me gather my things and put them in my bag. He swung the strap over his shoulder. "I got a pass from the office excusing me for being late to my classes so I can carry your things to each of your classes until you get the sling off your arm next week."

That's something Jaden should be doing. But, no. It's not about him. Thank God for Tim and Jenna.

"Thanks." It was the first word I'd said since walking into the building with Jenna that morning.

Tim and I walked silently to my English class. I hesitated outside the door. Tim waited quietly beside me. The warning bell sounded, and I knew I had to go inside, but I couldn't get my feet to move. I could feel the panic welling up inside me like a tumor growing. It was suffocating me. I couldn't take a breath. Blood rushed behind my ears and I felt sweat slither down my spine, causing my shirt to stick to my skin. My whole body began to shake and my teeth chattered like I was standing outside in the middle of winter, but the school was warm.

I can't do this.

Images of Brody played in front of my eyes. The night at his Aunt Bess's bar when we played pool and I made him think I'd never played before. The night in the tent, laying under the twinkle lights. How he looked as he leaned down to kiss me for the first time. His crooked grin, sapphire eyes… the images ran like a slide show in front of my eyes, faster and faster until I was dizzy. I reached out and steadied myself against the wall.

"Hey, are you sure you're up to this?" Tim put his arm around my waist, and I leaned into him.

Then the tears started. I couldn't get them to stop. They just kept coming, one after another after another until I thought I'd drown in them. I buried my head in Tim's shoulder and cried silently, trying not to draw attention to myself. I had enough attention without everyone seeing me have a mental break in front of my second-period English class.

"Let's go. We're outta here," Tim said, pulling me gently away from the door.

I shook my head and wiped the tears off my face. "I can do it," I whispered. I raised my head from Tim's shoulder. That was when I saw him. He was standing about five feet away, staring at me. His jaw set in hard lines. It was the first time I'd seen him since he left my house. Since I told him I didn't love him. I opened my mouth to say something, shaking my head slightly. There was so much I needed to tell him, but his face was closed off, and I knew I'd ruined everything I had with Brody. I looked at him once more, pleading with my eyes for him to give me some sign that he understood. When he just stared at me, his jaw clenching and unclenching, I dropped my gaze to the floor, turned, and walked into class.

I wished Tim had English with me so he could switch seats with Brody again. But, in the end, I didn't need to worry. Brody found someone else to switch with. I didn't know where he sat. I forced myself not to look. I just knew he wasn't near me. It should have made things easier, but for some reason, it didn't. It made everything worse. I didn't understand why, and I didn't have the energy to try to figure it out.

The rest of the day continued much the same way. Tim met me at each class and gathered my things for me, carrying them to my next class. In each, Brody had found another seat.

At lunch, I sat with Jaden and his group of friends. I didn't eat—I lived on high-caffeine energy drinks and nothing else—and I didn't go to Jenna and Tim's table to say 'hi' like I used to. I was afraid Brody would be there. Instead, I stared straight ahead, not speaking unless someone spoke to me. Jaden was oblivious.

When the day was finally over and Jenna dropped me off at home, I went to my room and lay on my bed, staring at the ceiling.

I didn't go down for dinner. I never left my room. No one noticed, or no one cared. Either way, they left me alone and that was how I preferred it.

My phone chimed around nine o'clock. I sighed and read the message.

JENNA: HOW'D IT GO?
ME: DON'T REALLY WANT TO TALK ABOUT IT.
JENNA: OK. I'M HERE WHEN YOU DO.
ME: THANKS.
JENNA: LOVE YOU.
ME: LOVE YOU TOO.

I must have fallen asleep right after Jenna's text, because when my alarm sounded the next morning, I was still lying on top of my blankets, wearing the clothes I wore to school the day before, my cell phone gripped in my hand.

I pulled myself out of bed and got ready for school.

The day was a repeat of the day before. And the next day and the day after that and the day after that, they all blended together. I went through the motions without paying attention. The only thing that changed was that I cried less. People who learned to close off their emotions were good at that, and I was becoming an expert.

I just tried to survive. I only had to make it to graduation. Just a few more months and it'd be over.

Breathe. I can do it. It can't get any worse. Just breathe.

TWENTY-TWO
Kara

"The worst feeling isn't being lonely. It's being forgotten by someone you'll never forget."
~Willow

T'D BEEN TWO WEEKS. I WAS ONCE AGAIN JADEN'S PRISONER. HE KNEW everywhere I went, who I was with, when I'd be there, and when I'd be home. He cut me off from Jenna and Tim at school and he spent most evenings at my house, making it impossible for them to visit me. I didn't care. I couldn't be with Brody. Nothing else mattered.

It was one of the rare nights that Jaden wasn't over. There was a party at Jamieson's house. I conveniently let it slip to my mother that there'd probably be drinking since Jamieson's parents weren't going to be home. That got me off the hook. She told Jaden I wouldn't be going to the party with him. For once, she stood up for me.

I called Jenna and asked if she could come over. She was there in five minutes. She had me in a huge hug in six. I was crying in seven.

"You look terrible," she whispered against my hair.

"Thanks. You look like a supermodel, too." I sniffed and wiped the tears from my cheeks.

"You've lost so much weight. Your clothes just hang off you like you're a hobo or something."

"Gee, thanks for the pep talk," I said with a small smile.

"Do you eat? Or do you live on these?" She picked up an empty energy drink can.

I shrugged. "This has been the best diet ever."

We talked for an hour. She filled me in on everything going

around the gossip hotline at school. Who was hooking up, who was breaking up, who was pregnant, who'd come out of the closet. She didn't tell me anything that'd been said about Brody and me. In fact, she didn't bring Brody up at all.

We ordered a pizza, and she force-fed me. I choked down a piece and a half before I started gagging.

"I don't want anymore." I pushed my plate away. "Wanna watch a movie with me?"

"Sure."

We put a comedy in the DVD player and settled on the bed. I lay my head on her lap. She combed her fingers through my hair. The movie was half over when my phone chimed. I forced myself up and grabbed it.

JADEN: WHAT ARE YOU DOING?

ME: WATCHING A MOVIE WITH JENNA.

JADEN: WHERE?

ME: HOME.

JADEN: FINE.

I tossed the phone across the room and buried my head in my pillows.

"He's worse than ever, huh?" Jenna murmured.

"Yeah."

"Hey, let's find a really snotty shirt for you to wear tomorrow. One that he won't understand. That shouldn't be too hard, huh?" She climbed of the bed, opened my closet door, and froze. "Oh, Willow."

I started crying. Again. Always crying. I was getting on my own freakin' nerves.

"You better not let Jaden see these," she whispered. She looked at each of the photos of Brody and me that covered the inside of my closet door. "You look so happy." Tears filled her eyes. "I'm so sorry, Willow."

I shrugged. "It is what it is."

"Look, I don't know if I should tell you this or not, but I think it's probably better to hear it from me than get blindsided." Jenna picked at the nail polish on her thumb. "Um, Kara asked Brody to the girl's choice dance Friday and he said yes."

I sucked in a breath. Pain ricocheted through me. It was like Jenna had hit me. My head started to pound, and the room spun around me. I bent forward and leaned my head on my knees. I didn't even try to hold back my tears. A half sob/half scream tore through me, leaving an open wound behind.

Jenna rushed over and knelt next to me. She wrapped her arms around me and rocked me back and forth like a mother would a small child. "I'm so, so sorry," she repeated over and over.

"I knew it would happen," I said through my sobs, "but it hurts so bad. It hurts so damn bad."

Friday. The girl's choice dance was that night. I was in constant pain, physical and emotional, from the knowledge that Brody was going with Kara. Was what we had that easy to forget? It was that easy to walk out of my life and into hers?

I decided it didn't matter. It was better that he move on with his life. Better for him, better for me. It didn't make it hurt any less, however.

I took Jenna's advice and decided to find a suitable T-shirt to wear to school. It needed to be long sleeved to hide my fresh bruises. I moved shirts across my closet rod, looking for the perfect one. When I found it, it was short sleeved. I'd have to wear a hoodie to cover my arms. I reached for a hoodie that would match, but my hand stopped just before touching it.

"Screw that. I'm not hiding anymore." I yanked the short-sleeved T-shirt off the hanger and pulled it on. Let everyone see the bruising—I didn't care anymore.

The saying on my T-shirt was perfect, although I'd probably get sent home for wearing something that had a curse word on it. It said, *Excuse me, which level of Hell is this?* I decided it was worth it. I looked in the mirror and paused, my hand skimming down the fabric. It was red.

Did I pick it because it's Brody's favorite color? Or is just coincidence?

I wore black sweatpants and my red Converse high tops—I

figured it'd be one day Jenna would give me a free pass and not lecture me on my wardrobe choices. I pulled my hair into a messy bun and put a little makeup on to hide the circles under my eyes.

I looked in the mirror one last time. Jenna was right. I had lost weight. My clothes looked a size too big for me.

Best. Diet. Ever.

I sat in the foyer, looking out the window, waiting for Jenna to pick me up. As soon as she pulled in the driveway, I hurried to her car.

"Let's get this day over with," I muttered.

We pulled into the student parking lot. Jenna parked and was out of her car before I could say anything. I just sat and stared.

"What's wrong?" she asked, opening my door. She followed my gaze. "Oh, shit, Willow. I didn't see them."

I shrugged a shoulder and climbed out of the car, still watching Brody and Kara walk across the parking lot. He'd given her a ride to school. I'd seen him open the door for her to get out of his Jeep, like he'd done for me so many times.

When I walked into school, I felt every eye on me. People parted in the hall as I walked through. I don't know if they pitied me or just wanted to see my reaction. I kept my head high and just tried to make it to my locker.

"Oh, no."

"What?" I looked at Jenna. She nodded her head toward our lockers. Jaden stood with his shoulder leaning against mine.

"Hey, Wills," he said.

"Don't call me that."

Jenna helped my get my coat off and sucked in a breath when she saw my arms. She didn't say anything as she grabbed my books from the locker, hefting my bag over her shoulder. I thought again how Jaden should be doing that. He was supposed to be my boyfriend. Wasn't that what boyfriends did?

"Still got the sling, huh?" he asked.

"I'm wearing it, aren't I?" I snapped.

"Watch the attitude. Nice shirt. See ya at lunch." He sauntered off.

"I told you he wouldn't get it." Jenna pointed at my shirt.

"He doesn't pay enough attention to get it."

Jenna laughed, but there was no humor in it. "Yeah, he's a real douche."

Nodding, I followed her into my biology class. I forced myself not to look for Brody. I just walked to my seat and sat down, laying my head on my books. At least I didn't share any classes with Kara. I wouldn't have to see the two lovebirds together.

Wrong.

Everywhere I went Friday, I saw Brody. And each time, Kara was with him. And to really make things horrible, like they weren't already, they were holding hands.

My body shook when I saw him with her. It was a cross between blinding anger and searing pain. My stomach roiled, and I was sure I would have puked if there had been anything in it, but I couldn't remember the last time I'd eaten.

I snuck one of my mom's prescription sleeping pills that night. I took it right after dinner and went to bed. It saved me from a night of sitting in my room, wondering what Brody and Kara were doing at the dance. If he pulled her close during the slow songs. Did he kiss her? My mind whirled with thoughts of them until I thought I'd go crazy. After I took the pill, sleep sucked me in and took away all thoughts of Brody, Kara, and the girl's choice dance.

Saturday, Jaden and I went to a movie and The Dive for dinner afterward. As soon as I walked in, I knew he was there. I hadn't seen him. It was as if my mind and body were still connected to him. They sensed him. I had Brody radar.

Jaden walked to the back of the restaurant where he always sat. I followed behind him, keeping my gaze locked firmly on the floor. I knew the second I passed the table where Brody sat. I could smell his subtle scent. And then I smelled something else. Something flowery and feminine... and I knew he wasn't alone. Tears pressed behind my eyes, and I tried to swallow down the lump that'd lodged itself in my throat. One lone tear escaped, and trailing down my cheek and dripping from my chin before I could catch it.

Are they freakin' everywhere?

When Jaden and I sat at our table, I made sure to sit with my back to the rest of the room. I didn't want to look up and see Brody with her. It was bad enough knowing they were there. I didn't need to watch them too.

Jaden and I ate our burgers—with freakin' mayo. We barely said two words to each other. I didn't know why he insisted on staying together. It was obvious we didn't love each other. We barely tolerated one another. But he wouldn't let go.

When he finished his meal, he wandered from table to table, talking and joking with his buddies. As usual for a Saturday night, The Dive was packed wall to wall with people from school. I sat in the booth, waiting for him to get tired and decide to take me home. I played with my leftover French fries, running them through the puddle of ketchup and using it to make designs across my plate.

We'd been there an hour when I got up to use the restroom. I walked by Jaden and his hand snaked out and grabbed my wrist, yanking me back to him. I let out a small yelp when he jarred my shoulder.

"Where are you going?"

"I have to use the bathroom. Is that okay with you or would you rather I pee myself in the middle of the restaurant?"

He dropped my wrist and turned his back to me. I let out a breath through my teeth, biting my lower lip to keep from saying something stupid.

I walked into the restroom and froze. My mind screamed at me to turn around and leave, but my feet wouldn't work. It was as if they were made of lead. I couldn't lift them. She saw me in the mirror.

"Hi, Willow." She gave me a small smile.

"Kara."

"This is kind of awkward," she said with a nervous laugh.

I just smiled.

Why should it be awkward? Just because you're dating the one person I love more than anything? Nah, not awkward at all. Twit.

"Well, I better get back…" She let her words trail off and gestured toward the door.

I moved away from the door. "Yeah, your date is probably

waiting for you," I said with an edge.

"I'll see you around," she said before she hurried out of the room.

I hope not.

It was two weeks later when I came face to face with Brody in independent study. It was the first time we'd come in close contact since the morning outside English class. We just stared at each other. Neither of us seemed to know what to say or do.

"Hey," Brody finally said.

"Hi, Ace."

There was another long, awkward pause.

"Well, I need to get back to work." He gestured to his things strewn across a table.

"Sure."

He started to walk away, and I panicked. I just wanted another few seconds with him. I needed it, even if it was filled with so much tension it was suffocating.

"Brody?"

He stopped with his back to me.

"I'm glad you found someone who makes you happy," I whispered behind him. I wanted to touch him so badly. Reaching out, I let the tips of my fingers graze his shoulder. He tensed, but he didn't pull away. I fisted my hand, and it dropped to my side.

I sighed. "Um, there's something I need to tell you." I paused, hoping he'd react, show some interest. Anything. He didn't. He kept his back to me.

I licked my lips and pushed a piece of hair behind my ear. "I don't know if you remember, but not long after we met, you told me reputations aren't always deserved. Well, I need you to know that sometimes things aren't always what they seem. Um... some... something can look like something else. Sometimes people do or say things they have to, to protect the person they love most in the world. They become great chameleons. It's the only way they can survive. It's how they protect themselves and the one person they love more than themselves. The one person they'd never hurt—if we lived in a perfect world."

I gave a bitter laugh and ran my tongue over my lips. "I'm babbling. I just, well, I hope one day you'll understand what's happened and why I did what I did." I swallowed back my tears. Giving up, I touched his arm. He didn't move away, but he didn't acknowledge it either. "When we were together, I meant every word I ever said to you, Brody. Every word. And when I broke it off, I didn't mean any of them. Not a damn one."

I waited for him to acknowledge me. Other than seeing his jaw working, he did nothing. Said nothing.

"I don't love Jaden. I never have. It's you. It was always you. I'm just sorry our relationship wasn't strong enough for you to see through the lie and believe in what we had—or what I thought we had."

I took in a big breath and let it out slowly before I said, "And I'm sorry I wasn't strong enough to stand up and fight for us. I let them break me. Goodbye, Brody. Be happy." I hurried away. I knew it would be the last time I'd speak to him. As soon as I reached the hall, I ran to the girls' restroom and threw up.

TWENTY-THREE
Time

"Time is the school in which we learn, time is the fire in which we burn."
~*Delmore Schwartz*

*J*ANUARY.
A new year, same bullshit. Brody and Kara were still a couple. And I still felt like someone shoved a knife in my chest every time I saw Brody with her, laughing, holding hands, kissing. It was torture.

I was still imprisoned by Jaden and his rules. And Ralph, Jaden's watchdog. Jaden was as inattentive to me as always. If anything, it got steadily worse. He went about his day like I was a burden, an albatross he carried. I couldn't understand what his reason was to keep me around.

Jaden's New Year's resolution was to stop hiding his extracurricular activities and flaunt his many hookups in front of me… and the entire student body of Cassidy High.

"If you're not going to give it up, I'm going to find someone who will," he'd told me when I confronted him.

I didn't bring it up again. Five months until graduation. I could make it.

FEBRUARY

"I hate Valentine's Day. It is a day for nothing but disappointment."
~*Larisa Oleynik*

The month of love and all that crap. It made me want to vomit. Whoever said time heals all wounds didn't know what the hell they were talking about. It still felt like the breath was sucked out of my lungs every time I saw Brody.

I just wanted to talk to him one more time. Touch him. Feel him touch me. I needed to tell him I loved him. He'd never listen and I didn't blame him.

The month of love. Yeah. Blah, blah and frickin' blah.

MARCH

Three months until graduation. Things were the same. Brody was still dating Kara, and Jaden and I were… whatever we were. I didn't even know anymore. He barely tolerated me. He hooked up with some skank whenever he got the chance. Once again, I wondered why he didn't just let me go. I thought he got off on making my life miserable.

Chess club was coming to an end. The regional tournament was held at Cassidy High on the last Saturday of the month.

"Are you ready for this, chickie?" Tim asked.

"Yeah. It should be cake."

"Good luck."

"You, too," I said.

I shook hands with my opponent and sat down in front of the board. My eyes traveled over the squares as I mentally prepared my strategy. The buzzer sounded, and the game began. The girl I played made her first move. I knew exactly what her strategy was as soon as she placed her first piece. I scanned the board, working out my next three plays. I'd have her in checkmate in five moves.

It took seven moves, but I won the game. I moved up in the rankings. Everyone from Cassidy won their game. We were in first place going into the second round.

My second game took longer to win. He was a good player, but made a stupid mistake that cost him the game. Once again, everyone from Cassidy won their game.

By the third game, I was really in my zone. I ignored the other games around me, blocking out the sound of the pieces hitting the board and the clicks of the timers. The game was over quickly. That round two of our players were eliminated. We were still in first place.

By the sixth and final game, Cassidy was still ranked number one. I won my game and walked to the table where the PTO had laid out snacks and drinks for the players. I grabbed an energy drink and turned to watch the games still being played. Movement in the bleachers caught my eye, and I looked up just in time to see Brody slip out the side door on the other side of the gym.

My heart skipped a beat, and then another. I was out the door before I had time to think. I ran down the hall and around the corner, but the hall was empty.

Maybe it was someone else. He wouldn't come to my chess tournament. It's not like it's a big deal. There are barely a handful of people here to watch. It wasn't him.

I shook my head and went back in the gym to wait for the games to end. Cassidy won the regional championship and went on to win state.

Jaden never came to the tournaments or even asked about them.

APRIL

The first day of the month, Brody's birthday. Yeah, that day totally sucked. I tried to hold back my tears, but more than a few leaked out. The pain of losing him tore through me, slicing my heart along the way. Almost like it was happening for the first time. I knew I should ignore his birthday. He didn't want anything from me, and why would he?

But I couldn't ignore it. I bought a birthday card, not too mushy, but with a short poem that talked of love and friendship.

I kept what I wrote simple:

"I miss us. Happy Birthday, Willow."

"Write something more, Willow. This is your chance to really say something." Jenna slid the card across the table to me.

"Like what? Please come back to me. I lied to you, but I still love you?"

"Well, no. We'll think of something great," she said.

"No. This is fine. I don't want to garf it up with a bunch romantic crap and fluffy apologies." I put the card in the envelope and closed it with the envelope seal that came with it. "There. Done."

"Do you want me or Tim to give it to him? We see him at lunch. He always has that growth attached to him, though. I mean, Kara is nice and all, but she is so ditzy. I can't believe he went from you to her. Talk about dating down, and down, and down, and down the dating scale."

I had to smile. Jenna usually found a way to make me smile. "No, I'm going to slip it in his locker. But thanks."

I slipped the card in the vent of his locker. I wanted to do more, so much more, but I settled for the card. If he actually read it and didn't toss it in the trash, it'd be a miracle.

April was also the start of baseball and softball season. I played softball on the varsity softball team. I was surprised to learn Brody tried out and made the cut for the varsity baseball team. I went to every one of his home games. I'd show up late and sit on the ground next to the bleachers where he couldn't see me, and I'd leave early. If he knew I was there, he never gave any indication.

He was a good player, strong and fast. Watching him, seeing his muscles flex as he hit the ball or ran the bases, was torture. The sight of him still warmed places in me only he could touch.

I never saw Kara at his games and wondered if they were still dating. I asked Luce. If anyone knew, it would be her.

"Nope. He's a free agent," Luce told me.

"Did he break up with her or did she break up with him?"

She looked at me for what seemed like minutes before asking, "Does it matter?"

"No, I guess not. Thanks, Luce."

"Anytime."

Brody is single. Would I stand a chance if I could get away from

Jaden?

My heart did a funny dance inside my chest. I had to remind myself that it didn't matter. He didn't want me, and I shouldn't want him.

It was the middle of April. My mom, Ralph, and I were having dinner and I mentioned that Jaden and I weren't a happy couple. That he'd been hooking up with other girls, and he didn't bother hiding it. And maybe it was time we went our separate ways.

I don't remember much after that, other than the blinding pain of the first punch that sent me flying out of my chair. Then Ralph was on top of me, slamming my head against the floor over and over and over.

I woke up alone in the hospital the next afternoon with a concussion, three broken ribs, and a punctured lung.

Within an hour of my regaining consciousness, the same case manager from the day my shoulder was dislocated came into my room. She asked me what happened, and for once, I didn't have to lie. I couldn't remember.

After the case manager left, I sat on the side of my hospital bed, looking out the window. It was raining and I stared at the fat raindrops as they hit the window, trying to forget where I was. The world seemed to slow, the raindrops pulling me away from my life. Just away.

I closed my eyes and tried to hold onto that feeling, but the smell of illness and antiseptic filled my nose, the constant beeping of machines in other rooms made my head pound, and the tubes hooked in my arms kept getting in my way. And I was pushed from my solitary world back into the hospital and the life that put me there. I just wanted to run away screaming.

I'd been there three days. My mother visited once. Ralph didn't come at all. I didn't really expect him to. Jaden was there nearly every hour. It'd been torture. Visiting hours were over in a little less than an hour. Jaden had just left.

I knew he was in the room before he spoke. I didn't turn around.

"I always knew he'd put you in the hospital one day," Brody said quietly.

I squeezed my eyes closed and bit my bottom lip to keep it from quivering. I nodded. When I thought I could answer without breaking down in tears, I said, "You called it, Ace." My voice trembled.

"Are you okay?"

I took in a breath to keep the tears away, hoping Brody didn't hear the shudder in it. "Never better." A knot formed in my stomach, traveled up my throat, and lodged there. It felt like someone was strangling me from the inside. My hands fisted in the bed sheets so hard my fingernails bent against my palms.

"Glad to hear it." I listened as he walked out of the room.

A sob ripped from my chest and I fell to the floor, pulling my IV from my arm. Blood and IV solution dripped on the floor and monitors blared. My nurse rushed into my room to find me lying on the cold tile floor, sobbing, holding my chest above my heart. It physically hurt. Could a heart really break? It felt as though mine had shattered.

"Honey, what happened? Are you okay?" she asked, kneeling beside me.

"No," I whispered.

The best thing in my life had just walked away from me. No, that wasn't true. I pushed him away. The one person I didn't want to live without—couldn't live without. I just pushed him out of my life like he meant nothing. Again.

Life was a vindictive bitch.

May

The first, my birthday. Jaden forgot. I don't know why I was surprised.

Jenna and Tim surprised me with a gift certificate for a spa day. I so needed that. A lavender footbath sounded like Heaven. Jenna and I made an appointment to go that Saturday.

"I want to get my feet babied, baby." I smiled at them. "Thanks, guys. This is perfect."

But the best gift came from someone who didn't leave their name. It was taped to my locker when I got to school that morning. A white chocolate and almond candy bar.

"Brody," I whispered.

And my heart soared.

Twenty-Four
Enough

> "Out of suffering have emerged the strongest souls; the most
> massive characters are seared with scars."
> ~*Khalil Gibran.*

I WAS DONE WITH JADEN'S CRAP. *IT WAS OVER, WHETHER HE WANTED TO* admit it or not. I didn't bother telling him. I just wore a new T-shirt I had made. It was the one time Jenna was excited to go with me to get one of my horrible—her word—T-shirts. She even paid for it.

I walked into school and to my locker like any other morning. Jaden was waiting for me, his back against the locker door.

"Hey, Wills."

"For the last damn time, don't call me that!" I shouted.

"Whoa, watch how you talk to me. What's up your butt anyway?"

"Nothing. Move. You're blocking my locker."

Jaden stepped aside. I opened my locker, got the books I needed, and threw in those I didn't. Slamming the door shut, I walked away. Jaden caught up with me and grabbed my arm. My books scattered across the floor. Everyone around us stopped and stared.

Tim knelt to help me pick up my books. Jaden kicked them across the hall. "She can do it herself," he said through clenched teeth.

Tim ignored him and picked up my things anyway. He carried them into class for me. I followed close behind him. I prayed the teacher was already in the classroom because Jaden followed me. He'd seen my shirt.

"Willow!" he bellowed.

I walked through the door into biology, and my heart sank. No teacher. Jaden came up behind me and jerked me around to face him. His fingers dug into my flesh, and I fought the urge to flinch away.

"What the hell is that?" He pointed at my shirt. Everyone in the room was silent as they watched the show.

"It's called a shirt, Jaden."

"I know it's a shirt. I meant what it says, *"Yes, I'm single. You're gonna have to be awesome to change that."* What does that mean?" He poked me in the chest.

"Just what it says. We're done. Through. Over. I'm single. You're single. Go hookup with Sarah or whoever your flavor of the week is. I'm finished with you."

He grabbed me by the collar and jerked me to him. His face was just inches from mine. I could feel his hot breath on me when he spoke. It made my skin crawl, like dozens of ants were swarming my skin.

"Remember the little secret I know? You wouldn't want the police to find out what your dear mommy did, now would you? We're through when I say we are." His face was red, and a vein bulged in his neck. Spittle formed in the corners of his mouth. "I wish you'd learn that little fact. It'd make life easier for both of us."

"Jaden, wish in one hand and shit in the other… see which one fills up faster. I said we're done. I wish *you'd* learn that little fact. It'd make this so much easier."

He jerked me closer. His hand fisted on the collar of my shirt. He raised his other hand, and I fought the urge to cringe. Realizing where we were, he let his arm fall to his side.

"We aren't done, Willow," he said through clenched teeth.

I kneed him in the crotch and pushed him away from me. "I say differently."

I was lying in bed that evening, staring at the wall, when my phone chimed. I rolled over and looked at the clock. Eleven-thirty. I picked up my phone, pushed the button to read the text, and my heart jumped into my throat. My head pounded in rhythm with my heartbeat, which was racing.

BRODY: YOU ENDED IT WITH HIM?
ME: YES. FOR GOOD THIS TIME.
BRODY: GOOD FOR YOU.
ME: THANKS.
BRODY: NIGHT, WILLOW.
ME: GOODNIGHT, ACE.

I knew it was a probably just a meaningless text. He didn't say anything in it to give me any indication that he wanted to see me or even have any type of relationship. But, still, the butterflies in my stomach gave me hope that maybe, just maybe, it was a sign that he'd let me explain everything. That he'd let me back in.

We might not ever have what we shared before, but I needed to tell him the truth. I needed to tell him I still loved him. Would always love him. It was him. Would always be him. No one else. Brody Victor showed me what true love was and in doing so, he ruined me. No other man would ever live up to the standard he set. I might find love again, but there would always be a piece of me left hollow—a piece that only Brody could fill.

Only he could make me whole.

"You little bitch," he roared. He knocked me to the ground and kicked me in the stomach. I pulled my knees up to my chest, covered my head with my arms, and waited for the next hit.

That was only the first one. There were always more.

Ralph grabbed my arm and yanked me off the floor. The attack caught me by surprise. He was supposed to be traveling.

He pushed me hard against the wall before backhanding me. I felt blood gush inside my mouth. The metallic taste made me gag as it slid down my throat.

"What do you have to say? Huh? Anything?" he yelled, and I winced.

"Yeah," I rasped.

"Willow! Just be quiet!" my mom cried from where she sat on the stairs.

"Shut up, Mom. Help me!" I yelled as loud as my voice would

allow. She looked away. "You're the reason I'm here. You did this. If you hadn't walked away that night." I turned back to Ralph. "I do have something to say, asshole." I spit blood and saliva in his face.

I knew I was asking for more abuse. If I'd just kept my mouth shut and let him have his temper tantrum, I would've been better off, but the urge to fight back was growing inside me, pushing out my weakness, my fear.

He wiped his face with his shirtsleeve. His other hand darted out and grabbed me around the neck. "Don't ever do something like that again or you will pay. And the price will be high, dear, sweet Willow," he whispered, staring in my eyes.

He squeezed my throat so tight I couldn't draw in a breath. I clawed at his hand. My nails left red scratches on his skin. Stars flickered in front of my eyes, and the room started to spin. I reached out and jammed my thumb into one of his eyes. He howled and dropped his hand. I fell to my hands and knees, gasping for air, and crawled toward the front door.

Ralph yanked me up by my hair. Holding me in place, he punched me. Pain sizzled across my jaw.

"You call us white trash. But you're nothing more than a con artist. Marrying for money and then hitting her around a little."

Another quick hit to my face split my lip. "Shut up, you little—"

"Little what? That's the problem, isn't it? You wanted her money because you were broke; you even wanted her... but me? Nah." I could feel warm blood drip off my chin.

A third hit. I could see blood drip from the corner of my eye. I could feel it swelling shut. I started feeling woozy, and it was hard to keep my thoughts straight.

"Yeah, a kid wasn't in my plans. You're a nuisance I don't need."

Another hit and another. I tried to block the blows, but I was too weak. His fists pushed past my arms, hitting me again and again—the face, the stomach, anywhere he could reach.

I hit back, something I'd never done before. It surprised him and took some of the force out of his hits. When I had a good shot, I kicked him between the legs, hard and fast.

Ralph pushed me away from him before he fell to his knees,

holding his crotch. A colorful string of cuss words spewed from his mouth. His face turned different shades of reds and purples that I would have found funny under any other circumstances.

When he pushed me, I slammed into the wall and felt my shoulder pop. I knew the hit had dislocated it. Gripping the entryway table with one hand to steady myself, I held my other arm tightly against my body. I stumbled toward the door and knocked over a vase as I passed the table. It shattered against the hardwood floor, sending Ralph back into a rage.

"Look what you've done," he screamed. A vein pulsed in his forehead. His face was red with fury. "You're useless."

He pushed me to the floor. The shards of glass cut into my hands and knees. Blood smeared across the floor as I tried to crawl away from him. He reached down and grabbed my ankle. I kicked at his hand with my free foot. When that didn't do any good, I tried kicking his knees, anywhere I could make contact.

As he dragged me across the floor, I grabbed a large chunk of the broken vase. I flipped over and sliced his hand. Satisfaction bubbled through my veins when I saw blood ooze across his hand.

My satisfaction was short-lived when he backhanded me with his free hand and I fell backward, my head hitting the floor with a thud. Stars circled in front of my eyes. My head bounced against the wood as he continued down the hall. The pieces of the vase sliced my scalp. Jolts of searing pain shot through my head and neck.

"Look at yourself. You're pathetic." He raised his hand, and I braced myself for his hit. "You should have been in that car with him."

The doorbell pealed through the house. Startled, I looked at the door.

"If you know what's good for you, you won't say a word," he warned through clenched teeth. "Janine, I'm warning you. Don't get any ideas or I'll make you both pay."

I stared at the door. I was closer to it than he was, but I could barely move. I tried to calculate my chances of getting to the door before he got to me. They weren't good.

The doorbell rang again.

I tensed and made up my mind. Rolling, I pushed myself away

from Ralph as hard as I could toward the door and screamed. I reached the door just as he reached out and grabbed my hair. He yanked me backward. I skidded across the floor on my back; my head collided against the wall.

But I'd done it.

I'd turned the knob and when he yanked me backward, I'd pulled the door ajar. I raised my head and tried to see who was there through the haze of blood covering my eyes and dripping from my hair.

"Brody," I choked. "Run."

Brody took one look at what was happening and slammed his fist into Ralph's face. Ralph landed on his back with a grunt. When he pulled himself up from the floor, Brody hit him again and again. Ralph slammed into the wall and sank to the floor.

Brody took his cell phone out of his pocket and quickly dialed 9-1-1 before sliding the phone across the wood floor to me. When Ralph tried to stand, Brody planted his foot on his neck and held him to the floor.

"I need the police," I whispered when the operator answered my call.

"What's your address?"

"912 Rose Terrace."

"They've been dispatched. What's your name?"

She was still talking, but I couldn't focus. The phone slipped from my hand, and my head dropped to the floor. Then everything went black.

I woke up in the hospital. Every single inch of my body felt like someone had rubbed it with sandpaper until it was raw. My stomach hurt, and I was almost certain he'd broken my already injured ribs. My shoulder had been reset—at least I was asleep during that particular bit of torture. Judging by the way my head pounded, I figured I had a pretty good concussion to go with everything else.

"She's awake," someone said. I tried to turn my head to see who it was, but it told me it didn't like that, so I stayed still.

Two men in suits appeared at my bedside. I looked up at them. One was dark-skinned, tall and broad. He looked like a bodybuilder. The other man was older. He had graying hair and was partially bald, but looked just as fit as the first man. They both had kind eyes.

"Willow Rutherford?"

"Yes." It was hard to talk. My throat felt like someone had lit a match to it. My voice came out gravelly.

"I'm Detective Renard," the balding man said. "This is my partner, Detective Samuels. Can you tell us who did this to you?"

"Ralph McKenna," I whispered. It felt so good to tell someone. Finally, that part of my secret wasn't my burden to carry any longer. I could be free of it.

"Is this the first time it's happened?"

"No."

"How long has he been hurting you?" the bodybuilder, Detective Samuels, asked.

"More than two years. Since my mother married him."

"Does your mother know he hurts you, Willow?" Detective Renard asked.

I felt my lip start to quiver. "Yes."

"Why didn't you tell anyone?"

"He's an important man. No one would've believed me. He said my mom and I were just white trash before he came around. No one would believe us over him."

"No one is that important," Detective Samuels said. "Is there anything else we need to know? Now is the time to tell us, Willow."

"Yes." My throat clogged. It was so tight it was painful to talk around it. I felt like my bed was spinning. I'd never told anyone what I was about to tell them. I'd locked the secret up so tightly I wasn't sure I could get it out. But it was time to let go.

It wasn't my burden to carry, and I refused to carry it around a second longer.

"Um, I was there the night Jack Moore died. My mom and I were passengers in the car he was driving. He was drunk and hit the tree."

"Yes, we're aware of your mother's first marriage and her husband's death. That case was determined an accident. The file is closed," Detective Samuels said.

I shook my head quickly and licked my dry lips. "If you look in the records, you'll find that Ralph McKenna was the witness to the accident. He said he'd lie about what he saw if my mother gave him half the life insurance she'd receive. He was going broke, almost bankrupt. He needed money."

I reached for my cup of water. Detective Renard picked it up and held it while I took a drink. "Thank you."

He nodded once and said, "So are you trying to tell us Mr. Moore's death wasn't an accident?"

I nodded. "I'm telling you that the car hitting the tree was an accident, but my dad's, Jack Moore's, death was not an accident."

I've done it. It's not a secret anymore.

"Willow, I think you need to tell us everything. Starting the night you met Ralph and work your way to today," Detective Samuels said. He placed a small recorder on the table next to my cup of water. "I'm going to record it so we have all the details when we fill out our report. Okay?"

"Um. Okay. I'm not really sure where to start." I tried to push a lock of hair out of my face. My hand shook so badly that I had to try twice.

"Okay, let's start with the night your dad was in the car accident," Detective Renard suggested. His voice was gentle and soothing, and I relaxed a bit.

I shook my head. "Jack was my stepdad. But he raised me for as long as I can remember, so I thought of him as my dad. Everyone thought he was my real dad. I never told them he wasn't. My mom didn't either."

"Where's you biological father?" Detective Renard leaned his hip against the counter lining one wall of my room.

I looked down and picked at the bedspread. My voice was soft. Barely a whisper. "I don't know who my real dad is. Neither does my mother. She used to be a… well," I cleared my throat, "she did a lot of things to survive when she was young."

"Okay. That's okay. What happened that night to Jack Moore?"

I looked at the gray screen of the television hanging on the wall across the room and started talking. As I talked, I saw the images on the television as though my life were a movie. The characters floated across the screen in brilliant color, acting out my words as I said them.

And then I was there. I wasn't just watching anymore.

I was living it again...

TWENTY-FIVE
Memories

"One of the keys to happiness is a bad memory."
~Rita Mae Brown

*T*HREE YEARS EARLIER…
"*Let me drive, Jack. You've had too much to drink.*" *My mom reached for the keys.*

Jack slapped my mom across the face. A perfect red handprint colored her cheek. "I'm fine. Keep your damn hands to yourself."

My stepdad slapped my mom around, especially when he'd drink. And he was jealous. She couldn't talk to any man or he'd accuse her of having an affair. He'd have to know where she was, who she was with, what she'd be doing, and when she'd be home, every time she left the house. And he'd check to make sure she wasn't lying. He was possessive and abusive.

But he never hit me. He was a great dad. Loving and attentive. He played catch with me in the yard when I decided I wanted to try out for the softball team. And when I wanted to play chess in the fourth grade, he bought a book and we learned how to play together. He was awesome. I knew he loved me, and I loved him. But he was different with my mom. I never knew why.

We were at a barbeque at Jack's friend's house. He'd been drinking. He shouldn't have driven, but he wouldn't let my mom drive. The car swerved down the road, crossing over the middle line before he'd jerk into our lane again.

The road we were on was curvy. It twisted its way through expensive properties and undeveloped woods. It was a dangerous road

279

on a good day.

My mom held on to the stabilization handle. "Jack, slow down. There're too many tight curves."

"I know how to drive, Janine. Just shut the hell up."

"Willow, sweetheart, are you buckled in good?" my mom asked looking into the backseat.

I nodded, but my mom reached back and pulled the belt tighter anyway. It was really tight against me. It almost hurt. But I was scared, so I didn't say anything.

We came to a sharp curve, and my mom told Jack to slow down. He braked and jerked the wheel. But it was too late. The tires screeched against the pavement. Jack swore and turned the wheel just as we hit a tree. The airbags blew, and it smelled like a gun went off.

My mom sat up and looked around. She seemed dazed, but it was only a few seconds before she tried to get out of the car. She pushed on her door, but it was crumpled and wouldn't open.

"Willow?" She reached for me. "Are you okay?"

"Yeah. I'm good." My voice shook and tears ran down my face.

"Can you open your door?"

I unbuckled and tried my door. It opened with a loud groan.

"Good, good." My mom climbed over the seat into the back with me. "Get out of the car."

I hesitated. "What about Jack—?"

"He's unconscious. I have to get you out first. Go. Go!" She pushed me, and I stumbled out of the car. She followed behind me.

I saw an orange light and smelled an odd odor. Looking over my shoulder, I saw the fire as my mom pulled me from the car.

I pushed at my mom, trying to get away from her. "We have to get Jack!"

She turned and looked at the car, holding both my arms so I couldn't move. We just stood and watched the fire.

And I heard him. I heard him yelling. He wasn't unconscious. He screamed for us to help him. His voice shook. He was scared

"Janine, help me. My buckle is stuck. Janine!" Jack screamed.

He shouted for help, and she just watched. She just stood there. The fire grew. And still, she didn't help. She stood there, listening to his *screams, him pleading for his life.*

The fire hit the gas tank, and the explosion vibrated the ground where we stood. I screamed, but Jack was quiet. All I could hear was the fire.

My mom let go of my arms and wiped her hands down her thighs. "Well, that bastard won't hit me again, will he?"

I took a sip of my water and wiped my mouth on the back of my hand. "We thought we were alone. There weren't any other cars on the road. So my mom and I sat on the side of the road to wait for the police. We knew OnStar would contact the local authorities when the airbags deployed. We just had to wait."

"That's quite a mess you have there," he said behind us.

My mom jumped up and let out a small scream. "Who are you? And where did you come from?" she asked.

"I came from there." He jerked his thumb toward the house behind him. Then a slow smile spread across his face. "And, as for who I am, I just became your worst nightmare."

"Wh...what are you talking about?" My mom pulled me to her.

"My name's Ralph, and I saw you stand here and watch your husband, boyfriend, father, or whoever he was burn to death in that explosion. I was coming to help, but I couldn't get here in time."

"You don't know what you saw," my mom said through clenched teeth.

"Oh, yes I do. I could hear him yell out to you all the way at the house... Janine."

My mom's face paled when she realized Ralph knew her name. The only way he could was if he'd heard Jack yelling it. I started to shiver. I wasn't sure what was going on. I think I may have been in shock, I don't know. But I didn't like the man. He had an abrasive presence. Malevolent.

"So, I think you have a little problem on your hands. When I give my statement of what I witnessed, it isn't going to go well for you." The man rocked back on his heels. His eyes never left my mother's face.

"I didn't think I had time to—"

"Eh, save it." He flicked his hand in the air. "We both know that isn't going to fly. You had plenty of time. You stood here and let him

burn to death. That's murder."

My skin prickled with goose bumps and my stomach fell to my toes. Murder? No, no, she didn't murder Jack. But… she didn't help him either. He was still alive, and she just stood there. A knot grew in my chest. It swelled until it became painful, pushing my organs out of its way. I rubbed my chest and tried to take a breath, but the knot cut off the air to my lungs and I could only take small, fast gasps.

What is it? I wondered. What's happening to me? It must be grief—Jack is gone.

But it wasn't grief. It was anger. Pure rage. At the man. At Jack for driving. At the road for its curves. At her for not helping him. Especially at her.

"Do you have an insurance policy?" Ralph asked my mother.

She nodded and looked over her shoulder. We could hear sirens in the distance. It would only be minutes—maybe less—before they were on scene.

He leaned in, eyes bright. "How much?"

"Two million," my mom whispered, "plus whatever I can sell his carpentry business for."

"Well, then, we may be able to work something out. You have money, and I happen to need money. Give me some of your insurance and I'll keep quiet."

The sirens were closer. Just around the bend. "Tell them I didn't have time to get him out before the explosion and I'll give you half."

Ralph smiled and held his hand out. My mom took his hand, and they shook once. Seconds later, the police arrived, followed by the ambulance.

We all gave our statements: "Jack had too much to drink. He took the curve too fast, lost control, and hit the tree. Janine's first instinct as a mother was to make sure her daughter was safe. When she tried to return to help her husband, the flames had overtaken the car and she couldn't get to him. It exploded seconds later."

The police were satisfied and the case was closed. After a small memorial service, Jack was out of our lives for good. We hardly talked about him after that.

Ralph had told the truth when he'd said he'd become my mother's worst nightmare. The night of the accident, he insisted that we move in with him and for the next week, he never left her side.

"I'm not letting you outta my sight and risking you taking the money and running. We stick together on this," he'd told her.

The first night we were at his house, his eyes raked over me and his lips curled in disgust. "Is that yours?"

"She, not a 'that'," my mom snapped, "and, yes, Willow is my daughter."

"Cripes. I didn't want to have to deal with a kid too. I hate kids. Hey!" He snapped his fingers and waved his hand at me. "Get over here."

I walked to the recliner where he was sprawled out. His gelatinous belly spread across the seat. "Be seen, not heard. Do what you're told, when you're told to do it. Stay out of my way. Don't touch my stuff. In other words, be invisible and we'll get along fine."

I opened my mouth to say something, and he gave me a look and raised his eyebrow. My mouth snapped shut. I nodded and backed away.

The seventh day we were at Ralph's, he dropped a bomb. "We're getting married." He smiled and kissed my mother. She pushed him off her and wiped her mouth with the back of her hand.

"Marriage was never part of the deal!" my mom yelled.

I sat in stunned silence. There was no way she was going to marry him. No way. He was a mean, nasty tool. And revolting. He reminded me of an egg, if eggs had arms and legs. My insides started to shake. But what could she do? He knew what she did. He could tell.

"Getting married is the only way I can be sure I get my fair share of the money. You're not cheating me out of one cent. I will tell what I know, Janine, make no mistake." He poked her with his finger. "But we can't get married yet. You need to have a proper amount of time to mourn the loss of your husband. Six months. That'd be good."

He stood and walked to the stove to fill his plate with more hash. Picking up the skillet, he scraped every last morsel onto his plate. My mom sat at the table, looking into her empty coffee cup. Her shoulders were slumped forward and her face pale. That was when I knew that Ralph was calling the shots. He was in charge.

"During your six months mourning, you won't spend a cent of the *life insurance money. Tell people there's a hold up or some governmental red tape... whatever. But you spend nothing."*

"What? How are we supposed to live?" My mom stood up so fast her dining chair fell behind her.

"I don't know and really don't care. Six months. Then we get married."

"How long are you going to stay married?" I asked Ralph.

He glared at me. A glare so dark and menacing that I flinched away. "I told you, you are to be seen and not heard. This is your last warning."

A few days later, my mom found a job in a diner. We couldn't afford the monthly mortgage payments on the house we lived in with Jack without his life insurance. And if Mom and Ralph got married, she didn't need the house anyway. So she listed it for sale. We planned to live in it until it sold. It sold two days after it went on the market and we had to move out.

We rented a small trailer in a questionable neighborhood. The trailer was rundown and dumpy, but it was clean and had plenty of room for the two of us. We lived there while Mom and Ralph pretended to meet, date, and fall in love.

They got married six months later.

Then the beatings started.

I told them about the abuse. The beatings. Jaden. The abuse to my mom. Everything. I was almost detached from it. The words tumbled out of my mouth.

Finally, Detective Samuels said, "Okay, Willow." He laid a hand on my shoulder and squeezed it lightly. "We've got enough. You can stop now. You don't need to keep reliving that."

Detective Renard clicked the recorder off and slid it into his jacket pocket. "Is there anything you need? Anything we can get you?"

"I'd really love a Coke," I answered, rubbing my eyes with the tips of my fingers.

The detective smiled and shook his head. "After all that, the memories you just relived, and all you want is a Coke?"

"Okay," I said with a small smile, "some M&Ms would be good."

He walked out of the door. "Coming right up," he called over his shoulder.

"You did really good, Willow. I think we have all we need in your statement to keep you off the witness stand, but that's going to be up to the lawyers." He shrugged a shoulder. "I tried to be as thorough as I could with your part of the investigation. I have a daughter your age. If she'd…" He cleared his throat. "I don't know what I'd do if someone treated her like you've been treated. I don't want you to have to keep reliving this part of your life over and over. So," he put his palms on his knees and pushed himself out of the chair, "I hope we have all we need. And you can start fresh at college." He grinned at me.

"Thank you." I reached out and squeezed his hand. "I appreciate you trying to keep me out of the courtroom. But I'll testify if I have to. If I do, will you be there?"

"Of course. There's not a damn thing that could keep me away," he answered, his voice thick.

I gave him a small smile and nodded my head once.

"Here we go. Coke and M&Ms. I didn't know what kind you liked so I bought them all." Detective Renard spilled bags of M&Ms across the table in front of me and sat four cans of Coke down.

I laughed. A real laugh. It felt good. I'd almost forgotten how good. I looked at him, and he chuckled. "Luckily, I like all the M&M varieties," I said with a giggle and grabbed a bag. "Thank you."

"Willow, I just have a couple more questions. Just so everything we've went over is perfectly clear." At my nod, he continued. "Did Jack Moore abuse your mother?" Detective Samuels asked.

I picked at the edge of the sheet. "Yes."

"Did he abuse you, as well?"

I shook my head, and my gaze found the detective's. "No. He was a great father to me!"

"Okay. Ralph McKenna, did he abuse your mother?" Both detectives stared at me.

My eyes dropped to the bed. I folded my hands to keep from fidgeting. "Yes, but not as bad. He didn't like that she came with a kid, especially since my mother doesn't even know who my real father is. He said that if she knew who my father was, they could've at least got child support payments for me."

Detective Renard patted my hands. "You did good, Willow. You're a strong girl. Ralph McKenna is in jail. We might need to ask you some more questions, but he won't hurt you again." The detective walked toward the door.

Detective Samuels smiled at me. "Be well, Ms. Rutherford. We'll be here if you have any questions."

Warm tears slid down the side of my face. "Thank you."

TWENTY-SIX
Goodbye

"You never leave someone behind, you take a part of them with you
and leave a part of yourself behind."
~*Unknown*

I WAS IN AND OUT OF CONSCIOUSNESS MOST OF THE DAY. *I WOKE UP ONCE* and saw someone in the chair next to my bed. A familiar scent mixed with the medicinal odors of the hospital. I tried to focus, but my eyes were so heavy. I let myself drift back into the cocoon of sleep where nothing hurt.

When I woke again, I knew immediately someone was in the room.

"You could have told me. I would have believed you," Brody said in the darkened room.

I didn't know what time it was. It must've been late. The hospital was quieter than usual, and my room was bathed in darkness.

"I'm sorry—"

"Don't," he said through clenched teeth. "Don't you dare apologize. You haven't done anything wrong."

I put my arm over my eyes and started to cry. I cried because I hurt and because my nightmare was finally over. But most of all, I cried because Brody was there.

He lifted my hand and kissed the inside of my wrist, letting his lips linger on my skin. I felt them move when he spoke. "I'm so sorry, Willow. I should've made you tell me."

"There was no way for you to know."

He threaded his fingers with mine. "He was the reason you stayed with Jaden? He forced you to?" Brody smoothed my hair from

287

my face. His touch was gentle. Always gentle, such a huge contrast from Ralph and Jaden.

I longed for him to say he forgave me and we'd try again. If he'd asked me, I would have stayed and gone to school in Ann Arbor with him. I could have stuck it out in Michigan if I had him.

"Yes. When you and I were dating, Ralph was out of town a lot, remember? When he stopped traveling and found out I'd broken up with Jaden to be with you, he went crazy. Every time I tried to break up with Jaden, he'd..." My tears came faster. "He made sure things were bad enough for me that I'd get back together with him. Ralph is good friends with Jaden's family. He said I was lucky someone like Jaden would even look at a piece of trash like me."

"That's what happened the day you kicked me out and told me you didn't love me, that you loved Jaden. When you came back to school, your shoulder had been dislocated." Brody sighed and ran his hand down his face.

I didn't answer. There really wasn't anything to say.

"What happened that made him go berserk this time? Did he know you'd broken up with Jaden?"

"Yes."

I was in the hospital for a week. When I was released, I stayed with Jenna and her family. I couldn't go back to the house on Rose Terrace. I couldn't go back to my mother. Not after she turned her head and ignored what Ralph had done to me.

The detectives and the District Attorney's office kept in close contact with me. The DA told me that Ralph pleaded no contest to child abuse and felony assault. His plea bargain saved us from going to trial.

Jenna and her family, along with Tim, went with me to his sentencing hearing for moral support. Ralph stared defiantly at me as I gave my testimony. I sat with my back straight in the witness chair and when the DA asked me to point out the person who'd abused me, I pointed with a steady hand toward Ralph.

"Him. Ralph McKenna abused me." My voice didn't waver. I

didn't cry. I finally felt stronger than him.

Ralph was sentenced to five years in prison. Because of Michigan's over-crowed jail system, he'd probably be out in less than two. He'd spend fewer years in prison than I'd spent living in Hell with him.

My mother pleaded guilty to child neglect and abandonment. She was sentenced to ten years parole. I wasn't sure how I felt about that. I guess since she was my mother I should've been happy. But she was also the woman who let her husband knock me around while she looked the other way and that girl wanted to see her in jail. I was confused by my conflicted feelings.

Jack Moore's case was reopened and an investigation was ongoing. Both Ralph and my mother were named as persons of interest.

I tested out of my classes at school and never went back. Instead, I withdrew the small college fund I'd managed to save, sold my car, and moved to California. I didn't see any reason to stay in Middleton. I wanted as far away as I could get. There were too many bad memories there. I'd been awarded enough in academic scholarships that, combined with what little money I'd saved, I'd be able to pay for my tuition at UCLA. It was a fresh start. One I desperately needed.

"Are you sure you have to leave? He's in jail. He can't hurt you," Jenna said.

"Yeah. I can't stay here. Just think—you'll always have somewhere to stay when you want to visit Cali. We'll scope out the star's homes."

"It won't be the same without you."

"I wish you'd stay, chickie," Tim whispered when he gave me a hug.

"I'll miss you guys, too." I hugged and kissed them both and stepped through the metal detector. I waved one last time before turning and making my way to my gate.

I hadn't seen Brody since the night at the hospital. I texted him twice to tell him I was leaving for California and wanted to tell him goodbye. He never answered. I guess that was my goodbye. It left a hollowness in my heart that I knew would never be filled. It was Brody's. Only he could take it away—only he could fill it.

I went to Aunt Bess' and said goodbye to everyone at the bar. Aunt Bess pulled me into a tight hug. "You love him, don'tcha? Things that happened… you were made to do that."

My throat clogged and I nodded, crying against the soft skin of her neck that smelled slightly of lavender and burger grease. "Yes," I finally said. "I've always loved him. Always will."

"If you ever make it back to Middleton, I expect to see your pretty face here. You and me, we'll have ourselves a milkshake." Aunt Bess stepped back and wiped the tears from my cheeks. "I love you, kiddo. You're a strong woman with an old soul."

"I love you, too. And if I'm ever in Michigan I'll be here to get that milkshake. You can bet money on that," I said with a laugh through my tears.

I called Anne when I got home from seeing Bess.

"I've missed seeing you, Willow. You know, I grew to love you. That hasn't changed."

"Thanks. I love you too. You always make me feel like part of your family…" I started to cry and couldn't finish.

"I wish you'd stay and go to school in Michigan, but I understood why you feel the need to leave. Maybe you'll find your way back one day."

"Maybe," I answered, knowing the chances were next to nothing of me returning to Michigan.

"You have a safe trip, Willow. Let me know if you need anything. I mean that. Anything at all, I'm always here."

I wiped the tears off my face with the back of my hand. "Thank you." My voice shook when I answered.

"Oh, sweetie, don't cry. This is a new chapter in your life. An exciting one. An adventure. You're finally free to do what you want. This is a good thing." I could hear the smile in her voice, and I didn't have the heart to disagree. But the truth was, it wasn't an exciting new chapter in my life. Not without Brody.

And Brody was never mentioned.

The plane shimmied and shook as it roared down the runway. I had a death grip on the armrests when I felt the wheels lift off the ground. A lump grew in my throat, and it felt like a hand was squeezing my heart. Sadness flowed through me. I knew I'd never set foot in Middleton again. Probably not even in Michigan.

As the miles ticked by, the less the hand squeezed and the more my heart sang. Was I sad? Maybe. Did I have regrets? Yes—I'd wanted to see Brody once more before I left. Was I happy? Yes. My nightmare was finally over. I didn't have any more secrets.

I was free.

Epilogue

"We cannot change the truth, but the truth can change us."
~unknown

"I CAN'T BELIEVE I'M GOING TO BE LATE FOR MY FIRST DAY OF CLASS," I muttered. "I don't even have time to stop for a freakin' Starbucks." I jogged across the campus to the building where my first class was held. I threw open the door and nearly hit the students standing in the hall talking. "Excuse me," I yelled over my shoulder. "Sorry."

I made it to the lecture hall just before the professor started his lecture, which was more a warning of what he expected of us and what we could expect to get out of the class. From what I could tell, it would be lots and lots of homework and even more exams. Sounded like lots of fun.

I was glancing through the syllabus when someone set something on my desk. I looked up and a Starbucks cup was next to my textbook. I turned, and his sapphire eyes stared into mine.

"Caramel Macchiato, right?"

"Mm-hmm." I nodded. I couldn't find my voice. I definitely couldn't form words.

"I'll meet you outside after your class is over." He turned and walked out of the lecture hall.

It was the longest class ever. I didn't think my professor would ever shut up.

"How'd you find me, Ace?"

"Were you trying to hide? Because if you were, you shouldn't have put your name in the campus directory." He grinned. The crooked one that always melted my heart.

"What are you doing here, Brody?"

"Trying to ask a girl out on a date. So far, I don't think it's going well."

"You came all the way to California to ask me on a date?"

"Who said it was you?" he teased.

I sighed and looked away, drumming my fingers on the strap of my messenger bag. "I—"

"Give us a chance, Willow. Things could've been different if it wasn't for Ralph and everything he put you through. Things can be different. I love you. I always have. My world wasn't complete until you entered it. It's been hell without you."

I shook my head, fighting tears. "I'm not looking for a long-distance relationship. And I can't go back to Michigan."

"Neither am I." Brody bit his bottom lip, rolling it between his teeth.

"Then I'm confused. Why are you here?" I blew out a breath. *I've worked so hard to forget you and move on. Seeing you is like a razor blade slicing open old wounds.*

"I needed to see you." He placed a lock of hair behind my ear, and I fought the urge to lean into his hand.

"That doesn't change anything. I live here. You live there. I can't do that. I'm sorry," I whispered and turned away.

My hands were shaking and my knees felt like jelly. I couldn't believe I was forced to walk away from him again. How many times would fate throw us together only to rip us apart?

"I don't live in Middleton anymore. I live one dorm away from you," he called after me.

I stopped. "What?"

"I moved out here to go to school… and to be near you. Mostly to be near you." He took me by the shoulders and gently turned me around to face him. His eyes searched mine. "So see, if you don't go out with me, it'll be a wasted trip." He stuffed his hands in his pockets, his arms held straight, making his shoulders rise.

My eyes narrowed at him and I shook my head slowly, trying to process what he was telling me. "There are a lot of things we need to work out, to talk about."

"I know, and we will. I'll talk to you every minute of every day for the rest of my life if you'll just give us another chance. We both deserve it," he said quietly. He ran his finger down the side of my face. "I love you and I'm lost without you, Willow. Give us a chance. Go out with me."

"Okay, I'll go out with you, but I'm picking the movie."

We started walking through the campus. Brody took my hand and brought it to his mouth, kissing the inside of my wrist before he threaded his fingers with mine.

"Just promise me you'll wear one of your famous T-shirts." He squeezed my hand.

"Oh." I giggled. "I have the perfect one."

"True love stories never have endings."
~Richard Bach

Unspeakable Playlist

Almost Lover—A Fine Frenzy
Already Home—Ha-Ash
Calling You—Blue October
Chasing Cars—Snow Patrol
Doesn't Mean Anything—Alicia Keys
Everthing Has Changed—Taylor Swift & Ed Sheeran
Far Away—Nickelback (Epilogue)
Figure it out—Maroon 5
Hanging By a Moment—Lifehouse
Here with me—Dido
I'd Lie—Taylor Swift
Kiss me—Ed Sheeran (Tent Scene)
Love Don't Die—The Fray (Epilogue)
Mercy—Duffy
Please Forgive Me—David Gray
Secret—Maroon 5
Secret Garden—Bruce Springsteen
Shiver—Maroon 5
Tattoo—Jordin Sparks
The Sun—Maroon 5
True—Ryan Cabrera
Turn to You—Michael Johns
What You're Doing to Me—Michael Bolton
You Comfort Me—Michael Bolton

A note from Michelle,

Hello, I hope you enjoyed Willow's story. It was not only one of my favorites to write, but also one of the hardest. *Unspeakable* is a story straight from my heart. Domestic violence has touched my life and left a scar that reminds me, even though I'm not fighting the war any longer, others are still battling, hurting, feeling alone, and broken. I want you to know, it can change. You can change. You are not alone.

According to the CDC, twenty people per minute are victims of some type of physical violence in their relationship. The United States Department of Justice estimates 960,000 cases of domestic violence occur a year.

Senator Dianne Feinstein is quoted as saying, "Domestic violence does not only happen to adults, forty percent of girls age fourteen to seventeen report knowing someone their age who has been hit or beaten by a boyfriend, and approximately **one in five female high school students** reports being physically and/or sexually abused by a dating partner."

The relationships depicted between Jaden and Willow, and Ralph and Willow were not based on love. They were relationships built on foundations of threats, abuse, and fear.

Love shouldn't include any of these. It's about mutual respect, security, and a desire to be together. It's not easy to make a relationship work, even when you love a person. It takes time and commitment. But threats from one partner to the other are never part of the process. Stalking isn't permissible. Touching your loved one in a way designed to inflict bodily harm is absolutely intolerable.

If you are in a relationship like the one I've described, there are programs that can help. It doesn't matter what your situation. Your background isn't an issue, neither is your race or religion. The people who volunteer at hotlines or emergency shelters are only interested in one thing: *Your Safety.*

Because Love Shouldn't Hurt.

Please seek help. I've included some websites that may answer your questions. They include confidential hotlines to give you someone to talk to. However, if you believe your computer is being monitored, please take precautions and use a library or coffee shop computer. Even empting your history doesn't completely erase where you've been, so be cautious.

The National Domestic Violence Hotline:
www.thehotline.org
Love is Respect: National Teen Dating Abuse Hotline:
http://www.loveisrespect.org/
Feminist Majority Foundation:
http://www.feminist.org/911/crisis.html
National Resource Center on Domestic Violence:
http://www.nrcdv.org/
Helpguide.Org:
http://www.helpguide.org/mental/domestic_violence_abuse_help_treatment_prevention.htm
National Coalition Against Domestic Violence:
http://www.ncadv.org/protectyourself/GettingHelp.php
AVAD:
http://avda-tx.org/

If these sites aren't helpful, run a Google search for organizations in your area.

Protect yourself. You are worth it!

Sources:
The Centers for Disease Control, "NISVS Infographic." CDC Home. 30 September 2014.
http://www.cdc.gov/violenceprevention/nisvs/infographic.html
The Department of Justice, "Bureau of Justice Statistics." Statistic Brain. 30 September 2014.
http://www.statisticbrain.com/domestic-violence-abuse-stats/

Acknowledgements

This is perhaps the hardest page for me to write. There are so many people to thank, and I know, before I even start typing, I'll forget someone. So if you are reading this and wondering why I didn't thank you, please forgive me. It isn't because I don't appreciate you or the hard work you put into bringing *Unspeakable* to life. I absolutely do! It's because my brain is somewhere between fried and mush.

First, I'd like to thank my family. You are so supportive of my writing. I couldn't ask for a better group of cheerleaders. From cover critiquing to proofreading, and even doing laundry, you do more to encourage my writing career than anyone else. I want you all to know that I probably don't tell you enough, but I see what you do, and I appreciate it, even the littlest things, like Mom having a stock of Coke in her apartment for me when I get a migraine. I love you all and I don't know what I would do without you. Larry, you always put a smile on my face when you come home each night and ask me, "How was work?" That little question shows me how much value you place on my writing. It's not a hobby, but a career, and that's how you treat it. It's in writing, my love, and words are eternal.

To the people at Clean Teen Publishing. Wow! I don't even know where to start. My eyes fill with tears when I think of you. From the acquisition readers to the editors and everyone in between—you have wicked skills! I couldn't have dreamed of a better home for *Unspeakable*. You treated it as if it were your own. You giggled over the silly things and gave me ideas for more. And, Marya, the cover is beautiful. I can't thank you enough. I'm so proud to be a Clean Teen author. *Unspeakable* was meant to find a home with you. You're all rock stars!

To my awesome beta readers: Erin (Albert) Rhew (AKA: The

Grammar Nazi), Mary Waibel, and Krista McLaughlin. All excellent writers and I encourage you to check them out. Each lady gave me advice on different areas of the manuscript and, when I pulled it all together, I think it came out a stronger book. Thank you! Your input was just as awesome as your friendship.

And I can't forget my bestie beta, Meradeth Houston, author of The Sary Society Series, which is ah-ma-zing. Meradeth, you were my beta reader, sounding board, rambling email reader, and everything in between. I can't thank you enough. I don't think you realize how big a role you played in getting *Unspeakable* dusted off and sent to a publisher. Thank you for everything. I can't think of any other friend that would read a book four or five times for someone, just because she wanted to. You are a friend unlike any other, and I'm so thankful for you. Even if you do, do gross things with people's DNA. Ick. (Actually, I think it's pretty cool.)

Book bloggers and reviewers, you all should all have bejeweled tiaras and wear them every day. You are the queens (and kings) of the writing community. Thank you for what you do to help authors spread the word about their books. You are priceless.

This is always the hardest thank you to write. To the readers of *Unspeakable*, saying thank you just doesn't feel like enough. There are so many choices for you when you walk the aisles of a bookstore or browse the pages of an online bookstore. I'm very grateful that you decided to spend your time reading my book. I can't express how honored I am. I hope you enjoyed *Unspeakable*, and that I'll see you around the pages of the next love connection I write!

Thank you all from the depths of my heart,

~Michelle

About Michelle

Ask Michelle to skip the serious stuff and tell you about the real her, and this is what she'll say:

I can't write without a hoodie. Yeah, I live in Texas. We all have our quirks.

I majored in accounting in college. I was required to declare a major, having no clue what I wanted to do, I picked the first thing listed in the booklet the counselor gave me.

Forget coffee. Hand over the Red Bull and no one gets hurt. Seriously, just set it down and step away. I will morph into a normal human after I guzzle my can of caffeine.

I hate to cook, but love to watch cooking shows on television.

I paint my nails weird colors just to see my husband roll his eyes and make my nine-year-old twin girls giggle (and also mortify my teenage son).

I'm a hopeful romantic and love swoon-worthy endings that keep the butterflies going for days, but I don't believe a HEA always ends with the boy getting the girl. Sometimes, a HEA is an ending we don't see coming, but is still best for the characters in the long run.

I write across genres in the young adult and new adult age groups while eating way too many peanut butter M&Ms (but we'll keep that second part just between us).

I was born and raised in Flint, Michigan, but now live in a suburb of Houston, TX with my very supportive family, two rescued dogs and a rescued cat.

And lastly, I'd love to hear from you. So drop me an email! Let's chat. You tell me what you like in books, what you'd like to see happen in the writing community, what type of books you'd love to see more of—less of—I want to hear it all. Because the one thing I wish I could put on my list, but I still haven't figured it out yet, is mind reading. But don't tell my kids—I still have them fooled.

Find me here:

Website:
www.Michelle-Pickett.com
Email:
Michelle@Michelle-Pickett.com
Blog:
www.Michelle-Pickett.com/blog
Facebook:
www.Facebook.com/michellepickettauthor
Twitter:
@Michelle_kp

CPSIA information can be obtained at www.ICGtesting.com
Printed in the USA
LVOW08s0527290115

424675LV00002B/2/P

9 781634 220200